Leather to Steel

Clint Goodwin

Copyright © 2017 Clint Goodwin

Hardcover ISBN: 978-1-63492-162-6
Paperback ISBN: 978-1-63492-163-3

All rights reserved. No part of this publication may be reproduced, stored in a retrieval system, or transmitted in any form or by any means, electronic, mechanical, recording or otherwise, without the prior written permission of the author.

Published by BookLocker.com, Inc., St. Petersburg, Florida.

The characters and events in this book are fictitious. Any similarity to real persons, living or dead, is coincidental and not intended by the author.

Printed on acid-free paper.

BookLocker.com, Inc.
2017

Second Edition

Also by Clint Goodwin

Mine Eyes Have Seen the Glory
U.S. Civil War Horse Perspective: 1861-1865.
ISBN 978-163492-533-4

Experience key U.S. Civil War battles through the eyes of a black stallion whose future generations will carry notable military leaders into American wars. *Mine Eyes Have Seen the Glory: A U.S. Civil War Horse Perspective: 1861–1865* is the first book in a series of historical fictions used to pay tribute to the American men who served honorably for our country. The main character, Lucky, finds the will to survive battles that defined America.

Mine Eye Have Seen the Glory reminds its readers that the U.S. Civil War was not that long ago. With a dose of imagination, the key book characters saw the same defeats and triumphs the men experienced fighting for their respective sides—North or South.

*****

Comanche's Wars
ISBN 978-1-63492-341-5

Award-winning *Comanche's Wars* delivers a story about a young black stallion from Virginia embarking on a journey of self-discovery during America's aggressive push to the West. Stonewall's journey will parallel that of a nation's story that embraces tribulations and triumphs on the battlefields. The book's key characters' fight for their land, cultures, traditions, and ways of life. *Comanche's Wars* highlights the struggles between American progress and peace.

*****

For Poppy

Leather to Steel pays homage to my beloved grandfather —Poppy— a distinguished veteran of World War I and World War II. Poppy's sacrifice and selfless dedication to duty, honor, and country set the bar for our family. My memories of him remind me of how one defines a great American. I had the privileged honor to listen to Poppy talk about the Great War with my other hero —my father— Russell Clint Goodwin, a World War II veteran.

On many a Saturday during the '60s, my father and Poppy sat inside in our screened-in front porch to play dominoes and drink Schlitz beer during the hot Texas summer months. Those moments in time helped define me as a child, a man, a brother, a father, a husband, and kept me alive during my own wars. I thank God those men gave me permission to watch them play a game that helped them open up about their wars and pains.

When I walked out onto the concrete porch, Poppy would say, "Come here - Mark. How is my grandson?" I would run over and give him a hug. I always scrunched my eyes when his unshaven face pressed against my check. Dad showed the same kindness by pinching my ears. I would then step back and ask dad and Poppy if I could watch. They would nod in silence: never turning down my requests.

Looking back at those times, I realize how privileged I was to watch two war-torn veterans play dominos, laugh about life, and bemoan war events that I could not possibly understand then as a child. During those times, my heroes talked about their service to our great nation, and of course the enemies they killed.

I do recall that my father and my grandfather had not one positive thing to say about whom they fought, and how they killed. Dad would mumble, "Those damned Japs." Poppy would nod in agreement, light his tobacco pipe, and quip, "The Jerries' never forgot the Great War. They fought harder the second time around."

For some reason, I was fascinated with Poppy's smoking ritual. He took out a small white cotton bag filled with tobacco. Holding the bag open with his left hand, he reached inside with his right to draw out a pinch of tobacco. The tobacco aroma permeated the air. Poppy then packed it into his ornate ivory pipe bowl; white with dark brown stains around the rim.

His pipe-lighting ritual was eye-catching. When Poppy used his flip-top lighter, a sharp metal clanking noise preceded the flame. He did so by opening the lighter top and igniting the flame using one motion of his hand against his khakis. Not sure how he did this magic trick. Once I joined the United States Navy, I figured it out. The same lighter skill Poppy mastered, I perfected using Zippos from the fantail on my first warship.

Poppy held the flame over the pipe bowl. He took several puffs of air to pull in the fire down onto the tobacco. Gray-and-white smoke rose, indicating the tobacco leaves were lit. Satisfied with the burning ash, he took a puff and exhaled.

The next act of Poppy's smoking ritual was even more impressive. He blew a circle of smoke into the air. I watched with amazement as a white halo expanded and floated toward my dad. Poppy would chuckle.

Now he was ready to further comment on his enemy. I recall him saying, "Those damn Krauts killed my friends in both wars." He would then blow a smoke ring up toward the porch eves.

My father would shake his head. "James, that smoke looks like an angel's halo."

Poppy replied, "Too soon to tell, Russell." Both men chuckled.

Growing up with two war veterans made me proud. I knew not what their hearts endured during my youthful years. It was not until decades later—when I carried a weapon myself onto the fields of battle—did I truly understand their realities and sacrifices. My father and grandfather were not alive during the moments I needed them the most during my war. Now I understand their silent pain when one takes another life.

I recall watching my father move a domino tile to set up for his next move. He would crack a smile that showed his missing upper

Leather to Steel

front teeth Dad said he lost them during a promotion ceremony on board a ship. Poppy said sailors were promoted that way back in the day when ships were made of wood and men of steel. Dad would scratch behind his ears and bellow out a broken laugh.

Though Dad never talked about the red scars near his ears, I knew they were caused by anti-aircraft artillery gun flash. Mother said he sustained injuries during the *Battle of Leyte Gulf* in the Philippines. Later in the years after his death, I found black and white pictures he hid in an old navy footlocker. The pictures confirmed he shot down Japanese warplanes. His sustained injuries also included major hearing loss. Funny, he never complained about it until years later as an elderly man.

I watched Poppy carefully make the next domino move. I remember how his short-sleeved shirt exposed scarred, tattooed dark-skinned arms. His inked anchor chains led up and over his shoulders to a large ship anchor tattooed on his back. During the Texas summer months, he often didn't wear any shirt. His tattoo's bluish artwork was literally melted together, creating raised scars that streaked across both arms.

According to Poppy, his injuries were caused by hot steam escaping from broken propulsion pipes; fusing together several layers of skin. He did not say it, but the family knew the scars were a visible reminder of saving several sailors from an inferno. Poppy's heroics were then forever etched on his body.

Grandmother Elsie said Poppy spent over a year in an Oklahoma military hospital receiving multiple operations and skin grafts. I can't imagine the suffering he went through. The military doctors did their best to give him a sense of normalcy. All the physical pain endured was because Poppy chose to be selfless. A true hero!

Poppy survived the horrific enemy bombings of his warship during the Sicilian Campaign in August 1943. For his heroism, President Franklin D. Roosevelt personally pinned the Navy Cross on my grandfather's chest. The president wrote of Poppy's selfless acts:

> The President of the United States of America takes pleasure in presenting the Navy Cross to Chief Watertender James William Daugherty, United States Naval Reserve, for

extraordinary heroism and devotion to duty while serving on board the Destroyer USS *Shubrick* (DD-268), in action against the enemy during the Sicilian Campaign on 4 August 1943. Hearing the cries of men who were trapped in the after fireroom when an enemy bomb inflicted severe damage on his ship, Chief Watertender Daugherty disregarded imminent peril to himself and promptly went to the rescue of his helpless comrades. To facilitate escape, he cut away a blackout device, then entered the fast-flooding, steam-filled compartment and assisted the imprisoned crew members to safety. The conduct of Chief Watertender Daugherty throughout this action reflects great credit upon himself, and was in keeping with the highest traditions of the United States Naval Service.

General Orders: Bureau of Naval Personnel Information Bulletin No. 333 (December 1944). **Action Date:** August 4, 1943.

Actual United States Navy Cross Awarded to Poppy: Author's Photo

Who is Poppy? Simply put, he was a man who loved life. He had every reason to be. His reminders were permanently engraved on his body, heart, and mind. If I could see his soul, I am sure there is an unwanted shade of gray.

On every Veterans Day—November 11—Grandmother Elsie showed us kids the sacred medal President Franklin D. Roosevelt presented to Poppy, Chief Watertender, United States Navy. Poppy said the Navy Cross should have come with a white cross. He always made humor out of his situations. After all, he earned the right to dismiss the idea of being a hero. Being a humble man, he did not consider himself a hero, just a sailor doing what any other sailor would do, if their men were going to die.

I remember the first time I got to hold the medal. It was heavy. The bronze Navy Cross was shaped into a cross-patty forged with four laurel leaves. Berries covered each of the reentrant arms of the cross. The dark navy-blue ribbon connected to the cross is divided by a thin white stripe. My father said the white stripe represented selfless service. He also said the dark blue hue represented widows—sad but true, more than not.

After Poppy passed away, the medal was given to my father. After my father died, the Navy Cross ended up in my hands, since I served in the U.S. Navy. At the time, I wanted to keep it. However, there was another family member more deserving than I—my grandfather's son—Uncle Phil Goodwin. I watched tears fall down his cheeks as he held it in remembrance.

One does not have to serve in the military to be a great American. My Uncle Phil was that man. Though he grew up between wars, he still contributed to building our great nation. The day I gave Poppy's Navy Cross to my Uncle Phil was the day my heartfelt at peace. It was the right thing to do. Poppy must have smiled upon us that day.

*****

This book speaks loudly —with great respect— to the children, grandchildren, and great-grandchildren of veterans who served during the Great War. Millions of brave souls fought heroically on

European soil, and the world saw much bloodshed between the years 1914 and 1918. Human blood was not the only sacrifice. Over eight million horses and mules died alongside their masters on unforgiving battlefields. Their lives assuredly paid the price for freedom that shifted between muddy trenches on four hooves.

The world transitioned from leather to steel armaments. The Bible says, "The horse is prepared for battle, but the victory is mine, says the Lord." The horses that carried thousands of brave troopers into battle survived because of courage and the willingness to ride into battle. Like those horses, my grandfather Poppy rode into those battles. He did so on a steel man-of-war over oceans where silent killers lurked below the water's surface. The Great War ushered in a transformation in military affairs on sea, land, and air.

Acknowledgments

Several notable historians' perspectives enlightened me. Authors General Jack Seeley, Barbara Tuchman, Robert K. Massie, and Margaret MacMillan provided delivered excellent perspectives of the Great War. Their research conclusions helped me defined why major twenty-first century challenges are rooted in the Great War.

How could I write a book through the eyes of horses without acknowledging General Jack Seeley's insightful narrative about his horse —Warrior— the real warhorse? The general clearly understood the value of properly training horses for the battlefield. During my research, both were referenced in official Royal Canadian Horse Artillery Brigade correspondence.

Other Great War veterans inspired me as well, such as Jimmie Johnston, who served with the Canadian Machinegun Corps. As well as Martin Gilbert, whose book *The First World War: A Complete History* helped me understand an era skimmed over in my '60s history classes.

My favorite author of all time is Pulitzer Prize winner Barbara Tuchman. She penned an unquestionable masterpiece—*The Guns of August*—that helped me justify to myself why I spend so much time alone writing. Mrs. Tuchman's writing impressed and inspired me. Her eloquent prose moved me to become a better writer. She crafted an amazing story about the beginning of the Great War. Her account, just like that of Massie's and other historians helped me understand why the war started—not because of an assassination but because of dysfunctional monarchies reining over countries with borders that periodically changed ownership, as with every European war.

Mrs. Tuchman clearly understood the four-year war would be impossible to cover, and give proper justice within one book. Instead, she wisely chose to write about the political details surrounding the weeks prior to August 1914, through the month of August, culminating with the Battle of the Marne in early September. I wondered why she chose the title *Guns of August*. I thought the book's title represented major combatants shooting one another from the trenches. From my perspective, that was not the case. In fact, the big guns she centered her research upon represented the profound beginning of a prolonged war between the aggressor and the innocent; the rich and the poor; and between dreamers and realists.

I enjoyed reading historian and author Margaret MacMillan's *Paris 1919: Six Months That Changed the World*. Ms. MacMillan's research produced an unbelievable story about how four world leaders negotiated a peace settlement that set the stage not only for World War II but also for modern-day world problems festering in the Middle East and the Balkans. I now have more sympathy for the people in those countries. History denied their culture, lands, and way of life by the *Gang of Four*.

The *Gang of Four* consisted of U.S. president Woodrow Wilson, British prime minister David Lloyd George, French prime minister Georges Clemenceau; and Italian prime minister Vittorio Emanuel Orlando. The men did the best they could, given the political climate in their respective countries. But in the end, history tells us they signed death warrants for millions of innocent people for future generations.

Expert sources enriched my understanding of how warhorses were most likely trained. I extend a hand of appreciation to my friend Mr. Ranse Leenbruggen. His expert equestrian insights added depth and clarity to horse training scene descriptions that otherwise would have been brief and oversimplified prose about early twentieth-century horse training.

Lastly, I want to thank the Canadian and United Kingdom Library and Archives Commission for providing superb online accesses to original government correspondence. The amount of source information provided is overwhelming. The world extensively documented the Great War—a war that was very complex from beginning to end. The abundance of newspaper accounts, military records, and personal diaries almost seemed endless. This author had little difficulty finding source materials to compliment a fictitious book scene.

I want to thank my publisher BookLocker, for assigning a top-notch production team that includes publisher Angela Hoy, editor Karen Goodwin, and Todd Engel at Engel Creative. Their grace and patience made me feel respected and inspired to stay focused on writing the best series of historic fiction possible. Thank you all.

Contents

Prologue	1
Bloodline Reflections	7
Tough Guy Recalls	15
Service to the Nation	23
Going Home	46
Texas Remembered	65
Magnolia Remembered	107
The Making of a Warhorse	114
A Suffrage Movement	148
The U.S. Army Needs Men and Horses	164
Preparing for War	181
The Great War Begins	197
Suffering in Every Trench	227
The Replacements	265
Those Poor Horses	291
Taking Advantage	292
American Expeditionary Force Men and Horses	316
1918: The Western Front	363
Second Battle of Ypres: Village of Passchendaela	374
The Armistice	388
The Last Ship Home	397
Save the Horses	407
Epilogue	417
Notes	423

Prologue

Between 1901 and 1919, industrialization and technological warfare transformation necessitated the movement from leather to steel. History proves wartime modernization is rooted in the human mind's susceptible destructive nature. A mind-set that once–combined with fear and imagination, created the world's first arms race.

Modern warfare evolved before and during the Great War. New and improved designs included steel U-boats, machine guns, tanks, flamethrowers, aerial bombers, and chemical warfare designed to efficiently kill all living things on the battlefield. One would question what motivated the world to *allow* such tools of death to be designed and developed. The motivations became clearer on the battlefield. Both men and horse would suffer from the effects of modern warfare.

Leather to Steel highlights historic events preceding the onset of the Great War. The story transitions into key battles fought between the Entente Powers (Australia, Canada, France, Italy, Russia, England, and the United States) and the Central Powers (Austria-Hungry, German, Ottoman Empire, and Bulgaria).

The war's conclusion does not end with newspaper headlines celebrating "Armistice Day, November Eleventh, Nineteen Hundred and Eighteen." The Great War was just the beginning of mankind's determination and struggle for power among greedy and misguided souls. The Great War gave mankind its first glimpse of true evil. An evil was embodied by a young Bavarian soldier's thirst for a perfect society. Unfortunately, he survived the Great War.

Leather to Steel introduces readers to world events shared by horse, men, and women before, during, and after the Great War: the consequence of which set the stage for World War II—another exasperating struggle between good and evil during the years 1939 and 1945. Those events will be addressed in *War-to-War*, the fourth book in this series.

Early twentieth-century warfare technology was efficient, yet had its limitations during inclement weather conditions. Horses and mules compensated for technology inefficiencies. Horses provided important tactical advantages on difficult combat terrains inaccessible by truck and tank. Motorized track and wheeled vehicles yielded to the most uncontrollable threat —Mother Nature— since she was unpredictable and uncooperative. Inclement weather conditions rarely impede our four-hooved friends.

Researching and writing *Leather to Steel* was daunting and troubling for this author. I am mindful that my '60s school history classes glossed over, if not oversimplified, why the *Great War* came to its violent fruition. The first world war redefined human suffering. I welcomed the challenge of sorting through documented firsthand accounts of horse artillery units and cavalry divisions fighting on both sides of Eastern and Western front trenches. The nagging question kept in front of me during my research was, why? Who was accountable for causing the outbreak of regional hostilities that transitioned to a global war?

From this author's perspective, the answer lay within the aristocratic European elite minorities. With God's help. the working people would ultimately hold the monarchies accountable. *Lest vengeance be mine.*

The source material cited in this novel clearly proved that European monarchies controlled Europe's fate between 1914 and 1918. The kings and queens of Austria, Germany, Russia, and England had a choice but woefully sanctioned familial differences and alliances to dictate the fate of over 20 million souls.

From this author's perspective, the assassination of Archduke Ferdinand was not the singular cause of the Great War. German, British, and French preparations for war were well in place before the assassination of Austria's king-to-be.[1] The arms race between Germany and England foretold the expected. France and Germany were drunken with historical vengeance. England's splendid isolation would be tried in a court of survival.

I used the same authorship approach to writing *Leather to Steel* as I did for my first two books, *Mine Eyes Have Seen the Glory: U.S. Civil War Horse Perspective: 1861–1865* and *Comanche's Wars*. *Leather to Steel* is the third book in a series of historical fictions promoting American history through the eyes of courageous horses. Brave animals that had names and enlistment numbers or in most cases, a brand. I am proud to continue espousing the importance of the horse's unmatched bravery and loyalty.

Leather to Steel offers insights to unique battlefield perspectives from the artillery and cavalry horses that served during the Great War. This book stimulates thought about a horse's perspective of war and peace. Did the horse feel the same shock during bombing raids and machine-gun fire? Did the four-legged beast rise to the occasion when conditions were unbearable? The answers are an unequivocal yes and yes.

Beasts of burden played very important roles during the Great War. The horse offered a tactical advantage that modern technology could not overcome when rendered ineffective by the muddied Western and Eastern Front trenches. The cavalry horse saved the day many times for armies that could not see behind enemy lines. However, few survived to enjoy the rewards of bravery. They gave up their lives in the process.

The horse did not die alone. Millions of brave souls died on the backs of horses, or by the side of their charges, for the latest military innovation—the machine gun—did not discriminate among the living. Mankind again invented one more way to kill a human being.

Most nonfiction books characterize soldier, politician, or a citizen's perspectives of the Great War. As it should be, notable historians—such as Massie and Tuchman—documented their findings that truly enriched the modern-day understanding of why so many souls perished in such a short period of time. Yet even at the time of their writings, author interpretation and inferences filled gaps caused by distance, time, and creeping Great War myths.

What would the history books say if the battlefield accounts were written by the horse or mule? *Leather to Steel* helps answer that question.

Animals, in fact, experienced the same shell shock, as did the men and women diagnosed as having soldier's madness. I personally understand this condition as a combat veteran. I often wondered at night when the next mortar round would hit my hooch. We lived through each night listening to the sporadic high-pitched crackling sound of mortar rounds hitting inside the camp. Those haunting war memories take up residence where none should be. The one memory I circle back to during sleep is witnessing a man's gut bleeding from a shrapnel wound. Several weeks later, I signed the paperwork to award one more hero's Purple Heart. My other war memories are not properly rated for this book. I choose to let them be.

Leather to Steel helps me to advance the legacy of my second novel's character—Stonewall—through his son, Tough Guy. A cavalry horse, whose sense of duty compels him to follow his family's tradition of heroism, courage, and dedication to service before self. Like his father, Tough Guy is willing to pay the ultimate sacrifice to protect his trooper.

*****

When one thinks about the survivability of horses during the Great War, as compared to horses during the *Comanche Wars*, there is a notable difference in survival rates. During the nineteenth century, Native Americans avoided killing horses during battle because their weaponry discriminated between soldier and horse. Horses were more likely to survive on the Texas Plains. Not so during the Great War. Modern weaponry did little to separate friend from foe. Soldiers, sailors, horses, and mules perished in unfathomable numbers.

For instance, the United Kingdom government archives estimate over eight million horses and mules died between 1914 and 1918 during the Great War. These beasts of burden were killed while pulling cannons, transporting rockets, toting medical supplies, and carrying cavalrymen onto the battlefield. These facts serve as the key premise for assigning the book's primary character—Tough Guy—with the U.S. Army Remount Service. He would more likely produce offspring this author will carry forward into the next book, *War-to-War: A U.S. Cavalry Horse's Perspective (1941–1945)*.

I used literary license to develop the book's characters, whose deeds are historic facts combined with a creative imagination. The character names used in this book represent twentieth-century personalities who contributed or fought in the Great War battles. Some character names simply satisfy a scene sequence that adds context to the story.

The Great War battle dates cited are true and accurate. The battle locations described are real. I sourced several vintage maps—accessible on the U.S. National Archives and the United Kingdom government websites—to visualize the firsthand accounts of cavalry engagements on the Western Front.

The best source materials used were newspaper accounts written over one hundred years ago. The U.S. National Archives provides access to billions of metadata files containing U.S. newspapers articles and pictures dating back to the early nineteenth century. These sources help me research unique information to tell a story that provides insightful historic facts readers will find interesting.

I did not include cavalry engagements on the Eastern Front. Russians' engagements with Austrian and German armies were short-lived. In fact, Russia struck a peace treaty with Germany and Austria years before the Great War ended. The reader should note that once Russia signed the Treaty of Brest-Litovsk, Kaiser Wilhelm immediately ordered his Imperial German armies to the Western Front. That one decision continued the slaughter of men and beasts well into 1918.[2]

*****

This book promotes American history through the eyes of a horse. The story lines will entertain readers who appreciative of historic fictions–about the Great War —although not all-inclusive— address interesting cavalry engagements. *Leather to Steel* pays tribute to horse and mule sacrifices made for the men and women they served.

As with my previous books, this project gave me another opportunity to write safely about feelings of going to war and coming home through the eyes of fictional character proxies. The words used to describe character emotions are real. I superimposed my personal combat experiences and perspectives onto an animate object—the horse.

*****

As of this writing, it has been ten years since I applied the concept of "writing is healing" as a healthier option for dealing with postwar challenges. I can share with my readers that core anxieties are less now, and more effectively managed. War changes us all forever. But we have to strive to survive, and find a way to cope with the "new life."

I recall what an army chaplain told us in Kuwait before flying back home. He said, "Men. First, thank you for your service! When you get home, remember it is you that changed on the battlefield, not your family and friends." I carry those words with me every day I wake up on this side of the grass. My soul reminds me that there are no more incoming mortar rounds, no more errant bullets sprayed into our compound, and, best of all, no more smells of human waste in the air we breathed.

Loneliness continues to haunt our minds when the right words cannot be found to express "been there and back." Understandably, we keep a safe distance from our family and friends because we do not know how to respond to the questions, "are you okay?" and "how do you feel?" Combat veterans loathe those questions. The answer is, "we will spend the rest of our lives trying to reconcile what we have done for the sake of another's freedom. In short, we pursue coping mechanisms that help us live with it."

Bloodline Reflections

Peace

As a proud black stallion, I can attest seven generations forged my family's legacy of unrelenting courage, enduring strength, and a spirited will to live. Thankfully, each generation produced horses who found a way to keep our bloodline going. Such was the case with my sixth-generation sire—Stonewall— and his chosen mare, Cinnamon. Both united in Southwest Texas during the Comanche Wars. Otherwise, I would not be telling this story. Thanks to them, my family's legacy continued well into the Great War.

My story begins with the saga of my father's great-great-grandfather, Tough Guy, who lived to serve our great nation on the Western Front. His spirit surrounds my every move today as the twentieth century nears its end. I am all that is left of him and our family's bloodline. My name is Peace. I am dedicated to telling the valiant heroics of great stallions and mares who have served our nation since the mid-nineteenth century. Their sense of duty is the rock I stand upon. I neigh loudly and boldly, "Proud to be an American."

*****

Old blood runs through my veins. I have been told that my breeding comes with a trace of a warm blood and thoroughbred breeds that defined my stature. Standing over seventeen hands high, the United States Army charged me with the humble honor of pulling, with five other horses, caissons loaded with flag-draped caskets of America's heroes.

We serve the Third U.S. Infantry Regiment (Old Guard), Third Squad Caisson Platoon at the Fort Myer army base in Arlington, Virginia. Twenty-four of us—twelve black and twelve white horses—reside at the Old Guard stables. Each of our stalls has brass plaques engraved with our names in black lettering.

Army regulations require six horses to pull one caisson. At the Old Guard, there are twenty-four of us horses assigned. We are divided into four teams of six. It takes six horses to pull one black-lacquered twenty-four-hundred-pound caisson. The first two horses on leather are called "wheel horses" because they are closest to the caisson's front wheels. The strongest horses perform that job. I am a wheel horse. Swing horses work the team's center. Lead horses take the front. All six of us move together in perfect concert.

It is our job to get the deceased veteran from church to their assigned burial plot reserved in the Arlington National Cemetery. The ceremony begins with the deceased veteran's fellow service members gracefully lifting the closed casket off our caisson. In rehearsed perfection, the soldiers, sailor, or marines carry their brother or sister to a final resting place—where heroes quietly sleep—in America's sacred ground. I am privileged to participate in this ceremony. I am saddened it occurs twice a day, seven days a week, three hundred and sixty-five days a year.

My assignment to the Old Guard is a long story. It began six generations ago with our family's patriarch, Lucky, who served during the U.S. Civil War. Evidence of his legacy persists, as I stand here in a Fort Meyer horse stall waiting patiently for my caretaker, Sergeant Major Kuiken.

I live in a stable most horses would consider spacious. For me, standing over seventeen hands high, it feels small to me. Comforts being not expected. As long as I have a roof over my head, water to drink, and food to eat, I won't complain.

I often wonder how a horse stable in Arlington, Virginia became the centerpiece of American history. Sacred ground where American history ends for so many who served. Horses before me said serving with the Old Guard came with an agreement to honor and respect those who paid dearly for freedom. For many soldiers and marines, the Old Guard was their farewell assignment. I hope the Old Guard was not mine. I still have fight left in my gut.

Leather to Steel

Our stable manager, Jim Kuiken, Sergeant Major, United States Marin Corps says the president of the United States handpicks honor horses assigned to Fort Meyer. I am not sure about that claim, but I certainly know many horses served here much longer than I. With that said, there is much Old Guard tradition and honor treading on this hallowed ground at Arlington Cemetery. I am humbled and honored to serve.

Between ceremonies, my handler takes me outside into the paddock to stretch my legs. Before entering the ring, I stop to resist the handler. He tugs and I don't move. I always stop for a few minutes to look down a narrow-paved street running east. It winds downhill toward the Arlington Cemetery main entrance. Each time I look down on the hill, I imagine a lone rider on my back; the same ghost that comforted me in Afghanistan. All I know is that my heart fills with appreciation and gratitude for the United States Army.

The U.S. Army—like the Navy, Marine Corps, Air Force, and Coast Guard—deploys brave Americans around the world to fight and defeat those who wish to do our country harm. A fine example of those servicemen is Sergeant Major Kuiken. He was willing to pay the ultimate sacrifice during multiple wars to protect our country. For that very reason, I serve an army that has provided my family a home for over 150 years. On this soil is where my family's story began.

*****

For generations, our family has pulled machines of war since 1861. My dad, Rusty, told me many war stories about our family's military exploits since the U.S. Civil War. While under fire, Rusty himself carried a famous army officer across deep rice paddies during the Vietnam War in the late '60s. My grandmother, Reckless, carried artillery and brave U.S. Marines up and across the muddy valleys of Osan during the Korean War.[3] Both of them learned from Jubal Early.

My great-grandfather, Jubal Early, pulled key artillery pieces out of the muddy German-held valleys of France and Belgium during the wars. My great-great-grandfather, Tough Guy and his son Jubal Early both served with the Royal Canadian Horse Artillery Brigade and American Expeditionary Force (AEF) during the Great War. This story is about them.

My father, Rusty told many stories about Tough Guy's father, Stonewall who served during the Comanche Wars and the Spanish-American War. He frequently reminded me that However, all of my father's fathers recognize and pay homage to the memories of our family patriarch, a famous black warhorse, Lucky who wrote the first chapter of the family's history during five major U.S. Civil War battles fought between 1861 and 1865. Lucky, indeed set the bar high.

During my tour with the Old Guard, my fellow horses have listened to me talk about Lucky and Stonewall. My friend Blackie graciously lends an ear when others turn away. Today, my team is off duty. I neighed at Blackie standing in the stall across from me., "Ready for another story? This one is about the Great War. You may remember Jeremiah Bates and Allison Drayton."

"Sure do, sonny. Jeremiah was a Buffalo Soldier and Allison was the young girl whose family owned the Magnolia Plantation down in South Carolina. Where your family bloodline began."

'You actually listen to me."

"Peace. I can eat and listen at the same time. Like an old mare. How about later this week? I have to pull this afternoon. Missy threw a shoe."

"No worries Blackie. We can connect next week." Blackie snorted and went back to eating his oats.

*****

A week's time has passed since winter closed her eyes for the year. Spring in Washington DC did not fail expectations. The wet and windy months made life miserable for humans. However, inclement weather was never a problem for me. Nature gave horses the ability to grow the right amount of coat to keep us cool or warm for each season.

Across the stable aisle from me was my other friend, Lucy. Her closed eyes and long breaths told me she was napping. That old white mare worked hard during the day, but needed her sleep to do so. For me, morning naps help me catch up on sleep I lost during the night. A full night's sleep was not possible since after I returned from the war. Three o'clock in the morning comes quickly. I wish it were not that way.

*****

Our stable manager, Sergeant Major Kuiken opened the stable doors at exactly zero four thirty every morning. He wore his weathered woodland utility uniform every day, except on Sunday. A set of gold wings were centered and pinned over his last name embroidered above the left blouse pocket. He always wore his uniform in perfect order.

The sergeant major bellowed out to us. "Ladies, today is Saturday, April 30. This day will be a somber day for our nation. We will bury the partial remains of U.S. Navy commander, Michael J. Smith, the shuttle's pilot in a common grave. Sadly, the other seven *Challenger* astronauts will be intermingled with his. You need to do your best. President Ronald Reagan will make an appearance to help comfort the families and friends left behind by the deceased astronauts. It will be a sad day, indeed. A sad one to remember."

I did not care for sergeant major calling all of us ladies, since he knows darn well I am a stallion. No matter. I always let the levity go, knowing he has more combat experience than all the horses and men together serving with the Old Guard.

Many a late night he would come sit by my stall and talk to us horses. He told stories of being in multiple wars. He was wounded twice and kept returning to service, keeping the marine faith, *Semper fidelis*—*Semper fi* for short—meaning "always faithful." His unchallenged devotion to our country inspired us.

*****

After we buried two astronauts in the morning, we returned to the stables. The soldiers unhitched our leathers and returned us to our stalls. The afternoon caisson team waited in the paddock for our team to get secured. Team White was tacked up and ready to go for the next burial.

The soldiers looked subdued. I watched sergeant major wipe tears from his eyes. He rarely showed emotion. That evening, the stable was silent out of respect for brave patriots. The nation's sudden loss of seven astronauts was almost unbearable for America.[4]

*****

In the mornings that followed, the sun rose earlier and earlier as the spring season reached its lunar limits above the nation's capital. The sun signaled to the living that summer would be here in Arlington before long. Until then, infrequent morning frosts would coat the grass with a sparkling glaze that looked inviting for a hungry horse. The mornings would be brisk for my friends and me.

The sun decided to suspend itself closest to the earth on the summer solstice. Last night, the soldiers put us up for the night without blankets on our backs. When I woke up, I could feel the wet dew on my back. I wanted nothing more than to go outside into the paddock and roll in the dirt. A horse's way of drying off, which made me feel hungry. We all started snorting in the barn. Before too long, like clockwork, the sergeant major would enter the stable.

Hearing the heavy stable double doors open, I stuck my neck out over the black metal stall guard to catch a fleeting glimpse of the sergeant major before he walked into the tack room. He reemerged and shuffled toward our stalls carrying a tin bucket of oats in one hand and cotton horse leads in the other. I noticed he left the stable doors open to allow the morning sunshine parse darkness from the stable.

While he filled our feed buckets, six other soldiers walked toward their assigned tack rooms to perform their duties. Each soldier polished every brass fitting on the black McClellan saddles and leathers hand crafted by the Old Guard's saddler.

I neighed anxiously towards the sergeant major. "Good. Sergeant Major Kuiken brought our oats and water. I hoped he put molasses in mine. The taste of molasses adds flavor to an otherwise dry meal." My father once proclaimed, "Peace, you will never have a

Leather to Steel

sick day in your life, as long you eat a teaspoon of molasses." I know he was right. I have yet to catch a cold during my first six years of life. Something in the molasses has kept me strong. The sergeant swears it's the iron, which is good for the blood. I have no idea what he means.

I liked the sergeant major. He was much older than the other soldiers attached to the Old Guard. He was not chatty around the younger men. However, when he's alone with us horses, he speaks much about his past. There are many days when he remained silent. During silent times, the sergeant major was reflecting. I could sense the trouble in his soul.

I come to know the sergeant major best during those he would come into the stable and sit down on the floor with his back to my stall door. I looked down at the top of his head. To get his attention, I tried to nibble at his short-cropped hair. He would ignore me most of the time when he was drinking. I could sense his pain. He must have sensed mine. I was the only Old Guard horse that had seen battle.

On one of those occasions, he looked up at me and said, "Peace. Who the hell gave you that name?" I could smell the whiskey on his breath. I neighed back, "The navy man who rode me bareback during a firefight." He raised his fingers up towards my muzzle. He carefully scratched my nose. He whispered, "Your shrapnel wounds are just like mine." He never said one word to me from that point on. We understood the pain of war.

The Old Guard soldiers called Sergeant Major Kuiken a hero, which he downplayed with indifference. I've overheard the young soldiers talking about how he bravely fought in many battles. He saved lives. They said he was an American hero.

For his heroism, the sergeant major earned the right to choose his last duty station before retirement. He worked a deal with the U.S. Marine Corps and the U.S. Army to let him serve his last year as a burial guard leader with the Old Guard.

I overhead two junior officers talk about Sergeant Major Kuiken. The officers discussed how the sergeant major willingly put himself in the enemy's line of fire during several campaigns. The officers also spoke of why Marine Sergeant Major Kuiken wanted to be near his friends laid to rest in Arlington Cemetery. A poignant act of his respect for the fallen.

Military leaders and peers could sympathize and understand his compelling need to not let go of those who sacrificed their lives to protect our nation's freedom. Sergeant Major Kuiken understood the unwanted feelings of a combat veteran of foreign wars. The battle scars and the wounds in both mind and body never go away.

*****

My old friend Blackie told me that he once met my father Rusty. I appreciated his reflections of a stallion I barely knew when I was a colt. He did not say it, but he acted as if he had heard my stories before. I tested the waters. I got his attention with a big snort and neighed, "Blackie, do you want to hear another family story"?

He neighed back, "Go ahead young feller. It has been some time since I heard about Lucky and his offspring."

I added, "You will like this story. It is about a war that forever changed the moral conscience of future human generations to come. The year is 1895. The year Lucky's grandson, Tough Guy was born. From that day on, his life's events would take him to the Western Front. Tough Guy was not to be alone on that journey. Others who loved him, played a role in his future. Let us get started."

Tough Guy Recalls

Tough Guy

On Thursday morning, April 13, 1895–my mother—Cinnamon—gave me life. She was the proudest Texas mare alive at the time. Standing over me in a cold stable south of San Antonio, mother nudged me to get up. It took some time for my wobbly legs to push myself upright on all four hooves. But I managed to do it. I was cold and wet. She licked me clean and nudged me away from the drafty stable aisle. Taking a step back, she neighed, "Son. You look just like your father. Solid black and built like a cannonball."

Unfortunately, I was sold to the U.S. Army and did not get to know him when I was a colt. My mother said life just works out that way. Questions go unanswered. I had many of them that only a father-son discussion could address. In my heart, I knew fate would not abandon me. I kept faith that the answers to my questions would be delivered. Years later, they would be delivered.

My existence began on a southwestern Texas ranch owned by an old man the locals knew as Mister Bill Black. He began his working life as a Texas cattleman. He started as a drover and ended his career as a trail boss. Within ten years, he made a small fortune driving cattle herds from Texas to Kansas City during the mid-nineteenth century. Mister Black pushed herds until he got too old and worn out for the trail. He made a change.

In 1886, Mr. Black purchased the old Baker Ranch for $3,000. His ranch spanned three thousand acres situated twenty-five miles southeast of San Antonio. His property abutted to the Zapata Ranch. The purchase was intentional. He formed a business partnership with his neighbor and friend, retired U.S. Army Colonel Clemente Zapata. The old men figured raising and selling horses to the army was a safer bet, than going after Comanche, or losing cattle to the unpredictable wrath of Mother Nature. Through their partnership, my parents, Stonewall and Cinnamon, came together. Ten years later, I was born.

Mister Black had a long history with Colonel Zapata who owned my father, Stonewall, a large black stallion standing seventeen hands. A cavalry horse, Stonewall was an experienced veteran of the Comanche Wars and the Spanish-American War. Always alert and always faithful to his trooper, Stonewall said he never let a man down, except once. Fortunately, during the Battle of Tule Canyon in 1874, the Comanche warrior could not get a kill shot on Stonewall's trooper, Sergeant Abercrombie. My father never lost focus on the battlefield thereafter.

Mister Black owned and raised my mother, Cinnamon. She was a beautiful sorrel standing fifteen hands high. She was not a veteran of war. Instead, she served as a brood mare—a job she did not care for until she met my father, Stonewall. According to her, it was love at first sight.

My mother and my father's union took place during the spring of 1895 at the Fleur de lis Ranch. Mister Black asked Colonel Zapata to bring my father, Stoney, to meet Cinnamon. It was not as easy a union as one might think. Dad said my mother played hard to get. He also said the bigger problem was another stallion living on the Black ranch. A Palomino stallion who challenged my father. It was no contest. My father demonstrated domination over the Palomino. Eleven months later, the result of Stonewall's union with Cinnamon gave me life.

My mother told me Stonewall served as a proud U.S. Army cavalry horse during the Texas Red River War. Battles fought on Texas soil between Comanche tribes and several U.S. cavalry regiments between 1873 and 1875. During this time, she said he was not just any cavalry horse. He never backed away from a fight, nor did he waver from serving the nation during his last chapter in life. He and his trooper, Colonel Zapata, volunteered to serve the nation one last time. They both fought during the 1898 Spanish-American War.

Mother said Stonewall demonstrated great courage carrying the Rough Riders commander—Colonel Theodore Roosevelt— during the Battle of San Juan Hill, Cuba, in July 1898. I was told Colonel Roosevelt never forgot how Stonewall avoided enemy fire while charging up the famous hill. The future president of the United States, Theodore Roosevelt vowed to locate my father and his trooper Colonel Zapata after the war. However, only my father would live on.

*****

Colonel Zapata died of old age at his Texas ranch in January 1901. He left a will directing his worldly possessions transferred to his only son, Manny Zapata. The colonel's property was not easily transferred to his son Manny living thousands of miles away to the east with his wife, Lucinda, near Arlington, Virginia. Knowing my father was old, the colonel willed Stonewall to Mr. Black. However, a different plan took effect after the colonel's death. My father would travel back east to live with Manny and Lucinda. A key turning point in our lives.

It began with Mr. Black and Manny exchanging cables that led to Stonewall loaded on an eastbound train to Richmond, Virginia. Once at the Richmond train depot, the plan was for Manny to take charge of Stonewall. As fate would have it, the United States Army put me on the same east-bound train.

*****

I never forgot the day Stonewall and I met in the train's last boxcar. I will always remember how we spent the first day studying each other from opposite sides in the boxcar. Those tense moments defined our future. I recall how the minutes passed by like hours. While we were staring each other down, the silence divided us. But somehow during that two-day trip, we found a way to get beyond ourselves.

The boxcar we rode was unforgiving. It was dusty, noisy, and rattled as we rolled on down the track. Our movements were limited. Short leads kept us secured to D-rings bolted to the floor. All we could do was stand and look at each other through shadows. Between us, not one sound was made, except for an occasional heavy sigh.

At the time, I sensed my father knew me as his son. However, he did not acknowledge the fact during the first day of travel. My gut told me it was stubbornness that delayed the inevitable. He was simply too prideful to approach me. Not sure what to make of the situation, we both just stared at each other. A knife could have cut the air between us.

Toward the end of the second day, the locomotive bellowed steam while whistling three times, indicating its final destination was near. During those last few miles of track, I watched the old black stallion raise his head up. He turned aside to peer out at the morning sunrise quickly making its appearance over the eastern horizon. The sunlight slipped through the boxcar's wooden slats. The light reflected off floating dust swirling inside the car. The glimmering flecks of dust reminded me of fireflies.

As the sun moved higher over the horizon, the yellow-hue light moved across Stonewall's chiseled long face and broad chest. He must have sensed me staring at him. He turned his head toward me. Stonewall's eyes shined through the shadows casted upon his face. I stood tall to make sure Stonewall knew I was not afraid of him, though somewhat intimidated by his battle scars, which spoke of a warrior.

Minutes before the train stopped at the station, the daylight subdued the boxcar's shadows. The sight of him made me nervous. Stonewall was an impressive-looking stallion. Raised scars formed diagonally across his neck, chest, and withers. I wondered how he got them. How did he get those wounds? Stonewall raised his head to the ceiling and arched his neck to form a high carriage.

I stepped closer toward him. Silver whiskers and coat encircled Stonewall's muzzle. He had aged. The gray muzzle made his nose brighter than the rest of his head. I heard him make a heavy sigh. He neighed, "You look just like me, but act like your mother. She never did back down from me. She was a stubborn mare." I looked into my father's eyes and knew he was the one. I replied in a smart way. "Funny. At least she was around to raise me. I had to learn the hard way. Where have you been?" Before he could answer, the train's breaks squealed. The train came to a full stop at the Richmond rail yard.

Several minutes passed. Stonewall neighed, "Son, I would have been there for you, if not for the wars. There is much family history to share with you." I neighed back, "How do I know it is you?" Several more minutes of silence passed. I had mixed feelings about him. At that moment, my first inclination was to bow my head to the stallion that made me. However, my second instinct was to challenge him to a fight for leaving my mother—Cimmy—alone. Fortunately, the later subsided from my heart.

My father took a couple of steps towards me. He stopped. Holding his neck high and arched, he shook his head north and south, snorted, and said, "Your mother's name was Cimmy. She was my mare." His words caused my eyes to water. Tears ran down my cheek. A sense of joy prevailed.

I tried to break free from the D-ring to get closer to him. It was impossible to do so. The wire rope kept me secured to the boxcar deck. It could not stretch. The steel leader buckles rattled as I struggled to move toward Stonewall. The corporal handling me woke up from his deep slumber. He stood up and uttered, "Calm down, boy. They will be opening the boxcar door before long." He had no idea why I was getting excited.

*****

A platoon of U.S. Army troopers watched the stock unload into the livestock corrals. Each trooper secured one horse with a lead. Once on tether, myself and the rest of the purchases formed up into a two-column formation. A sergeant led the mounted platoon out of the rail yard onto the main street leading toward the city center.

We covered two miles over asphalt, the platoon halted alongside a thirty-foot bronze statue of a Confederate soldier mounted on a horse reared up on his two hind legs. The cavalry officer held a saber in his right hand. His extended the sword over his horse's ears, pointing toward the statue. The rest of the troopers remained motionless and silent in their saddles.

The sergeant bellowed out, "Men! In front of us stands the greatest cavalryman to fight on the battlefields during the U.S. Civil War. His name was General James Ewell Brown Stuart, a Confederate. He is mounted on a courageous horse that General Stuart's men knew as Lucky. Remove your covers!"

The troopers turned their horses right to face the memorial, then removed their slouch hats. For me, the movement brought into view more than just bronze heroes. My father, Stonewall, stood proudly on the other side of the monument circle. He arched his neck and pointed his ears up and toward me.

I could see my father's eyes fill with pride and approval. We both gazed at each other while the sergeant continued to narrate the history of General Stuart. Then without warning, my father jerked the lead from his new owner's hand. He took two steps forward and reared up on his hind legs. While extending his hooves toward me, he snorted and neighed. I acknowledged him. "I will do my best." Stonewall neighed out, "Son, I am proud of you. Soldier on. Soldier on."

Stonewall returned his hooves to the ground and bent his left front knee on the ground. The poignant moment stirred a hidden love in my heart. He showed me the precious gift of respect. From that day forward, I kept my hopes alive that we would meet again.

We were physically closer now to our family's monarch born on the Magnolia Plantation near Charleston, South Carolina. Providence was indeed at work. Only the Father knows what the future holds.

*****

While Tough Guy began his military training in Virginia, Allison Drayton transformed her Magnolia Plantation to better support America's quest for peace and tranquility. No longer would cotton serve as the Magnolia's economic mainstay. An opportunity for change was presented to Allison Drayton and her mother, Elizabeth, and they seized it. Together, they worked hard to transform the Magnolia Plantation into a horse farm. A farm that produced highly sought-after horses bred for strength, agility, and endurance.

Allison and her mother were business partners. Allison took care of the horse training while Elizabeth ran the breeding business. They both traveled all over the country, —from Kentucky to Texas and all states in between—to purchase the best-of-best horse breeds. Eventually, they settled on a tried-and-true mixture of warmbloods and Thoroughbreds. Her colts and fillies became highly desirable horses amongst ranchers, farmers, and eventually... the United States Army cavalries.

After her mother's untimely death in 1888, she became a recluse. She made faint efforts to be social with men. Over a twenty-year period, she did have one or two close relations, but resisted committing to a life she called *servitude*. She did not need a man in her life. In spite of it, Allison became a wealthy woman who defied traditional thinking.

Allison did not mind the locals calling her a redheaded spinster. She paid no attention to what was socially expected of a Southern lady. However, she did pay plenty of attention to her Magnolia Horse Farm. There was always plenty of work to keep her busy. She managed the breeding and training of world-class horses, the animals she loved dearly as a child and continued to do so as a grown woman.

Each spring on the Magnolia brought new worries for Allison. The spring of 1904 was no different. She worried about the mares foaling during the night. It was springtime now. The mares impregnated in the previous year would be foaling soon.

For five straight sleepless nights, she would do it alone. If absolutely need be, she could hire a local veterinarian to help her. However, she rarely called for help during foaling season. She already had the knowledge and the skills. Having graduated from Boston University with a degree in medicine, she became an expert horse doctor and trainer. Those skills paid for her education, and then some.

*****

Life events helped transform Allison's societal beliefs. Her insatiable determination for equality drove her to reconcile how women should be treated. Her Irish blood forged her tenacious diplomatic skills. Too many times, she encountered gender discrimination that challenged her horse business. Through determination, unwavering business acumen, and self-reliance, she found a way to successfully assert herself into the Southern gentry world.

Allison knew horses did not care if a man or a woman's hand held the reins. Horses responded to handlers who understood how to respect a horse's abilities and limitations subjecting the animal's ability to perform in an arena or on the battlefield. The latter had never been tested, except for one horse Allison loved during the Civil War. His name was Lucky.

Her middle-aged years, equestrian expertise, and wisdom would serve her well during an ever changing world. The turn of the twentieth century already felt the effects of the industrial revolution. Allison anticipated the effects on farm and ranch. She chose not to raise farm horses. Instead, she pursued breeding the perfect horse built for speed and endurance. Only two professions required both, polo and war. The later would bring the Magnolia Horse Farm onto a world stage.

Service to the Nation

Tough Guy

The young army corporal escorting me from Kansas City to Richmond gave me my name, Tough Guy. I reckon he saw how I never backed down from the black stallion standing opposite from me in the boxcar. When the train pulled into Richmond, he said, "Your service to our nation begins now. You are a rock of the U.S. Army Cavalry." The year was 1901.

Proud to say, my first duty station was located in the beautiful Commonwealth of Virginia. The countryside was much different from what I had known as a colt in Texas and Kansas. Virginia pastures were covered with tall blue grass. Avenues of trees filled with oak, walnut, hickory, and maple trees defining property lines of many farms we rode by. Once outside the Richmond, green valleys extended for miles across the countryside. I saw many old farms, streams, rivers, and thick forests divided by roads and hills.

It took the platoon two days to reach our final destination in Northern Virginia. We covered over eighty miles of roadside and trail between Richmond and Arlington County. I was glad for a short trek. My hooves ached. I was not fitted with horseshoes. The corporal riding me said new horses would see the farrier first thing in the morning. I could not wait.

*****

As we approached the army training grounds, I took note of all the farms surrounding the post. I would surely check out the post's perimeter once free to roam the fields.

Our platoon columns passed through two large wooden swing gates that served as the post's main entrance. A lone soldier stood guard. Once inside the compound, the soldiers guided us over to the first green gable-roof barn to the right of a red-brick tack house. We halted in formation. The company sergeant commanded the troopers to dismount. Within seconds, ninety troopers slid off our backs.

While the troopers dusted off their britches, the company sergeant walked his mount over to the main barn. Half of the company followed while the rest of us remained in place for further orders. Within a few minutes, an older-looking man emerged from the tack house and approached my trooper, Corporal Gaines. The corporal extended his hand towards him.

The-man looked old and grumpy. I smelled his foul body odor. A long gray beard covered his throat. I noticed the black slouch hat he wore did not have army crossed-rifles badge attached to the front. It was even missing the traditional yellow hat cord. It was hard for me to figure out if he was a soldier or a civilian.

Looking down at his boots, I guessed he must have been army. He wore blue uniform pants, a dirty white T-shirt, and yellow suspenders keeping his baggy trousers above his hips. To top off his disheveled-look, his pant legs were tucked halfway down inside his black riding boots. His upper pant legs look like bloomers.

I watched the old guy extend his hand to Corporal Gaines. Speaking in broken Irish, he said, "Good morning, laddie boy. My name is Sergeant Robert V. Abbott. That will be *Serge* to you, sonny." The corporal removed his white leather riding gloves and grasped the old man's hand. The old man was not so old. I could see him grimace as the sergeant squeezed the corporal's hand. Sergeant Abbott looked over at me and took my reins from Corporal Gaines. He said, "Glad to see you boys made it back from Kansas City. Looks like the major purchased some good quality mounts."

Staring at me, the corporal replied, "Serge, you bet he did. Looks like this one has some royalty in 'em."

"What do you mean, corporal?"

"While we were on that train to Richmond, there was another black stallion hitch'n a ride with us. His handler told me this fella and the older stallion are related."

"You don't say! So why did you use the word *royalty*?"

Brushing down my withers with his right hand, the private said, "Looks like this one's grandfather carried ole General Jeb Stuart during the Civil War."

"How do you figure?"

"Serge, you won't believe it. Turns out that a big black stallion with us on the train was the son of Lucky, the famous U.S. Civil War horse. Do you remember that bronze statue of General Stuart in the Richmond city center?"

"Yes, I do. What does that statue have to do with this horse and the other stallion?"

"Because the bronze horse General Stuart sits on had a distinctive brand on the left rear quarter. The same brand the stallion standing across the street from us had."

"I be dang! Then this one must be his grandson. What is his name?"

"The cowboy we bought him from called him... Tough Guy. He said this one was quite a hell-raiser when he was a colt. So I kept the name."

"That is good characteristic we need in a cavalry horse. He will be a horse we can count on during battle."

"Why do you say that, Serge?"

"Easy. Horses are no different from soldiers. The timid ones run away from the explosion. The crazy ones run toward the action, saving a few along the way. These types of horses are the ones you go to war with. Be forewarned corporal. You will want the same from the man fighting next to you. Now take him over to the paddock. Get him some oats and a teaspoon of molasses. That should fix 'em. After you are done, go get yourself some grub at the mess tent."

Corporal Gaines made quick time leading me over to the barn. Once inside, I noticed two white pole fences connected to the barn, one on each side. The soldiers arranged the fences in an oblong circle. The center looked about fifty yards across. The private called the fenced-in area a paddock. I could smell sawdust laid down inside the ring to keep the dust down.

Gaines slipped a halter over my head before unhooking the thin leather straps securing the bridle to my neck and behind my ears. I opened my mouth to free the hackamore bit I had been chewing on for the last three hours. The corporal opened the paddock gate and shushed me inside the ring. I was alone for only a few minutes. Soon thereafter, a few dozen other horses joined me in the ring.

The soldiers divided us up equally into both paddocks. I meandered around, getting a feel for the place. The sawdust felt good under my hooves. I smelled water in the long metal troughs on the other side of the paddock fence. I trotted over to the far end and stopped just close enough to stick my neck through the fence and take a long drink from the trough.

After getting my fill, I looked up at the darkening sky. The sun was setting. A gentle breeze began to flow across the rolling hills. I extended my nose upward. Traces of a particular scent alerted me. I picked it up not too many days ago. It came from another stallion not far from this post.

*****

Manuel Zapata's one-hundred-acre farm butted against the expansive army training grounds. Over one thousand acres of cleared pastures with soldier quarters, mess hall, hay barns, tack houses, and stables occupied what the soldiers called the Stables. At this post, I would spend a year learning how to carry rockets, troopers, and big guns meant for the battlefield. I would not do this alone.

The army assigned trooper Sergeant John Weatherford to train me and a dozen other specially selected horses to run, jump, and, oddly enough, lie down during simulated explosions. During the initial training, the lying-down part was difficult to do. The explosions set off in the fields temporally deafened us. But over time, we learned to respond to our trainers' hand signals, regardless of the background noise.

During the first few months, we spent most of our days running in and out of mud-filled trenches. I was unsure how pushing through mud was a military necessity. At least the regimen strengthened our legs and improved balance. Not much could be said about cleanliness. When we exited the mud shoot, the only color we wore was red.

After completing the mud-shoot runs, the trainers took us into a large shallow pond the Army Corps of Engineers dug out near the south end of the Stables. Sergeant Weatherford said the engineers lined the pond's bottom with oil mud that prevented the water from seeping out. We were pretty much guaranteed to have water during the summer months.

The first time I waded across the pond, I struggled to keep myself upright even though the water came up only to my chest. The waterline was high enough to cause resistance to my forward motion. Determined to win, I persevered and always crossed the pond first. The rest of the horses were at least four or five lengths behind me.

Since I was a colt, my competitive instincts motivated me to win. Proving my point, the trainers rewarded the first horse out of the water. Sergeant Weatherford pulled my reward out of his pocket. A handful of sweet oats to feed me. At the end of the training day, he told me, "Tough Guy, you are a magnificent horse. I only hope you never have to go to war. The weapons have changed since the Indian Wars, mister. They are more deadly."

After four months of learning control and physical conditioning, the trainers eventually let out dozens of us at time to graze in the north forty in the early mornings to run and warm up before the training day began. When the paddock doors opened—within seconds—I was at a full gallop. I neighed out to the horses behind me. "Try to catch me." None could keep up. Running faster was exhilarating. The summer morning breeze pushed my forelock above my ears.

When the night's air cooled down, morning dew collected on each blade of grass. Since it was summertime, the heat wasted no time drying out the wet grass. The dry ground felt good under my hooves. Each stride taken lifted my mane up off my neck. Excited, I switched my tail back and forth. I wanted to be the first to the center hilltop. I wanted to be first to graze. My legs never let me down. Once on the hilltop, I stopped to catch my breath.

One morning, I decided to change the scenery. The left side of the hill sloped to the northeast. Untouched grass covered it. I walked halfway down to stop and view rolling hills, farms, and many pastures fenced off from the training grounds. Scanning from left to right, I could see six-foot cedar-pole fences surrounding the training site. Little did the army know I could easily clear that fence.

The army intentionally built wooden fences to enclose the training grounds. If a horse spooked and failed to jump the fence, the worst injury would be a broken rib. The alternative barbed-wire fence could kill us. I overheard an old cowboy back in Kansas say Texas outlawed barbed wire during the ranch wars. Not sure how true that was.

Sergeant Abbott told Corporal Weatherford a story about a Texas dairy farmer who strung up three strands of barbed wire around his farm to keep the Jerseys from pushing over the fence line to graze on better grass. Unfortunately, the farmer's draft horse escaped the barn and ran across the field toward the creek. Thick fog had settled low over the pastures, limiting visibility for both man and beast.

The mare was at full speed before running sideways into the barbed-wire fence. The wire sliced up the horse's chest. The farmer could not save her. The wounds were beyond stitching. The horse lost too much blood. She had to be put down. That story would come back to haunt me in a future place and time.

*****

One of my fondest memories at the post was when I decided to run along the fences just to see how fast I could get around the training grounds. Perhaps it was fate again acting on my behalf. But the day came and my life's journey would cross paths with my past.

I was probably one-quarter of a mile into my run when I heard a loud neighing sound from a large tobacco field extending alongside the east-side fence. I stopped to figure out exactly where the sound was coming from. The neighing grew louder as I trotted towards the tobacco farm. Before long, I could not believe mine eyes. My father, Stonewall was neighing at a mare. He did not see me. Standing next to a beautiful bay mare, he neighed, "Luna. Why do you keep bothering me?"

She replied, "Because you are old and onerous. Some mare has to keep you in line. That is my job mister."

I neighed and snorted to get their attention. Our eyes locked on each other.

I shook my head and pointed my ears up to let him know I come in peace. Stonewall and his mare, Luna, walked toward the fence. I did the same. We stopped within a foot of each other's noses.

Stonewall turned toward Luna. "I want you to meet my son, Tough Guy." Hearing this, I arched my neck up and lowered my head toward Luna. I neighed, "Pleased to meet you." Stonewall added, "He serves in the U.S. Army cavalry." I lowered my head and then looked back up. I neighed, "I am glad to see you again."

"Son, I see the army has put some muscle on you."

"Thanks. I guess I am following your journey with the army."

Stonewall pawed the ground with his front right hoof. He neighed, "Tough Guy, I have watched you over the past few months run up the center hill. I was wondering when curiosity would get you over here. We have much to catch up on. How much longer will you be here?"

"About seven more months."

"Good. Then let us make time for each other."

I could hear the soldiers yelling for my return. I snorted at Stonewall and Luna. "I have to go. I will return." Running back toward the stables, I turned back to see my dad and Luna watching me. He rose up to his hind legs, and pawed the air while neighing, "Come back soon, Tough Guy."

The remaining months at the post provided my father and me time to get to know one another. I made an effort to graze in the east forty. My father would trot over and rest his neck on top of the pole fence to tell me stories about our family. Each time he spoke, I listened closely to his every word. Stonewall told me of the many winding roads I had ahead of me, and that eventually one road would carry me back home. Every story he told was a life lesson to learn.

On a future battlefield, my father's words of wisdom would serve me well. I was grateful and privileged to have a father like him.

For seven months, we shared many moments of enlightenment. During that time, my army trainer Sergeant Weatherford and Manuel Zapata became acquainted. Both men recognized and respected the honorable history between the stallions. Our family's history was told again and again.

Manny shared stories he learned from Stonewall's first trooper, Sergeant Abercrombie. He talked about Stonewall's sire—Lucky—and his Civil War exploits on the battlefield. Manny told of how Lucky became the property of President Ulysses S. Grant. Manny knew about Stonewall. How he shared the same brand with Lucky. A brand that was missing on my hind quarter. Manny said, "Tough Guy, you are missing your family's mark. The Magnolia brand."

With Manuel Zapata's permission, the army coordinated a special event for me with the command blacksmith. What awaited me was the permanent marking of our family's legacy—the Magnolia brand on my rear. Sergeant Weatherford said, "Tough Guy. You are not going to like the pain. I am sure you will appreciate the enduring mark it leaves upon your hide."

Sergeant Weatherford and the blacksmith secured me inside a tight box called a squeeze chute. The box yielded little movement for my body. I waited and watched as the blacksmith took a quarter-inch steel rod and hammered it into the shape of the same brand burned into father's left rear quarter, the magnolia tree with a quarter moon. The sergeant blindfolded me. Standing in front of the chute, the sergeant rubbed my nose and whispered, "You are going to be just fine. It will be quick."

While the Weatherford talked to me, I could smell the blacksmith behind me. Then without warning, he plunged the searing hot iron into my flesh. I could not buck. A set of leather hobbles were attached to my hocks. My front legs were hobbled together. All I could do was snort and whine.

After a long two seconds, the blacksmith removed the branding iron from my hide. He stepped back from the box. He spoke with his deep voice, "There you go boy. You are branded just like the Rebs branded my granddaddy during the war." I could smell the stench of burnt hide. I never forgot that smell. Sergeant Weatherford threw some cold water on my rear quarter. He applied a yellow salve that cooled down the burn.

The branding worked. After a couple of weeks, the scabs fell off and the mark of our family raised up from my hide. The brand was in a way, a befitting army gesture of tradition. The sergeant said the brand represented respect to a line of warhorses the U.S. Army embraced as their own. I looked forward to sharing my badge of honor with Stonewall.

The next time I met my father at the fence, he saw the raised Magnolia brand scar on my quarter. He reared up and neighed loudly. His snorting was so loud he frightened all the mares, fillies, and colts grazing in surrounding pastures. He neighed, "Son. How did you get that on your hide?" I explained the story. He showed great approval and said, "Son, maybe someday you will have a bronze statue built for you."

I snickered, "You will get one before I do."

*****

My time with Stonewall would not last long enough. The sergeant said I would soon transfer to the U.S. Army Eleventh Cavalry, and pair up with an experienced trooper. Until then, I put the idea of leaving the stables aside. I wanted to enjoy each remaining moment with my father. I needed to hear his stories about our family's history. He gave me a sense of belonging and tradition. His wisdom helped me grow up. I needed to learn more.

I received orders to transfer in October 1901. Stonewall and I were not surprised. He understood transfers from his own military service. An army change of station comes with serving our nation. Sergeant Weatherford said it would be a week or two before I left. However, when week two came, Sergeant Weatherford told me I may not be transferring to the Eleventh Cavalry at Fort Myer. His words confused me. He said a very powerful man was coming to acquire the best stallion from the Stables. I was indifferent. To me he was just another human that would separate my father and me. A noble man the sergeant referred to as President Theodore Roosevelt.

*****

Sergeant Weatherford told me the Secretary of War, Elihu Root offered to escort the president to inspect army equestrian training centers located around the country. They would start in Virginia. Their first stop was our equine training post in Arlington, Virginia.

The president cabled his desire to inspect every horse. Both horse and men recognized me as the top-performing horse at the Stables. The trainers agreed that the president would inspect me first. The sergeant told me several times I was the modern cavalry horse the army wanted for all cavalrymen.

The soldiers spent the week cleaning up the facilities. On the day of the president's visit, every soldier on post wore their best army dress uniforms. The trainers tacked us up with brand-new black U.S. Army saddles, pads, and bridles. The farriers trimmed our manes, tails, and forelocks, and then shined our hooves. Sergeant Weatherford said we all looked like a million bucks, whatever that was.

President Roosevelt and Secretary Root arrived at our post Saturday midmorning. The visiting Fort Meyer Eleventh Cavalry Commander, Colonel Francis Moore escorted them around the training grounds. Their first stop was Paddock Number One, my paddock. I trotted around the ring, while keeping my neck in a high carriage. I turned counterclockwise to give him another view. It worked.

President Roosevelt pointed at me. He ordered, "Colonel Moore, I want that black horse brought to me. He bears the brand of a brave horse I rode once." The colonel signaled to the trainer sitting on the paddock fence. He jumped down and whistled at me. I promptly trotted over to him. In his hand was a cup of oats. I munched them while he secured the lead to my halter. We then walked over to the men standing on the other side of the fence. The one man wearing a funny-looking hat spoke with authority. The others nodded in agreement. I overheard the president tell the colonel about a brave

Leather to Steel

horse he rode during the Battle of San Juan Hill. The president said it was me. I knew who he was referring to—and it was not I.

The colonel asked, "Sir, if you will. How could that be?"

"Certainly colonel. A horse looking just like that stallion carried me up a steep grade during the battle. We were taking enemy fire. The black stallion —I rode— zigzagged from side to side, preventing the Spaniard sharpshooters from getting a shot at me. However, this horse is obviously too young to be the same horse. Where did you get him?" The president stopped the colonel from answering.

While pointing at my rear-left quarter, he continued, "That magnolia tree and crescent moon brand tells me his father—wherever he may be—left his mark on this earth. I want this horse transferred to my horse farm in Winchester. What is his name?"

Sergeant Weatherford stepped towards the president. He said, "Sir, his name is Tough Guy. I would like to add, his father grazes on the Zapata farm not one mile from here." The sergeant pointed east, saying, "Sir, they spend quite a bit of time over that hill together in between Tough Guy's drills."

President Roosevelt ordered, "Take me over to him. I want to meet the old black stallion."

The colonel stood at attention and clicked his boots. He looked at the president and smartly replied, "Yes, sir. Do you want—"

The president interrupted, "Colonel, take me there now. This horse's father was owned by a colonel who served as one of my interpreters at San Juan Hill. It will be good to see old Stonewall again, and his trooper Colonel Zapata." Sergeant Weatherford understood what the president said. The sergeant remained silent and smiling.

Colonel Moore leaned closer to the president. He said, "Sir, I think the Zapata Farm is run by a much younger man—his son Manuel."

Roosevelt nodded, acknowledging the fact his old friend may have passed on. The president's bushy eyebrows arched as he scowled. His smile faded into a look of sadness. President Roosevelt shook off the moment and walked over to me. He ran his right hand over my neck and patted my nose. He looked at me straight in the eyes and said, "Tough Guy, your father was a hero. Let us go see him."

The Twenty-sixth President of the United States walked with Colonel Moore and me to the tack room.

The colonel commanded Sergeant Weatherford, "Tack up Tough Guy. Make it quick."

I watched the sergeant salute and do an about-face. The sergeant took my reins and led me over to the tack room. He secured me to the hitching post. While Sergeant Weatherford got my gear, I looked back at the three men walking toward me. Behind them were two men carrying rifles. They looked rather serious.

Within five minutes, Sergeant Weatherford had the saddle cinched up on me and the swivel bit in my mouth. The president walked up and took the reins from the sergeant who was all smiles. Sergeant Weatherford whispered to me, "Tough Guy, they are going to take you to the back forty of the Zapata farm."[5]

Colonel Moore asked the president, "Sir. Should we get two more horses for your security detail to ride with you?"

President Roosevelt replied, "Thank you. But no thank you. I would rather ride by myself. I want to see what this horse is made of."

The colonel replied, "Sir, are you sure you don't want mounts for your security detail?" The serious-looking men standing behind the president stared at their protectee.

President Roosevelt turned toward the men and extended his right hand up toward them. He said, "Gentlemen, I will be perfectly safe on this horse." He glanced at the colonel. "As I said once before… I will be fine. Dismissed." The colonel backed away, realizing his error in judgment.

President Roosevelt mounted up on my back with little effort. His seat felt like that of a man who knew how to ride a horse. Once mounted, President Roosevelt yelled towards the colonel, "Where is your north forty? I want to see how fast this mount can go."

"Sir, just point Tough Guy toward the east, and he will take it from there."

"What do you mean, 'take it from there'?"

"Tough Guy has explosive speed. I can't guarantee your safety, sir."

I felt the president's knees put slight pressure on my sides. That was my cue to go. He held on to my reins, but did so loosely. He learned forward on the saddle and yelled out, "Let us see what you got, mister!" I picked up my front legs and planted them firmly into the ground in front of me. My hind legs pushed me forward. The ground was wet from last night's misting, giving my hooves better traction.

We raced across the field and up the hill. President Roosevelt spoke over my ears. "Tough Guy. Your strength reminds me of the time a relative of yours and I made it up San Juan Hill back in 1898. I snorted out. "I know. My father told me. I will get you to him shortly."

I made it to the top of the hill in record time. The president pulled back on my reins to stop us. I relaxed my lungs while we stood still for a moment. The president patted my withers. "Thank you, boy. I needed this." I could feel him looking at the farm where my father lived. He yelled out, "Boy. Let us go over to that farm. I see a couple of horses acting up. Let us go see what the commotion is all about." He clucked once, and off we went.

Within a couple of minutes, we stopped just a couple of feet away from the pole fence that separated the army training ground from the Zapata farm. My father and his mare, Luna, were chasing each other on the other side. Actually, it was Luna chasing my father. I could hear her neigh loudly, "You are too old." My father, up in age, still had some speed left. As she ran after my father, Luna showed her teeth. It did not look like a pretty situation.

A man's voice bellowed all sorts of expletives. It was Manny Zapata saying, "Knock it off you two. Luna. Stop! Luna, stop!" She heeded the next command. Luna came to a slow stop and turned toward Manny. My father stood down and turned toward Manny. In the process, he caught sight of me and the president near the fence. Stonewall trotted toward me. I heard Manny in the background. "Get over here, Stonewall."

The president raised his hand to get Manny's attention. Manny caught sight of us. President Roosevelt said, "Hello, friend."

Manny waved his right hand to acknowledge the president. Manny was a couple of hundred feet away from our position. It was clear he had no idea the president of the United States was sitting on my back.

My father trotted to the pole fence, while Manny and Luna followed. Stonewall stuck his nose over the railing and snorted. President Roosevelt loosened my rein to move closer to my father. The president smiled at Stonewall and asked, "Do you remember me, mister?"

My father sniffed the air and snorted loudly. He shook his head up and down and neighed, "Yes."

President Roosevelt dismounted from my back. He gathered the reins and stood by the fence grinning from ear to ear. The president ran his right hand over my father's nose to establish trust. My father pulled back and neighed loudly. My father's snorting did not intimidate the president. The president said, "It is okay boy. All is right."

After a few calming moment, my father settled down. He said to me, "Son, the human you are carrying rode on my back during the Battle of San Juan Hill in Cuba. Many men died that day. The smell of death only comes with certain humans. The colonel has blood on his hands. War does that to a man. War does not discriminate between man or beast."

"Father, he did not kill men, nor horses."

"This is true, but he ordered it so. No different than the troopers who rode my back during the Red River War, or at the Battle of Little Big Horn."

"Sorry father, I do not understand what you say, since I have not been in battle. However, this man will be taking me from the army back to his farm in Winchester."

"Son, I hope you never see battle. *No one wants war.*"

My father calmed down after hearing the words *take me from the army*. Stonewall understood the meaning of the words No one wants war.

Manny and Luna stopped a few feet away from the fence. Taking one more step than Manny, Luna nipped at my father's withers. Manny jerked on her lead. With consternation in his voice, Manny ordered, "Stop that Luna. Leave him alone."

Luna expressed her consternation by pawing the ground. She neighed, "Your stallion does not know how to properly treat a mare."

I neighed out, "Luna, you know my father is old. I am sure he did not mean to do whatever bothered you." Before I could respond, the president came into Manny's view and said, "Hello, sir."

Manny immediately responded, "Sir. Mister President I... I did not know it was you. Please forgive me for not getting here quicker."

"No worries mister. What shall I call you, son?"

"Sir. My name is Manuel Zapata. I own this farm with my dear wife, Lucinda."

"Nice looking farm you have here, Mister Zapata. Say. I hope you could help me. I need to know, what is the name of that black stallion?"

"Sir, his name is Stonewall."

"How old is he?"

"My father —God rest his soul— told me he was born in 1871. I suppose that would make him thirty years of age."

"Who was your father?"

"Sir, Clemente Zapata. I remember him telling me how you made America victorious during the Spanish-American War."

President Roosevelt replied, "Son, it was not just me. Our victories were won on the shoulders of the brave men, like your father's. I take it he is no longer with us?"

"No, sir. He passed away not too long after my mother died. He was heartbroken. I think he died of a lonely heart." Before the president could respond, Lucinda caught up with her husband and the two horses. The president tipped his hat toward her, as gentlemen do in the presence of women. He said, "Pleased to meet you." Lucinda raised her hand, signaling the conversation to continue. The president looked back at Manny and continued, "I am sorry to hear that. Your father served our nation with honor and bravery. Tell me something. Is this his horse Stonewall? The same horse he brought to Cuba?"

"Yes, sir. He is the same stallion." About the time Manny said yes, Stonewall turned his left flank toward the president.

Pointing at the Magnolia brand, the president said, "Now I see. He bears the Magnolia brand. Your father told me this stallion's father, Lucky—I think that was his name—carried a few troopers during the U.S. Civil War."

"Yes, sir. His sire was indeed Lucky. It is told President Ulysses S. Grant owned Lucky and Stonewall."

Manny said, "Sir, not to change the subject, but sorry to know President McKinley was assassinated by a stinking thief. He was a good man. I understand you are now the youngest man to ever become president of the United States at the age of forty-two."

"Mister Zapata, you are correct. I now have a security detail that is with me every moment of the day, except today. I wanted to be alone with Tough Guy. He rides just like I remembered that old boy did." The president pointed at Stonewall. Stonewall neighed, shaking his head up and down at the president. President Roosevelt laughed. "Looks like he knows who I am now. If you will excuse me, I need to return to the commander's office. The men are probably getting worried about me. It was a pleasure meeting you and seeing my old friend Stonewall."

Stonewall neighed at Tough Guy, "Now you and I have something else in common. We both carried an American hero."

The president mounted back up on my back. He pulled the left rein to turn us around. Before he nudged me to gallop, he tipped his hat to Lucinda. The president said, "It was nice meeting you Mister and Missus Zapata. Thank you for telling me about Stonewall's service. I will make sure this one is well taken care of." The president pressed his hat on his head and clucked his tongue once. I did the rest. Little did I know then, those brief moments standing at the fence would be my last at the Zapata Ranch. The last time I would see my father alive.

*****

I learned months later, during the winter of 1902, a communicable horse disease called Glanders ran its destructive course across the states of New York, Pennsylvania, and Virginia. The disease infected and killed many horses on the East Coast. Fortunately, Luna was young and strong enough to survive. Several other horses on Manny's ranch did not make it. Stonewall reached the edge of death.

My father did not have the youthful advantage during the outbreak. At thirty-two years of age, he had one more battle to win. It was told that Manny and Lucinda spent every hour in the stall taking turns applying cold water to Stonewall's head. The Zapatas rubbed aloe oil all over Stonewall's body to draw out the poisons. Manny ground oats and molasses into a paste he applied to Stonewall's tongue every couple hours.

After two weeks of touch-and-go fevers, the Zapatas saved their prized heirloom. My father Stonewall refused to give up. He won the battle with Glanders. It was simply not his time to go. He still had enough will to live. That same kind of heart he showed on the battlefields.

*****

My army training soon ended after meeting President Roosevelt. Within weeks, the army discharged me into the service and pleasure of the president. Sergeant Weatherford said I was fortunate to be chosen. I had mixed feelings about the change of ownership. Where was I going? What would I be doing?" Key questions I wanted answers to, sooner than later.

In spite of what my father said about war, I still yearned to carry a cavalryman into battle. It was my family's legacy. At that time, I was not pleased with the idea of working for the president. I wanted to be on the battlefield. However, fate took charge of my life once again.

*****

Saturday morning came sooner than expected. President Roosevelt's old friend and stable farrier, Mister Allan McBride rode a pack mule through the posts' main gates. I was tied to a hitching post waiting to be picked up. I watched his mannerisms. He was quite the sight to see. His long hair protruded from under his dirty slouch hat. His red-checkered long-sleeved shirt hung out over his black britches. The man's riding boots had small spurs attached to his boot heels. They clanked with every step the mule took.

When I first Mister McBride up close, I thought I was looking at Sergeant Abbott's twin brother. The both looked old and scruffy. The fact he rode a brown pack mule made no sense to me. Stonewall told me mules were used for hauling, not riding. The mule told me later on our trip about how McBride became employed by the president, and that horses were no option for the old man.

After securing his mule next to me on the hitching post, McBride approached the commander's office. He knocked on the door twice. He yelled out, "Hello in there! I come to pick up a black stallion for the president. Hello. Good morning!"

There was a shuffling inside the office. Within a few minutes, a young army officer stepped outside. He carefully adjusted his army slouch hat, stood at attention, and saluted. "Mister McBride."

"Yep. That would be me. I take it that horse standing next to my mule is the one the president wants?"

"Yes, sir. That is the one. The sergeant has him all tacked up and ready to go."

McBride replied, "Don't call me sir. I know who my parents are."

The captain snickered and asked, "But you were awarded the—"

McBride interrupted him, "Sonny, that there horse don't need to be tacked up. I will not be riding him. By God, where is your colonel?"

"Sir, the colonel is out in the north forty. In regards to the tack, the saddle he wears was owned by his father, who was owned by the late President Ulysses S. Grant."

McBride took off his hat and slapped it against his britches. He replied, "Well, I be dang. Then so it will be."

The captain asked, "Mister McBride. Where are you taking him?"

"I am trailing him over to the president's horse farm in Winchester, Virginia. It is only a day's ride from Arlington to

Winchester. We will cross over the Blue Ridge Mountains running north and south near the western side of the Commonwealth."

"Thank you, sir, but I am familiar with the terrain."

"Well, in case you forgot, sonny, the Blue Ridge Mountains separate the Shenandoah Valley from the east."

I looked at the young captain and could tell he was not amused with the exchange of words. The captain walked over to me. He untied my reins from the hitching post. He said, "Tough Guy, thank you for your service. The other horses learned from you what it means to have a heart and courage. Godspeed. Maybe I will see you on the battlefield someday."

McBride mounted up on his mule he called Little Sorrel. He reached down to take reins from the colonel's hands. He turned Little Sorrel around and led us out of the post's gates, without saying a word to the captain.

Once outside the gates, McBride halted the mule. I stopped. He dismounted and walked to the left side of Little Sorrel to untie a lead rope hanging on the side. Inside the saddlebag, he pulled out a hemp-rope halter. He walked over to me, removed my bridle. McBride then secured the halter to my head. He clipped the lead rope to the bridle and said, "Here you go, Tough Guy. No need for you to be on the bit for the next thirty-five miles."

I was grateful he took the snaffle out of my mouth. I never cared for the army-issued bridle bits. That type of bit put too much pressure on my tongue. McBride returned to mount Little Sorrel. He tied the twenty-foot rope to his saddle horn. I did not mind being in tow.

We rode west alongside the Little River Turnpike to get out of Fairfax County. McBride said he did not care for riding roads cluttered with a new-age invention called the automobile. I do not blame him. Us horses did not care for all the noise and smells those contraptions made. The smoke produced from underneath the car smelled horribly bad.[6]

As we traveled along Snickers Turnpike through Loudoun County, McBride told Little Sorrel and me about the Civil War battles that took place between Arlington and Winchester. I was most interested in hearing about the Civil War battlefields where

Stonewall said my grandfather, Lucky carried Confederate troopers: until a U.S. Army cavalry captured him south of Richmond in 1865.

After about ten miles, we arrived at the small town of Aldie in Loudoun County. From there, we turned northwest onto a trail that ran parallel with the Snickers Gap Turnpike. Within sight of the Blue Ridge Mountains, McBride said aloud, "Boys and girls, time to stop and grab some grub before we cross through the gap. Looks like there is good grass over by that creek for you both to eat." He steered Little Sorrel and me away from the trail over to a large draw between two small hills divided by a running creek called the South Fork of Beaverdam. Tall oak trees grew like giants standing guard along both of its banks. The old oaks cast shadows directly beneath their low-hanging limbs. That meant one thing to me. I looked up at the sun directly above us. It was about noon.

McBride stopped us by a dead cedar tree trunk laying on the ground under an old oak tree. I smelled cool water running just on the other side of it. In fact, we both smelled fresh water two miles back. Little Sorrel and I were thirsty. McBride said, "Figure you two need some water. So do I." He dismounted from Little Sorrel and secured her to a low hanging tree limb. He then walked over to me.

The sergeant unhooked my lead from the saddle and walked me down to the creek. Little Sorrel whinnied loudly, wanting her turn. After I had my fill of water, McBride led me back up to the tree line. He secured the rope, then took Little Sorrel down to the creek. A good ten minutes passed before they returned. I guess she was thirsty.

Little Sorrel and I stood side-by-side under the shade tree while McBride sat on a tree log to consume his lunch. While he ate, I thought it would be a good time to socialize with the mare mule I had been following for the last twenty miles.

I neighed at Little Sorrel. She perked up her ears, turned her head toward me. She asked, "What do you want?" Her tempered response took me by surprise. I expected her to be friendlier. The words I wanted to say to her wisely stayed in my head. I replied, "Nothing from you. Just want to talk while your rider mindlessly whistles old Confederate songs and eats his lunch."

"What do you know about Confederate songs?"

"Well, my grandfather served in the U.S. Civil War. He served under General Jeb Stuart himself."

"You don't say. I know that name. Do you know who General Stonewall Jackson was and what side he fought on?"

She got me on that one. I knew *Stonewall* was my father's name, but I never did ask him how he got it.

"Let me educate you," Little Sorrel said with a smug tone.

I looked at her and surrendered my pride. I said, "Please. Go ahead. I am always impressed with a Jenny's ability to tell a story."

Little Sorrell knew that response came from a stallion's arrogance. She kicked her left hind leg out, which barely clipped my right shin.

"Ouch! Why did you do that?"

"The tone of your voice—I don't like it. Show me some respect. I know the human men treat their women like second-class citizens, but you are not going to treat me irreverently, or any other Jenny on four legs!" I recognized she was right. No sense in creating hate and discontent for the remaining trip.

"Little Sorrel, you are right. I will not make that mistake again."

"Good. Then you and I will get along just fine during the rest of the trip."

McBride stood up and started to pack his tin box back into the saddlebag hanging off the right side of Little Sorrel. He said, "Boys and girls. It is about time to get back on the trail. Before we go, I need to take care of some business behind those trees over there."

As he walked away, I continued questioning her about the name *Little Sorrel*.

"How did you get the name *Little Sorrel*?"

"Can't you see my coat has sorrel colors? Plus, I am a mule standing only fourteen and a half hands high. My big ears are another giveaway."

"I am thinking there is another reason why you are called Little Sorrel."

"So you say. Tell me, smarty-pants. What is the other reason?"

"In fact, my dad was named after General Stonewall Jackson, and he told me the general called his horse Little Sorrel, the one he rode during the Battle of First Manassas. The same battle my grandfather Lucky served in. The place where he first met Little Sorrel."

"You got to be kidding me."

"Not one bit. I will tell you one thing my grandfather told me about the first Little Sorrel. She was female like you. Tough on the outside. She relentlessly protected her trooper in battle."

Before Little Sorrel could speak, I neighed a little louder, saying, "And Miss Little Sorrel, I might add. My grandfather said she was a good looking mare with the same reddish coat you have. Like the redheaded Irish women men complain about."

Little Sorrel looked at me and resigned herself to the fact she had met her match. I had won. Regardless of my arrogance, she must have recognized that I was a rather handsome stallion. She kicked me in the shin again.

*****

Standing on the western side of the Blueridge Mountains, we looked down to the valley. McBride said, "The Shenandoah Valley is an ominous sight." He continued, "My four-hooved friends, this is the place where battles were fought and lost between brothers during the civil war. I know. I lost many a friend during those dark days."

McBride guided us down a patched dirt road crossing a bridge over the Shenandoah River. Within a quarter mile, the trees gave way to open pastures McBride said were cleared over two hundred years ago.

After traveling eight more miles, we turned south toward a farm that extended from the Route 1 turnpike to the west, back over to the Shenandoah River to the east. Since we made good time, the sun still had another hour before setting for the day.

We stopped at a crossroad off Route 11, not more than one-mile south of Winchester. McBride turned us left onto a graded road, and continued for two more miles until numerous barns and houses come into view. Several structures were clustered together around a small pond in the distance.

MacBride guided us right onto a dirt road leading to the farm entrance. The road snaked downhill toward a semi-circle driveway in front of an elongated log-cabin style house surrounded by large oak trees. As we got closer, two horse stables in back of the main house came into view. Much to my delight, two oval paddocks were connected to the gabled-roof structures.

As we passed through the main gate, everywhere I looked, from east to west and north to south extended towards nude horizons. The property was beautiful. In one section, golden wheat swayed on a rolling field. The angle of the sunlight shining on the wheat made the grass look like moving waves of water. Even Little Sorrel could smell the beauty before our eyes. I snorted and neighed at her, "This place was to be my home for the rest of my life. I was blessed."

*****

Peace

Tough Guy arrived at President Roosevelt's horse farm in 1904. He was six years old—the prefect age for siring. It was the president's intent for Tough Guy and top-end brood mares to produce offspring purveyed to the wealthy around the world. To those on the inside, the farm was a perfect place providing food, shelter, and safety. Those comforts would not endure over time. The Roosevelt farm's occupants had no way of knowing that in eight years, the world would quickly turn into a bastion of human suffering. Tough Guy and his offspring would write history that their troopers' generations would not want to talk about.

Going Home

Jeremiah Bates

In the year 1897, retired First Sergeant Jeremiah Bates stared at his framed U.S. Army retirement letter hanging on his bedroom wall. Each day before going to work, Jeremiah gave a quick look at the silver-framed certificate. The parchment letter memorializing his best and worst memories. Jeremiah rubbed his chin and slightly shook his head. He whispered to himself, "There has to be a better way."

Jeremiah turned away from the picture and looked down at his wife, Mary, sleeping peacefully under the patch-quilt she made. He noticed the early-morning light coming through the window made her long black Seminole hair reflect blue hues across her chest. Looking at the love of this life, Jeremiah gazed at her peacefulness. He whispered to her, "I do this for you and the children, Mary. Our family."

Since retiring from the United States Army, Jeremiah discovered society had not changed much since the civil war. The only local jobs a black man could get required a strong back and a tight lip. He certainly had strength. He also articulated a sharp mind and wanted to use it.

Jeremiah told Mary he could offer much more to the community. Unfortunately for him, prejudice turned employers the wrong way. Hence, he bemoaned working the odd jobs around Fort Sill as a maintenance man. In his mind, he honorably served his country and deserved a "white man's" job.

With no risk, there is no reward. Jeremiah understood prejudice very well. As such, he set his sights on moving out of the Oklahoma Territory. A territory that was quickly changing hands. The Oklahoma Territory was quickly becoming crowded with settlers that many called "Sooners," who anticipated statehood before the turn of

Leather to Steel

the century. It would take time for the Bates family to prepare, but they needed to relocate before there was no room to live and grow.

Four years later, the Bates family made the change. The family had saved enough money to move back east. Jeremiah wanted to live where he was born—in Arlington, Virginia. His elderly father, Bo, wrote that he knew people looking to hire good horsemen. Jeremiah jumped at the chance. A chance to simply start anew where black men were more welcome. That day came.

Jeremiah and his wife, Mary, agreed that there were three good reasons to move away from the Oklahoma Territory. One, the oldest son, Abraham, a boy of mixed color, could get a good education and, with the right attitude, could earn a decent living. Two, get a better-paying job. Jeremiah's father said he knew someone at a local horse farm looking for a trainer. Jeremiah qualified for the job, since he became an expert horseman during his stint as a U.S. Army cavalryman. Three, Jeremiah wanted to be closer to his elderly father, Bo Bates—a man freed from slavery during the U.S. Civil War.

*****

The spring air swirled around Fort Sill, thanks to the previous eve thunderstorm, it smelled fresh and cool. Jeremiah and Mary thought it to be a good sign. Standing outside their two-bedroom house, the Bates held hands on the front lawn with their five children. Jeremiah said, "Family, this home has provided us shelter and warmth over the past years. Let us bow our heads and pray." The Bates held hands while Jeremiah raised his head to the clouds. He said, "Father, who art in heaven. Bless our family. You continue to provide us strength, health, and encouragement. Keep us safe as we journey to our new beginning. Amen."

Mary squeezed Jeremiah's hand. "We have one more place to go before we leave."

Jeremiah nodded in silence.

The Fort Sill cemetery provided the resting place for many a soldier who fought and died during the Comanche Wars. Jeremiah led his family to the one headstone he knew represented the sacrifice of the troopers he served with. The cavalryman buried beneath was decorated as a hero who on his horse, Stonewall, fought bravely on the battlefields chosen by chance.

He scanned the cemetery's sea of headstones and crosses. Jeremiah said to Mary, "The old oak tree marks the place where the three cavalrymen were laid to rest. Men who fought at the Battle of Tule Canyon during the fall of 1874. The same battle myself, my friends Bill, Joe, and the rest of the Tenth Cavalry chased Comanche warriors from the Llano Estacado back to the Oklahoma Indian Territory."[7]

Mary replied, "I remember you participated in the military honors rendered to the three men." Jeremiah nodded in agreement. At the time, Jeremiah made note of the two oak trees that grew near their gravesites. The trees were not hard to find once inside the cemetery. The trees' trunk girths expanded twice in size. The trees' canopies cast cooling shadows over the three graves.

Jeremiah, Mary, and the kids walked up a trodden dirt path that ran between the trees. Once between the oaks, Jeremiah said, "Mary, we are looking for three side-by-side graves. One of those crosses has the name *J. W. Abercrombie* embossed on the cross."

Mary replied, "I see the cross just behind you." Jeremiah turned around. "You always were a good tracker. That Seminole blood gave you some good eyesight."

Aligned in front of the trees, the three graves faced east. Jeremiah took off his slouch hat to pay his respects. He knelt down and looked at Abercrombie's cross. Moments of silence were observed. He then turned toward Mary and said, "This man was ambushed and killed by a young Comanche who was never found. This man also had a connection to my friend Joe. My friend who should be buried here. Someday I will make it right."

Mary replied, "Your friend Joe Drayton."

"Yes. A man who saw much life. A man who was my father on the trail and a trusted friend."

Mary reached for Jeremiah's hand. Holding it, she said, "I know how much it hurt you to bury Joe on the Texas prairie. You did the right thing not leaving him…"

Leather to Steel

Shaking his head, Jeremiah added, "Not so much the fact Joe was killed by a Comanche, but the fact he did not get a proper military burial. He told me he would have liked to have spent his retirement days back at his home in Charleston, South Carolina, on the Magnolia Plantation."

"I understand your sorrow and sense of loss."

"Of course you understand. The white man raped and killed your family. Stole your tribe's sacred burial grounds."

"Husband, we all have to pay for freedom. Joe did his part."

Jeremiah stood up. He coaxed his children and his wife into a semicircle facing the three graves. The family formed a chain of hands connecting Jeremiah on one end to Mary standing on the opposite side. The Bates family made the sign of the cross on their chests. Jeremiah turned to Mary and said, "Time to go. Time to go home."

*****

The army cargo truck dropped the Bates family off at the new Kansas City Union Station. Jeremiah looked at Mary and grasped her hand. "Well, this is it. Once we are on the train, we are not coming back." Mary looked up at her husband and added, "It will be a nice change for all of us. Before we go into that big building, let me secure the little ones to this twine. I keep in my pocket for occasions like this." She tied the twine to the arms of the two youngest children. She did not want the children to wander off while making their way to the train station ticket counter. Jeremiah did his fatherly duty by holding the hands of the next two older children. The oldest child, five-year-old Abraham, was old enough to walk beside his father.

The family made their way inside the massive train station. Jeremiah located the ticketing office. Standing at the ticket counter, he looked up and read the train schedules. The next train to Virginia was in two hours. He walked up to the ticket counter. A short older man wearing a long-sleeved white shirt, black vest, and a white visor cap asked, "Can I help you?" Jeremiah removed his worn brown army-issued slouch hat and said, "Yes, sir. I would like to purchase two tickets for the next train to Virginia."

Clint Goodwin

"Mister," the ticketing agent said, "You need seven tickets—one for each of you."

Jeremiah scratched his head. "Well, I thought since the children did not take up much room, we would only need two adult tickets. The children will sit with us—two on our laps and three at our feet."

The ticket agent took off his visor to push back what little gray hair he had on his head. He replaced the visor and spit tobacco juice into a brass spittoon near his feet. He shook his head and remained silent for a few minutes. Then he mumbled to himself. A few minutes passed by as he looked over the seven-member family. Staring at Jeremiah, the ticket agent noticed the army slouch hat in hand. He asked, "Did you serve, mister? The cavalry hat you are holding in your hand."

"Yes, sir. I did. Between 1872 and 1898. I rode with the Tenth Cavalry Regiment out of Fort Reno and Fort Sill until I retired in '98."

"Well, I be dang," said the ticket agent, smiling now. He added, "My cousin was stationed at Fort Sill back in those days. He is gone now. My mother says he was killed by a Comanche."

"What was his name?"

"My mother, God rest her soul, called her nephew JW, I think. Anyways, does not matter now. He is gone. So you served as he did. Okay, mister, what is your name?"

"Jeremiah Bates, sir."

"Well, Mr. Jeremiah Bates, this is what I can do for you. Since you are colored, you know you have to ride in the colored-only passenger car. That will be the last car on the train. I will get you and your family on the four fifty-five for the price of three tickets. Seven people for the price of three tickets."

Jeremiah reached down into his pocket and pulled out several greenbacks and change. He looked at Mary. "We will need to eat beans and rice for a couple of days."

"Husband. We have gotten by on far less. Pay the man."

Jeremiah handed twenty-six dollars to the ticket agent. The agent stamped the paper tickets and handed seven tickets to Jeremiah. The agent said, "Now listen closely. These tickets are not transferable.

The conductor will punch them once your family is on board. Those tickets will get your family from Union Station to Richmond, Virginia. From there, you will transfer to a short-haul train to Fairfax, Virginia. You should arrive in Arlington on Saturday, May 16."

Jeremiah reached through the ticket window to shake the agent's hand. The agent accepted Jeremiah's hand. After shaking hands, Jeremiah pulled his hand back to tuck the rest of his money back into this front pants pocket. He looked back at the agent. "By the way, sir, what is your name?"

"Abercrombie. Billy Abercrombie."

Jeremiah put the slouch hat back on. He nodded towards Billy. No further discussions were needed. Jeremiah decided it best to keep it to himself.

*****

With train tickets in hand, the Bateses made their way to the train station platform. Several wooden benches lined the passenger waiting area. The Bateses occupied three benches for two hours. Patiently waiting, the kids played hopscotch while Jeremiah and Mary held hands and prayed. When the train arrived, the Bates family walked to the last car to wait for the train conductor. Several other colored families waited with the Bateses. Once the conductor situated the white passengers, he then walked to the last passenger car to take tickets for passage to the east.

*****

The trip from Kansas City, Kansas to Virginia took one and a half days. Mary was glad the trip would be short. Her five children tried her patience being cooped up in a passenger car that rode rough on the tracks. Modern transportation took less time compared to the horse-drawn wagon days Jeremiah and Mary lived through. A time where horses required rest and passengers needed food for the long haul.

During the trip, Jeremiah enjoyed having his family sitting close together in back of the passenger car near the windows. He wanted the children to learn about the countryside. Crossing through Tennessee and Kentucky, Jeremiah pointed out the significance of several U.S. Civil War battles that were fought in places like the Shiloh-Pittsburg Landing in Tennessee. When they crossed into Kentucky, Jeremiah told his children the U.S. president that set colored men free was born in Hodgenville. He was President Abraham Lincoln.[8]

*****

The elder Bo Bates anxiously waited at the Fairfax train station for his son's arrival. Standing above the shoulders of others waiting on the platform, he could easily see the train push itself around the bend. He listened to the train's engineer pull on the brakes, causing the locomotive's wheels to screech, metal on metal. Bo covered his ears to deaden the shrilled noise. The conductor pulled the whistle three times to signal the train's stop.

*****

Bo carefully watched each passenger car door open, one by one. It took a few minutes for all the passengers to start unloading. He figured Jeremiah and his family would be in the back cars. So he limped over to the end of the station platform with great anticipation. Bo had not seen his son Jeremiah, daughter-in-law Mary, and the grandkids in several years. The twins would be new to him.

Bo moved slowly but surely. Startled by a sudden noise, he looked to his left up the track. The train blew out another three, quick loud whistles. The engine's steam lines spewed white clouds of mist across the tracks. Bo shook his head. He mumbled, "Never got used to those sounds after the war. Not since the Siege of Richmond."

Trying to get a glimpse of his son, Bo put his hands over his furrowed eyebrow to deflect the afternoon sunlight from his eyes. He scanned each car to ensure he did not miss them. He was getting nervous. The station platform was getting more crowded. The locomotive released steam again. White puffs of smoke bellowed

Leather to Steel

across the tracks. Bo backed away from the edge of the platform to avoid the white steam bellowing across the platform. He waited.

*****

Jeremiah sat next to the passenger car window throughout the whole trip. As the train slowed by the platform, he kept watch for his father, Bo. Mary nudged Jeremiah. He turned to look at her and said, "What did you do that for?"

"Husband. It had been too many years in between visits. Do you remember what he looks like?"

"Of course, I do. No one could miss my father in a crowd. A giant of a man standing six-foot six. Weighing about two hundred and twenty-five pounds. My father stands well above others." Jeremiah returned to looking out the window and noticed an older-looking black man wearing faded overalls over a red plaid shirt looking at every passenger car. Jeremiah stared at the man he respected most in the world. He patted the window to get his father's attention. Bo saw his son's hand waving back.

Jeremiah helped Mary and the five kids step down from the passenger car. Bo walked up and looked at his son with approving eyes. He said. "Come here, boy. It has been some time." Jeremiah walked toward his father with arms open. The two men embraced. Looking into Jeremiah's eyes, Bo spoke softly, "Son, I have missed ya boy."

Jeremiah replied, "Me too, Pops. It has been too long. That changes today. We got much to catch up on."

After the men hugged, Mary interrupted, "Excuse me. My turn." She stepped in front of Jeremiah and tried to wrap her arms around her father-in-law. He placed his large hand on her right shoulder. "Thank you for kicking my son in the rear to get out here." She looked at Jeremiah, who shrugged off the remark. She turned back toward Bo. "So good to see you." She tried to kiss Bo on the cheek but could not reach his face. Bo bent down.

Jeremiah turned his attention to the end of the train where railroad porters unloaded boxcars and the caboose. He said, "Good. I see our luggage on the platform. I will take little Abraham with me to pick up our stuff." Looking at his dad, Jeremiah said, "Pop, please stay here with Mary and the rest of the kids." Bo acted as though he wanted to help but realized his son was giving him an honorable excuse from performing a task he probably could not physically handle.

After the Bateses had secured their luggage, Jeremiah and family followed Bo to his friend's Ford truck. Bo stood by the driver's door. A grin spanned Bo's face from ear to ear. "Son, I bet you thought I would never drive one of these things." With eyes wide open, Jeremiah replied, "No, sir. I never would have imagined it in a thousand years."

"Well, I reckon that is to be expected." Bo continued, "We don't have far to drive. The city roads are paved here in the east. I am sure the roads, or should I say *trails*, are still potted and rough back west."

Jeremiah smirked. "Not really, Pops. There is modern progress back west. There are even water pipes running into the houses."

Bo reacted, "You don't say."

"I do say," laughed Jeremiah.

*****

Jeremiah had no problem getting a job working at Fort Myer. His father had labored as a blacksmith for almost thirty years at Fort Wipple [renamed Fort Myer], after the civil war. Bo knew all the horse trainers still working at the fort. He had also made a reputation for himself. He earned every cavalry trooper's deepest respect during his service. This respect helped Bo pull a few strings to land his son a job taking care of horses. Special horses. Horses that pulled caissons of dead heroes who were laid to rest with honors at the Arlington National Cemetery.

Finding a home was not a problem. Bo insisted Jeremiah, Mary, and the kids move in with him, until they could save up enough money to get their own place. The three-bedroom house was a tight fit for all eight, but they managed. Close families do so during tough times. For Jeremiah, the temporary sacrifice of space was worth being near his father. He would be with Bo until his last breath. Jeremiah did not want to make the same mistake he did with his

Leather to Steel

mother who passed back in 1897. A military leave situation Jeremiah could not control.

The United States Army would not give him leave to attend his mother's funeral. He regretted not being with his mother during her final days. Consumption took her life very quickly. He did not have a chance to say his last good-bye. However, his faith in Christ comforted him, knowing he would see her again in heaven. Jeremiah was also comforted by his father, who said the good Lord was with her. She did not suffer too long.

*****

Living in Northern Virginia meant Jeremiah and Mary could give their children a better life. The public schools were more modern than the one-room schoolhouses back at Fort Sill. Jeremiah understood the importance of the kids getting a solid education. He and Mary believed that education equated to more respect and opportunities for their children. Better jobs meant making a better living; instead of working as a farmhand or a housemaid for the rest of their days.

Mary still had her concerns. They came from the country. She had her moments fretting about moving their five children to a place where "city folk" may not understand their ways. Jeremiah put her at ease, knowing the eastern people were more accepting of colored folks than those down South.

*****

The months flew by at the Bates home. During their first year, the children adjusted to the town schools, making friends of other colors they had not known back in Fort Sill. There were light-brown-skinned folks called Italians, white folks called Irishmen, and tallow folks called Chinese. People from all walks of life. Mary was relieved. All was well at the Bates home, until an unrelenting cough attached itself to the eldest Bates.

Bo's health deteriorated to the point where he could not walk. He needed assistance with getting around the house. Even getting dressed was difficult. A prideful man, Bo refused assistance from Jeremiah and Mary in the beginning of his discomfort. Eventually, the pain in his body forced reluctance to give way to necessity. The pain in his joints was too great.

The Sunday before their first Thanksgiving together, Bo could not get up out of bed. He mumbled, "The time has come." He called out to his son, "Jeremiah, son. I need you."

Jeremiah and Mary rushed into his bedroom. Since the bed was pushed up against the window, the headboard cast a dark shadow onto Bo's face. Jeremiah hurried to his father's bedside. After switching on the floor lamp, he knelt down by the bedside and grasped Bo's hand. Jeremiah asked, "Pops, what can we do for you? How can we make you comfortable?"

Bo looked up at his son's long face. He motioned Jeremiah to lower his head. He released his son's hand and placed it on Jeremiah's cheek. He whispered. "I love you, son."

Tears immediately formed up in Jeremiah's eyes. He leaned over Bo, his tears falling onto Bo's cheek. Jeremiah looked into his father's brown eyes. Eyes that were now covered with gray spots. Jeremiah attempted to provide comfort. "Pops. You are going to be okay. Everything will be fine here. You don't have to struggle anymore on earth. You don't need to worry about us. We will be fine. I know you have been hanging on, not wanting to let go."

Bo took a deep breath. He motioned Jeremiah to get closer.

Nose to nose, Jeremiah asked. "What is it you want to say?"

Bo whispered, "Son, there is a branding iron under my bed. You must never lose it. Your mother brought it with her from the Magnolia Plantation. You will know what to do with it."

The elderly Bates gasped again for air, and then slowly breathed out. Jeremiah watched his father's eyelids slowly close. Bo's chest heaved up once more, then back down. His body then went still.

Jeremiah looked up to the bedroom ceiling and said, "Mother, he is coming home to you. Please show him the way." He laid his face onto his father's chest and quietly wept.

*****

On the next day, Jeremiah traveled to Fort Myer, Virginia. His goal was to gain approval for burying his father in Arlington Cemetery. He wanted the army to honor and respect Bo's service. The answer he sought could only be answered by the Fort Myer commanding officer.

Jeremiah had no trouble getting on the post. There were no guards at the main gate, so he walked along a main road winding along the hill Fort Myer buildings and officer housing were situated overlooking the Arlington Cemetery. As he walked, he noticed several large Victorian houses lined up in a secluded area surrounded by big oak trees. Jeremiah mumbled, "Them army officers live pretty good here."

He knew to walk along the sidewalk. Each house had a small white sign placed in the respective house's front yard. The first sign on the corner did the trick. Stenciled on it in black letters were the words "Commanding Officer." He walked to the front door and knocked. A colored woman answered the door. "What do you want n—"

Jeremiah replied in a terse tone, "Miss, I don't know you, but I am no n—. I am an American, like you."

The older colored woman relaxed her jaw. She wiped her hands on the white apron she wore over a light-blue dress. "I am sorry. I was not polite. How can I help you at this time of the morning?"

"I know it is a holiday week. I was hoping to catch the colonel."

"Mister, first of all what is your name?" Jeremiah removed his slouch hat.

"Jeremiah. Jeremiah Bates."

The woman replied, "My name is Ellie. Ellie Cannon. I am the head housemaid here."

Jeremiah bowed. "Pleased to meet you, Miss Ellie."

"Mister Bates. Colonel Moore is working over near the new stables. Just walk back to the way you came in and turn left. The stables are being built closer to the main road about two blocks down."

Jeremiah put his hat back on and smiled at the woman. "Thank ya, ma'am."

Before Jeremiah could turn around, Ellie stopped him. "Excuse me. Why, might I ask, you look'n for the colonel?"

"I need his permission to bury my father in Arlington cemetery."

"I see. So--- who was your father, sonny?"

"Bo Bates. Mister Bo Bates. He retired as a government civilian working for the United States Army. As a matter of fact, he was the head blacksmith for Fort Whipple back in the day."

"I am sorry for your loss." Ellie's eyes started to tear up. Jeremiah put his hand on her shoulder. "It is okay. He died peacefully at home."

"I am sorry. I--- I am without words. You better get on."

Jeremiah tipped his hat to Ellie. "Much obliged," Ellie replied. "Godspeed."

Jeremiah left the house and walked back to the fort's main entrance. Eyes watched him. Miss Ellie had more to say, but could not find the words. She knew Jeremiah's father back during the Civil War. In fact, they were both slaves of Colonel William Cannon's plantation in North Carolina. A colonel who pledged his life to the Confederate States of America.

*****

The Fort Myer commander expressed his condolences to Jeremiah. However, the conversation did not set well with Jeremiah. The colonel said it was department policy not to bury nonmilitary men in the Arlington National Cemetery. Jeremiah was disappointed. Bo was not a veteran, but he did serve the Union once he became a Freeman. Jeremiah suspiciously thought otherwise. The army would not allow him to bury his father in the military cemetery because Bo was colored.

Though Jeremiah's anger could be justified, he had to let it go. If he made ill of the situation, the army could easily take his job away. He did not want to push the issue. Instead, he relented and made arrangements for his father to be buried next to his mother in a colored cemetery near the District of Columbia.

*****

Leather to Steel

After Bo's funeral, Jeremiah, Mary, and the kids returned home to host the wake. Many of Bo's old friends showed up at the Bates' home to pay their respects. Their wives brought food dishes to celebrate the life of Bo Bates. Jeremiah and Mary were not surprised so many came to pay their respects. One older man was grateful to have made it. His name was Jack Welford.

Wearing his best and only black suit, Jack moved from room to room looking for Jeremiah. He found him standing in the kitchen. The spitting image of a younger Bo was nursing a glass of Kentucky bourbon. Welford approached Bo to express his condolences. He spoke to Jeremiah. "Son, I am sorry for your loss. You don't know me, but I used to work with your father on Fort Whipple back in the day. Right after the war. Well, now they call it Fort Myer." [9]

Jeremiah nodded and thanked Welford for coming. Welford continued, "After your father retired, I soon followed his lead. Now, I manage a horse farm out near Winchester, Virginia. A five-hundred-acre farm about seventy miles west of here."

Jeremiah said, "Thank you for coming. I know my father would be pleased."

Welford rubbed his chin and said to Jeremiah, "Jeremiah, the last time I spoke to your father, he said you were very good with horses. In fact, you served with the Buffalo Soldiers, Tenth Cavalry Regiment."

"Yes, sir. I did."

"Your father told me you fought at the Battle of San Juan Hill with Colonel Teddy Roosevelt."

"Yes, sir, I did." Jeremiah started getting fidgety, not really wanting to talk about himself. He wanted the day focused on his father. He turned his head aside from Mr. Welford.

"Sir, if you would, please excuse me. I need to get over into the living room to help Mary serve the folks. It was a great pleasure meeting you. Follow me and we will get you a plate of food. Good vittles. Chicken and dumplings, collard greens, cream of corn, and many deserts the women folk brought. Come on, I will dish out some food for you."

"Thank you, son," Welford replied with a smile. "I think I will. But before we go, Jeremiah, I have something for you." Welford reached into his inside jacket pocket and pulled out a white piece of paper. He handed it to Bo. "Here. This is how you can get hold of me. We are expanding the Winchester horse farm. We will need another experienced horse trainer."

Jeremiah took the piece of paper. He looked it over, then looked back at Welford. After stuffing the paper in his front shirt pocket, he grinned at Welford. He nodded and said, "Much obliged, sir. Can I think about it?"

"Why, sure you can. Take all the time you need," bellowed Welford. "Just send me a cable when you are ready to talk." Jeremiah nodded his head again, turned, and walked into the living room. Welford did not follow. Instead, he slipped out the kitchen back door. He had many horses to tend and was, at the moment, a one-man show.

*****

With both parents gone, Jeremiah knew it was time to move out of his childhood home. It would never feel the same with his father gone. The feeling drove him to think about the future and what he could do to better situate his family.

Sitting on the front porch drinking iced tea, Jeremiah remembered his father's last words—the branding iron. He spoke with urgency: "I almost forgot." He immediately stood up from his rocking chair and ran back into the house toward his father's room.

Once in the room, he got down on his knees beside his father's old bed. He reached under the bed and waved his arm from side to side trying to locate the branding iron. He mumbled. "Nothing on the floor on this side." He got up and went to the other side of the bed. This time he lay on the floor to reach farther under the bed. No luck. Jeremiah pushed himself back out and sat back up on his knees. He said, "Where in heck is that branding iron?"

By the time he said iron, Mary walked in. "What are you doing, husband?"

"Trying to find that branding iron Pop told me about when he was taking his last few breaths on this earth."

"Did you try looking on the other side of the bed?"

"Yep."

Mary put her hands on her hips. She said, "I know. Your father complained about how the box springs squeaked with the slightest movement of his body."

"So...what are you saying?"

"He must have reinforced the box springs with something stiff. Over the last few months, he never complained about the bed squeaking."

Jeremiah stood up and said, "I see where you are going with this. Let's pull off the bedding." They piled up the blanket, sheets, and pillow on the dresser. Jeremiah said, "Now, help me with the mattress and box springs."

Jeremiah and Mary leaned the mattress against the wall.

"Those old box springs must weigh at least a hundred pounds," Mary complained.

Jeremiah observed. "Mary. I can see something dark lodged inside the springs."

Mary attempted to put her hands inside, but Jeremiah stopped her. "Darling. Take care reaching into these old metal springs. Those stiff metal springs will pinch your hands something awful."

Mary nodded her head in agreement.

With the box springs leaning against the wall, Jeremiah and Mary stepped back and saw what prevented the springs from squeaking. Jeremiah reached inside the springs to loosen them. He pulled on each spring enough to enable Mary to slide the iron out.

Holding the branding iron in her hands, she commented, "Looks like your father found good use of the iron."

Jeremiah looked at the unusual design his father, a blacksmith himself, forged out of hot steel. He looked closely at the tip of the iron. The shape was in two parts. He asked Mary, "What does that look like to you?"

"Hard to tell, since you can really only tell by branding something."

Jeremiah contemplated Mary's comment. After a minute of thinking, he said, "Mary. Let us go into the kitchen. You still have the wood stove fired up?"

"Yes, I do. Just getting the coals fired up for cooking some pies later today."

"Great. Come on."

Jeremiah and Mary left Bo's bedroom and hurried over into the kitchen. Abraham was sitting at the kitchen table eating something. After taking a bite from his sandwich, he looked up at his parents. "Dad, what is that you're holding?"

Jeremiah replied, "Son, first, don't talk with your mouth full. To answer your question, this is a branding iron. Not sure what the brand shape is. We won't know until we brand something." Abraham's young mind could not understand the concept of a branding iron. He replied, "Sounds good to me. I think I will go back outside to play."

"Good idea," replied Mary. Then She added, "Also, make sure your brothers and your sister keep it down while the twins sleep."

"Okay, Mamma."

As he was walking out the door, Mary called to him. "Don't forget to come back in and clean up your mess."

"Yes, Mamma."

Jeremiah was standing by the potbellied stove that was already hot to the touch. He put on an oven mitt to lift off the stove's top cover. He then inserted the tip of the iron into the glowing red coals. After about five minutes, the iron started getting hot to the touch. The tip turned red. Jeremiah's forearm briefly touched the stove's edge. He shouted, "Ouch. Getting hot quick."

Mary reached over to the kitchen countertop to grab the second oven mitt. She handed it to Jeremiah and said, "Here, put this on. Two is better than one."

Jeremiah quickly put the second mitt on before twisting the iron in the wood coals.

Jeremiah peered into the stove and noticed the end of the iron was glowing orange and red. He looked backed at Mary. "Mary, open the kitchen door up when I say, go. I will then pull out the iron and quickly run to the old oak tree near our backyard fence."

Mary asked, "What are you going to do, then?"

"Brand the tree."

Mary walked over to the kitchen door. She peeked through the kitchen window and said, "All is clear. No kids between here and the fence."

"Okay. Here we go. Open the door!" Jeremiah pulled the hot iron out of the stove and ran out through the kitchen door to the fence. Standing by the oak, he pressed the end of the iron into a smoothed circular oak knot with a six-inch radius. The knot began to smoke.

Mary yelled from the porch, "What does it look like?"

Jeremiah replied. "Shut the door and come on over and look. You will be amazed when I tell you the story about the Magnolia Plantation.

*****

Jeremiah remembered the names of several horsemen in the area his father mentioned. He followed up with several farm owners in Northern Virginia that his dad talked about, but none were hiring. He did not get discouraged. He kept trying.

One day, while eating breakfast in the kitchen, Jeremiah read the Richmond paper. He read an interesting article about how popular the polo pony sport was becoming. The word *polo* nagged at him. Mary was sitting across the kitchen table trying to feed the twins. He looked at her and asked, "What did you do with my good shirt after the wake?"

"Darling, since you did not get it dirty, I simply hung it back up in our closet."

Jeremiah said, "Excuse me, dear." He scooted his chair back, got up, and hurried out of the kitchen. Inside their bedroom, Jeremiah moved toward the closet. He only had a few shirts hanging. He slid the long-sleeved white shirt toward him. Jeremiah reached into the front pocket and said to himself, "Got it. He looked up at the ceiling and said, "Thanks, Pops. I know what to do now."

Jeremiah's reputation as a horse trainer got the ear of Jack Welford, who trained horses owned by Teddy Roosevelt. The horses were specially trained animals. Roosevelt's farm turned them into polo ponies and sold them to very wealthy families competing in polo games around the world.

    A few cable exchanges between Wilfred, Roosevelt, and Jeremiah sealed the deal for the job offer of a lifetime. Jeremiah and Mary talked about it. Using the money made from selling the old house, Jeremiah and Mary relocated their family to Winchester, Virginia.

Texas Remembered

The summer of 1904 brought many blessings for the Bates family. Since moving to Virginia, retired U.S. Army sergeant Jeremiah Bates finally landed a white man's job training horses, on a farm no less owned by President Theodore Roosevelt. The farm boss, Jack Welford, recommended hiring Bates to meet the growing demand for polo horses. During his conversation with Welford, the president asked, "Bates. That name sounds familiar. Who is he?"

"Sir— well, he did retire from the U.S. Army Cavalry."

"I wonder if he is the same Sergeant Bates who served with me at San Juan Hill."

"Sir, I think he did say he served during the Red River War and fought at San Juan Hill."

President Roosevelt had the memory of an elephant. He never forgot a face. In 1898, then, Rough Riders Colonel Teddy Roosevelt vowed to never forget the brave men who served with him. In particular, the black soldier who ran between shots to bring the colonel a big black stallion. A horse that took the colonel up San Juan Hill to claim victory. A magnificent moment for both rider and horse. Remembering his commitment, the president told Welford to offer Bates the job of training horses. A job that an experienced cavalryman understood too well.

*****

Sitting on the front porch of his new Winchester home, Jeremiah Bates looked back at his life and thanked the Lord for every day he lived. He was grateful for making a positive difference in the lives of others. His father told him, "Son. Two feelings in life you must know in your heart before you leave this earth. One, experience joy. The second is give joy." Jeremiah did just that.

Jeremiah and many Freedman—like him—after the civil war endured and continued to struggle for equality in America. He learned to take it. Being the bigger man, he always found a way to improvise and overcome each one of them, for the sake of his family. He remembered what his deceased friend, Corporal Joe Drayton, told him while patrolling the Red River back in 1874. "Never get angry. Let your heart guide your soul. Always remain calm."

After taking a sip of hot coffee, Jeremiah looked down at his herding dog Yank and said, "Well boy, we did good moving back east. Mary and the kids are happier here. The folks around these parts do not much care we are of color. I suppose it could not get any better than this."

Yank looked up at him and barked. Jeremiah rubbed the dog's neck. He heard a rustling up in the big black walnut tree to the right of his yard. Jeremiah looked up and grinned at the sight of two gray squirrels chasing each other for the rights to a weathered walnut. He looked down at Yank. "I wonder who is going to win that race. My, how fast the years go by."

Jeremiah often thought about the United States Army Tenth Cavalry, better known as the Buffalo Soldiers, stationed in Fort Sill, Oklahoma. A military service that provided First Sergeant Bates an opportunity to work twice as hard for army promotions when compared to his white counterparts at Fort Sill. He had to overcome the fact that he was a soldier of color. Fortunately, the army recognized his strength of character and willingness to obey orders, by approving every reenlistment. His uncompromising work ethic was what the army demanded from all troopers. Jeremiah proved he had the temperament to serve his country.

During his service, the good Lord did not want Jeremiah to walk on the earth alone. Thus, Jeremiah was given the choice to take a wife, who gifted him five children to love and care for.

His wife-to-be came by fate. He met and married a young woman from the reservation. She had been attending the same church Bates frequented when not on patrol. The preacher said the Seminole tribes banished her from their tepees. The pastor's wife took her in out of compassion. She could not speak English. However, Mary

Leather to Steel

quickly learned to work in exchange for room and board. She learned English along the way.

Bates shared with a fellow soldier that it was a spiritual obligation to help the squaw. That obligation evolved into a sense of commitment and love between Bates and the Seminole woman whom he eventually fell in love with. Jeremiah prayed to Jesus, asking for guidance. Working with the church congregation, the Seminole squaw was baptized in the name of Christ. Her reborn name would be Mary.

*****

Jeremiah and Mary had a tough time raising a family in Fort Sill, Oklahoma. All the more reason to move east. Northern Virginia would be more accepting of mixed colors. In Oklahoma, the Bateses experienced racially charged maltreatment by whites on a daily basis. However, this torment did not deter them. Jeremiah always preached to his children that forgiveness was better than vengeance. That the Bible says,

> *For we know him that hath said, Vengeance belongeth unto me, I will recompense, saith the Lord. And again, The Lord shall judge his people.* (Hebrews 10:30 KJV)

Jeremiah drew spiritual strength from the Lutheran Church family he worshiped with since 1898. The Bateses prayed and lived by His words. Fortunately, they joined a good Christian church in downtown Winchester. With the church, the Bateses gained spiritual peace and moral strength that extended to their five children: Abraham, five years of age, Isaiah, three years old, Corinth two years of age, and the one-year-old twin babies, Luke and Daniel. Through faith and Providence, the Bates family's moral courage provided them a humbled and respected life. They were a true reflection of an American family.

Sunday was the day for rest, relaxation, prayer, and reflection. After the traditional Sunday supper, Jeremiah, Mary, and the kids would gather in their living room illuminated by burning wood in the fireplace and two lit oil lamps hung on each side of the front window. The children would sit cross-legged on horse blankets in the center of the room. Mary rocked in her worn oak chair in the family room, while Jeremiah settled into his cracking leather chair, where only he sat.

During family time, Jeremiah told days-of-old stories to his children. He wanted them to remember how things came to be for the family. He repeatedly reminded them, "Our nation is condemned to repeat history, if we do not understand it."

Jeremiah often told stories of his time in the United States Army. His favorite war story was about a horse he rode during the Battle of San Juan Hill in July 1898. He would tell the beginning of the story with pride. He said to his wife and children, "While standing outside the Fort Sill commander's office, the post's quartermaster happened to walk by and handed me a notice calling for volunteer troopers to sign up with the First United States Volunteer Cavalry. I looked at the notice and exclaimed, 'What is this all about?' The quartermaster spat tobacco juice on the deck and then replied to me, 'Sergeant, the United States is preparing for war with Spain. I reckon it has to do with helping those Cuban revolutionaries gain their independence. Kinda like what we did back in 1776 with Britain. You interested?'

"I looked down at the notice, then back up at the quartermaster, and proclaimed. 'You know... I think I might need to talk to the missus about it.'

Mary always appreciated it when Jeremiah tossed respect her way.

Bates continued his story. "In his grumpy tone, the quartermaster said, 'Well, you need to let us know by tomorrow, Bates. The cavalry commander, Colonel Roosevelt is requesting all volunteers be present for duty in San Antonio by May.'

Bates looked at his wife Mary and said to his kids, "I returned home and shared the First United States Volunteer Cavalry Call for Volunteers notice with your mother."

The children looked at their mother and said in unison, "Mother. What did you say? Did you cry?" Mary looked into the eyes of each child. "I did not speak much English then. I suppose he thought I said yes, when I actually meant no." The family broke out laughing. Jeremiah laughed so much his eyes started to water.

Mary saw a few tears roll down her husband's cheeks. She knew it was happening again. The tears of sadness were for his friend Joe Drayton. A brave soldier killed by a Comanche warrior's arrow. The mental episodes were triggered without warning. She commanded, "Children, enough stories. Go outside and play."

The memories of battle would never go away. During these moments, Mary finally convinced her husband to talk about what had happened. Wiping tears from his eyes, Jeremiah let out a heavy sigh. "I held my dying friend Joe Drayton out in the middle of nowhere in the Texas Panhandle. I watched him bleed out on the battlefield. I could do nothing to stop the bleeding with one hand while shooting at Comanche with the other." Mary showed empathy. She said, "Sergeant Jeremiah Bates, time for a cup of tea." Her voice broke through his thoughts. "Of course. That would be good," Jeremiah replied.

On the next Sunday afternoon, the Bateses gathered together in their family room. Jeremiah sat in his old chair reading the Sunday paper. Mary sat on the couch darning socks, while the children quietly played a marble game.

Abraham broke the silence. "What happened next? You have not finished the story about the war with Spain. Please, please, go on." Jeremiah looked at Mary and winked. He then nodded at Abraham and sighed, "Well, okay, son, I will finish it." All the children clapped with excitement.

"Now, kids. Your mother and I prayed together about the decision to go or not to support the war effort against Spain. At the end of the day, the answer was yes. Children, remember, being an American means we are willing to die for freedom. Freedom is not free. So I packed my horse and left for San Antonio on May 5, 1898. You know what comes next in the story?"

The children knew the answer. They said in unison, "The black stallion is coming!"

"Indeed, children. This is where I meet a legacy. A cavalry horse called Stonewall, for the second time."

He never forgot the first time he saw Stonewall in east Texas back 1874 when he and his friend Joe were patrolling along the Red River. Jeremiah often told the story about how a Comanche's arrow killed Joe after the Battle of Tule Canyon. Jeremiah could never forget how his friend, a brother of skin, died in his arms. Jeremiah was ordered to bury Drayton where he lay dead.

Jeremiah Bates lived by every word the Freedman, Joe Drayton taught him. The battle stories Joe spoke of were unkind reminders of an unforgiving past. Lessons were learned and passed on.

One story Jeremiah loves to share has to do with a black stallion. He tells of an excited Corporal Joe Drayton who recognized a mounted black stallion traveling with an army cavalry regiment column patrolling across the Red River. Drayton thought the stallion was the same horse he raised and fought with during the U.S. Civil War. Both men knew the stallion with the magnolia tree brand was too young to be that horse. But the hopeful Drayton was emphatic about it. "That has to be Lucky!"

Jeremiah had doubt and knew better then. However, years later while fighting at San Juan Hill, Cuba, Jeremiah crossed paths with a black horse bearing the magnolia brand—Stonewall. Fate had brought them together for a reason. A reason not be realized until 1904.

*****

Jeremiah lived for years with the silent pain of knowing his friend Joe Drayton was buried alone on the Texas Panhandle plains. He always thought about Joe and that mournful day in September 1874. The day a band of Comanche warriors ambushed Jeremiah's platoon. The day his Buffalo Soldiers patrolled back to Fort Sill. Feeling high in the saddle and filled with good spirits, the troopers were honored to know Colonel "Bad Hand" McKenzie commended their courage after routing the Indians during the Battles of Tule and Palo Duro Canyons.

Leather to Steel

Jeremiah said to Mary, "Darl'n, you know I have been wrestling with many pains from the battles I fought. The battle I fight right now is in my heart. I need to go back to the plains and find my friend Joe. I and several other Buffalo soldiers buried him out in the Texas Panhandle, east of Abilene. My heart sinks every time I think about how his remains rest in the middle of nowhere. At least his grave has God's headstone. Two hundred pounds of pink granite sticking out of the ground; marking his grave. But Joe still deserves better."

"Yes, dear husband. I understand." Mary walked over to hug Jeremiah. She whispered, "You go. The children and I will be fine. You must journey to the past to get to the future."

Jeremiah puts his hands on Mary's shoulders, looked into her brown eyes. "God blessed me bringing you into my life. I am proud to call you my wife. Always have."

Mary released her hug and stepped back. She said, "I know. I love you too."

*****

Mister Welford gave Jeremiah permission to take no more than one week from work. He told Jeremiah that ten mares would be foaling during the first week in October. Jeremiah knew his job depended upon coming back, as directed. He had to be home by October 1, no later. Jeremiah figured two days back to Fort Sill. One day to the site. One day's ride back in time to bury Joe at the fort cemetery. Only two days needed to return home. If all went well, Jeremiah would have a one-day cushion.

Jeremiah packed his old cotton duffel bag with a change of clothes and his army dress uniform. Mary walked in while he packed. She asked, "Why take the uniform?" He replied, "Need to make things right. I remember being at the Fort Sill cemetery presenting honors to a white soldier killed by a Comanche after the Red River wars. If my memory serves me right, that soldier's name was Abercrombie. The fellas said he was a good trooper.

During his burial, I and two other troopers fired our rifle three times to honor that man. Each time I fired, I thought about my friend Joe, buried out in the middle of nowhere in the Texas Panhandle."

Mary reached out to hold Jeremiah's hand. He continued. "The army needs to do right by him. I plan to bring his bones back to Fort Sill for a proper burial." Mary nodded her head. She stepped up close to her husband to wipe the tears from him eyes.

Friday was payday. Jeremiah collected his wages and went down to the train station to get his ticket. Jeremiah bought a twenty-dollar boarding pass that covered his fare from Winchester, all the way to Fort Sill, Oklahoma. The station's ticket officer said getting there would not be easy. There would be train changes in Martinsburg and Richmond, then on to Kansas City. From there, Jeremiah would take a bus down to Fort Sill.

Once in Fort Sill, he would meet up with his old friend Bud White. Bud returned a telegraph assuring Jeremiah he would have four horses ready to ride. They would ride hard from Fort Sill to the Red River, then into East Texas. From there, travel northwest across the Texas plains. Jeremiah knew the trail to Joe's burial site all too well. He rehearsed the moment in his mind a million times; since the day he buried his friend near God's granite headstone.

*****

Jeremiah woke up early Saturday morning. Sitting on the edge of the bed, he reached over to the nightstand to turn on the reading lamp. Mary lying next to him mumbled, "What time is it?" Jeremiah picked his pocket watch off the stand. He flipped open the cover. "Five o'clock. The stopwatch starts now, September 24, 1904."

He rolled out of bed and walked briskly to the bathroom to clean up and shave. Jeremiah returned to the bedroom. Mary had gotten up and gone into the kitchen. Thoughtfully, she laid out a clean pair of Levis, a brown corduroy shirt, and socks on the bed. Mary placed Jeremiah's black work boots near the dresser, and his favorite slouch hat on the bedpost.

He heard Mary yell out of the kitchen. "Come on, Mr. Bates. I got your breakfast wait'n for ya."

He replied, "I can smell the coffee. As soon as I get dressed. Com'n fast to ya, Missus Bates. I will just follow my nose."

Jeremiah sat at the kitchen table with Mary and his oldest son, Abraham, who insisted on getting up to see his father off. Jeremiah always sat at the head of the table to get a clear view through the kitchen window. He watched the morning sky gradually turn into shades of blue and purple. Minutes later, the reds, oranges, and yellow color bands dominated as the sun broached the horizon. Jeremiah reached over to gently shake Abraham's shoulder. The boy had laid his head down on the table and fallen back asleep.

"Wake up, boy." Jeremiah gently nudged Abraham.

The boy lifted his head and said, "Sorry, Dad."

Jeremiah directed Abraham's attention to the kitchen window. "See that horizon of many colors?"

"Yes, sir." Abraham rubbed the sleep out of his eyes.

"Always remember, God owns those colors. Only in Him can we see them. Otherwise, life is just black, white, and gray."

Mary chimed in, "Husband, too early for wisdom. He is just a boy."

Jeremiah chuckled and nodded in agreement.

Mary flipped the eggs out of the cast-iron skillet onto a plate laden with ham and potato fritters. She carried the plate over in one hand while holding a hot cup of black coffee in the other. She placed both in front of Jeremiah.

"Here ya go, mister. Only good meal you are going to eat for a week."

Jeremiah took her hand. "Thank you, dear wife. I know what you say is true. I will savor every bite."

"I also packed some hardtack and dried venison to keep your stomach from growling on the train. I wrapped them in wax paper to keep fresh during your trip."

"Mary. You always know how to take care of me and the kids."

Abraham became alert at the table. "Mom, what about me? I am hungry."

Mary replied, "I will fix you some biscuits and gravy in a little bit. We need to spend some time with your father before he goes."

Abraham frowned, but understood. He looked at this dad and asked, "Why are you going west?"

"Son, I need to make things right with a friend I served with in the army."

"When you were an army trooper?"

"Yes. When I was a Buffalo Soldier."

"Can I go?"

"I wish I could take you along, but you need to stay here and be the man-of-the-house while I am gone."

Abraham sat up straight in his chair. He spoke with confidence. "I will not let you down. You can count on me."

"Son, you are a good soldier."

Mary put away the dishes while Jeremiah sipped the rest of his coffee. He stood up and said, "Wife, that was a great breakfast. Thank you."

Mary smiled and winked back at Jeremiah.

He continued, "Well. It is time. I best be go'n. The train pulls in around half past six o'clock. The ticket master said I should be there fifteen minutes early. Sometimes the train shows up early."

Mary quipped, "You have always been an early bird."

Jeremiah stood up and went back into the bedroom to retrieve his bag. He returned to the hallway and headed toward the front door where Mary and young Abraham waited.

Jeremiah walked over to young Abraham standing near the coatrack. Jeremiah extended his arms toward his son.

Abraham stepped back. "No, sir. I am a man now. Men shake hands."

Jeremiah glanced at Mary, who cracked a smile. He looked at his son with pride. "I reckon you are right, young man. Then we can shake on it." Jeremiah extended his right hand toward young Abraham, who was expecting a handshake. Instead, Jeremiah took his boy's right hand and pulled him into his chest. Abraham protested, yet surrendered to his dad's loving arms.

Holding his son, Jeremiah said, "You will always be my baby boy. Take care of your mother, brothers, and sister." He kissed Abraham on the cheek.

Abraham stepped back. "Yes, sir. You can count on me. I love you Dad."

Leather to Steel

Jeremiah released Abraham and stepped over to Mary. They embraced. She looked up at him and touched his nose with her right hand. "You be safe, mister. Go take care of your friend. Settle your business. God will be with you."

Jeremiah picked up his duffel bag and placed it on the foyer shoe box. He opened it up and peered inside to ensure he had everything. Mary handed Jeremiah a small burlap tote bag filled with three days' worth of grub. Jeremiah replied, "Thank you dear. I appreciate it." He placed the tote bag inside the duffel and closed it up. Using one arm, Jeremiah swung the duffle over his shoulder. He looked down into his wife's brown eyes. "Well darl'n. It is time for me to go."

*****

At the Winchester & Western train depot, Jeremiah waited on the station platform for the train to arrive from Gore, Virginia. There were only a few other passengers waiting with him outside the ticket office. One of them was a young army soldier wearing his dress green uniform. Jeremiah looked at him. Both tipped their slouch hats toward each other. No words were exchanged, but the sense of respect was clear.

As the train approached, the engineer blew its whistle three times one mile from town. Jeremiah looked down the track and watched a column of black smoke rise toward the morning sky. The locomotive pulled a coal car, two coaches, and three freight cars. A red caboose brought up the rear.

As the trained pulled into the depot, the trains brakeman wasted no time clearing her brakes to stop. A few minutes later, the train conductor stepped onto the platform. He hurriedly spent the next ten minutes getting all waiting passengers on board.

The train departed the Winchester Station on time. From there, it made its next stop in Martinsburg, West Virginia. Jeremiah debarked there, and caught the Chesapeake and Ohio Railway (C&O) locomotive going to Richmond. From Richmond, Jeremiah traveled the rest of the day and night to Kansas City, Kansas.

Twenty hours on the train from Richmond to Kansas City gave Jeremiah time to think about Buffalo Soldier, Corporal Joe Drayton.

He could have sat in the passenger car, but he chose to be alone. The conductor agreed with his request, but told him to look out for any hobos or bums trying to hitch a ride when the train slowed for curves.

While the train rolled over miles and miles of track, Jeremiah slept. He did a lot of sleep-talking. He mumbled, "Yes, sir" to the Company D captain directing Bates to place Drayton's body by a pink granite rock that seemed out of place in the middle of nowhere. Half of the rock buried under the ground, the other half jutting out toward the sky in the shape of a pyramid. He replayed the same conversation in his head over and over.

When he opened his eyes before dawn, the sunlight rudely reminded him he was on a train to Kansas City. Jeremiah rubbed his eyes and looked at the opposite side of the boxcar. The darkness was giving way to the sunlight beams slipping through cracks in the boxcar's split oak planks.

He gasped at a vision at the other end of the car. He recognized several apparitions come together on a grassy plain. Jeremiah could not believe his eyes. He watched his old cavalry commander, Captain Keyes, walk over to a ghostlike Jeremiah kneeling down by Drayton's prone body. The captain noticed Corporal Drayton's shirt torn at the right shoulder. A Comanche arrow sliced open the shirt, exposing Drayton's skin. Both the captain and Bates saw the scar.

Jeremiah watched the vision become brighter as it moved with the train. He watched the captain carefully pull Joe's torn shirt back to get a better look at the shoulder wound. Instead, Joe's black skin had a pale raised scar shaped like a magnolia tree. At that moment, Jeremiah came out of his trance. He raised his voice in the boxcar. "My, my, Joe was telling the truth. That black stallion we saw on patrol across the Red River was the horse from—where?"

Searching his memory, Jeremiah at that moment could not remember the name of the place Joe called home. Then a ray of sunshine pierced the boxcar shadows, triggering his memory. Jeremiah spoke out loud. "Thank you. Thank you, sweet Jesus! That was it. The Magnolia Plantation in South Carolina. That was where old Joe worked as a slave. The design on my father's branding iron. I remember now. That first black stallion branded with the Magnolia seal was called Lucky."

*****

Jeremiah had to be at Fort Sill on September 25. He wanted to get on the trail to Texas as soon as possible. He had to find the grave. The plan was for Jeremiah and Buddy to bring picks and shovels to inter Drayton's remains. From Plains' gravesite, the two men had to push the horses back to and hold proper burial at Fort Sill. He had to bury Joe on September 29, 1904; the thirtieth anniversary of his death, September 29, 1874. Jeremiah told Bud he prayed the burial would include military honors, but that depended upon the fort's commander.

The Crown Coach Bus trip from Kansas City to Fort Sill achieved record time. The driver and owner said there was no speed limit, so he could drive a speed of his choice. He went by the name of *Bobbie McGill*. Jeremiah sat on the first seat behind him, because the white folks sat in the back close to the windows.

Jeremiah leaned forward and asked. "Hey, fella, what is that clear stuff you drink'n?" Bobbie replied, "Just a little homemade brew I call Everclear. Made it out of corn."

"Mind if I take a swig?"

"Sure. Go ahead. Be careful you don't burn your nose." Jeremiah took a good sip. His eyes watered, and he choked some. "By golly. That tasted worse than the old firewater we drank with the Apache on the reservation."

"Suit yourself. Now you know. When were you on the reservation?"

"Back in 1874, off and on up through 1898. I served in the U.S. Army Cavalry. Put many miles in a saddle across that country."

"You served? Well, I be dang. I am sure you ran into my older cousin, Captain Miles Keogh."

"No, Bobbie, but everyone in the army knows who he was after the fact. He transferred up to Fort Lincoln before I had a chance to meet him."

"Darn'ist thing ever happen to a man, Jeremiah. I understand every soldier died at the Battle of Little Bighorn except three horses. Two were put down. The one survivor, I think his names was Comanche, became a hero."

"Bobbie. You are right about that. The army paraded that poor horse around the country for many years. Suppose ole Comanche was supposed to be a recruitment tool." Bobbie took another swig.

"Well, it did not convince me to join. Besides, I was only about ten years of age then."

"Bobbie, how did you come into the bus business?"

"Funny you should ask. My mother and my father live out in California now. The Crown Carriage Company out there started selling these buses during the first part of this year. We made an investment. Since the world Summer Olympics were hosted by St. Louis, we got this bus to haul all them visitors around. Made a good bit of money. Now I own two buses. My brother Tom drives the other one across the river. I like to drive these long-haul routes."

Jeremiah sat back in his seat. "Better let you drive. Don't want to distract ya, Mr. McGill."

"No worries mate." Bobbie took one more drink. The bus rolled on.

*****

Bud waited at the Fort Sill bus terminal. He had brought four horses for the trip. Each was tied to the water trough. Two horses were tacked up and ready to go. The other two wore only halters hooked up to leads.

When Jeremiah stepped down from the bus, he saw his old friend leaning against the hitching post, chewing tobacco and spitting on the street. A stray dog was nearby looking for food. Bud spat on the dog. "Get out of here."

Jeremiah walked up to him. "But I just got here."

Bud chuckled. "Not talking to you, old horseman. Ain't you look'n' worse for wear. Good to see ya, old friend."

"Look at you, Bud! Sport'n a gray mobius mustache. I could hang Christmas ornament off those waxed handles." Bud twisted the ends of his mustache. "The gray hair means wisdom and class." He continued, "Looks like you made it up there with the rest of them rich cats back East." Both men took a few steps toward each other and embraced like old veterans. Veterans who understood each other without saying a word.

Bud asked, "Jeremiah, do you need to get a bite to eat, or a drink before we go?"

"Thank you kindly, but no, thank you. I see you got the horses ready. I am thinking we need to mount up and get on out of here. My heart has been racing since KC. You understand why time is not my friend right now? Did you get what I asked?"

"Yep, I got it packed in my saddlebag."

Jeremiah walked over with Bud to the hitching post. They untied the horses. Holding his horse's reins, Jeremiah looked around at the town. The population had built up around Fort Sill, he noticed. "Bud. This place has changed some." Bud turned his head to the side and spat tobacco juice. Bud cleared his throat. "You bet this place changed. Don't hear horses' hooves clopping around like we used to. Mainly them dang motor cars making a racket and spewing out the devil's black and gray breath. What troubles me is the occasional engine bang sound those contraptions make. Gets me into a nervous spell every time."

Standing by the horses, Bud said, "Jeremiah, go ahead and take Bucky's reins. He is a good buckskin geld'n. I picked him up down at the Four Sixes ranch in South Texas. His relief will be that chestnut quarter horse I call Trouble. My palomino mare is Misty. The geld 'n beside her is Killer. He is a geld'n I bought from a Cheyenne squaw on the reservation."

Jeremiah raised his eyebrows a bit. He looked at Bud and mumbled, "Man is going to get me killed yet."

Bud asked, "What did you say? You know, my hearing ain't what it used to be." Jeremiah just shook his head. "Never mind, friend. Killer sounds like a good horse."

Bud and Jeremiah mounted up on Misty and Bucky. Jeremiah double-checked the stirrup lengths to make sure his knees were not up to his chest. The western saddle he sat in was worn and had a comfortable padded leather seat. Jeremiah pointed his finger over Bucky's head. He said, "Move out. We got many miles to cover, my friend."

Jeremiah leaned over and shook hands with Bud. Both looked at each other and nodded. They spurred the horses and moved out on the road.

*****

Jeremiah and Bud stayed mostly to the roadsides until they reached the Wichita Mountains. Breaking toward the mountain trails would avoid switchback roads that added time to a trip. Jeremiah and Bud rode many cavalry patrols knowing the shortest distance between two points is a straight path.

Crossing south of the mountain range, the old migration trails took Jeremiah and Bud west, toward the Red River Valley. Coming down from the mountains into the valley was an easier ride than expected. The horses sniffed the air. Within seconds, the horses picked up the pace knowing there was water ahead. Jeremiah got Bud's attention. "Looks like we are about ten miles from the river. The ponies seem to be in a hurry." Bud spat and then replied, "Yep. Always trust the horse. They get you to paradise, when you think you're ride'n in a desert."

Once at the Red River, they stopped to water and feed the horses. Bud said, "Jeremiah. We need to tack up the other two horses to give these mares a break. We have forty miles to cover tomorrow morning. We can walk, trot, and gallop. Then swap horses again."

By the next morning, the Red River was in front of them. The dry season made it possible to cross without using a river taxi. Once they reached Doan's Crossing, the rest of the trip would be over flat country.

At Doan's Crossing, much had changed since the Buffalo traders camped outside the trading post walls. Dirt roads and ranch houses dotted the area surrounding the old post. Leaving early in the morning, Jeremiah turned in the saddle to look back at the Red River. He pointed out to Bud and said, "We sure crossed that river many a time."

Leather to Steel

Bud chewed his tobacco and spat. "Darn right about that, trooper."

Jeremiah said, "No one has called me that in some time."

"Well, that is what we are, brother. Two old black Buffalo Soldiers who don't have two cents to rub between us."

"Actually, we do have two cents worth of food. Mary packed some trail food for us. Same as money out here on the Plains." Jeremiah reached in his saddlebag and pulled out some venison jerky. He pushed Bucky over next to Misty. "Bud, here. You will like this venison. Shot this doe with an old cap-n-ball. Two hundred yards using a two-foot elevation."

"Dang good shot. But then you always were," Bud said while tearing off a piece of jerky with his gapped teeth. "I remember when all we had to eat was hardtack, salted ham, and rock-hard sourdough biscuits. Say, do you remember that story about the Christmas tree crossing over the Clear Fork River in Texas?"

"Sure do. I think an old drover told us about how their cook messed up a mixture of sourdough bread. Got so mad he threw the dough toward the river. Instead of going into the river, the lose dough dripped out over the mesquite tree branches. Each drip of dough hardened in the Texas sun within minutes. The hardened dough looked like white Christmas tree ice cycles. Not sure if it is true, but sure sounds reasonable." Jeremiah reached into his saddlebag and pulled out two hard biscuits. He said, "Bud, catch it." Jeremiah tossed the biscuit over the Bud, who did a one-hand catch.

Bud tried squeezing it, but the biscuit did not give. He said, "Looks like we are going to have Christmas breakfast." Both men laughed.

Bud and Jeremiah crossed over several creeks and valleys that one could not see from level ground—at least not until they were upon them. The Plains of Texas were deceiving that way. But maps were not needed. The old Buffalo Soldiers had no problem following their instincts and the trodden cattle trails under the stars, where they slept for months at a time.

By midmorning on the third day, Jeremiah and Bud were getting somewhat discouraged. The tall buffalo grass made it more difficult to spot the half-buried pink granite rock they remembered marking Joe's burial site. The farther west they rode, the more the terrain changed. Bud yelled over to Jeremiah, "What in the heck is that awful smell caught in the breeze?"

Jeremiah stuck his nose in the air to sniff. "I don't know, but it smells like rotten eggs."

Bud pulled out his handkerchief and tied it over his face to help reduce his intake of the odor. Jeremiah yelled over, "Come on, Bud! The stench is not that bad. You have smelled worse."

He turned toward Jeremiah and shook his head sideways. Within twenty more minutes of riding through several draws, Jeremiah and Bud identified the mysterious smell source. The smell came from oilrigs. Dozens of dark silhouette toil derricks dotted the prairie. They stood like inverted pyramids rising one hundred feet above the ground. Rotating pumpjacks connected to each derrick. As the pumpjacks rotated long connected pipes pump up and down from the ground, he pump-pulled up the black gold from underground.

Jeremiah looked down at tire ruts leading to each oil well. Several makeshift roads crossed back and forth over old Indian trails the men desperately tried to follow. Modernization had made its way to the Texas Plains. Locating Joe Drayton's gravesite just became less likely. Jeremiah got Bud's attention. "Looks like finding Joe may be a little more difficult. I envisioned the Texas Plains to be like they have always been—open for the eye to see."

Bud agreed. "You are not alone on that sentiment. I only expected to see prairie dogs and buffalo grass."

Jeremiah and Bud pushed their horses forward. As they proceeded northwest, the rising morning sun cast a gold light across each blade of buffalo grass moving with the breeze. Jeremiah and Bud were fascinated with how bright the landscape emerged from the night's cover. Several wheat fields to their north shined like gold.

Jeremiah halted his horse to gaze at Mother Nature. Bud brought his horse over near Jeremiah and did the same. Jeremiah said, "Bud, looks like waves of gold moving across a lake. Have you ever seen anything like it?"

"Reckon I can't," said Bud after spitting his tobacco juice on the ground. He added, "Yep. If the buffalo were alive and migrating, this grass would be short as all get out."

Jeremiah nodded, "You are right. I guess I'd better pay closer attention to the knolls we ride through. The pink granite stone is shaped like a pyramid. Sticks out of the ground where we laid Joe down. That stone stuck out a good three feet. The grass is two feet high. We will find that rock. Lord is my witness."

The men continued looking. Each time they crossed over a hill going northwest, Jeremiah stopped and looked to match the horizon against the rolling hills. Bud spread out to Jeremiah's left to look west. He stopped and whistled. "Jeremiah! I am thinking we are getting close. I feel it."

Jeremiah extended his right hand above his shoulders and gave a thumbs-up and yelled, "I think you are right, Bud. I see some familiar vales to our right."

Bud rode over toward Jeremiah. He said, "I think we should dismount and start looking."

Jeremiah turned around and recognized the horizon. He gave a nod to Bud, and they dismounted from their horses.

Leading Misty and Bucky on foot—with Trouble and Killer in tow—both men spread out to cover more ground. Jeremiah looked left and right, hoping to see the pink granite rock. Bud kept his nose to the ground, looking south to west as they slowly pushed through the tall grass.

Jeremiah studied every foot of ground with each step forward. Bud acted in unison, but not as quietly. For every step his horse took, his five-star boot spurs jingled. The rhythmic sound of Bud's spurs became a beacon for what they could not see. A loud clank broke the silence. Jeremiah stopped and looked at Bud, who just stood still, not knowing if the sound came from behind or in front. Jeremiah walked over to pull away at the grass surrounding Bud. The pink granite rock glistened in the sun—a sun it had probably not seen since the last winter.

Jeremiah brushed away the dust and the roots covering the rock. With his bare hands, he dug alongside the rock to uncover the side facing east—the side where Jeremiah laid Joe's head facing east. The deeper he dug, the more careful he became.

Bud asked, "How deep did you bury him?"

Jeremiah looked up and said, "At the time, I thought I did not bury him deep enough. I just wanted to ensure his bones would not be pulled out by the wolves and coyotes."

Bud replied, "Let me start six feet from your spot. I will try to find his leg bones."

They labored for hours. Time was not their friend. By midafternoon, Jeremiah looked at his hands— blistered and bleeding. He held them up for Bud to see. "Third time I bled for this man."

Within a few minutes, they uncovered the upper torso bones. Jeremiah stopped and looked up at the sky. He closed his eyes. Bud looked over and asked, "Are you okay, partner?"

Jeremiah let out a heavy sigh. "I am fine. It feels like the weight of the world is now off my shoulders and in my hands. Let us get him home."

Bud nodded in agreement. Within the half hour, the men separated dirt from Joe's bones. Now it was time for the ritual.

Jeremiah and Bud had to be careful removing Joe's dried and brittle bones. Jeremiah asked Bud, "Partner, please bring over Joe's Civil War haversack."

Bud got up and walked over to Misty. He ran his hands over her mane and whispered, "Girl, we found what we came for. My, my, my." He stepped over to the saddle and reached into the saddlebag and pulled out a package wrapped in brown paper. He untied the package string and carefully peeled back the paper. He shook out the oiled cotton haversack. He admired the black markings "C.S.A." stenciled in bold black letters on the outside flap.

Bud walked back over to Jeremiah, holding the haversack out in front of him. "Here it is. Just as you asked. This haversack has not seen sunlight since I wrapped it back in 1875. I figured he would need it someday."

Bud knelt down on his knees beside by Jeremiah. He held open the old haversack, while Jeremiah carefully placed Joe's remains inside. Jeremiah looked at Bud. Tears formed in the corners of his

Leather to Steel

eyes. "We need to say a prayer for our old friend Joe." Bud nodded in silence.

"Father, thank you for keeping us safe on this journey to recover our friend and brother, Corporal Joe Drayton. Please protect us during our journey back to his final resting place. Thank you, sweet Jesus. Amen."

Bud mumbled, "Amen."

Jeremiah reached around his neck to pull off his leather necklace. Attached to the center was a wooden cross. It swung like a pendulum when he held it up to the sky. Watching the cross swing, Bud asked, "Is that the cross? The one you made after Joe died?"

Holding the cross up between his fingers, Jeremiah replied, "Yes, I made it using the Comanche arrow I removed from Joe's chest. Now I give it back to him with God's blessing and protection forever." Jeremiah carefully laid the leather necklace across the bones, which were also carefully arranged in the haversack. He then removed a snow-white cloth from his short pocket and gently laid it over Joe's bones and the cross. After making the sign of the Maker, Jeremiah stood up. "Time to go home. Mount up, soldier."

Jeremiah and Bud switched tack between the horses. They needed fresh mounts to ensure they could make quick time back to Fort Sill. The clock was ticking. They only had a little over a day to get back. Before the men mounted up, Jeremiah looked at Bud. "Thank you, soldier. I could not have done this without you."

Bud replied, "You are my friend. We survived many battles back in the day. We owed it to Joe. I know ole Colonel Henry Kingsbury will be surprised to see us back with Joe."

"What do you mean, Bud?"

"I am sure he thought hell would freeze over before we found Joe. However, he did say Joe would be buried at his Fort Sill with honors, if we get Joe back."

Jeremiah's eyes lit up. "Then Lord as my witness, let us make this last ride out of this place one to remember." He and Bud healed their horses into a gallop.

The warm Texas wind blew against Jeremiah's face as they galloped eastward. After covering three hundred yards, he suddenly held up Killer. He turned in his saddle to face north. The vale where the Comanche ambushed the company dipped just before him. Staring at the horizon, he saw the ghostly mirage of a Comanche sitting bareback on a black horse. The horse had a prominent marking on its left hind quarter. The warrior had his own marking. A black hand painted on the side of his face. The black stallion had a white hand painted on its chest. Jeremiah remembered the mark of the hand was earned by a warrior who killed another in hand-to-hand combat.

Jeremiah stared at the rider and horse. His mind wandered to the past. Suddenly, Jeremiah grasped his chest. A tingling session ran down the back of his neck. He lowered his head toward the saddle horn, as if he was ducking. Jeremiah raised his torso back up onto the saddle. He blinked eyes to make the haunting vision go away. He looked again. The ghosts remained. Jeremiah tried to raise his arm to wave toward the lone rider. A numbing feeling ran down his left arm, freezing his body in position. He gasped for air while looking at the Indian and the horse.

Jeremiah rubbed his eyes and looked again. The Comanche warrior had raised a feathered lance toward Jeremiah's direction. Expecting a charge, Jeremiah lowered himself over his horse's withers for protection. He reached for a rifle that did not exist. After a few seconds passed, he looked up and breathed a heavy sigh. The charge did not come. The warrior had turned the black stallion away from Jeremiah. He watched the ghosts disappear over the horizon.

Jeremiah relaxed. He sat up on the saddle to make sure the warrior and the horse were gone. Within a few minutes, a warming sensation overcame his body. He was able to sit up and move his arms freely. Jeremiah wiped his eyes and forehead. He looked again to make sure. The vision was gone.

He looked over at Bud, who was holding his cowboy hat with one hand and the reins in the other. He raced over toward Jeremiah and yelled, "You okay, partner?"

Jeremiah looked back. "I am fine now. Just had a bad spell of indigestion."

Bud stopped his horse just short of Jeremiah's position. He put his slouch hat back on. "Partner, we need to get on back to the fort. Come on."

Jeremiah raised his left hand and gave a thumbs-up. As Jeremiah rode, a sense of calmness overcame him. Just one more day until salvation.

*****

Jeremiah and Bud made it to Fort Sill in the early morning on Thursday, September 29. Jeremiah asked Bud. "You think Colonel Kingsbury's office is open this early in the morning?"

Bud pulled out his silver pocket watch and said, "Yep. Only seven o'clock. We have time. The colonel works until five. We can get 'er done."

"Good. We need to let him know we made it back. Joe must be buried today."

*****

The colonel was very pleased to see the old Buffalo Soldiers had brought home their fellow soldier. He ordered his staff to make arrangements for a military ceremony for an afternoon burial. The colonel's staff hastily executed his order to honor a fallen soldier deserving of the U.S. Army's respect.

Corporal Joe Drayton earned it as a slave, a Freedman, and a soldier who saw battle during the U.S. Civil War and the Texas-Indian Wars. The United States Army would properly bury Corporal Joseph Drayton on the thirtieth anniversary of this death.

Colonel Kingsbury expressed to his First Sergeant that not for one second, did he think two old Buffalo Soldiers would give up on a comrade resting in the Texas Plains. The old troopers proved him right.

Anticipating a moment not shared by many colored soldiers, the colonel wired an old Buffalo Soldier who shared a common interest with Jeremiah and Bud. The special soldier accepted the colonel's invitation. He would come to Fort Sill attend the burial ceremony.

The decorated soldier would also lay the United States flag on Joe's casket. His name was First Lieutenant William McBryar, Tenth U.S. Cavalry, Medal of Honor recipient.[10], [11]

Wearing his best military blue uniform, Colonel Kingsbury stood by the Old Post Cemetery gate entrance waiting patiently for the guest of honor, Corporal Joseph Drayton, United States Army Cavalry.[12] Looking down the entrance path, the colonel watched two soldiers stepping in unison towards him.

As the two men got closer, the colonel noticed Jeremiah and Bud had dressed up in their formal cavalry uniforms. The colonel pulled out his gold pocket watch to check the time. He said to himself, *it was a little after three o'clock. Now all I need is one more to show up. Where are you, Mister McBryar?*

Medal of Honor Recipient Sergeant Major William McBryar agreed to overseeing military honors planned for Corporal Drayton. Not because the colonel was unwilling to officiate the ceremony, but because Joe Drayton was a Buffalo Soldier.

It was now half passed three o'clock. Colonel Kingsbury had grown impatient. He could not wait for McBryar much longer. Once Jeremiah and Bud were within three steps of the colonel, the old soldiers rendered salutes. The colonel replied in kind.

"Good afternoon, gentlemen. Where is Corporal Drayton's urn?"

Jeremiah held up the haversack and replied, "Sir. Joe is in here. He wore this haversack during the Battle of Petersburg. He shouldered it on the day the Comanche killed him. It is best he be buried in this."

The colonel's eyes softened. He said, "Corporal Drayton deserves a proper military burial. "Let us go now. I want to get him buried before taps. Most fitting, I think."

As they walked, the colonel added, "So you know, I invited an honorable guest to lead Corporal Drayton's burial ceremonial. Unfortunately, it looks like he got waylaid."

"Who might that be?" Bud replied.

"Does not matter now. I am just trying to do right by Joe."

The colonel, Jeremiah, and Bud walked up the long path toward the northern end of the cemetery. Jeremiah noticed several tomb markers that had Native American names. He looked at the colonel and asked, "Are Indians buried here?"

"Yes. At least the famous ones are, like Satank and Sitting Bear."

Jeremiah spoke. "Now I know why a black man can be buried here."

The colonel just shook his head, knowing he was right.

The colonel said, "Gentlemen, I had a pine casket brought up to the gravesite. You can place the haversack in the middle of the casket once we get there. I will call us to attention while the bugler plays taps. I will then offer either of you to speak your piece."

Jeremiah and Bud replied in unison, "Thanks, colonel. We appreciate the offer."

The colonel nodded his head once in silence. He then cleared his throat and adjusted his olive-green campaign hat. Out of the corner of his eyes, he saw movement. The colonel turned toward the direction of the gravesite. Someone was trying to get his attention.

The silhouette of a small man stood by the casket. The colonel could not see his face with the sun behind him. The three men approached the lone man. Once within twenty feet, the colonel recognized the stranger. It was First Lieutenant William McBryar.

Colonel Kingsbury spoke. "I thought we were going to meet at the gate."

Lieutenant McBryar saluted the colonel. "Forgive me, sir. I wanted to spend time reflecting here alone. It probably should be me in this grave."

The colonel replied, "Well, it is not, Mister McBryar. I do appreciate you answering the call." Once they were within a few feet, the officers exchanged hand salutes.

Jeremiah and Bud looked at Lieutenant McBryar with amazement. Each stumbled for words, not knowing what to say. McBryar said, "Don't look so surprised, gentlemen. Yes. I am black. I am a Buffalo Soldier just like you. Let the Lord guide our hands as we lay U.S. Army Corporal Joe Drayton to rest."

Jeremiah and Bud looked at each other and then watched the Medal of Honor recipient move into place. Jeremiah spoke first. "Sir, I know Joe is smiling in heaven right now."

Lieutenant McBryar responded, "Perhaps so. Let us get on with this."

Two of the colonel's staff closed up the casket with Joe Drayton's remains inside. Once done, the men stepped back to signal the colonel. The ceremony was ready to begin. Colonel Kingsbury turned toward the burial guard. He looked at the corporal in charge of the detail. He said, "Mr. Suggs, carry on."

The corporal and three privates stood down from attention. The soldiers marched smartly by twos to each end of the casket. The corporal barked orders to pick up the casket. In unison, the soldiers slowly stepped toward the open grave. "Halt," the corporal said with authority. On a silent queue, the soldiers slowly lowered the casket to the ground. The men stood at attention.

Colonel Kingsbury ordered, "Right face!" The soldiers turned right, using proper turn-heel movements. "Forward...march!"

Then men returned to their original positions to remain at attention after the last command: "About face."

Jeremiah and Bud marched side by side to the casket. They halted exactly even with the casket's center. Jeremiah took one more step forward and then did an about-face. He now faced Bud, who took one side step to the left. Jeremiah grasped the blue end of the flag. Bud untucked the red-and-white-striped end. Bud took careful backward steps to open the flag. Once the flag was fully unfurled, Jeremiah looked down at the forty-five stars that shone brightly on the blue. Bud stopped once the flag became taut, ensuring it never touched the ground.

Jeremiah and Bud took two side steps to align themselves over the casket from end to end. Looking directly into each other's eyes, Jeremiah looked down, then back up at Bud, giving the silent queue. They both lowered the Stars and Stripes onto Drayton's casket. Satisfied with the flag's center, then men released the flag. Each remained at attention, not knowing what to do next.

Leather to Steel

Colonel Kingsbury saw that the old soldiers were having a moment. He would help. "Buffalo soldiers!" barked the colonel. "Return to your positions."

Tears flowed down each man's cheeks as they marched quietly back to their positions near the grave.

The colonel gave the next command, and two soldiers marched to their rehearsed positions. One stood at attention at one end of the casket, while the other took position on the opposite side. The colonel gave them another ready command. In unison, the soldiers lifted the flag off the casket and began folding it into two halves. They stopped once the flag was properly even on both long sides.

The soldier holding the stripes end began folding first. He held the left corner tight while his right hand pulled the right corner toward the left edge to form a triangle. Both soldiers kept constant tension between both ends during the folding proves. Once the folding soldier made it to the stationary soldier, he released his hands to allow the stationary soldier to properly tuck the blue and stars inside the top fold. A properly folded flag only showed blue and stars. The soldier holding the flag did an about-face and took three steps toward Lieutenant McBryar, who was standing by to receive the flag.

Lieutenant McBryar secured the folded U.S. flag underneath his left arm. He then marched seven paces over to where Jeremiah was standing at attention. He stopped directly in front of Jeremiah. He looked up at the big man and commanded, "At ease, soldier."

Jeremiah relaxed from attention, but kept his eyes straight forward.

The lieutenant presented the flag to Jeremiah, who extended his hands to receive the flag. He placed his right hand on top of the flag and the left underneath. The lieutenant continued to hold the flag with him. He said, "First Sergeant Bates, United States Army, Retired. Please accept this flag on behalf of a grateful nation. It would be best for you to have it, as his friend and comrade in arms."

No additional comments were made. The colonel led the men in reading Psalm 23 from the Bible. Upon completion, the colonel ordered a rifle detail of three black soldiers standing on the hill render a three-gun salute appropriate for an enlisted man.[13]

The burial with military honors was complete. The colonel commanded all in attendance to carry on. Jeremiah and Bud shook the colonel's and lieutenant's hands, thanking them for making it right for Corporal Drayton.

The colonel asked, "Did you men see the headstone?"

Jeremiah replied, "No, sir."

"Well, go take a look at it. It is temporary until we get the marble version done. That will take a few weeks. Until then, the men built Drayton a temporary headstone out of old oak. Go read the words." Jeremiah and Bud walked to the head of Joe's grave. Inscribed on the maker, were these words:

> Corporal Joe Drayton,
> U.S. Civil War Battle of Petersburg
> U.S. Army 10th Cavalry, Red River Wars
> Born: Unknown Date
> Died: September 30, 1874.
> God rest his soul.

After the funeral, the soldiers gathered at the colonel's office for a farewell. Sitting behind his cherry desk, the colonel pulled out a bottle of Scotch whiskey from the right drawer. He then pulled open the left and removed four short crystal glasses and set them on his desk. He looked up at the three old soldiers. "Let us warriors make a toast to Corporal Drayton." The colonel poured equal amounts of whiskey into each glass. Lieutenant McBryar, First Sergeant Jeremiah Bates, and Sergeant Smith stood side by side in front of the colonel's desk waiting for their cue.

Colonel Kingsbury pushed a whisky shot toward each man. Promptly picking up the glasses, the four soldiers were ready to execute an age-old tradition for a fallen comrade. Colonel Kingsbury held their glasses up and initiated the toast. The glasses clinked and remained suspended while in contact. The colonel spoke in a low, solemn tone. "Gentlemen, today we laid to rest one of many who died fighting for our great nation. The United States Cavalry did not

Leather to Steel

forget Corporal Drayton on the Texas Plains, nor in our hearts. On behalf of a grateful army, thank you for bringing him home." The men gulped their drinks. They placed the empty glasses back down on the colonel's desk. A couple of glasses sang.

The prideful McBryar grasped his Medal of Honor lanyard and looked at the colonel. He bellowed out. "Buffalo Soldiers! Attention!"

Jeremiah quickly glanced at Bud, who nodded. All three stood at attention facing the colonel, who rose from his chair. McBryar spoke towards the colonel's direction. "Men. In front of us is a United States Army officer. He proved this fact today."

The three black Buffalo Soldiers saluted the colonel, who returned the same. The colonel wore a face of genuine respect. He proudly ordered, "Carry on Buffalo Soldiers. You may be dismissed."

Colonel Kingsbury walked around his desk to escort the soldiers to the front of his office. Standing on the front porch, the colonel said, "Bud, now I know you live here and will walk home. Lieutenant McBryar. I understand you are headed to New York state tomorrow. Jeremiah, when are you going back to Virginia?"

Jeremiah replied, "Sir, I will head over to the bus stop to catch the morning bus up to Kansas City. From there, I will be on the rail."

The colonel nodded with approval. Colonel Kingsbury spoke three last words to his fellow veterans. "Soldier on, men." And all three men walked in silence together toward the gates.

Standing by the fort's main gate, Jeremiah, Bud, and Lieutenant McBryar shook hands one more time. The men nodded at each other: then walked away in three different directions. A poignant part of life experienced because of loyalty and respect. For those moments spent with Corporal Drayton, all souls were equal. Outside the gates of Fort Sill, the three men also knew they would return to the reality of what most colored people experienced during those times—segregation.

Jeremiah's journey was not complete. He walked onto the steps of his house at five o'clock in the morning. It was October 1. He had one hour to get on over to the farm to begin his workday. Though exhausted, he kept his promise to Mr. Welford. Otherwise, there would be no job waiting for him.

Mary was in the kitchen stoking the oven stove when she heard Jeremiah's heavy footsteps on the front porch. She quickly put down the iron poker and shut the fire door before exiting the kitchen. At the living room window, she pulled back the curtain to see who was on the porch at such an early hour.

Seeing her husband, she hurried to the front door to pull off the chain lock. She swung the door open to see a very tired-looking man standing before her. Jeremiah took a deep breath and let out a heavy sigh. "Oh, sweet Mary. I made it home. I have little time. I need to get on down to the farm before the sun rises."

Jeremiah stepped into the house and embraced Mary. He then kissed her.

She pulled back and said, "You need to get on. We have enough time for that later. I will take your bag. Before you go, let me get you a couple of biscuits and slices of ham to eat on the way. So glad you are home, husband."

Jeremiah replied, "You always know what is important. See you this evening." He hastened his way to work.

*****

Welford walked back and forth in front of the horse barn. He pulled out his pocket watch to check the time. Normally, Jeremiah showed up to work in the morning fifteen minutes early. His watch read five forty-five. He mumbled to himself, "I hope Jeremiah gets here soon. I would hate to fire him. I have my word to keep."

As soon as he put the watch back into his pocket, a large black man loped up to the circle drive. He waved his hand and yelled out, "Good morn'n captain. I made it back."

Welford breathed a sigh of relief. "How was your trip?"

"We accomplished what we set out to do. My friend Joe Drayton lays to rest at Fort Sill, Oklahoma."

"Glad to hear all is well Mister Bates. You can tell me all about your journey later. We have some brood mares getting ready to foal.

Leather to Steel

If they all come in today, we will be busy. I know you must be tired. Assuming the foaling goes well, why don't you take tomorrow off and get some rest. You look like you could use it."

Jeremiah hesitated. After a few moments, he replied, "Thank you Mister Welford. I do appreciate the consideration, but I need to make the money."

"Don't concern yourself Jeremiah. I will reward a man who keeps his word. Now, we got eight mares to tend. Between the two of us, we can bring into the world some warhorses."

Jeremiah raised his eyebrows when the boss man uttered the word *warhorse*. "You mean polo ponies?"

As they walked inside the barn, Welford replied, "Nope. President Roosevelt wants us to train them for the battlefield. That means we get educated on this Europe dressage–type training. Supposed to make the horse move better during the fight."

Jeremiah said, "Derrr... sarrgit, what the heck?"

"I know. Took me a couple of days practicing how to say it. In any case, Roosevelt invited his European friend to come here and teach us. I think his name is Ranse something. Never too old to learn something new Mister Bates."

Jeremiah shrugged. "I reckon so. We will cross that bridge when we get there."

Welford nodded in an agreement.

*****

At the end of the day, eight foals were born on the Roosevelt farm. Four bay fillies, and one black and three sorrel colts. Welford and Bates were exhausted. Both men wanted the day to end before the good light disappeared: the sun was thirty minutes from setting.

Standing near the hay loft, Jeremiah looked at Welford with tired eyes. He asked, "If you don't mind, I am ready to get on back home."

"Jeremiah, before you go, stop by and say hello to Tough Guy. He was a stinker while you were gone."

"Dag nabbit. You are right. I should have taken the time to see him earlier today. I will head over to the paddock right now." Jeremiah washed his hands in the horse trough; then walked over to

Tough Guy's stall. He did not want the foaling smells make Tough Guy any ornerier than he was.

*****

Tough Guy

I saw Jeremiah come into view as he rounded the corner of the house. He moved in slow motion. He wrung his hands and looked as though he was on his last legs. I knew Jeremiah had been gone, but I did not understand why he left. I walked over to the fence to extend my nose to him. Like always, he scratched my nose and scratched me behind my ears. He looked me in the eyes. "Sorry, boy. I had many things on my mind lately. I did not forget you. In fact, I wish you were with me when I saw Stonewall standing proudly on the horizon."

I snorted. "Were you at the Zapata Farm?" Jeremiah shook his head and continued telling me his story. "I went back to Texas to search for an old friend. It may have been the heat, but I swear I saw a Comanche warrior straddled on your father's bare back. A black stallion baring the same Magnolia brand you have."

I neighed and shook my head up and down to tell him that I understood. In fact, I had a similar vision last week out near the river. I was saying good-bye to my father, Stonewall. To me, the vision meant something was wrong back in Virginia.

Jeremiah mumbled to himself, "God Bless Texas." Something was not adding up.

Jeremiah pulled a handful of oats from his jacket pocket. He held them under my chin. I smelled the oats. Once he said "go ahead," I took the liberty of eating them. He told me, "It will be all right, Tough Guy. Here are oats for the night. I will be back tomorrow morning."

I neighed back at him. "All right for what?"

Jeremiah turned and walked away. Once he was out of sight, I trotted toward the paddock water trough. I needed a drink to wash down the oats. After taking a few slurps, I turned around and saw Jeremiah had stopped near the barn. He was looking at me. He waved, then turned and walked away. Something had changed in him. I sensed it.

*****

Inside the comfort of his warm home, Jeremiah sat deep in his leather easy chair. The chair seemed to wrap its arms around his body. He looked at Mary standing by the kitchen door. "Darl'n, if you don't mind, I think I would prefer to sit in this chair and not move."

Mary replied, "Honey, I will bring your supper to you on a tray. I told the kids we all needed to stay quiet until you have had a chance to rest. I also told them that if they were good tonight, you would tell them about your trip tomorrow evening, before their bedtime."

Jeremiah waved Mary over to his side. He reached out and held her hand. Looking up at her, he said, "Thank you. You know me. I appreciate you taking care of things while I was gone."

She replied, "Oh, we had no problems. Abraham stood up to the task. He acted like the man of the house while you were gone. He cut wood, shot some rabbits and squirrels for dinner, and even helped his brothers and sister with school'n. You need to let him know how proud you are of him."

Jeremiah released her hand. "I will do that tomorrow. He is going to be somebody someday."

Mary returned to the kitchen to fix a plate of vittles and freshly baked bread with thick apple butter spread all around. She placed the plate on the tray and then returned to the living room where Jeremiah was waiting, standing by his chair. "Here you go, Mr. Bates. Fresh vittles."

He did not respond. She tapped his shoulder. There was no movement. She shook his shoulder; he took a deep breath and started snoring.

Relieved, Mary mumbled, "Don't you go anywhere, mister. We still have work to do in this world." She bent down to kiss his forehead and whispered, "You are the love of my life. God will not call you home yet."

*****

Jeremiah woke up on October 2 thinking he had to go to work. Mary rolled over and said, "Don't you remember? Mister Welford gave you the day off. That means you get to work for me."

Jeremiah let out a big yawn and then stretched his arms out. Wait a minute, what day is it?"

Mary tried to control her giggling. "Darling, today is Sunday. You never work on Sunday. He was just pulling your leg. Being so darn tired, you knew no difference."

Jeremiah rolled over toward Mary, who was already standing up with her robe on. He mumbled, "I need to pay more attention to things said to me."

"I suspect you do, Mister Bates. Now get yourself out of bed. We are going to church and thank the Lord for your safe return. Then we are going to go to the store to pick up the Sunday paper. Then we are going to come home and spend time with the children. Then—"

"Now, wait a minute, Missus Bates. Where is our time alone built in there?"

"The same time we have every day—when we go to sleep. Now stop complaining and get yourself ready for church. I will have some scrambled eggs, ham, and slices of sourdough bread wait'n for you in the kitchen. We will eat together like a family this morn'n."

"Sounds like a great plan, dear. You are always right. My friends say, 'Happy wife, happy life.'"

Mary proudly said, "You have the smartest friends in the world!" Jeremiah got up out of bed while Mary went to the kitchen.

*****

Tough Guy

The morning came quick for me. I was back in the paddock just killing time. Mister Welford came out to check on me. Little did he know I was in the barn all night trying to reassure the mares and foals that all was calm and safe. There had been a pack of wolves coming down from the Blue Ridge Mountains into the Shenandoah Valley causing all sorts of problems with the neighboring farms. It was my job to protect them. I would not fail.

Mister Welford brought over a bucket of oats for me. He poured them into the tin bucket tied up on the top cross rail. I stuck my muzzle in the bucket and began to eat breakfast. Welford liked to talk to horses, just like Jeremiah. He said, "Well, ole boy. Looks like you have four daughters and four sons. One of them looks just like you."

I neighed back, "I know. I smelled them last night, though the darkness was unforgiving."

Mister Welford went on, "I am thinking things will change around here some. President Roosevelt wants to start training your horses up to be effective in battle. A far cry from the safety of a polo field. He says the army has been complaining about horse purchases that are hit-or-miss for the cavalry. I reckon your brood will be the first generation of warhorses never before seen in this country."

I knew what the word *war* meant. My father, Stonewall, told me about the Red River Wars, the Spanish-American War; and in both cases, good horses and troopers died on the battlefield. I shook my head back and forth, trying to tell him of my concern about war. He extended his hand toward my head and scratched me behind my ears. While doing so, he told me, "Don't worry, ole boy. President Roosevelt is bringing a horse trainer from Europe who knows how to prepare horses to survive during battle. It will be all right."

He got my attention. My father said it was our honor and duty to serve this nation. I never forgot the words he told me back on that train we rode together from Kansas City to Richmond. I was younger then. I am much wiser now. It was times like these when a human said something to me, I wished I had my father here with me to interpret. He was so good about that during my training at the army's training camp. I hoped he was okay. Something had been gnawing inside me since last week.

*****

The Bates family returned home just after the midday sun had passed the top of the old oak. While standing on the front porch with the children and Mary, Jeremiah proclaimed, "Today is the day your mama is going to make magic out of these fall apples. I am thinking she is going to make some apple pies!"

The kids started clapping and jumping; and together they said, "Is that true, Mama? Is that true?"

Mary brought her children to her side. Looking down at the four of them, she said, "Your papa is right. We are going to make apple pies that will put good dreams in your little heads."

Abraham looked his mama directly in the eye. "Mama, can we make some whipped cream from the fresh milk in that gallon jar? I see two inches of cream settled on the top."

Mary grinned. "Sweet son, you bet we will make some whipped cream to put on top."

The kids went inside to change out of their good clothes into their play clothes. Jeremiah and Mary sat in the living room, taking the time to talk while all the children were outside. Mary sat in her flowered wingback chair. She set her cup of hot tea on the small round-top mahogany table that separated Jeremiah and Mary's chairs. Jeremiah came into the room wearing a clean pair of overalls over a white long-sleeved shirt. He sat down in his chair and let out a gasp of air. He said, "Mary, feels good to be home. You know, we brought eight foals into this world last night. Four fillies and four colts. In fact, one of the colts is as black as I am."

Mary replied, "That is nice. Now you know what I want to talk about. Don't change the subject. Did you find what you were looking for? Did you get closure?"

Jeremiah cleared his throat and said, "Yes, I found what I was looking for, and he is in a better place. I think it is time for me to let go of him."

"Jeremiah, I know your friend's death has been heavy on your heart for years. If you took the arrow, there would be no me or kids. You did what you could do in that hell. I am proud of what you just did for him. No one can ever take that away from you."

"Thank you, dear wife, for standing with me. I know my moodiness over the years did not create good relations between us. Nevertheless, you were patient. You kept me away from the bottle. Now it is over. I do not have to cope anymore. I can move on."

Mary reached over and took her husband's hand. "I will always be here for you. We took vows—good or bad. We have had more good than bad."

Jeremiah squeezed Mary's hand and said, "What do you say we go outside and sit on the porch? We can read the paper while we watch the kids play."

Mary replied, "Well, only for a little while. I need to get those apples cut up and soaking in some cinnamon and sugar."

*****

Sunday-morning breakfast, church, and rocking on the porch helped Jeremiah recover from his long journey to inter the bones of a friend. A friend killed by a Comanche's arrow nearly thirty years ago.

Jeremiah rocked back and forth in his old oak rocking chair. The chair creaked with every backward movement. He looked over at Mary. She rocked in her padded mahogany chair Jeremiah made for her back at Fort Sill in 1895.

Mary knitted while Jeremiah read the Sunday paper. The cool fall breeze swirled across the porch, kicking up dried brown oak leaves against the porch steps. The crackling of leaves sounded like campfire burning in the forest.

The kids ran around trying to tag one another. Mary yelled out, "Now, kids. Be careful running around, not paying attention. Don't want you getting hurt."

The four children waved and spoke at the same time. "Don't worry, Mama." Mary went back to concentrating on her knitting.

Jeremiah straightened out the front page to a story headline that caught his eye.[14] He said, "Mary, looks like your brethren down in the Indian Territory are having issues with federal money and schools. Says here the federal government denies there is any trouble over the question of my people attending school with your people. You would think in 1904, our country would become color-blind after that damn civil war."

"Honey, I think us Indians can go back farther than that. Maybe three hundred years. We were here first."

Laughing, Jeremiah tried to swat her with the paper.

Jeremiah straightened out *The Times Dispatch* pages. The breeze kept ruffling the paper, which made it difficult for him to read. When he finally got control of the paper, he noticed an announcement in small print. The title read, "Famed U.S. Cavalry Horse Peacefully Passes." Jeremiah continued reading. He let out a deep sigh.

Mary looked up from her knitting, concerned. "What is wrong, husband?"

"Well, my sweet Lord. A horse Drayton told me about passed away last Wednesday."

Confused, Mary replied, "I hate to say this, but it was just a horse."

"Not any horse. The newspaper says Stonewall, a U.S. Cavalry horse—veteran of two wars—died peacefully at his owner's farm near the army equine training grounds."

"So this Stoney... did you know this horse?"

"No. I only saw this horse twice. Once in 1874. Just before the Battle of Tule Canyon. The second time I saw him was—well, last week." Mary's eyes widened.

"What do you mean last week?"

"After packing up Joe's bones, I mounted my horse and sat there for a moment to rest my eyes."

"You mean, shed a few tears?"

"No, no. I am a grown man. I don't cry. I was about to nudge my horse forward when out of the corner of my eye, a dark silhouette of a horse and rider suddenly appeared on the horizon. The sun was behind them. I stared in that direction for a few moments, thinking it was a mirage. My head felt fine. I was not tired. I rubbed my eyes and looked again. The rider did not move."

"What happened next?"

"A cloud passed in front of the sun. The rider and the horse came into view. I recognized the Comanche warrior sitting bareback on a big black stallion. Something else. The stallion had a brand on its left hindquarter. The same brand a horse I saw back in '74. It was Stonewall. After the warrior extended his lance toward me, he turned the horse to the north. They vanished into the clouds."

"You know. In my old ways, that meant the God of Life took Stonewall to where he belonged—with my people."

"I don't understand, Mary. Why do you say that?"

"Do you remember what the Bible says about Joseph and his brothers who betrayed him in Genesis?"

"Yes. Joseph correctly interpreted the Pharaoh's dreams. The King then elevated Joseph's place in Egypt. In the end, Joseph put away his anger in exchange for seeing his family again."

"Husband, perhaps the ghosts represented you forgiving the Comanche warrior who killed your friend. The black stallion represented your friend Drayton. They both now have peace in the afterlife. You must have peace now."

"Mary, you are wise and right. I guess I'm more at peace now. The wrongs have been righted. I suppose it is time for me to let go of the war."

Mary got up from her chair and sat on Jeremiah's lap. She put her arms around Jeremiah's thick neck and kissed his cheek. She whispered into his ear, "We are living in the now together, and for tomorrow. You will still have your bad days, husband. Those memories never go away. You can simply look at them with a different perspective. My people took the same path, considering what the white man did to us. We forgive and move on."

*****

The Zapatas and Stonewall

At the Zapata Farm, Manny and Lucinda wanted to till their fields one more time before the winter set in. Stonewall was tacked up with the plow harness connected to a curved steel blade Manny guided across each row of dirt. Once in the middle of the field, Stonewall stopped and lowered his head and began snorting. Something was wrong. His breathing became very shallow. Manny noticed that Stonewall's legs started to tremble. He wasted no time removing the plow harness. Manny slowly led Stonewall back over to the barn stall.

Manny saw Lucinda standing on the porch looking at him. He hurriedly waved her over. Lucinda jumped off the porch and ran toward Manny and Stonewall. She had concern in her eyes. "What is wrong? Why did you stop plowing? Something wrong with ole Stoney?"

"Honey, he may be lame on the right hind. He has irregular breathing. Help me get him back into his stall. Please. Run ahead and get some fresh hay laid down."

By the time Manny got Stonewall to his stall, Lucinda had the hay spread out across the stall from side to side. Once inside, Stonewall immediately went down on his front knees. He then brought his hind legs down to the side. Manny stepped alongside Stonewall while running his hand over his back, across the mane, until he reached Stonewall's head. He got down on his knees facing Stonewall. Eye to eye, tears started to well up in Manny's eyes. He stuttered, "Old boy, I know you are in pain. I can't remove what hurts you. But perhaps these treats will help."

Manny pulled out a handful of oats rolled in molasses. He placed them in front of Stonewall's muzzle. Stonewall did not take it. Manny looked at Lucinda and said, "It must be his time. I will leave these oats in front of him. Maybe things will change. I will stay here with him. Would you mind bringing me some dinner? I don't want to leave him alone."

Lucinda nodded her head and said, "Of course. I will be right back." Manny left the stall door open and hurried across the barn to get a stool. When he came back, Stonewall was lying down with his head extended forward. Manny sat his stool in the middle of the stall door. He looked to the right through the open, double barn doors to see the sun starting to set. He said, "Stonewall, Lucinda will be here soon. We will not leave you alone."

After a few minutes passed by, Lucinda came into view holding a tray of food. "How is he doing?"

"Looks like Stoney decided to lay down. I am watching his breathing. His chest slowly rises with each breath. I wish there was something we could do to make him more comfortable. By the way, today is a special day for him and my father. It was thirty years ago my father led his company during the Battle of Tule Canyon."

"How can you remember such a thing?"

"Papa said Stonewall was defiant to a devilish colonel who spurred him hard enough to draw blood."

"What did Stonewall do?"

"He just took it. Papa said Stonewall was a gift from President Ulysses S. Grant to Bad Hand McKenzie. Evidently, the colonel did not want a stubborn horse. That worked out for the trooper who rode him. I remember his name was Sergeant J. W. Abercrombie."

Manny looked down and watched Stonewall struggle to breath. Lucinda and Manny remained silent. Stonewall blew out heavy sounds out through his nose. Manny noticed a small trickle of blood seep out of Stonewall's nostrils. Manny grabbed Lucinda's hand and sighed. He kept his eyes on the childhood friend he grew up with back at the Zapata Ranch in Texas. Stonewall's breathing slowed. He took one last gasping breath, and then his chest rose no more. The barn's silence could not be broken at that moment.

Manny and Lucinda wrapped their arms around each other. While holding Lucinda tight to his chest, Manny rested his chin on her shoulder, eyes closed. The tears fell like rain between the two. Then a strange feeling ran down Manny's back. He lifted his head up and stared out the barn door. He saw the sun fall just below the horizon, painting the sky with shades of green, blue, indigo, and violet. His eyes went wide. A white mist moved quickly over the creek, running by his property line. Unlike fog, this mist moved toward the barn. Within seconds, the mist formed up into a herd of white horses. The lead stallion stopped and reared up on his hind legs, pawing the air. Manny pulled back from Lucinda and whispered. "Papa was right. I can't believe it. Look. They are out there! The ghosts of Tule Canyon." When Lucinda turned around, the white herd had moved across the field.

The ghosts of Tule Canyon. Original artwork
by Russell C. Goodwin.

"What do you mean ghosts of Tule Canyon?"

"It does not matter right now. Just a sign that a courageous horse has left this life."

"I am so sorry for you, Manny. I know how much Stonewall meant to you. He was the last living reminder of your father and your mother, God rest their souls."

Lucinda pulled Manny toward her bosom. "Let us go put a blanket over Stonewall's body. We can borrow Mr. Monroe's tractor to move Stoney down to the creek tomorrow. There is a nice willow tree down there to bury him near."

Manny released Lucinda. He pulled off a horse blanket from the stall door and placed it over Stonewall. He looked at Stonewall one more time and said, "Gracias por tu vida. Gracias por proteger a mi papá." Thank you for your life. Thank you for protecting my papa.

Magnolia Remembered

Allison Drayton

Lying in her goose-down bed with eyes wide open, Allison Drayton stared at the bedroom ceiling watching the fan turn. She mumbled, "I need to get up." She rubbed her eyes. Allison continued to lie in bed watching the rattan ceiling fan slowly rotate, pushing air down to stir the heavy South Carolina air. She loved that fan. She bought it during her business trip down to the Florida Everglades back in December 1903.

Driving down Florida Route 11 in her Ford coupe, she saw a roadside marketplace bustling with farmers and artisans selling their goods. She pulled into the gas station parking lot just beyond the makeshift fruit stands lined up along the road's shoulder. She parked underneath a large billboard sign that said, "Gas. 20 Cents per Gallon."

Allison got out of her car and walked over to a tiki hut covered with dried palm leaves providing shade where a middle aged–looking man sat behind a wooden workbench. She walked over to get a better look at the artisan's work. He had hung several intrinsically designed ceiling fans from a wooden display frame. A three-foot-by-two sign was nailed to the frame's top. The sign read, Phil's Fans.

The man's leathery brown skin had seen much outside living over the years. Even more noticeable was a long white beard that hung down to his chest. The only clothes he had on were a pair of faded Levi overalls and a white bandanna tied around his neck. He paid no attention to Allison standing in front of the hut. He focused on shaping four palm-shaped fan blades made out of wicker.

Allison took a few side steps to get under a palm tree, providing shade from the hot Florida sun. She watched the artisan's hands with amazement. The Floridian put the final touches of glue on the fan blades. He constructed the blades to easily attach or remove from the electric motor. Allison could tell he took great pride in his creations.

Allison loved the fan. She had to have it. In fact, she would pay him more than what he asked for. She reached into her purse and pulled out a bag of Morgan silver dollars. She counted out ten and handed them over to the artisan. The man looked at each coin carefully to make sure they were real. He stuck a coin in his mouth and bit down, feeling a little give in the metal. He looked up at Allison. He said in his heavy Southern accent, "Ma'am. Not seen one of these in 'while. Just make'n sure. All due respect."

Allison replied, "No worries, friend. Those were just minted this year. By the way, what is your given name?"

While the artisan wrapped the four blades in dead Spanish moss, he replied, "Philip. Philip Diehl. Glad to meet you." He used hemp twine to secure the moss around each blade for protection. Diehl added, "This moss will keep the fans from getting scratched or broken." He then packed them with the electric motor into a four-foot-long wooden crate. Diehl then helped Allison pack the crate in her car. She thanked him and drove away.

*****

Allison watched the fan blades slowly rotate in a circle. The blade's movement induced her into deep thought. The fan moved the room's air to cool her face and body. The air temperature was most pleasant during the evening in the spring, summer, and fall. Between April and October, Allison kept the bedroom windows cracked during the night. She could not stand stagnant air. During the winter, the cold air robbed her of sleep with the windows shut.

Now sitting up in bed, she turned her head right to check the time. The old Irish wall clock's pendulum swung back and forth, producing a rhythmic *tic toc* sound. The hands, made of wooden feathers, indicated six o'clock. The hand-carved walnut clock meant much to Allison. Her grandmother, Nancy Powers, brought it with her from Ireland back in the mid-1800s. She and her husband, daughter Elizabeth, and her prized warmblood mare, Grace, crossed over the Atlantic to settle in Charleston, South Carolina.

Allison rubbed the sleep from her eyes. She said aloud, "Come on, Ms. Allison Drayton. You need to get your lazy tail out of bed. Those horses need feed'n. Much work to be done today." Allison swung her long legs over the bedside, stood up, and stretched her arms out to yawn. She turned around and stepped toward the bedroom window. Looking outside, she took a deep breath of fresh air to induce another deep yawn.

A familiar sweet scent in the air made her smile. A light breeze carried aromas of the white magnolia blossoms and pine trees across the pasture. The smells were one of South Carolina's natural greeting cards during the spring. She loved living on the Magnolia Horse Farm, though that was not its original name. During her formative years, it was called the Magnolia Planation. Even though the mansion was not the original house she grew up in, it was still home. The first mansion had burned down during the U.S. Civil War. It was not by the hand of Union General William T. Sherman. Instead, it was her own Confederate soldiers that were forced to burn down all the farms and fields before General Sherman could take the spoils.

She turned around from the window and quickly tiptoed across the cold oak floor into the bedroom's walk-in closet. She pulled on the light cord to help her choose from her apparel options for the day. While scanning her wardrobe, her toes found warmth on a thin blue Persian rug runner that covered the closet floor.

Trying to decide what to wear, she slid several frilly blue, white, and peach-colored dresses across the hanger rod to the left side. She murmured, "One of these days, I might actually have an occasion to wear those lacy things." She looked at practical clothes organized to the right of the closet in rows of blue and white cotton shirts, Levi britches, and several pairs of riding boots. She replied to herself, "The work clothes will do."

Allison let her cotton nightgown fall to the floor. She then pulled a blue cotton pullover blouse off the hanger. The blouse was easy to put on. Next were the riding britches. She had to sit on a small chair in the closet to pull up the tight-fitting brown britches. Britches she had a tailor sew brushed leather patches onto the seat, inner thighs, and on front of the knees. She did not invent the idea, but she surely appreciated how the leather seat and the inner thigh patches reduced saddle chaffing.

She put on a pair of silk-lined cotton socks. Then the brown high-top field boots were next. She stood up and walked back to the bed, were she had kicked off her work boots before going to bed. Allison picked them up and walked back to her bed.

Sitting on the mattress's edge, she grasped both leather bootstraps and pulled up to slide her toes to the boot's toe. She placed her thumb sideways between her big toe and the tip of the boot to make sure there was exactly one inch between her toe and the tip. Allison knew that an ill-fitting pair of boots and regular jeans would not help her feel the horse. The riding pants helped her sit deep in the saddle. The leather-seated pants and the tight-fitting boots could not fail her during a jump.

After tucking in the britches, she walked over to the full-length mirror. She admired her body. "Still fits after all these years. I guess the kind of body a woman keeps when they bear no children. If I had ever had kids, these thin pants would be just a memory." She laughed at herself.

Lingering a little longer than usual in front of the full-length mirror, she said, "There you go. You are a fine specimen of a woman. A horsewoman, that is." Using her mother's old horse brush, Allison pulled her long wavy red hair into a ponytail tied in a thin pink ribbon. "There," she mumbled. "I have one prissy thing that will not get in the way of my business."

Before turning away from the mirror, she did a double-take on herself. Something caught her eye. She took a step closer to look at herself, or the sparkle that briefly showed itself. She stared into her own green Irish eyes. Working outside in the weather had carved crow's feet near her eyes. Her face looked leathery. She chuckled at herself. Looking into the mirror, Allison said, "Mirror, mirror on the wall, I am beautiful in mine eyes and et al." She grabbed her work gloves off the register and left the bedroom.

Allison Drayton did not dress herself like a typical Southern woman. She grew up on horses and would always be a horsewoman—not a horseman. Her social attitude hardened over the years. She never cared for man's domination of the English language. Words created inequality. Perhaps her tenacious drive for equality kept here single for so many years. That did not bother her. One thing for sure, Allison was as good as the rest of the men running horse farms. She did successfully without a man standing in front of her.

Allison's Magnolia Horse Farm's reputation for producing sought-after horses garnered praises throughout the South. The wealthy clamored for her warmblood and Thoroughbred-mixed stallions and mares. In fact, President Teddy Roosevelt himself purchased a top-notch brood mare from the Magnolia Horse Farm back in 1903. He told Allison the mare would produce world-class horses trained to compete in international polo competitions throughout Europe.

Always concerned about where her horses ended up, she asked the president, "Where will my mare—strike that, *your* mare be going to?"

The president replied, "I own a large horse farm myself near Winchester, Virginia. She will have a good life there."

Satisfied with his answer, she sold him the mare without further question.

*****

Allison walked downstairs and rushed toward the kitchen. She was running a little late. She hurriedly opened up the icebox and snatched the glass milk bottle and a couple of buttermilk biscuits previously baked for the workweek. She could now quickly heat up the biscuits with her new oven. A new energy called natural gas fueled her cooking stove, along with several baseboard heaters installed throughout the house. The gas was fed by a ten-foot-long cylindrical steel gas tank mounted aboveground behind the mansion. It contained pressurized natural gas. The utility man connected and buried small underground copper pipes from the tank to a distribution box designed to supply gas to her stove and baseboard heaters. She loved the idea of not having to fire up wood in the potbelly stove every morning to heat up breakfast.

After eating her breakfast, she put the dirty glass and plate in the kitchen sink. She said to herself, "I will clean these later. I hope they invent an automatic dishwasher someday. I hate doing dishes." Allison left the kitchen to make her way toward the mansion's large twelve-foot oak double doors.

Before going outside, she took a small sidestep to peer out of one of many six-inch square glass panes that outlined the doorframe. Taking note of a clear sky, she stepped back and glanced at the coat rack where a half dozen hung. "No need for a jacket today," Allison quipped. She grasped the left door handle, pressed down on the lock, and pushed out the double doors. She stepped onto her wraparound porch and yelled out, "Good morning, Magnolia!"

Closing the doors behind her, Allison stepped across the front porch to a set of cascading steps leading down to a red-brick path. As she walked, every step taken caused the wooden planks to creak. Before going down the steps, she stopped to lean against one of six tall twenty-foot white pillars supporting the second-floor porch that extended from her master bedroom.

Allison had the best view of the Magnolia property at ground level. To see how far the Magnolia front lawn extended, she had to look under and through all the large trees that overhung the west and east property lines. Spanish moss blocked her view. The greenish-gray plant hung down from the lower tree limbs and blocked her view of a creek that flowed into the Ashley River.

The majestic Magnolia front lawn was first cleared back in 1676 by Allison's grandfather, Sir Thomas Drayton. Her mother, Elizabeth, said it took many hands to keep the lawn in shape. Allison changed it. Her front lawn was now a pasture. A pasture she now used for grazing her horses. She looked down at the porch deck and stomped it with her boot heel.

She stepped toward the railing and ran her hands over the smoothened wood. She grinned, knowing her father had constructed the porch out of hard oak he cut from a massive oak tree brought down by lightning in the spring of 1859. She also knew he did not

Leather to Steel

build it alone. A black man working for the Magnolia—known as Mister Joe—did most of the heavy lifting and wood hewing. Together, they constructed a porch and railing that endured the test of time.

She looked across the left side of the yard to the barn. Her fondest memories were of her mother's mare Grace, and the colt she gave birth to where the original carriage house once stood. She watched the colt grow up into a young black stallion, until the Confederate States of America Army appropriated him for service. His name was Lucky.

Once at the bottom of the steps, her eyes followed a narrow brick path toward the barn, which was remodeled to accommodate twelve horse stalls. She left the first original inside stall untouched. The stall she watched her beloved black stallion Lucky be born, and, sadly, the same one where his mother, Grace, died on April 13, 1859

The Making of a Warhorse

> If you desire to handle a good war-horse so as to make his action the more magnificent and striking, you must refrain from pulling at his mouth with the bit as well as from spurring and whipping him. [...] but if you teach your horse to go with a light hand on the bit, and yet to hold his head well up and to arch his neck, you will be making him do just what the animal himself glories and delights in.
>
> —Xenophon, *The Art of Horsemanship*, 360 BCE

Tough Guy

After the foals were born, I waited to see them. All I could do was neigh loudly enough, hoping the mares would reply, letting me know what sex they gave birth to—colts or fillies. I wanted to know what the little ones looked like. I did not understand why Welford confined me to the paddock for the last few days.

I was in terrible shape not knowing. Then it hit me: the six-foot pole fence is an easy height for me to jump. I galloped to the opposite end of the paddock. Turned around and ran full-speed. Within ten feet of the fence, I dug my front hooves into the dirt to push up. My rear legs did the rest. I extended my neck up and over the top cross pole. My front legs cleared the height, bringing my chest high and over. As I started to fall forward, I arched my back to bring my rear legs over the pole. I came to a dead stop. I looked back at the fence and neighed proudly. "I easily cleared that fence with a foot to spare."

I trotted over to the barn, where I could hear the mares giving suckling to the little ones. I walked over to the front barn door, and of course, it was latched. That did not deter me. Mr. Welford forgot to

Leather to Steel

insert the chain pin. My nose became the perfect tool. I stuck my nose under the latch handle to push it up and away from the lock edge. I used the right side of my chest to push in the left door. That created enough separation between the doors to allow me to nudge the right door out towards the field. Now the only problem was light. I had no idea how to turn the lights on. Once inside, I walked down the stable aisle. Each stall had a mare and baby.

At the far end was Grace's stall. I stopped and looked over the stall door. She had given birth to a healthy black colt. She stood in the corner while the colt fed. His long legs wobbled a bit. He stopped sucking and turned to look at me. The colt could not see me. His eyes were still adjusting. Grace neighed, "Let him be. He needs to eat."

Recognizing I was not needed, I returned to the paddock to wait for the morning sun to rise.

*****

The hard Virginia winter was finally over. It was springtime, a season for new life. I stood proudly on top the pasture hill watching over the new additions to our herd. They were growing up fast. The farm's highest point on the property provided me a 360-degree vantage to observe the goings-on. Looking down into the river valley, one could not help but appreciate Mother Nature's offering of red, blue, purple, and orange blossoms dotting the fields and tree limbs. The day was shaping up to be perfect: blue sky with a few wispy clouds hanging over the horizon.

Sticking my nose up in the air, I detected faint smells of the thawing Shenandoah River making its way north to Harper's Ferry. It would join the Potomac River at the confluence under the railroad bridge connecting Virginia and West Virginia. Mister Jeremiah said Harper's Ferry made its name known during the Civil War. I suppose my father knew more about that than me.

As the morning sun rose, a southwesterly breeze kicked up over the Blue Ridge Mountains. I felt its warm breeze rush down over the river, drawing up river mist rising up from the broken ice and rapids. I could taste snowmelt in it. It was cool. I loved the smell of the springtime runoff. All the scents made another day at the farm normal—except for one thing.

A loud machine noise coming from the west startled me. I quickly spun around. Coming into view was a fast-moving gray motorcar making a loud honking noise. Two black motorcars kept the same speed behind the lead car racing toward the western farm road entrance. The commotion on the road quickly caught the attention of nervous-tempered fillies and colts. They did not like the sounds. They certainly did not care for the site of strange-looking machines. They reacted.

The frightened little ones quickly turned away from the main fence line. The colts scattered about looking for safety. Several bucked and flatulated, as they galloped across the field. Within a few minutes, the colts eventually regrouped and calmed down. Only one problem remained; they headed toward the river.

I warned the mares to keep them away from the trails paralleling the riverbank. The mares and I knew predators were coming down from the mountains searching for newborn prey. During the previous eve's graze, we heard a wolf prowling by the river. His high-pitched howls told us one thing: he was very hungry.

It was not but a week ago when an older mountain lion made his presence known to the farm and five unsuspecting colts. Unbeknownst to them, danger lurked nearby the river's edge that morning. It began with the four bay colts chasing each other all over the property. The playfulness escalated when four bay colts turned together and ganged up on the lone black colt. The four bays gave chase to the black one, who raced toward the river. The four bays aggressively pursued yet could not keep up with the much faster black colt.

Grace watched the colts. The wind brushed under her nose. She smelled it and sensed the danger. Within seconds, the colts were already over a hill and out of sight. I witnessed the same. Concerned, I neighed at Grace to chase after them. Another mare heeded my command and joined her. While they pursued the colts, I put my ears up to get a better position on the lion. I could hear a low growl emanate from the river's edge. The sound meant the lion was preparing for a kill. Wasting no time, I sprinted down toward the river.

By the time I made it to the river's edge, the mares had already herded the four bays back to safety. Within a minute, they neighed out, indicating all but one, returned to them. The black colt was still missing.

I frantically searched for Grace's colt. We called him No-Name. Walking north along the bank, I rounded a large willow tree near the riverbank. The colt came into my view. He did not move. No-Name remained steadfast in the midst of a four-foot blackberry thicket growing along the riverbank. His ears were pointed up. His withers remained still.

I galloped toward No-Name. Within twenty yards of him, I sensed danger between our positions. No-Name must have heard me coming, but he did not turn to look at me. He held his neck up in an arch-shape. I had never seen a colt hold a combat position. The colt did not waver or shake. He showed no fear. I cautiously walked toward him, noting the smells of overwhelming willow tree blossoms and new green leafs growing on low-hanging limbs suspended above us.

Once by his side, I nudged No-Name to get his attention. As No-Name turned his head away from me, at that moment, the lion pounced onto my back. I immediately reared up and bucked several times, trying to shake him off my shoulders. I snorted and neighed loudly. No-Name remained silent.

The lion's front claws dug into my withers. I felt a stinging sensation. I could smell blood. My own blood. The lion tried to secure his back claws into my hind quarters, but was slipping on my unsteady backside. If he had leveraged his rear legs, his fangs surely would have broken skin and sunk deep into my backbone.

Seizing the harrowing moment, I quickly reared and jumped on my hind legs to use gravity against him. It worked. He fell off my back. I glanced to my rear and noticed the lion was low on his haunches. He was preparing for another attack. The lion growled louder, getting ready to jump again. I turned away and braced my front legs for the attack. A few seconds passed by. The lion did not come. Instead, he screamed crazily like a human baby.

The predator did not see the hooves coming towards his head. No-Name backed out of the rambles and into a position perpendicular to me. He delivered the fatal kick to the side of the lion's temple. The attacker became the victim. I turned around to see the lion's limp body lying motionless against the base of the willow tree.

I got closer to the lion's body to make sure he was dead. I stood over him and watched his breathing get shallower. Blood trailed from the side of his mouth and ears. No-Name's rear hooves certainly dealt the lethal blow to the lion's temple. The lion took one last gasp of air. As he exhaled, blood seeped out his nostrils. His breathing stopped. I turned and looked back at No-Name. I neighed, "You killed the lion."

I turned back toward the lion to study his lifeless body. He did not look healthy. His rib cage stuck out. Patches of fur were missing around his legs. Clearly, he was starving and in bad shape. The hard winter must have pushed his food sources into the valleys. He had no choice but to follow his instincts and hunt closer to civilization.

I looked back at No-Name. He just stood in silence gazing at the river. I do not know what he was feeling. I had never taken a life like he did. I neighed at him to get back to the barn. He slowly made his way up the river embankment, and then trotted toward the main paddock. I followed him to make sure he was okay. From that day forward, the black colt never neighed again on the farm.

*****

By the time I arrived back at the main gate, the gray motorcar had already parked in front of the house. The two pursuing black motorcars stopped and parked at the farm's main entrance. I was not sure of their purpose. They were parked at an angle facing each other to block the road's entrance.

The gray motorcar's occupants were already standing outside the vehicle. I saw two men standing near Jeremiah and Mr. Welford. My memory and instincts alerted me to a familiar face and scent. I

Leather to Steel

recognized the shorter, stout man in the hat. However, the tall silver-haired man was not familiar to me. He looked in my direction and made eye contact with me.

I raised my head and put my ears forward to show interest in his attention. He waved at me. Curious, I trotted toward the men. As they spoke, I listened. The strange-sounding man was from England. I would appreciate whom he truly was six months later. That Englishman would eventually teach us horses battlefield skills based upon our natural abilities to maneuver with tact and grace, while carrying a rider into combat. The first time I heard the word *dressage*, it was uttered by the tall, silver-haired stranger. The word *dressage* would become our future identity.

While the men conversed outside the main house, I noticed No-Name had run to the highest point in the pasture to study the motorcars and the men. After the killing, he vigilantly watched over the farm's goings-on. Since the attack, he behaved differently from the other colts. He did not know it then, but on the killing day, No-Name had unwittingly become a veteran of war.

I left the men and walked over to the paddock areas to ensure the mares had caught up with the spooked running and bucking fillies and colts. Knowing the mares had eyes on the young ones, I returned to the main gate. I continued to observe and listen to the men talk. The gray motorcar's engine was still running. The irritable sounds and smells emitted did not concern me. What concerned me most were the men and their body language.

I moved to the other side of the paddock to get a better view of the strangers' faces. The identity of the shorter man standing nearest Jeremiah was confirmed: it was Mister Roosevelt. Mister Welford addressed him as President Roosevelt.

The president leaned on the motorcar's right door. He was wearing his classic tan Wasey cowboy hat—the same hat he wore back at the army training center in Arlington, where I first met him. Though something looked different. I studied the hat. The difference was that President Roosevelt had pinned up the left brim.[15]

Welford and Jeremiah invited the president and stranger into the house. The president walked on point. The three men followed.

Perhaps it was a respect thing. Once inside, the four remained sequestered for a couple of hours.

When the sun hit midpoint in the sky, President Roosevelt, the stranger, Welford, and Jeremiah reappeared on the front porch. All were laughing about something the president said.

The president's driver revved up the grey motorcar's engine. The driver appeared to be restless. The president yelled out. "Hold on! I know you boys have to get me back to the capital." The driver eased up on the gas pedal.

I stayed close outside the main gate, listening to "Good-bye" and "Until next time" among the men. Welford moved closer to the president and said, "Sir, we will do as you ask." He then looked over at the stranger and nodded.

Welford stepped toward the tall man and extended his right hand. "Ranse, the president's cables described your specialty in training horses. He also said you hail from England."

Ranse replied, "Yes, I do. I am bloody glad to be here, Mister Welford. I will be at the president's pleasure for the next six to ten months."

Welford added, "Ranse, we have much to learn from you. That ancient battle training technique sounds interesting. Dressage, did you say?"

Jeremiah observed and remained quiet.

Ranse replied, "Yes. Dressage is an ancient horse training technique used to condition warhorses. A collection of methods practiced in Europe three hundred and sixty years before Christ's birth."[16]

Welford looked down at the ground, and he scooted his boots back and forth. He looked back up at Ranse with an arched eyebrow and said, "Well, I'll be. I reckon it has been the preference of many a king and queen."

Ranse returned a slight smile and then excused himself from the conversation. He turned and walked towards Jeremiah. Both extended their right hands to each other. Jeremiah held Ranse's hand with a firm grip. Jeremiah said, "Looking forward to working with you, sir." Ranse replied, "My dear fellow, no need to address me as, sir. You can just call me Ranse."

Jeremiah replied, "Very well, then."

Ten minutes passed while individual conversations continued. Then silence. The four men grouped up and walked to the main paddock. They entered through the side gate, then walked in my direction. I was now standing outside the paddock.

Jeremiah yelled out to me, "Come on over here, Tough Guy! We have visitors wanting to meet you."

I neighed and trotted over to the gate. Jeremiah always had a pocket full of oats. He knew how to entice me on command.

Once at the corner gatepost, I used my front right hoof to paw at the latched swing gate. Jeremiah looked at me. He recognized I wanted to come in. As Jeremiah reached over to unlock the gate, I then stepped in. As I nibbled the oats from Jeremiah's hands, the stranger said, "Jeremiah, there is an old wound on his withers. I see dried blood."

Ranse stood beside me on my left side. He kept his left hand on my neck while he walked around my rear to my right side. He mumbled to himself, "No blood here. No breaks there." On my right side, he stopped. "Looks like he has two sets of claw marks. What do you make of that, Mister Welford? Jeremiah?"

Jeremiah replied, "He got into a scrap with a mountain lion. He obviously won. We found the predator's carcass down by the river."

Ranse nodded. "I see. A warrior's blood. Very good. I want to see how he reacts when a stranger tries to handle him."[17]

I waited for Ranse to walk around to the front of me. He kindly asked Jeremiah to stand back. Jeremiah nodded and complied. Ranse then aligned himself with the front of my chest. While he looked me over, I studied him. He was a tall man, standing over six feet. Just about the same height as Jeremiah, judging from his chest, he weighed over two hundred pounds. He wore clothes that I had not seen before—a short-cut brown jacket over a white shirt buttoned up to his neck. His pants were tight around his legs and tucked inside high leather boots coming up to his knees. Ranse's hat looked like a black bowl with a narrow felt brim rolled up around the edges.

Ranse stepped closer to me and looked into my eyes. He whispered, "The only way a horse can show their discomfort is through his legs. I am going to walk over here, then call you to me." Ranse turned around and walked to the other side of the paddock. He turned around and clucked his tongue twice. I was interested in why he was calling me. I trotted straight on toward Ranse. I got within three feet of him, when he extended his right hand. He commanded me, "Stop."

President Roosevelt, Welford, and Jeremiah joined us moments later near our position. With the men looking on, Ranse ran his hands across my withers, chest, and front legs. While always keeping a hand on me, he walked around behind me, periodically stopping to check out my haunches, hindquarters, and forehand positions. He eventually made his way back around up front and stood with his arms crossed and talked to me, not the men. "Looks like you are well-balanced, ole boy. Balanced muscle mass on each side of your chest. You squared up on your own. That means a rider has not ridden you more on one side or the other. When I get you on the lunge line, we will check your confirmation."

Welford commented. "Looks like we need to learn a new language, in addition to a new horse training style."

President Roosevelt removed his glasses. He pulled a neckerchief out of his pocket and started wiping the lenses clean. While cleaning, Roosevelt looked at all three men and directed them. "What I want to see in every horse I own is for them to demonstrate a confirmation that will save these horse's life on the battlefield. In other words, each horse must have a quiet disposition, unwavering balance, healthy muscling, high carriage, and structural correctness."

Ranse responded to the president. "Sir, by year's end, you will see a difference in all your horses. Mind you, it will take several more years to get them to become the best warhorses they can be. But all I need is six months to train Mister Welford and Jeremiah on movement techniques and conditioning. This black stallion looks like a perfect candidate for the training."

"Of course, I understand that, Ranse. I need to see results. My friends are expecting it."

"Yes, sir. You will see results by year's end."

"I expect so. If you gentlemen will, I need to make my way back to the capital. The damn driver is going to have a heart attack if we don't leave now." Jeremiah, Jack, and Ranse each shook President Roosevelt's hand. Ranse spoke with confidence. "Mister President, we will not let you down."

President Roosevelt replied, "Thank you, Ranse. I appreciate you coming across the Atlantic to do this job for me. We will talk again in a few months." The president turned toward Welford and Jeremiah. Laughing, he said, "I need to get going gentlemen. The security service fellas at the end of the driveway are waving at me to come back to the motorcar. You know, the driver used to play football for the Chicago Cardinals. Hell of a strong man."

Before the president got into the motorcar, I snorted and neighed loudly at him. The president turned around and grimaced. His eyes told me what he was about to say. He spoke to me. "Tough Guy, sorry to hear about your father, Stonewall. He was a great stallion. He demonstrated great courage taking me up San Juan Hill." I reared up on my hind legs and pawed the air toward the president. I wanted him to know my father's courage ran in my blood as well.

The president pulled the motorcar door open and slid into the passenger's seat. After shutting the door, he rolled down the window. He waved and yelled out, "God bless America." The car sped up, kicking dust up into the air. The other two cars joined them at the end of the road. Within minutes, the president's motorcade was out of sight.

*****

During our evening feeding, Jeremiah told me later that he and Welford talked alone, while Ranse was getting settled in at the main house. Jeremiah said they were not looking forward to learning the horse training methods used by Europeans. I, however, was very curious about the idea of learning how to move on a battlefield. For horses, our survival depended upon leveraging our natural abilities, as much as the trooper did his own riding skills. However, our abilities had its limits between our ears.

Stonewall told me that during a battle between rider and rider, I was to simply zigzag over the open field toward a tree line to confuse the attacking rider, or dismounted shooters. My father also told me that most shooters back in his day used single-shot muskets and an occasional repeating rifle. That was over forty years ago. Weapons had changed since.

*****

After the president departed, Jeremiah walked over and whispered to me. "Sorry, ole boy. I was thinking it would be best to tell you later. I read that your father passed on from old age. He was with the Zapatas. I understand you were blessed to have spent time with him over the last year." I snorted in reply.

Jeremiah continued, "The newspaper interviewed Stonewall's owner, Manny Zapata. The story said Stonewall had served our country during the Comanche Wars in Texas and Oklahoma. Tough Guy, the nation may very well call upon you and your little ones to do the same—carry soldiers into battle."

I knew what he meant. I reared up and turned around on my hind legs before lurching forward into a gallop, then into a run. I jumped the paddock fence and headed toward the creek to be alone.

Ranse turned to Welford. "By George, Duke William Cavendish. Looks like I will be working with an unexpected surprise here in America."[18] Welford took a couple of steps back, scratching his morning beard. Then he turned around toward Ranse. "Who is Duke—whatever was the last name you said?"

"No worries, my dear fellow. I will tell you all about him in time. His famous name goes hand-in-hand within the world of dressage. Until then, look at the superb-looking black stallion run. Magnificent animal. Impressive, indeed."

Jeremiah came after me. By the time he got to the river, I had walked away from the bank's edge, dripping wet. He stood on the high bank looking down at me. He called out, "Tough Guy, come on back. We have some work to do. I know what it is like losing a mother and a father. Times are changing. That new horse trainer, Mister Ranse, wants to help you become the best you can be.

Learning new techniques will help you and the rest of the herd. Come on now. We need to go back." He reached into his pocket and pulled out a handful of oats. How could I resist.

I had to dig in my front hooves to get up the steep embankment toward Jeremiah. Once at the top, I faced Jeremiah. He stepped around me to rub my withers and neck with his right hand while patting my chest with his left. Then he told me, "You got a big heart, ole boy. Use it. We learn as much from death as we do from life. Time to move on."

He hooked a hemp-rope lead to my halter and led me back across the field toward the paddock. As we walked, I looked across the pasture and saw my little ones and mares grazing near the western fence line. I would have rather spent the rest of my day with Grace.

Reluctantly, I reentered the paddock, not knowing what was expected of me. The tall man walked over to where I stood by the gate. His gait was slow, yet sure. Welford yelled out, "Ranse. Are you scared of that big boy!"

Ranse turned around and lifted his hand up toward Welford, who smirked.

He reintroduced himself. "Do you remember me? My name is Ranse. Perhaps you and I can work together to show how you will become one of the best warhorses I've ever ridden." He put the back of his right hand in front of my nose. I smelled it. I could tell his hand was recently in a feed bucket with oats. I also smelled a hint of molasses. He held a thirty-feet lunge line, which was clipped to my halter. I put my nose down by the dirty white bag tied to his belt. I could smell the oats mixed with molasses in the bag. He pushed back, "Hold on lad. You will get rewarded if you do as I say."

I noticed he carried neither crop nor whip. There was no crop in his back pockets. That was unusual, since Welford and Jeremiah always carried a trainer's aid designed to reinforce a desired behavior. I neighed at him. He replied, "I know boy. You are wondering how I am going to get you to move when I say move. In fact, I am not going to say much. Our communication will be between you and my legs, seat, torso, and hands. You will learn."

Ranse walked to the center of the paddock while letting the lunge line slack fall to the ground. He stopped and then got my attention. He clucked his tongue twice. I took a guess and started walking clockwise. Evidently, I made the right choice. Ranse gradually gave me more slack while I moved around him.

I kept my eyes focused on his. When he blinked several times, he always made a command to turn, stop, or go forward. Each time I satisfied his command, he always stopped me. He then walked over to me and give me a handful of oats. The pain-free reinforcement worked for me. I started to like this funny-speaking man. He had a gentle spirit about him. He obviously understood how to work a horse. We were building trust.

By the end of an hour's time, I had worked up a good amount of white lather inside my legs. Not once did Ranse get on my back. I figured he needed to tack me up before he took that step. In the ensuing weeks, that would not be the case.

Ranse explained to Jeremiah and Welford the approach to developing warhorses. He used three phases of training. The first phase was four weeks of *groundwork*. Teaching us how to get squared, balanced, and relaxed. He called the second phase *techniques*, in addition to the groundwork. The last phase brought it all together. He started with groundwork, then techniques, and then conditioning.

*****

After eight weeks of performing repetitive groundwork, Ranse added the technical training regimen. The first time he rode me bareback, I could feel his leather-seated riding pants. He then started carrying the crop—not to cause me pain, but to act as a signal to make a movement. He spoke words during our training that I started to associate with certain leg movements I would make for him. I guess he was pleased with my progress. At the end of each session, he said, "Tough Guy. Your elevation of movement is coming right along. You are an amazing horse."

During each technical session, Jeremiah and Welford stood outside the ring watching Ranse run me through my relaxation drills.

Leather to Steel

He had me pivot on my forehands, then on my haunches. During one session, Ranse asked Welford to come out and mimic every move, and speak the commands Ranse used to get me to respond. Ranse yelled out, "Gentlemen, next week, we will work on Tough Guy's pole and carriage. He must learn to develop and maintain a high-neck carriage position to protect the cavalryman. To do so will require my custom-made tack for such occasions. I will need my bridals and saddles. They should be delivered by then."

*****

The following week, a delivery truck from Norfolk dropped off Ranse's special gear. He wasted no time tacking me up with a hornless saddle and lighter bridal. I, in fact, enjoyed having a much lighter saddle on my back. I was not so sure about the bridle and bit.

Ranse asked Welford to saddle up and take the reins. He approached my left side. Before getting on, Ranse said, "Mister Welford. Go ahead and get on. I need to adjust those stirrups to create the right bend angle in your knees.

Welford grumbled, "I am used to keeping them straight."

"Very true, if you ride a McClellan saddle. However, as you can see, the saddle on his back has no saddle horn."

"Well, I be dang. How do I hold on if he takes off?"

"That will be one of many movements you and Jeremiah will learn to do—total control."

Welford mounted up on me. The first uncomfortable thing I felt was the pull on the bit. Fortunately, Ranse quickly corrected him. Once he loosened the reins, the sides of my mouth returned to form.

I could not feel Welford's seat. He sat too close to my withers. Again, Ranse corrected him. "Mister Welford. You need to sit back further to get deep in the seat. I might add you also need to start wearing leather-seated riding pants. Those old Levi coveralls are not going to work for you during workouts with Tough Guy—or any other horse, for that matter."

Welford mumbled under his breath. "Dang limey. Thinks he knows everything." Ranse stood in the middle of the paddock barking off commands my rider tried to execute. While I trotted around the paddock, I periodically glanced at Jeremiah leaning on the fence. He scratched his head, looking bewildered. Ranse requested again, "Mister Welford, please come back to the center."

He looked over at Jeremiah and waved him over. After Welford dismounted, he walked over to stand by Ranse. Jeremiah stood nearest to me. Both men looked at each other, while Ranse pulled a paper copy of a small book. It had dogged-eared edges on all four corners. Ranse handed it to Welford. "Here, my good man. Please look this over the sections that talked about collection, extension, pirouettes, half passes, and flying changes. Several commands and drawings illustrate those dressage movements we want the horses to learn. Once you are done with it, please pass it on to Jeremiah."

*****

One week later, Jeremiah, Welford, and Ranse stood outside the paddock gate talking about the book. While handing the book back to Ranse, Jeremiah said, "Well, I reckon we got some learning to do. My wife helped me read some of the words I did not understand."

Welford added, "Ranse. That was about the same conclusion I came to. However, I think I get the gist of the book's high-school training descriptions."

Ranse nodded in agreement and said, "Very good, gentlemen." He continued, "I will add expert rules-of-thumb I learned while training Royal cavalry horses for Queen Victoria herself. For example, both legs signal the horse to move upwards into a different transition. The inside leg controls the position of the horse's hindquarters. Your butt position in the saddle, or seat, affects the horse's length of stride, speed, balance, and all downward movements. Do not—I repeat, *do not* use the reins to control these things. Instead, slightly move your hands and move your horse's shoulders toward a particular point you see ahead of you. Whips, clucks, applying leg pressure, and rein control all that's synchronized with the horse's movements."

Jeremiah asked, "What does leg pressure have to do with anything on a horse but to make him go forward?"

Leather to Steel

Ranse replied, "Good question. For example, the rider's right leg pressure influences the right hind leg. Conversely, the rider's left leg affects the horse's left hind leg. Applying both leg pressures is the cue asking the horse for movement. At that point, leg pressure simply asks the horse to hold or maintain a direction or gait. When I say 'Right leg off' or 'Left leg off,' that means you apply no leg pressure for that side. Through all this, the horse must learn to be supple. That is your job to give him soft eyes."

I could not understand what Ranse was saying. He spoke human words that I had not heard before. He used his hands to guide the conversation with Mister Welford and Jeremiah. He said, "Men, using the right hand, leg, and body movements—without a sound—are very important behaviors for both rider and horse to learn. On the battlefield, the loud noises will deafen the horse and rider's ears. Both have to 'feel' each other to survive on a smoke-filled battlefield. Now one more thing we need to talk about—tack and clothing."

Ranse walked over to the pole fence and removed a different black leather bridle. He held out an unusual looking bit I had not seen before. The snaffle bit was replaced with an arc-shaped silver piece of metal that was centered between two D-rings.

Ranse held up the bit portion. He said, "I've brought with me a tongue-friendly snaffle bit. The snaffle does not rotate in the center. It is a rounded piece of thin, smooth steel forged to provide a clear space for the horse's tongue. A double-jointed bit or snaffle with rotating mouthpiece shaped to allow tongue relief. This helps the horse focus on the commands, and less on where his or her restless tongue ends up during the ride."

Welford commented, "Well, I guess that is a pretty darn good idea. Who would have thought?"

Ranse said, "The English did. The bridle is just one part of a system I teach to keep the rider and horse safe. I think we have had enough for the day. I need a cup of tea."

After letting me out into the pasture, the three men walked back to the main house. I trotted over to where Grace stood on the hill watching over the little ones. The sun was moving closer to dusk.

The setting sun cast a beautiful red hue behind her. Her body cast a shadow on the hill in front of me. As I walked up, she neighed down at me. "So, how did it go? What did you learn today?"

"I learned that we have two hundred more days to go before we are ready."

"What does that mean, ready?"

"I don't know right now. In time, we will both know. The Ranse man speaks much different from what we are used to hearing. Don't worry, Grace. Your turn in coming." Grace snorted at me and pawed the ground, with a little sidekick. That was my cue to leave her alone.

*****

Training-month number four. Ranse expressed the importance of wearing leather-seated pants during this training. Ranse raised his voice at Welford and Jeremiah. "I noticed you men regrettably wear boots with spurs. Those spur rowels have sharp points. Before your next ride, make sure those rowels have been taken down to a smooth round nub, or don't wear them at all." Using a sarcastic voice, Welford asked, "Anything else you want us to do, Mister Ranse?"

"Yes. Thank you for asking. I have two more English saddles coming in from England. When those saddles get here, we will start training the remaining horses at the same time. Gentlemen. We need to be sensitive to President Roosevelt's tight timeline for getting the job done."

Welford asked again. "Now remind me—what is wrong with our good ole western saddles?"

"Let me explain. The high saddle cantle combined with the horn height will interfere when a rider leans forward during the moments a horse jumps a fence. The English saddle has a flat seat, very low pommel and cantle. I made modifications to allow for forward seat riding. When they arrive, you will notice a shorter stirrup length that requires a more forward flap. I use padding under the flap to lessen saddle slippage—"

Welford interrupted, "I am sorry, but Ranse. Can we hold off on the descriptions until we get the saddles? What you are saying now is going over my head."

Ranse said, "No worries ole man. You are right. It would be best to get the saddles in hand. So until then, I believe horse conditioning and a cup of hot tea is in order. Let us retire to the main house to enjoy the later. We begin again tomorrow."

Jeremiah recognized Welford's temper begin to flare up. Asserting himself, Jeremiah said, "Fellas. Hot tea sounds good to me." Ranse nodded in agreement. Welford huffed, abruptly turned, and began walking back to the house.

I could sense tension between Ranse and Welford. Jeremiah did not engage with them. He remained silent and calm. Once they were out of sight, I turned my attention back to the heard.

*****

While grazing near Grace, she asked me, "What were the men talking about?"

"Our owner wants us trained to basically carry a trooper on our backs during a battle."

"Tough Guy, what would that be like?"

"I do not know, Grace. I have never known battle and have always worn heavy U.S. Army cavalry saddles. My father, Stonewall, understood war. He carried troopers on western saddles during the Red River Wars, and during the Spanish-American War. One thing he said about both—it was rough moving cross an area overwhelmed with loud noise, reduced visibility, and just being plain scared."

Grace got nervous. "I am not sure I would like that one bit."

"Don't worry, Grace. You are the president's prized brood mare. I think I am his prized stallion. Then again, who knows what the future holds for both of us. I do know the little ones will eventually be sold. I do hope the black colt stays. He reminds me of—well, me. He is the American horse men want."

"Tough Guy, you think every black colt will be just like you?"

"Grace, I hope they become better than I do. Their survival will depend upon it."

*****

Ranse's two English saddles arrived just in time to begin the next phase of his dressage training program. It was already April, and he had only five months left. He had to get Welford and Jeremiah skilled enough to continue the training—on their own—after Ranse's departure.

*****

Monday morning began the work week on the Roosevelt Horse Farm. Horse feeding, grooming, and warm-up lunging began promptly at seven o'clock in the morning. The dressage relaxation drills ended one hour later. After I was properly warmed up, Ranse had Welford and Jeremiah meet at the main paddock gate by eight o'clock, on the dot. Ranse asked them to bring Grace and me into the far end of the paddock. Ranse had already set out the three English saddles on the top paddock fence pole. He took each piece of leather into his hands to ensure it was clean and not cracked.

Jeremiah asked, "What you are doing to the leathers?"

Ranse turned and looked at Jeremiah. He said, "Jeremiah. As you know, the fats and oils used to tan an animal's hide will dry up if the leathers are not cleaned. A dry leather strap can mean the difference between life and death for a rider. I like to use a small amount of saddle soap to ensure the leather is free of damaging dirt that clogs up the leather spurs."

Jeremiah nodded. "I see. Do you clean your tack every day?"

"No. Only if the leather fails my inspection."

Welford listened on with great interest. He cleared his throat then added. "Smart idea."

Ranse replied, "Thank you. Better to be prepared than be surprised flying off the horse. Shall we get the horses?" Jeremiah and Welford agreed. They turned around and walked toward Grace and me.

Jeremiah saddled me up I enjoyed the benefits of a light leather saddle on my back. The sheep's woolen blanket was a bonus. It did not slide when I breathed in and out. Wellford tacked up Grace at the same time. While we stood by the rails, Ranse walked back and forth between Grace and me. Ranse stopped by Grace's side and reached

Leather to Steel

down to slip two fingers in between her chest and the cinch strap. He double-checked to ensure the leather was secured to her chest, lest Mister Welford would lose his balance.

Ranse stepped over to my left and adjusted the stirrup lengths for Jeremiah. He asked Ranse, "Tell us, why are you making these stirrups shorter? My knees are now more forward."

"Jeremiah, the back of your boot heel needs to be aligned straight with your tailbone. By the way, don't lean over or back. Leaning back too much causes your lower back to get hollow. We don't want that. The horse needs to feel you balanced on their backs."

Ranse's eyes glanced back and forth between Welford sitting on Grace and Jeremiah sitting on me. He directed, "Now, men, I want you both to turn your boot toes slightly inward. This will cause your hips to open up, thus creating a deeper seat in your saddle. A tell-tale sign of not doing it right is when your boot heels are tapping the horse's rib cage."

Ranse said, "Now, the last thing to do for now is to talk about how you hold and control the reins. We want the horse to have a high-neck carriage, while putting their power on the back end. The horse has seven jointed hind legs. Six-jointed front legs. Therefore, they need to use their haunches more than the front. Now, gentleman, give yourself seven-horse lengths between yourselves while walking your horses around the paddock. Give the horses enough room from the fence to allow them a proper turn."

Jeremiah and Welford acknowledged they were good to go.

Jeremiah clucked once. He said, "Get on, Tough Guy."

I started to trot. Ranse yelled over at us, "Jeremiah, use your legs and hips to slow him down. Try your inside rein using a slight pull to bring him around. Calm your seat, and he will come to a walk."

Jeremiah complied. I went from a two-beat trot to a four-beat walk. I could feel Jeremiah holding both reins too tight.

Ranse yelled over again, "Jeremiah, mind your reins! Bring Tough Guy's topline down by softening your reins. Remember, men. Pressure on the reins is only through your thumbs. Again, pressure on the reins is only through the thumbs."

We did a couple of laps around the paddock. Ranse then instructed Jeremiah and Welford do figure—eight patterns. We switched directions after each loop. Welford asked, "Ranse. What is the point of doing figure-eights' and switching directions?"

"Good question," Ranse replied.

"We want to ensure the horse develops durability using all their muscles on both sides of the body. This exercise will help keep their skeletal structure in balance. It will also help you old men avoid getting more aches and pains as well."

Both Jeremiah and Welford grunted, knowing Ranse was right.

*****

After an hour of working, Ranse called us to the center of the paddock. He said, "Gentlemen, dismount."

Jeremiah patted my withers and ran his hands down my neck toward my nose. He told me, "Good boy. You did good."

Ranse walked over and handed Jeremiah a handful of oats. Jeremiah put the oats under my chin. I gently nipped them up from his hand. He stepped over to Welford and gave him a handful of oats. Ranse said, "Here you go Mister Welford. Feed these to Grace. She earned it."

I watched Welford extend his hand just under Grace's lower lip. She must have been hungry. Grace took most of his hand in her mouth. He quickly pulled his fingers back. "Dang, girl. Almost took my hand off."

She looked at me and neighed. "I was trying to bite his hand because he deserved it. He has got to stop jerking my reins when he feels off balance."

I replied, "Be patient. He is an old man who is trying to undo forty years of rough horse riding. Give him just a couple more weeks. He is almost there."

Grace snorted back at me, knowing I was right.

Jeremiah and Welford led us back to the barn to remove the tack and get a brush down. Ranse insisted that after every workout, us horses should get brushed down, fed, and watered. He really knew how to take care of a horse.

Leather to Steel

While the men removed our tack, Ranse approached them. "Next week, we start conditioning the horses. The horses must have stamina."

My ears perked up, wondering what he meant. Jeremiah had the same question. He asked, "How are we going to build up stamina in these horses?"

Ranse replied using two words. "Mud shoots."

*****

During the following week, a digging machine carved out one hundred feet of ground in the back side of the barn. The ditch was ten feet wide, twenty feet long, and three feet deep. Workers braced the walls with old automobile tires of every size. The bottom was planked with split pine logs. A dump truck hauled in a layer of sand spread on top of the planks. A different truck hauled in two tons of river mud drudged up from the Shenandoah.

Welford, Jeremiah, and Ranse walked around the shoot sides and ends. Ranse said, "Looks like the boys got it right. They installed thirty-degree wooden ramps going in and out of the shoot." Welford asked, "Ranse. Why are the old tires secured to the shoot walls on the inside?"

"Good question. It helps protect the horse from injury. If hard wooden cross beams were used, then a horse trying to jump out would certainly impel itself."

"Makes perfect sense. How will this shoot work?"

"It will take two men. Each man will connect a lunge line each side of the horse's halter. Then walk together on opposing sides, going in the same direction. The horse will be led into the shoot filled with three feet of thick mud. As the horse enters, each man will step with the horse's rhythm. The horse will instinctively pull its legs up and forward to move. It is during this stepping movement the horse will learn to keep its knees high. The horse will build stamina and muscle tone."

Jeremiah added, "A horse with stamina to endure a long battle."

"Exactly," Ranse replied with a smile.

Jeremiah said, "Then the first horse will be Tough Guy. He has to set the example for the other horses to follow."

Mister Welford and Ranse nodded their heads in agreement.

When I first stood in front of the mud shoot, I was unsure of the dark-brown liquid. The narrow shoot made me a little nervous at first. Jeremiah and Welford hooked two lunge lines to my halter. They then walked forward away from me on opposite sides. I looked left and then right. I saw Grace and the yearlings looking at me from the hillside. I neighed out at them to ease their concern. The only way for me to go was forward into the shoot.

I slowly walked down the ramp into the shoot. I carefully placed one hoof in front of the other. The ramp had a sticky, soft feel to it. I did not slip. Ranse said, "See, men. Nailing flattened tires to the boards gives the horse sure footing."

I continued walking in. With each step, the cold mud rose a little higher on my legs until it was just above my knees.

Eventually, I stood in the shoot with my legs evenly sunken into the mud. Jeremiah commanded me, "Come on, boy. We will keep you well. Pull your legs up and move onward."

I shook my head up and down, neighing loudly. I wanted to back up, but the men kept the lines moving forward. I finally relented and stepped high and out. With each step I took, the mud pulled at my hooves and hocks. The men yelled out to me, "Good job Tough Guy. Keep it going." I must admit, I was somewhat inspired by their encouragement.

After what seemed like an hour, I finally made it to the end ramp. I walked up and stopped. Jeremiah and Welford gathered the loose ends of the lunge lines while they walked over to me. Both men praised me. I was a little tired. I could hear Grace and the little ones neighing at me. They were as proud as I was.

Ranse walked up to us and said, "Well done, men. We will run the horses through this mud shoot twice a week. Eventually, they will be in good-enough shape to run it every other day."

Jeremiah replied, "Why not every day?"

"Good question. The horses will need rest. They are like athletes. Their muscles break down during the stamina training. They will need a day for their muscles to rejuvenate."

Welford commented, "You sound like a veterinarian, Ranse."

Ranse chuckled. He replied, "Ole chaps. I guess I failed to mention that I graduated from the Royal Veterinarian College.[19]

*****

The Zapatas

In Arlington, Manny needed a sire to replace Stonewall. A horse that would revitalize his horse farm. He sat on the front porch every evening after dinner discussing the future with Lucinda. They wanted to get a new stallion before winter. Manny wanted to ease the stallion into the herd before mating the brood mares in the spring.

While sitting on their front porch watching the sun set, Manny made the decision. He touched Lucinda's arm. "Honey, I know what we need to do. Tomorrow is Sunday. We need to take a drive out to the Roosevelt Horse Farm in Winchester. I want to see if there is a two-year-old stallion for sale."

Lucinda replied, "Manny, that would be a great idea. However, aren't those horses bred and trained for rich people friends of his?"

"Perhaps. However, I have a feeling he will work with us. Remember four years ago, the president took Stonewall's son—Tough Guy—from the army. I am thinking that stallion has sired quite a few fillies and colts. Surely, there must be one we can buy. He would show consideration to my late father, Colonel Clemente Zapata—and of course, Stonewall. Both served with President Roosevelt during the Spanish-American War."

"Do you think he will remember all that?"

"I think so. President Roosevelt is a sentimental man. Look what he has done with preserving millions of acres of wilderness areas in the west. He is passionate about life. It does not hurt to ask."

"Husband, first, we need to make sure such a horse exists. No sense in having this discussion if there is no stallion."

"You are right. I will go next Saturday morning."

Lucinda reached over to hold Manny's hand. She gazed at him. "It is worth a try."

"Lord willing, if we are lucky, we get a colt out of the deal. If not, we try again."

Lucinda raised her eyebrow. "Excuse me. Fillies are just a valuable as colts."

Manny and Lucinda arose from their chairs, and walked over the left side of the porch. The horizon's dusk colors were magnificent. Blue streaks outlined white clouds that turned gray near its edges. The northern star brightened in the sky as the sun sank below the hills. Manny put his arm around Lucinda. They gazed at the sunset that colored a narrow slice of orange and red near the spot where the Zapatas buried Stonewall.

Lucinda tugged at Manny's arm. "Can you imagine a young black stallion running with Luna out there in the pasture?"

Manny smiled. "Lord willing, we will have another Stonewall."

*****

Tough Guy

Jeremiah said our first year of dressage training was almost done, but that we needed several more years to perfect the high schooling moves we learned. Grace, a half dozen other horses, and I learned to be warhorses. Or at least move like one. Standing in the north forty pasture, all seemed well, until the wind carried a familiar smell to my nose.

I ran to the top of the hill to take a look. I heard a horse and a rider coming up the dirt road. My heart skipped a few beats. The scent was associated with my father, Stonewall; however, that could not be the case. He had passed away a few months back. The rider and horse looked like a speck on the horizon. I closely watched their approach, trying to make out who it was.

The hoof clops got louder as the rider and the horse neared the farm entrance. Once they rounded the corner, I could now see it was my father's owner, Manny Zapata. The horse he rode was Luna. I neighed over to Grace, "Looks like we have visitors."

Grace neighed in return, "Do you know them?"

"Yep, I sure do."

I ran toward the paddock while Grace remained grazing in the field.

*****

At the barn, Welford heard the unknown visitor coming up the driveway. He put down the pitchfork and mumbled to himself, "Not expecting anyone this morning. Who is it today? Ever since Teddy Roosevelt became president, this farm has become a circus."

Welford took off his work gloves before opening the barn door. Once they were outside, the bright sunlight made his eyes water. Rubbing them made the white spots he was seeing disappear. The unknown rider had stopped near the front of the main house. While walking over, he studied the man sitting on a bay horse.

To Welford, the man was some sort of foreigner. The rider wore a white-collared, long-sleeved cotton shirt that had the cuffs rolled up. A three-button leather vest kept the rider's gold pocket watch and chain tucked inside the front vest pocket. The rider's sombrero hat was not a common sight in Virginia.

Before stepping closer to the man, Welford used his eyes to carefully scan for any signs of a weapon on the rider's person or saddle. None noted. He walked toward the horse and rider. He said, "Hello stranger. How can I help you?"

Manny tipped his hat and replied, "Good morning, sir. I understand you have a stud here named Tough Guy."

"Yes, we do. Might I ask of your name?"

"My name is Manny Zapata. I own a working farm over in Arlington, Virginia. I also used to own the father of that black stallion you have standing near the paddock."

Welford glanced at Tough Guy standing by the fence rail neighing and pawing at the ground.

"Looks like he knows who you are, Mister Zapata. My name is Jack Welford. You can call me Welford. What is your business here?"

Manny dismounted and stepped over to shake hands.

"Yes, sir. Thank you for asking. I am interested in procuring Tough Guy's services for this mare I am riding. She is in season, and I would like to get a replacement for Tough Guy's father. He passed away last year. You see, Stonewall, Tough Guy's sire, was the stallion my father rode when he served in the United States Army Fourth Cavalry. He also served with the Rough Riders during the Spanish-American War."

"You can stop right there, mister. I think I know who probably sent you. President Roosevelt—is that right?"

"Well, sir, I did not send a cable to him requesting so. It is true, Tough Guy's father, Stonewall, carried Colonel Roosevelt at the Battle of San Juan Hill. Actually, this has nothing to do with him. I simply want to mate Luna with Tough Guy."

"We don't stud out Tough Guy, since he has been in training with the rest of the animals." Manny's head dipped down while he sighed. Seeing disappointment, Welford reacted.

"However, I think the president would be appreciative knowing Stonewall's past walked onto this farm. When is your mare going to be in season?"

"As a matter of fact, this week." Welford whistled over at Tough Guy. "Got some work for you to do, Tee Gee."

"You call him Tee Gee?"

"Yep. My nickname for him. Easier to say. The black stallion responds to it. He responds to both names. Go ahead and take your mare into the end stall in the barn. The one across from the tack room. I will go fetch Tee Gee."

Manny grinned from ear to ear. He had to ask, "But, sir, we did not negotiate a price."

"Don't worry about that right now, Mister Zapata. We will work something out. First, she has to get pregnant, and secondly, she has to birth the colt you want. Hopefully, a black one."

Manny nodded in agreement and replied, "We certainly will know in eleven months."

Manny led Luna into the barn. Standing in front of the stall, he removed the saddle, blanket, and bridle. He then slipped a halter onto Luna's head and led her into the stall. Manny looked in. He said,

"Girl, I know you are still young enough. I hope you understand. We need a colt. It has been too darn quiet around the farm since Stonewall passed on."

Luna stuck her nose out and snorted at Manny. Manny rubbed her nose and said, "I know. We shall see."

*****

Manny returned to Roosevelt's horse farm one week later. The new black Ford Model F truck he drove made much noise over the dirt road. He did not mind the noise. The trip back home would be quicker than riding on horseback. As the truck rolled down the farm's dirt road, the empty horse trailer's large white-walled wheels bounced across every road pothole. Periodically, Manny looked in the truck's rear-view mirror to make sure the trailer did not tip over. With only two center wheels, Manny had to slow down for almost every road obstacle, no matter how big or small. He had to be very careful driving the truck. He did not own the truck. His neighbor Max Eilenberg graciously loaned it to the Zapatas because his wife, Kate, ordered him to do so.

The horse trailer was another wild idea at the time. Manny's welder friend built what Manny's wife, Lucinda called, "a portable horse stall on wheels." All Manny cared about was safely transporting one horse over commercial roads. Going beyond what Manny expected, the welder friend designed and built a mini feed trough inside the trailer's front nose to keep the horse occupied with hay and oats.

Tough Guy

The first time I saw the horse trailer, I thought of my time spent in a boxcar hauling me from Kansas City to Richmond back in 1901. That was the first time I had been cooped up in a small area, for which there was no escape. Grace galloped over to stand by the fence separating the road from our pasture. I saw Manny driving the truck. Grace looked at me. She neighed, "What is that truck pulling behind it?"

"I don't know. I suppose we will find out. I saw Welford and Jeremiah coming out of the barn with that mare named Luna."

"You mean the mare who tried kicking you to death?" I pawed at the ground. "That was just her introduction. She calmed down later in the week. All is calm."

Manny drove the truck around the circular driveway. He stopped the truck facing toward the road leaving the farm. He got out and walked over to where Welford, Jeremiah, and Luna were standing near the main gate.

Manny said, "Good morning Mister Welford. I made it back with an easier transport." Manny looked over at Jeremiah and said, "Good day to you, sir." He extended his hand to Jeremiah, "My name is Manny Zapata. What is yours, sir?"

"Jeremiah. Jeremiah Bates. I am one of the horse trainers here on the farm."

There was a brief silence between the three men. Manny took a deep breath. He held out both hands with fingers crossed. He breathed out and asked, "Well, did we get lucky, gentlemen? I am not talking about Stonewall's father either."

Jeremiah's face lit up. His rubbed his chin and shook his head. He asked, "What do you mean, Stonewall's father. Was his sire's name, Lucky?"

"Yes. It was. My papa, Colonel Clemente Zapata rode Stonewall in the U.S. Fourth Cavalry. Papa said Tough Guy's sire—Lucky—served during the U.S. Civil War."

Jeremiah shook his head some more and mumbled, "Lord willing. God's plan."

Manny said, "Excuse me. What did you say?"

"Nothing. How do we get Luna inside that metal contraption?"

"My friend cut out a window on the front half of the trailer. He also cut out windows on the sides, but kept them open just enough for the horse to stick a nose through. I already opened the back door. He also built in a slide-out ramp for the horse to walk over and into the trailer. I will hook two rope leads up to Luna. You can control one lead on her right, and I will control the left lead to ensure she does not get too spooked. We will put some blinders on her."

Welford asked, "What can I do?"

"If you would stand in front of the trailer—just stand on the hitch. My friend cut a hole just below the little window. The hole is big enough for you to stick your arm in to remove the leads from Luna after I shut and latch the back door." Welford nodded and walked toward the front.

Jeremiah and Manny led Luna into the back end of the trailer. She stepped on the ramp and slowly moved into the trailer while being coaxed by the small bag of oats inside the trailer's mini-feed trough. Manny looked at Jeremiah and asked, "Please hold her still while I move to the side. I will have to temporarily drop the lead. I need to move to the side, reach through the side bars to regain control of the lead and her. Once I get that done, you will do the same."

Jeremiah nodded in agreement.

After completing a complicated choreography, Luna was safely inside the horse trailer. The men stood outside admiring their work. Welford said, "Manny, I think I know how we can work out the stud fee."

"How so?"

"Do you think your friend can build me a horse trailer?"

"Just say so, and it will be done."

Welford extended his hand to Manny. The men shook on the deal. Manny said, "I will cable you to let you know when he can get it done."

"That would be fine. Do you know how long it would take him?"

"He did it for me in three days. Now let me see. He already had the materials lying around his junkyard to do so. You see, he sells junk for a living. Metals, old furniture, scrap wood. He told me once, 'One man's junk is another man's treasure,' I think he was right."

"Sounds fair to me. Just let me know."

Manny walked around the trailer one more time to make sure the safety chain was attached to the truck's undercarriage. He got into the front seat and started the engine. He rolled down the window and waved at Jeremiah and Welford. In perfect Spanish, he said, "Adios, amigos."

The truck slowly pulled forward. Luna took a half step sideways to keep her balance in the trailer. Manny yelled out, "Well, wish me luck, men. It should be interesting getting over the pass."

I stood by the paddock with Grace. Both of us watched out of curiosity as the truck sped down the dirt road. I neighed at Grace, "Well, looks like we know what that contraption is used for now. To carry us away."

Grace looked at me with bewildered eyes. She said, "I suppose riding in a trailer could be good or bad, depending on where it is going."

I raised my head and arched the neck. I snorted and neighed. "Come on Grace. Enough entertainment for the day. We should trot over to the creek and get some fresh running water to drink."

*****

The Zapatas

August 1906 rolled in with the cicadas. The hot summer sun beat down on the Zapata barn's tin roof, which did not make things any more comfortable. Inside, Manny and Lucinda waited patiently by Luna's stall. Fresh grass had been laid down, which comforted her. Lucinda placed a wet towel on Luna's head during the labor pains.

It was very warm in the stall. Manny looked at Lucinda and said, "Until the sun goes down, we need to lower the temperature in this barn. She is going to lose her water." Lucinda nodded. "I know. Please get our fan out of the bedroom. The air needs to be moved."

Manny left and returned within minutes holding a portable electric fan and extension cord to a power outlet in the tack room. He placed the fan near the stall door and turned it on. "There," he said proudly. "Now we can get some relief until night."

"Do you think we will be here through the night?"

"Yes. When I was a boy in Texas, my father and I sat by many a birthing mare in those days. Some labors took two days." Lucinda's eyebrows furrowed. "I hope that is not the case with Luna. Either she will die, or you and I will see the future born on our farm."

Manny cracked a smile and replied, "Goodness. Watching her give life is worth the effort, trust me."

Luna lay on the stall floor sweating and sighing every few minutes. She raised her head briefly to look at Manny and Lucinda. Both had tirelessly stayed watchful over her for the last sixteen hours. They both surrendered to exhaustion, sleeping in their chairs. Luna decided it was time. Within minutes, the head and the shoulders of a foal emerged from her. Luna and Mother Nature did the rest.

After five minutes of birthing, Luna's newborn foal lay breathing and pawing at the air. Luna took a few deep breaths. She pulled her front legs up underneath her chest. She then slowly positioned each front hoof on the ground. The hind legs were next. Once in position, she pushed herself up to stand on all fours. She was exhausted. She had to lick the foal to clean him up. She turned toward her foal and neighed. The foal neighed back. She stretched down toward her baby and started licking the foal's face to ensure his nose and mouth passageways were clear for breathing.

The foal neighed louder. He woke Manny and Lucinda from their deep sleep, and they immediately got out of the chairs to see the newborn. Lucinda turned to Manny and said, "We did it. I mean…Luna did it. We have a baby!" Manny walked into the stall and looked under the black foal. He peered back at Lucinda and winked.

His noticeable smile meant one thing. In a state of excitement, he said, "And…we have a black colt! Thank you, God." He stretched out his arms toward Lucinda to embrace her. Holding Lucinda's face in his hands, Manny whispered, "Este potro va a cambiar nuestras vidas. Sólo sé que." (This colt will change our lives. I just know it.)

Manny put his finger up to the air, and placed it on the colt's rear quarter. He declared, "By the spirit of all that have come before him, I name him... Sonny."

*****

Tough Guy

Ranse Xenophon left the Roosevelt farm in August 1906. His job was finished. Jeremiah and Mister Welford clearly understood how to train horses to move within dressage rules of engagement. He also told them there was only one horse he would ride during the time of war. That horse was me. After all, everyone was impressed with my new abilities to move sideways without stumbling sideways on all fours. I held my neck carriage higher and felt good about receiving "high school" commands.

Welford had us horses exercising three times a day. He said to me, "Tough Guy, the president issued an order to all U.S. Army soldiers performing garrison duties to march three-day marches every month. The bottom line is--- he wants his army in shape. That means you horses as well."

I neighed back, "But we are not in the army now. Do you know something I don't?"

Evidently, back in March, President Roosevelt promulgated a famous order that required a regiment engaged in garrison duties to perform three-day marches every month.[20]

Grace and I showed our fillies and colts how to move across the field using dressage movements designed to protect the horse and rider. There were times on the field we watched all seven horses move in perfect synchronizing. The oldest black colt stood on top of the hill overlooking the pasture. He watched his brothers and sisters run in perfect unison. I looked at Grace and said, "Why do you think he wants to be alone?"

Grace neighed back, "Because he is different. He was born first. Unlike the others, the black colt is clumsier, and certainly hardheaded. Regardless of his faults, No-Name possesses the best instincts of them all. You know that?"

"Yes. I agree with you. I just hope he can keep up."

"Tough Guy, don't worry about that. You can see he is keeping up in his eyes and heart. It will take some time for his body to catch up. He is going to be a big one."

"I dratted the day he gets bigger and stronger than me. That means it is the day he has to leave."

Grace and I knew that by year's end, the yearlings would become two years of age. That meant President Roosevelt would decide upon their future. We hoped that the black colt would mature quick enough to ensure he ended up in a good place. All parents want their offspring to end up in a good place in life. For horses, those options were limited in 1906.

*****

You must in all Airs follow the strength, spirit, and disposition of the horse, and do nothing against nature; for art is but to set nature in order, and nothing else.

—William Cavendish,
1st Duke of Newcastle

A Suffrage Movement

American women of the year 1917 are no braver, no more patriotic, no more self-sacrificing than women have been in all wars of all times. Earth's women of every generation have faced suffering and death with an equanimity that no soldier on a battlefield has ever surpassed and few equaled.

—Olive Schreiner,
Antiwar campaigner, 1917

Tough Guy

The years spent on the Roosevelt farm raced by me. Many seasons came and went; marking precious time we had left on earth. Each time of year a horse could expect to be cold, cool, warm, or hot. This year was different. Spring should have been cooler. However, I concluded Mother Nature was on a vengeful rant. For weeks, the sun mercilessly deprived all living things, the giver of life... water.

The drought started well before winter. The winter snow did not come. The higher mountains were deprived of rain and snow. None to melt and refresh the creeks and rivers. The shortage of surface water forced Jeremiah and Welford to haul water from the underground well to our troughs. However, from my perspective, this was a teachable moment.

Grace and I taught our fillies and colts how to find water when there was none. My father, Stonewall, had taught me tricks to survive—the terms of survival he learned while on patrol under a withering Texas sun that blinded horses with thirst.

In the morning, the dew temporarily suppressed our thirst. When the sun reached midpoint in the sky, the shade trees kept us cooled.

Leather to Steel

The uncomfortable heat caused tempers to flare up. I watched Grace get irritated over little things she normally would dismiss.

One day, the heat ignited a conversation about which horse was in charge of the herd. Naturally, Grace always defended the mare's role as the caretaker. I had to remind her I was the protector. She differed. In fact, she neighed loudly at me. "Tough Guy, just remember one thing. We mares are just as important as the stallion. You can't deliver foals—we do— and don't forget it."

I raised my head high over her and pushed out my chest. "That may be true. However, without us stallions there would be no foals, nor protection for the herd."

"I differ. I heard Missus Welford tell the farm boss she had as much equality as he did. They both fought over it. Naturally, she won that argument. He did not have dinner for two days."

Grace continued, "In fact, Missus Welford yelled out, worldwide, all females are demanding change. She said all human women—mothers, daughters, grandmothers, and nieces—would pull together to form one perfect union of rights. She said females from all walks of life understood their place in the home, but could contribute more to the family. Mister Tough Guy, that means mares deserve the same."

"Okay, I get your point. Then the next time you smell a mountain lion coming down to the valley, you take care of it," I snorted.

Grace pulled back her ears and attempted to nip my shoulder. He simply stepped aside while watching her turn and trot away to the fillies and colts that never complained about their mothers. Grace found solace with the little ones, after having a spat with the alpha male of the pasture. The protesting sentiments must have been in the air. For the mares were not the only females wanting to change the world.

*****

The Bateses

After church on Sunday afternoon, April 15, 1906, Jeremiah and Mary Bates rocked in their chairs on the front porch. Sunday was a much anticipated day for the Bates, since the blessed day came once a week. Jeremiah labored the remaining six days; Mary took care of the home. Their rocking chairs represented solitude.

This particular Sunday was full of news. Mary and Jeremiah talked about the children, horses, and a devastating earthquake. Letting out a deep sigh, Jeremiah stopped rocking and said, "Mary, when I was in town yesterday, I heard some bad news."

"What? Nothing wrong at the job, is there?"

"No, no. The job is fine. While at the post office, I overheard a couple of fellas talking about a big earthquake that basically leveled San Francisco yesterday. People up and down the California coast felt it."[21]

"My gosh! How many were hurt?"

"The fellas said many were killed and missing. I am not sure of the exact death count. That information will not be known for some time."

"We need to pray for those souls."

"Of course, Mary. All we can do for them is pray and hope the men got to the survivors."

Mary put down her newspaper section and looked at Jeremiah.

He noticed Mary's eyebrows were furrowed, her lips thinned out. He asked her, "What? Did I say something wrong?"

"I find the use of the English language interesting."

"How so? You can speak in your native tongue and have good command of the English language."

"Jeremiah, that is not my point. I actually listened to what you said—not just hear you. Every man I have known since birth refers to guys, or fellas doing the act. You referenced men as finding the survivors."

"Yes. So that is who will save them."

"I beg to differ, husband. A woman is just as capable of saving a man."

"Mary, women are not strong enough to pull another out from under—"

Mary interrupted him. "You know darn well I am not just talking about strength. Of course, men are stronger than us. I am talking about what is between the ears. We can make lifesaving decisions."

"Mary, I am sure there are times when—nope, you are right. I stand corrected. Women can make decisions just as well as men."

Mary's eyes grew softer, but she remained leery of how quickly Jeremiah agreed with her. She picked up her paper and raised it high enough to block her sight of her husband. She flipped through the pages, periodically looking over at Jeremiah. She mumbled, "I think he just played me."

*****

Lucinda and Kate

Lucinda Zapata and Kate Eilenberg met for tea most every Saturday morning at their spot under an old oak tree near the driveway corner leading to the Zapata Virginia farm. The women had known each other for over ten years.[22] Both loved each other like sisters. The two thirty-two-year-old women had everything, except for one of life's gift—babies. Only God decided if a new soul was to walk the earth. Prospective mothers understood and accepted the fact it was God's plan, not theirs. They believed this since the day they met in Austin, Texas.

Lucinda and Kate's friendship grew during their college days at the University of Texas in 1885. They studied nursing together. They prayed in a Catholic church together. When Lucinda met Manny in the university library, she and Kate were helping each other study for exams. When Lucinda married Manny, Kate was Lucinda's obvious choice as maid of honor. The two were inseparable then, and inseparable in Virginia. They shared a strong and unbreakable bond of trust, respect, and affection.

Today's teatime took advantage of another beautiful Northern Virginia spring day. The morning brought cause for sharing special treats—sugar-dusted crumb cakes and a cup of hot black English tea—under their favorite oak tree.

When Kate arrived, Lucinda was already sitting on the bench positioning a rough-cut table Manny had made by hand for the occasions. Lucinda looked up at Kate. "Great. I can help you with the tray." She received the tray from Kate, and with skillful hands arranged the teacups and copper kettle full of hot water on the table.

They sat on outdoor chairs Manny hewed from the wood of a special tree. Lucinda loved the fact that each chair had a fascinating story behind their construction. The story began with a thunder and lightning storm:

During their first month living on the farm, a storm rolled in from the south. Dark gray thunderclouds towered up into the sky. Eventually, the warm southeast wind pushed over the Zapata farm. During that storm, lightning bolts streaked sideways across the sky. It was quite an impressive show Mother Nature put on for many to see. Interestingly enough, during that pop-up storm, only one lightning bolt struck the ground, and it did so on the Zapata farm. Manny saw it hit near the creek.

After the storm passed, Manny went to the barn to tack up Stonewall and pack up the repair tools. From there, they rode down to the creek to do two things: one, ensure the fence was not damaged, and two, put out any burning embers. They kept close to the fence line, studying every piece of ground, fence pole, and tree. Eventually, Manny saw a large American elm tree lying across the fence.

Manny dismounted from Stonewall. He unstrapped his burlap sack from the saddle and pulled out a rip saw and a pair of leather gloves. He first cut the elm tree limbs away to assess which part of the tree was still good enough to make a single log; however, the tree was not perfect.

The lightning bolt had split open the middle. Charcoal marred its center. Fortunately, the rain put the fire out before it consumed the whole tree. Manny studied the tree and concluded half of it was worth taking back to the barn.

After cutting the tree into three sections, he tied ropes to the first log and secured the rope to the saddle horn. Stonewall pulled what was easily a five-hundred-pound log up from the creek to the barn. Manny and Stonewall repeated the same for the remaining two logs.

It took several months for the Elmwood to age. Once completely dried, Manny cut planks of all sizes to make slats and spindles. He sanded and dovetailed chair joints together. He carved out by hand dozens of pegs needed to secure the wooden joints without the need for glue.

Once the two chair frames were assembled, he sanded and varnished them. Lucinda sewed together padded-burlap seats and back cushions for the chairs. When not in use, she simply brought the seats back to the house.

*****

Lucinda noticed Kate's new outfit. "Did you make that dress?" Kate returned a smile.

"Why, thank you for noticing dear sister. No, I did not make it. My sweet husband, Max, got it for me while he was at the docks picking up a shipment from France."

"Kate, it is a lovely gored dress. I like the light-green and yellow flower print. Nice touch with the yellow belt."

"You are looking pretty darn good yourself, Missus Zapata. Where did you get that hat?"

"Same hat I have had since Texas. Quit pulling my leg."

Both women giggled. Lucinda continued to speak. "So. What is in the news today, Missus Eilenberg?"

"Don't know. Paperboy just delivered it. One of these days his paper-throwing aim will get better. I hate digging the paper out from the rosebushes."

Lucinda chuckled at the idea. She poured the tea into the cups. Kate picked up her cup and took a sip.

"Lucinda, I brought some honey-sweet crumb cakes to go with it." Kate turned back the corners of a small yellow linen towel she used to cover a basket on the tray. "What do you think about these sweeties?" A light breeze carried a mixture of honey, cinnamon, orange, and nutmeg under Lucinda's nose.

"My goodness, Kate. You outdid yourself on those, darl'n."

Kate took the paper out from underneath her arms. She looked at Lucinda. "Would not be gossip if we did not have a gossip column." Lucinda winked at Kate. "Let us waste no time. Open it up. I enjoy reading about those Washington hoity-toities."

Kate turned the pages and stopped midway between the Want ads and the local announcements. Black-and-white pictures of two women caught her eye. Lucinda asked, "Keep turning, girl. We are not there yet." Kate held up her right index finger. "Hold on. Look at these two women. One is dressed like a man. The other looks like a Civil War soldier."

Lucinda's eyes widened with surprise. "What does it read?"

"Says here that the woman dressed like a man is Dr. Mary Edwards. She was the only woman to receive the Medal of Honor during the Civil War. The woman dressed like a Union soldier is Rosetta Wakeman.[23] Seems she was one of many women who actually fought alongside the men."

Lucinda mumbled, "Well, I be dang. Never thought a woman could do such a thing."

Kate looked at Lucinda and said, "We can do anything a man can do, if we put our minds to it."

Lucinda nodded in agreement. "Well, let's get to the gossip column. I want to see what Teddy Roosevelt is up to these days."

While Kate flipped through the newspaper, Lucinda asked, "Kate, how are your brothers Ethan and Jon doing? You have not mentioned them in some time."

Kate stopped and looked over at Lucinda.

"Thanks for asking. Little Jon is now big Jon. He moved out west to Oregon. He is logging in the mountains somewhere in the Northwest. He sends us Christmas cards every year. His wife, Jennie, keeps up with the five kids they brought into the world. The main thing is he is happy and healthy."

"Glad to hear he is doing fine. What about Ethan? Has he gotten better?"

Kate began wringing her hands. She looked down and then back up at Lucinda. Her eyes narrowed as she replied, "Ethan, my oldest brother is not doing so well. As you know, he lives by himself back home in Little Springs, Texas. He is almost forty and has yet to marry. I rarely hear from him since I moved back here to Virginia. He did not come to my wedding because he said he was ill. He always has an excuse for not leaving Littleton Springs."

"Do you think it has to do with what happened to your family in 1873? The Comanche raid?"

Kate became noticeably fidgety in her chair. She shifted from side to side. She rearranged her skirt at her knee. She took a deep breath and said, "Yes. I think he wants to be near where Papa and Mama are buried. He was older than Jon and me at the time of the attack. He understood what was happening to Mama. I was just a toddler then. Jon was just a baby."

"I am sorry to bring it up Kate. I know how much you love and miss your brothers. I was just concerned how it affects you."

While holding hands, Kate said, "You are the sister I never had. I love you, Lucinda."

Lucinda replied, "And I love you too. Now let us finish these treats before the tea gets cold."

The day's conversation sparked a burning desire for change. Before going to bed, Kate sat down at her vanity desk and wrote down her thoughts of the day.

> The true irony about women's suffrage grew from the idea of women leading the way during times of trouble, yet not fully recognized for their selfless efforts as true drivers of positive change.
>
> Since the dawn of humanity, women selflessly disregarded their own disadvantages in all societies to help others. During the U.S. Civil War, American mothers, sisters, and daughters defended the helpless, to eradicate slavery in the United States. Those women did not give up knowing their own journey paralleled that of the slaves who gained freedom. Yet, women did not have true freedom. Our dreams and goals are limited to what the male-driven cultures deemed

appropriate for females performing child bearing, household containment, and stand behind the man.

The right to vote would be the first step towards our equality depending upon the National American Woman Suffrage movement. American women will prove our case. Perhaps my old college roommate and friend, Kate Gherty will join the movement with me. A movement that would encourage the U.S. Congress to recognize women's right to vote.[24]

*****

The Zapatas

Manny and Lucinda Zapata were grateful for Luna's young colt. Manny knew the little one would grow into a fine black stallion. Like his father, Tough Guy; his grandfather, Stonewall; and his great-grandfather, Lucky, the solid-black colt was special. The Zapata farm would again prosper. It was fate's decision.

The Zapatas had yet to give a name to the farm's new addition. Lucinda wanted to name the colt Sidekick since she was the receiver of the colt's first rambunctious act of defiance. Manny did not care for the name. He said *Sidekick* could mean a couple of different things. The name could mean pal, or, as Lucinda quipped, "rambunctious act of defiance."

Manny maintained holding off naming the yearling until it was one year of age. At that time, the colt's personality would have taken shape. Until then, Manny just called him Boy.

Manny touched Lucinda's arm and said, "Honey, I know what we need to do. Tomorrow is Saturday, June 9, 1906."

"Yes. What is so special about that day?"

"Lucinda. Tomorrow is the forty-third anniversary of the Battle of Brandy Station. The largest cavalry battle fought during the U.S. Civil War. Let us take a drive over to Brandy Station. I want to see where Lucky fought on the Rappahannock River. Maybe we will find some old stuff."[25]

Lucinda asked, "Manny. Why?"

"Sentimental reasons, I suppose."

"I don't understand. I know your father fought in the war, but he did not serve here in the east."

"You are right. But Stonewall's father did."

"Husband, okay. Why not. We can make a nice day trip out of it. We can leave right after breakfast. What do you think about inviting Kate and Max along for the ride? We just need to get back early afternoon. She and I are working the church bake sale on Sunday. We need to get some pies into the ovens before dusk."

"Great idea. I don't think Max has ever seen the other side of the Potomac River."

"I will talk with Kate later in the week. She loves to travel, you know."

Manny and Lucinda rose out of their chairs and walked over to the left side of their porch. The sky's colors were magnificent. Blue streaks outlined white clouds that turned gray near its edges. The northern star brightened in the sky as the sun sank below the horizon.

Manny put his arm around Lucinda. They gazed at the sunset that colored a narrow slice of orange and red near the spot where the Zapatas buried Stonewall.

Lucinda tugged at Manny's arm. "Can you imagine? In two years, Boy will be a young black stallion running with Luna out there in the pasture."

Manny said, "Lord willing."

*****

The Eilenbergs

Kate and Max Eilenberg sat at their kitchen table and ate dinner together just about every night, around six o'clock. Their conversations were limited at the table. Max rushed through his meal. Kate was left to clean up the kitchen. While washing the dishes, Kate looked at her reflection in the windowpane. She said to herself, *Our lives in Arlington Virginia consist of sleeping, eating, working, and more working. There has to be something else?*

*****

Since immigrating with his mother to the United States in 1881, Max took advantage of America's reward of hard work and dedication. It did not take Max too long to build a profitable mercantile business. With Kate's encouragement, he realized his dream the day he sold a bolt of Italian silk from their import-export storefront in downtown Richmond, Virginia. A popular store, the Eilenberg Imports/Exports catered to politicians, businessmen, and well-to-do tobacco farmers living in the Commonwealth of Virginia.

Looking to the future, Max anticipated supply and demand. To avoid middleman expenses, he and Kate purchased warehouse space in Portsmouth, Virginia, near shipping facilities. He figured the middle-man costs for handling, storage, and transporting products was an unnecessary expense. One business approach that kept money in his pocket.

Max also calculated that his imported goods were more susceptible to loss and damage using a transportation company. The warehouse space served as temporary storage of European imports originating from Germany, Italy, and England. The middleman cost avoidance put more money back into this business.

When a shipment arrived, the dock master's office would send a cable to Max's Richmond store. Max promptly drove to the port of Richmond docks, or in some cases, to Norfolk. He then inspected the receivables, paid customs fees, and reconcile taxes in one place. Max's success boded well for him and Kate's financial security. The only thing money could not buy was a child. Kate could not conceive.

Max voiced stern expectations of suppliers he did business with. Standing six feet two, weighing two hundred and twenty pounds, Max could present himself as an intimidating man to an unsuspecting swindler. Max's piercing blue eyes and chiseled face expressed intolerance for poor artisanship. His customers demanded quality products. Max always put his customer's quality needs first.

Kate understood her husband. She told Lucinda, "Max inherited his disciplined and rational thinking from his mother. If the goods received were flawed, he immediately shipped them back to the manufacturer. On those occasions, Max included a cable explaining how to improve the product. He was determined to achieve the American dream. In his mind, nothing would deter him. I am so proud of Max."

In the beginning of their blissful marriage, Kate was content being a successful businessman's wife. She also desired motherhood. They both wanted lots of children. She and Max tried for years to get pregnant, but Kate resigned herself to believing it was God's plan. It was not meant to be.

Over the years, the stress of a childless home strained on the Eilenbergs. Max became unhappier with the fact his heirs were not being born. He further buried his frustration in his work. Kate knew her husband was displeased. However, having no children would not deter their life together, or at least that was Kate's thinking.

After putting the dishes away one evening, Kate turned to Max still sitting at the kitchen table. She asked, "We need to talk, honey. I have been thinking—"

Max interrupted, "Wait a minute. Now we both know what happens when you start thinking." Both of them laughed.

"Yes. But this is serious, Max. I would like to start volunteering down at the hospital. I know you have a rule about women working outside the home. But my request involves volunteer work. I would not be working per se. I would be helping the infirm feel better about their ills."

"Honey, the only thing I don't like about that idea is you being around sick people who could get you sick. Then you come home and get me sick."

"I see. This is about you being inconvenienced."

"No, I did not mean it that way. I just like things kept in order. You leaving the house and not having dinner ready for me by the time I get home would be a change—"

Kate interrupted, "Husband, I don't just exist in this world to just make you dinner."

"Wife, I am again sorry. That is not what I meant."

"You seem to be saying a few things you don't mean. Now I am going to go down there on Monday to offer my services. If they accept me, then I will state my time availability in only three days a week—Tuesday, Wednesday, and Thursday mornings."

"Okay." Max sighed in a sarcastic tone.

"Then who will be home to watch the house?"

"I will ask Lucinda to check in on the place during those days. Before we go any farther, what I want to hear from you is how we can do it, not how we can't, Mr. Eilenberg." Kate got up from the dinner table and walked out of the room. She peeked back inside and said, "By the way, you can do the dishes. I am going to pour myself a glass of Irish whiskey, then go sit on the front porch and watch the sun go down—alone."

Max let out a deep breath and said, "Frauen . Kann nicht mit ihnen zu leben und kann nicht ohne sie leben." (Women. Can't live with them and can't live without them.)

*****

Allison Drayton

Allison Drayton had had enough of the South Carolina good ole boys network. She inherited the Magnolia Plantation from her mother. She had no other siblings to share the work. It was all hers, which was both a blessing and a curse. There were days she wanted to sell out. But her memories of her father, her mother, Mister Joe, Lucky, and the Civil War bound her to the land she loved.

Unmarried, but tougher than nails, Allison turned over every plantation cotton field to grow tall, blue alfalfa grass for the horses. She hired local hands to cut, bale, and stack it for the winter months. Any excess hay harvested was sold at the Charleston market. The money she made from selling hay and horses kept the Drayton family name in good standing with the local community.

Allison alone turned the Magnolia Plantation into the Magnolia Horse Farm. She was a natural with horses. Her reputation as a breeder and trainer preceded her everywhere she went. However, community respect did not always come with it. At every horse auction, the men treated her as if she was invisible to the rest of the Southern gentry sitting in the bleachers waiting for the next horse to bid on. Every time she raised her hand to signal an offer, the auctioneer looked elsewhere. She lost the bid not because of bad timing, but because of her gender. After one Saturday sale, she made her mind up. She was not going to take it anymore.

Allison rode on horseback into Charleston every Saturday to attend livestock auctions. The rest of the wealthy drove their new four-wheeled automobiles, which were loud and stank up the air. While in town, she would pick up groceries, medical supplies for the horses, and the *Charleston Gazette* newspaper.

On a warm Sunday afternoon, Allison was relaxed on her front porch to read the week's news. One article buried in the middle pages mentioned her old college roommate at Boston University School of Medicine class of 1885, Reverend Anna Howard Shaw. A strong-willed membership of women chose Anna to lead the National American Women's Suffrage Movement (NAWSM).

The NAWSM was actually two different groups that formed after the Civil War in 1869. In the same year, the U.S. Congress passed the Fifteenth Amendment to the U.S. Constitution, giving black males the right to vote. American women took note and vowed to make equality not restricted to men.

The NAWSM relentlessly lobbied Congress to pass equal voting rights for women. Ann and many women like her led the way. Allison would join the fight and, like her prized horses, cross the finish line first.

After reading the *Charleston Evening Post* story, Allison wasted no time getting involved. The following Saturday, while in town, she stopped at the Western Union telegram office to send a message to Anna requesting information for how to support the movement. Anna replied within the week. Reverend Anna Shaw was delighted to know her old college friend Allison Drayton was willing to join the cause. A cause dependent upon self-sustaining women professionals who could afford to go the distance. She telegrammed Allison with three sentences.

Start. BU Sister. So good to know the Lord has walked with you since our days. Begin your journey by contacting Missus Virginia Durant Young of Fairfax South Carolina. God be with you. End.

Allison heard about Virginia Durant Young going across the state to bring attention to women's suffrage. According to the *Abbeville Medium* newspaper, Mrs. Young started working tirelessly to energize the South Carolina women's suffrage movement back in the 1890s. She was fortunate to have her husband's emotional and financial support. Doctor Young owned a medical practice in Abbeville.

Allison also had the financial means to support the suffrage movement. Virginia Young joined the suffrage cause through the Women's Christian Temperance Union. Allison wanted to join not because of vindication and unsubstantiated anger toward men, but only wanted to make a societal wrong a right. She simply wanted equal terms at an auction.

Allison sent a telegram to Virginia Durant Young requesting more information about the women's suffrage movement in South Carolina. She wanted to be an active participant for change. Mrs. Young mailed Allison a copy of the *Fairfax Enterprise*, a South Carolina Equal Rights Association (SCERA) periodical written by Mrs. Young.

Between Allison's personal relationship with Anna Shaw and the local movement icon—Virginia Durant Young—Allison soon aligned her personal philosophies with the SCERA and the National American Woman Suffrage Association (NAWSA) lead by distinguished members such as Elizabeth Cady Stanton, the first NAWSA president, and Susan B. Anthony of Massachusetts.[26]

*****

By the end of 1906, the country was standing tall on the world stage. President Theodore Roosevelt did an amazing job propelling the United States into a world power. He believed in preparedness. His care for humanity and

Leather to Steel

Mother Nature were hallmarks of his service to the nation. He set aside millions of untouched acres in the west to preserve wildlife and the historical value the lands provided.

His efforts in promoting global peace was recognized by the distinguished Nobel Prize Committee. On December 10, 1906, the Nobel Prize Committee awarded President Roosevelt the Nobel Peace Prize for his role in ending the Russo-Japanese War during the Portsmouth Conference in 1905.[27]

The U.S. Army Needs Men and Horses

> Far better is it to dare mighty things, to win glorious triumphs, even though checkered by failure... than to rank with those poor spirits who neither enjoy nor suffer much, because they live in a gray twilight that knows not victory nor defeat.
>
> —Theodore Roosevelt,
> President of the United States (1901–1909)

In 1906, several U.S. territories had yet to achieve statehood: New Mexico, Arizona, Alaska, and Hawaii. The United States flag displayed forty-six stars representing each state. The west was still a wild and dangerous place to live. Mustang horses that roamed the free countryside multiplied over generations beginning with Sixteen Centenary Spanish explorers. Spaniards whose job was to spread Catholicism and bring back gold—on the backs of horses—for Spain's monarchy. Instead of saving souls, gold was all they brought back. The Spaniards left many horses behind to survive on their own; and they did.

The mustang bands adapted to the environment. They flourished in the high-desert areas of New Mexico and Arizona territories for the next few hundred years, expanding their range north, west, and southern United States. Those horses would become worth more than gold for the Native American, but not necessarily for the United States Cavalry.

*****

Recognizing the need for quality horses, the U.S. Congress authorized the establishment of the United States Army Remount Service, in 1908. The Remount Service dedicated itself to procuring,

Leather to Steel

conditioning, training, and issuing quality horses to army units that had a cavalry mission.

Before that time, the U.S. Army Quartermaster Department procured horses and mules through government contracts advertising bids. The bidding practice became quite unsatisfactory over the years in terms of receiving a number of older horses, many in poor physical condition, and thousands of unbroken mustangs. Professional horse farms stepped in to meet the army's breeding needs. Farms owned by President Roosevelt and Allison Drayton would fill the need out of patriotic duty.

The law changed the lives of horses like Tough Guy and Grace. Young mares and colts were recruited into a U.S. Army horse-breeding program that would transform average horses into warhorses. In two years, the United States Congress funded a program designed to solve the United States Army's remount problem of using domestic horses not bred for the purpose of military service. It is through the army's Remount Service that a new breed of horse would change cavalry tactics on future battlefields. Horses like Tough Guy and No-Name became the faces of the modern warhorse.

The Departure

England has heretofore been content to rely upon the resources of her colonial possessions and the United States for such horses, but her experience in the Boer War 10 years ago, when she was forced to drain North America of a large proportion of the horses suitable for military purposes, has compelled her to accede to the demands of the army, and a grant of $200,000 has been made by the Board of Agriculture to encourage the breeding of military horses at home.

—George M. Rommel, Chief of the Animal Husbandry Division, Bureau of Animal Industry (1910)

*****

Tough Guy

Exuding a somber mood, Jeremiah stood by the swing gate watching us run freely across the paddock. Jeremiah whistled once at Grace, then at me. We trotted over, knowing he had a pocket full of oats. He spoke in a low voice. "Tough Guy, Grace. The United States Army needs you both. According to President Roosevelt, the first three army remount depots will form up in Fort Reno, Nevada, Fort Sill, Oklahoma, and Front Royal, Virginia. Within a few years, the depots would be operational."

Jeremiah continued, "Luckily for you two, that means Front Royal is in your future. President Roosevelt committed you both to the remount depot program."

Grace and I did not understand the words *remount depot*. However, in short order we soon would understand the remount depot mission and where Front Royal was located. We would become the first among one hundred and fifty horses chosen to produce the best cavalry horse ever trained for battle.

The government purchased twenty-five top-breed mares and twenty-five stallions for each depot. The Roosevelt Farm produced horses meeting the army's standards. As a result —over a few months' time— Grace and I sadly watched our brood loaded one-by-one onto government horse trailers, and whisked away.

Eventually, Grace and my transfer would come; as did our black colt, No-Name. He was special. In fact, President Roosevelt personally oversaw him loaded up onto a U.S. Army horse trailer parked outside the farm's stable. He was the only horse loaded up in the trailer. Where No-Name was going, we did not know. We just watched the loading process with sad hearts.

A burley army soldier led No-Name over a narrow metal ramp that was previously stored under the trailer's floorboard. A second soldier stood inside near the front of the trailer to help guide No-Name into the trailer. Since the trailer was not covered, we observed the two soldiers hook up crosstie leads to both sides of No-Name's halter. The soldiers exited the trailer, slid the ramp back underneath the floor, and shut the rear gate. The burly soldier slid a long metal bar across the double-gated trailer end to latch it shut. The men then walked around and jumped into the truck cab and started the engine.

No-Name turned his head toward our direction. Perhaps he was going to finally neigh something to us. His side profile resembled me. He held his thick neck in a natural high carriage. Grace said he looked proud and accepting. In fact, No-Name did not snort and neigh like his sisters and brothers did when they left the farm. He simply shook his head up and down a couple of times. I turned to Grace. "You know. He has the temperament of his grandfather. I used to think he was like me. Not at all. He is just like Stonewall." Grace agreed.

The separation of the young from their mothers cast shadows over the herd. I did all that I could to comfort the mares during the transfers. However, consoling was to no avail. For days the mares would moan about their losses. We were not the only ones affected by the separations. Jeremiah and Welford expressed their dissatisfaction. What would they do once all of us were gone?

The most unsettling aspect of our own transfers reflected sadly in the eyes of Jeremiah and Welford. The day Grace and I were loaded up on the army transport, we watched both men wipe tears from their eyes, as their past and present prepared to leave the farm. Jeremiah even said once the trucks left, there would be little hope of seeing again the horses they trained to become warhorses.

Grace and I always told each other over the years that we would live and die on President Roosevelt's horse farm. In the farm's beginning, we produced some of the world's best polo ponies for the wealthy. That was the farm's business. Well, the horse business changed.

Welford understood the president's intentions. The president's plan began with bringing Englishman Ranse from England to teach dressage to the president's hired hands, who in turn trained us the methods specifically designed to develop warhorses. Jeremiah's questions were answered when the first Roosevelt horse was transferred to a remount depot.

*****

During the spring of 1910, former president Teddy Roosevelt decided his horses would contribute to breeding and producing superb warhorses—necessary to keep up with the modernization of military technology and weaponry. The cavalry horse and trooper, together, had to evolve into effective mission support roles on the battlefield.

By the end of 1910, global modernization in military affairs permanently affected the Roosevelt farm. As a consequence, Mister Roosevelt saw it better to discharge his horse sporting business to a gentleman farmer who had a different vision. The new owner wanted to grow a new crop not known to many: soy beans— the future of agricultural growth on America.

The farm still needed a manager to oversee the operations. Mister Welford and his wife were asked to stay on, and they accepted. The new owner had no time for managing daily farm operations, since he lived and worked in Washington. A type of professional many in the local area called "a gentleman farmer." Managing the farm would be Mister Welford's lone responsibility; without the help of Jeremiah Bates.

Unfortunately for Jeremiah, the business transaction did not offer the same opportunity for him and his family. The new owner's plans included using new farming equipment inventions that did most of the work, with less people. Jeremiah was not a farmer.

*****

The Bateses

At the age of fifty, Jeremiah Bates woke up on a cold December morning—just before Christmas—not having a job. He had to make money. Doing nothing was no option for him. Even though his army monthly retirement stipend was enough to get by on, it was not enough for five kids' college educations. He swore to Mary that their children would not be like him, uneducated. Faithfully, Jeremiah and Mary prayed and prayed to the Lord, asking for guidance.

His answer came Christmas morning. While in the kitchen cooking pancakes, Mary looked out the window and saw an old man

Leather to Steel

shuffling alongside the road. Snow swirled around his shoulders. She yelled out to Jeremiah sitting in the living room. "Come here. There is an old man walking out in the snow!"

Jeremiah got up from his chair and went into the kitchen. He looked dumbfounded. "I am sorry, dear. What did you say?"

"Jeremiah, there is an old man looking no better for worse out there. Look out the window. See?" Jeremiah stepped over to the window and brushed off the fog. He peeked out. Mary asked. "See him? Please go invite him in for a warm breakfast. He is obviously without home and family on Christmas Day of all days. Lord help him." Jeremiah grunted and moaned. "All right, Mary. You know there is no guarantee he will want to come in."

"I don't care. You do what you must to convince him so."

Jeremiah walked out into the foyer. He put his winter boots on, and then pulled an old wool jacket off the hat tree and buttoned up. He opened the front door and quickly stepped out, while shutting the door behind him. Standing on the porch, six-inch-high snowdrifts lined the porch railings.

He rubbed his hands and shrugged his shoulders complaining. "Dang cold out here. Better button up the sleeves." He wrapped his head with a black wool scarf, leaving enough openings to breath and see. The wintry breeze quickly sapped the warmth from his hands. Fortunately, a pair of sheepskin gloves were left in the coat pockets. Jeremiah pulled them out, slapped them together before putting them on. Satisfied he was warm enough, he stepped down the porch steps and walked toward the street.

The old man shuffling on the street heard Jeremiah's footsteps crunching through the snow from behind him. He turned around to see a large man coming up on him. Not intimidated, he used his cane to wave Jeremiah away. Jeremiah stopped a few steps to right side of the stranger not interested in charity. Jeremiah could not see the man's face. It was covered up by a tattered strip of gray wool wrapped around the cheeks. Only his eyes were exposed.

Jeremiah stepped close enough to tap the old fella on the shoulder. The old man continued shuffling with his cane through the snow. Jeremiah reached out and tapped him again on the shoulder.

"Mister, why don't you come back with me to get some warm vittles in your belly. Pretty darn cold out here today." The old man finally stopped and turned toward Jeremiah. "Go away, young feller. I ain't need'n no handouts, youngster. Now leave me be."

Jeremiah looked at the man's gray coat. It had a faded yellow patch on its sleeve. Jeremiah mumbled, "Either he was given this coat, or it was issued to him. Lord, I will not give up on him." Jeremiah pressed on. "Sir, I am an old army man myself. Let one brother help another. My wife, Mary, will be mad as a hornet at me, if you don't come back inside with me. She wants you in the house so she can feed you. Then do as you please. Don't make me look foolish. The missus is watching us."

The old man pulled down the rag from his face. Jeremiah noticed the long gray beard covering the old man's neck. The dirty face made the eyes look white as snow with piercing blue centers. The old man relented. "Oh…all right. If it gets you out of my business."

Jeremiah nodded at the old man. "Very good then. Follow me this way. We need to get back to my house sooner than later." Jeremiah looked up into the sky, "The snow is starting to come down harder." While they walked, Jeremiah studied the gray wool coat adorning the old soldier. He took note of the old man's heavy limp that required assistance of a cane.

Once on the porch, Jeremiah stopped and grabbed the broom leaning against the door frame. He swept off the snow from their boots and coats. Just as Jeremiah finished, Mary opened the front door. She greeted the stranger. "So glad you chose to come inside. On a day like this, a warm meal and a house makes for a perfect Christmas." The old man grunted and cracked a half smile. He limped into Bates' house.

*****

Once inside the foyer, Mary stepped behind the old man to remove his jacket. She looked at Jeremiah standing beside him. She could smell the stench. She immediately reacted. "Sir, let me take your coat. I will hang it up in the kitchen while you and Jeremiah head

Leather to Steel

into the living room." Jeremiah helped him slip off the tattered grey-wool coat, then hand it to Mary.

Mary returned to the kitchen, while trying not to gag from the coat's unpleasant odor. She quickly stopped in mid step. Turned around and asked. "Sir. If you don't mind, I will give your coat a good brushing."

He mumbled. "Eh—don't matter to me. Suit yourself."

Jeremiah held the old man's arm while they slowly walked toward the living-room fireplace. Once near the far window, Jeremiah positioned a straight-back chair behind the guest. "Please, sit down, sir."

Now sitting, the old man's shaking hands held his black cane until Jeremiah took it.

Jeremiah stepped around the front of the old man to get a better look at the unwrapped face. The fireplace cast a wavering light across the stranger's cheeks and forehead. He was semi-balding. The man's unevenly cut, short-cropped hair was silver in color. An unkempt white beard extended down to his chest. His clothes were in no better shape. Jeremiah noticed several kneeholes on the gray britches tucked into high leather black boots. The boots looked too small. Jeremiah knelt down. "Let me help you with those. Looks like your boots have seen some days." The old man snickered. "Just like me, sonny."

Jeremiah nodded in agreement. He grabbed the man's left boot heel and toe. Looking at the old man, he carefully pulled the boot off. Jeremiah asked. "So—now that you are here. What should we call you?" There was a good two minutes of silence. Jeremiah waited for an answer, while the old man's eyes fixated on the flames burning in the fireplace. His blues eyes sparkled in the flickering light.

Jeremiah repeated his question. "Sir, what is your name? What should we call you?"

The old man blinked and rubbed his eyes. He let out a heavy sigh. "Sonny, you can call me Silas Addison." Jeremiah sat back on his ankles. "Just like the name of Paul the Apostle's friend in the Bible," Silas replied. "Yep, my daddy and momma pulled that name out of the New Testament. Figured they would get me into church with at least a name."

Jeremiah did not react to the man's sarcasm. Instead, he reached for the right boot. Silas extended his right hand out to stop him. "That is okay, sonny. I can get it. The doctor quacks left bits and pieces of grapeshot in my right thigh. I just learned to live with it." Jeremiah stood up. "As you wish." Silas used his left foot to push on the boot's heel while the man inserted his fingers to loosen up the high leather. Silas sat back in the chair and took a deep breath.

Jeremiah placed a patched-quilt blanket on Silas's lap. "Excuse me for a moment. I will get us some hot coffee from the kitchen." Silas nodded and returned to watching the flames crackle in the hearth. The fire mesmerized the old soul.

*****

Jeremiah returned to the living room holding two cups of hot coffee. Steam swirled up from each. Jeremiah stood by Silas. He extended the cup. "Here you go, sir. Mary just percolated a fresh pot. It is fresh." Silas sniffed the cup held with both hands. He looked at Jeremiah and took a sip. "There was many a time in the field, we would take eggshells and throw them in to the coffeepot."

Jeremiah pulled up another chair and positioned it to the slight front right of Silas's fireplace to his back. "You don't say," he questioned.

Once sitting down, Jeremiah carefully kept his cup level to avoid spilling the coffee on the floor. He looked at Silas. "Yes, sir. I know that coffee trick all too well. I spent many a morning waking up on wet grass and dirt in the Oklahoma Territory and Texas Plains."

Silas looked straight at Jeremiah. "I am curious. What were you doing out there?"

"Chasing Indians. To be more specific, I served in the United States Army Tenth Cavalry Division. We chased them Comanche, Apache, Cheyenne, and buffalo."

"Well, I be dang. You served in the army! Why, I'll be! I did not think they let—well, you know, colored people serve in the military."

Jeremiah surmised the old man was a confederate veteran and expected the discussion. Silas added, "No disrespect, mind you."

Jeremiah replied with sincerity, "None taken, my friend."

Jeremiah continued, "Sir, I reckon times changed after the war. A war you must have served in based upon the coat and boots you wear now."

The old man stretched his right foot toward the fireplace heat. His big toe stuck out through the hole in his sock. He looked at Jeremiah with a sad face. "Sonny, you are right about that. That was long ago. I wished I had never seen or done what we had to do."

"I know what you mean. Not a day that goes I don't think about the men I served with. The men I saw butchered during the fight…Well, enough of that. Now what Confederate regiment were you attached to?"

"Like many of us during war, we started off serving with one group—maybe infantry, then ended up in another pulling artillery, because the Yanks killed all our horses first. I can't remember all the battles I fought. I just know I enlisted with my friends in the Virginia Thirty-Seventh Regiment in Washington County, Virginia, May 1861. I was an infantry soldier. Many enlisted together, but few mustered out. I was one of the unlucky few."

Jeremiah continued his query. "If you don't mind answering, what battles were you in?"

Silas paused to collect his thoughts. He ran his fingers through his long white beard and scuffed his feet on the floor. After a couple of minutes, Silas replied, "Well, my units saw action in many battles. The ones I remember the most were Antietam and Gettysburg. We finally gave up at Appomattox in April 1865." Silas lowered his chin and stared at the floor.

Jeremiah tried to find the words to comfort the old soldier. "Silas, I am sorry. I understand death, but not the kind you witnessed."

"Thank you, sonny. Much obliged. Coming from a fellow serviceman—well, means much to me. Many a fella told me over the years they understood war, but they never served."

"Silas, so you mustered out and went back to Washington County after the war?"

"Yes, I made it back in one piece. Got a job working on the railroad. The one ole Stoneman tore up. Started a family."

"Sounds like you made out okay."

"Not really. The years since were not kind to me. The kids grew up and left. They don't talk to me. I reckon they are still angry with me for treating their mother so badly. My wife left me because of my drinking. My daddy and my momma passed on. I chose to have no friends. I figure living alone was the best option for me. No one to hurt again."

Jeremiah listed intently to Silas, jumping from one year to another. Silas stopped to collect his breath in between decades. Jeremiah did not want to push the old soldier too much. Silas raised his right hand to signal that all was fine as he could be. He continued, "You see, sonny, I am on my journey back to where my pain began. To see my friends. I need to make sense of things before my last breath is taken."

"Antietam and Gettysburg?"

"No. Just Antietam. I lost my school friend Jake there at the Bloody Lane on September 17, 1862. You see, we were getting the best of the Yanks positioned on the ridge above us. We got reporting the Union put their greenhorns up front first. We all knew greenhorns moved with fear on the battlefield. Instead of crawling to the edge, they remained upright. During that morning, we shot many boys standing on that ridge."

Over the next couple of hours, the situation changed. The Yanks positioned experienced soldiers above us. Those fellas knew better. They crawled on their bellies to avoid hot fire. Once on the ridge, they put volley upon volley down on us. We were slaughtered."[28]

Jeremiah asked, "How did you get out of there?"

Silas took his time answering the question. He wrung his hands and rubbed his knees. Beads of sweat appeared on his forehead. He took a deep breath and sighed. "Sonny, I—"

Jeremiah placed his hand on the old soldier's shoulder. Silas looked and cracked a smile. He whispered. "If you must know, I am heading to visit my friends. That is all I am gonna say about that."

Jeremiah recognized it was time to stop talking. Mary appeared from the kitchen. "If you don't mind, sir—"

Jeremiah interrupted. "Mary, this is Mister Silas Addison. He is on his way to Antietam."

Mary nodded. "Then, Mister Addison, I am sorry. I spilled some coffee on your coat. I washed it up in the deep sink. I think I got it all out. Your wool coat is hanging near the potbelly stove drying out."

Silas replied, "No worries. How long do you think it will take to dry?"

"Probably a whole day. Since it is my fault—I am sure Jeremiah will agree—you can stay here with us for the day. Besides, it is Christmas. The weather is horrible with the cold and snow." Silas rubbed his hands together toward the fire. He looked at Jeremiah. Then at Mary. "Well, thank you. I appreciate your kind offer. But only until tomorrow morning. Need to get these old bones to where I am go'n before year's end." Silas would have one good day ahead of him.

*****

Early Christmas morning was quiet and calm in the Bates house. The children were still sleeping. Jeremiah and Mary were up and in the kitchen getting breakfast ready together. Jeremiah help set the dishes on the table while Mary cooked bacon and eggs. She looked at Jeremiah. "Do think Silas is going to be okay?"

"Yes. I think he is getting close to peace of mind."

"What do you mean?"

"Do you remember when I had to get back to Texas to make sure my friend Joe Drayton was properly buried?"

"Of course, I do. You needed that to help you become whole."

"Yes, that is what Silas is doing. He wants to become whole again. Which is why I am going to help him get there."

"Where is there?"

"Antietam. I am going to drive him there today. He said he has one friend there to stay with, which eased my mind."

"When are you leaving?"

"Right after breakfast. Sharpsburg is only forty miles from here. I don't think his bum leg will allow him to cross those mountains on foot."

"Husband, you are a good man."

"Mary, he earned it. He is a veteran like me. We take care of our brothers. Thanks to you, he will be leaving with a clean coat, mended socks, and new britches and long johns." Before Jeremiah could add another sentence, Silas hobbled into the kitchen. He was standing upright, looking stronger. Mary exclaimed, "Why, Mister Addison! You trimmed your beard down to just below your chin. Your hair is also trimmed."

"Thank you, Missus Bates. I hope you don't mind. I took a birdbath and cleaned up using your snippers."

"My goodness, Mister Addison! You look very handsome all dolled up."

Silas limped over to the kitchen table and sat down. "Well. I slept pretty well on your couch. Thank you. I feel I am ready to cover the next miles."

Jeremiah spoke. "About those miles. Let me take you there. You said you have a friend there who could take you in for a while."

"No, no. You and Mary have shown me enough kindness for one lifetime. I can walk."

"Now, Silas, you can't deprive a fellow veteran the chance to talk with you some more. We can do that during our drive."

Silas put his hand up to his chin and stroked his beard downward. "I suppose that would not be right of me to deny you more words of wisdom. Okay."

Mary and Jeremiah chuckled at his humor.

After breakfast, Jeremiah and Silas stood on the front porch buttoning up their coats. Mary stood at the front door wearing her Christmas apron. "Looks like the storm blew over last night. Good weather for traveling. Now, both of you, be careful. Even though the sun is out, the roads are still covered with snow. Do be careful."

Leather to Steel

Jeremiah replied, "Don't worry, wife. I will put wheel chains on before we head up the pass." Jeremiah stepped toward Mary and gave her a kiss on the cheek. Mary winked at Jeremiah. "I love you." Looking over at Silas, she said, "It was a pleasure meeting you, Mr. Addison. God give you comfort and peace."

Silas nodded. "Thank you, Mary. You are a good woman. I wish mine had been the same."

*****

Once on the road, Jeremiah adjusted his driving to accommodate slick patches of ice and snow on the road. Once they made it over the Shenandoah River Bridge, the hills got steeper. He stopped on a flat spot to put chains on the tires. Once the car was in gear, the chains did their job. Driving up the hill was a noisy proposition.

Silas said, "Do these contraptions normally make this much noise on the road?"

"No, sir. Only when the chains are grabbing at the asphalt. Once we are down on the other side, Sharpsburg is a straight shot. Did your friend give you an address?"

Silas let a few minutes pass before responding. "Yes." He yelled out over the noise. He lives nearby the Dunker Church."

Once they'd gone over the pass, a flat winding road took them the rest of the way. At the bottom of the hill, Jeremiah slowed the car down to a stop. "Silas, I need to stop here on the side and take off the wheel chains. It looks like a tractor cleared the road ahead of us." Silas nodded and continued to look out the passenger window. Jeremiah got out of the car. He glanced at Silas before closing the car door. Silas was fixated on the pastures he marched upon long ago.

*****

Jeremiah pulled the car up into the Dunker Church parking area. He looked at Silas and said, "Well, are you sure I can't take you to your friend's house?"

Silas opened the passenger's door and then closed it. Jeremiah reached over and rolled down the window. He said again, "I don't mind driving you to his house."

Silas lowered his head down to see Jeremiah. "Thank you. But I can walk from here."

Before walking away, Silas extended his right hand to Jeremiah. Feeling the pain in his leg, Silas grimaced. He waved at Jeremiah, looking Jeremiah straight in the eyes. "Thank you for serving. I know you lost much. Before you leave this earth, make sure you clear the mind to find peace. That is what I am doing. So long, friend."

Jeremiah rolled the passenger window back up and put the car in gear. He drove away from the church. Slowly driving away, he checked the rearview mirror to see Silas waving his cane. Jeremiah mumbled. "Funny. He did the same thing when I first met him."

Once the church was out of sight, Jeremiah rolled down the driver's window to clear the fog expanding inside the windshield. He looked out at the same pastures Silas stared at during the drive over. He spoke to himself. "Private Silas Addison. Thank you for the sacrifices you made. God bless your soul." He looked over at the empty passenger's seat and noticed a bulky brown envelop lying on the floorboard. It looked as though it had been rolled up.

Jeremiah pulled the car over to the side of the road. He reached over the centerboard and picked up the envelope. He held it up to the light and read the scribbled writing. It had a note written in front. "Jeremiah and Mary. God Bless you. Inside is something for your future. I have no use for it where I am going. Signed, Silas Addison, Private – Confederate States of America."

Jeremiah carefully opened the envelope using his pig sticker. Cautious curiosity guided his hand. He reached in and pulled out a stack of bonded blue-colored paper folded in half. He pulled the papers apart. "What in the world!"

The papers were identical. The title on each read, "Union Railroad Company." The subtitle read, "Capital stock, $1000.00." Jeremiah read on. The text in the center read,

> *This certified that the Bearer of this Instrument is the owner of twenty shares of the Capital Stock of Union Railroad Company transferable only on the Books of the Corporation in person or by Attorney on surrender of this Certificate.*

Jeremiah laid down the stock certificate in the passenger seat where the Bates family's Christmas angel had sat. He wept with joy. After collecting himself, he started the car back up and put it into gear. On the way back to Winchester, he sang songs of praise. Jeremiah thanked the Lord for Silas Addison. The Bates children would have a future.

*****

Silas did not have a friend to stay with in Sharpsburg, Maryland. He hated to lie to the good Bates family. But he had to make sure Jeremiah and Mary did not suspect anything other than his destination and safety of a friend's home. Silas could only think of one thing; getting back to the friends he left behind during the war.

He walked over the farmland he remembered not five hundred yards from the main battles at Antietam. Not much had changed. Luckily, the farmer cut the cornstalks down to the ground, making it easier for him to see farther west toward the confederate's position. As he walked westward along the cornfield's edge, he glanced left and right, making sure he was going in the right direction. The dirt field road he walked upon sloped downward toward another road that ran perpendicular, north to south. The locals called it Sunken Road. The soldiers called it something different. Once below the ridge of death, he stood on ground the soldiers called Bloody Lane.

Looking up at the ridge, Silas mumbled, "I wonder what the Yanks saw from up there." Silas walked down the lane far enough south until a narrow deer trail came into view. He limped up the trail running sideways toward the top of the ridge. Standing on high ground, Silas looked out across the fields from which he just came.

He walked toward the north ridge overlooking Bloody Lane. Standing on the edge, he looked down and whispered, "So this is why my shots flew over their heads, and why their shots were true." Tears welled up in Silas's eyes. He looked down at his right leg and touched it. The same leg that received a bullet from a repeating rifle fired from the very spot he stood. The same rifle that most likely killed his friend Jake, whose body fell on Silas. A body that shielded his from the thousands of bullets that rained down upon the Confederates that day.

Silas looked up at the clouds and took a deep breath. He sighed. His heart struggled to beat. The climb up the hill made him winded. After catching his breath, he spoke loudly. "Dang it. Should have just stayed down there. Better yet, I should have just stayed home in 1861."

Silas lay down on his back on the frozen brown grass that crackled. He looked up at the partly cloudy sky. He spoke to the heavens. "I will do this." He stretched his arms to the sides and spread his legs out as far as he could. Ignoring the pain, he brought his arms and legs back together. Silas cried out, "Jake, this is your angel. What should I do next?" He remained on the ground in silence. Waiting for an answer.

Preparing for War

The mounting of troops in an army is a most serious problem. Not only must provision be made for a supply of horses sufficient to equip the mounted service for the ordinary routine work during peace, but horses multiply slowly, and a reserve must be provided for use in case of an outbreak of hostilities.

—George M. Rommel,
Chief of the Animal
Husbandry Division Bureau
of Animal Industry (1910)

Tough Guy

The army trailered us from the Roosevelt Farm to the Front Royal Remount Depot on a Saturday morning. We were the last horses to leave. Mister Welford said we earned the consideration by the good graces of former president Teddy Roosevelt. Jeremiah said he directed the United States Army to keep us together. After all, Grace and I represented the army's reason for breeding exceptional cavalry horses, an experiment that began at Fort Reno in 1909. How could the army disagree with a former president of the United States?

The trip was easier than walking all the way from Arlington to Winchester, like I did back in 1903. The truck made our lives easier, in spite of the cold breeze blowing across our backs and the loud engine noises. As we traveled on the roads, Grace and I were not fearful of our prospective new life. In fact, we embraced the change. During the two-hour trip, we let go of the Roosevelt Farm.

The army truck parked just inside the depot's front main gate. While waiting to be unloaded, the open bay trailer gave us a bird's-eye view of the depot being built before our eyes. I studied the property. It bustled with many workers framing buildings and laying brick.

The compound looked expansive; it probably covered a thousand acres situated between hillsides and tree lines bordering large fenced-in pastures. In between the fences, hundreds of two-foot wooden stakes marked locations to build two barns, two more stables, and two barrack-type buildings. A large red stable was the only completed structure on the property.

The stable's gabled roof was covered with green shingles. A lengthy paddock extended from the stable's right. The paddock was much larger in circumference than the one back on the Roosevelt farm. This paddock occupied a flat area carved out of a hill rising up behind the stable. I neighed at Grace. "The white fence poles look perfectly round. I wonder what they are made of?"

Grace replied, "Not sure. I am sure we'll find out soon enough."

The soldiers unloaded us from the trailer. They walked us over to the front of the stable. The youngest of the two spoke. "Corporal, what do we do with these horses now?"

The corporal answered, "Stand by. The head trainer is supposed to receive the horses, and only him."

The younger soldier nodded and stood fast. A few minutes later, an older-looking civilian—sporting a scraggly gray beard—took his time walking through the stable doors. I neighed to Grace. "He looks like the old sergeant I knew back at the army's Arlington training ground. He smelled like a new piece of leather coming from a tannery."

The corporal holding Grace's lead called out, "Hey Gramps. Looks like you got your hands full!" The old man lifted up his head. "Well, boys, one thing for sure. These two horses probably have more sense than you two put together." The soldiers returned smiles and laughed as they handed the leads to Gramps.

*****

Gramps led us toward the stable. I could sense there was something special about him. Grace confirmed the same. We sensed his love for horses. When his leathery hands touched our withers, I could tell he

Leather to Steel

was a kind human being. Grace and I felt safer, and certainly less anxious about our new home.

He led us across the stable aisle to reach the back side of the barn. Since the back doors were open, we kept going until we stopped at the paddock gate. He unlatched and pushed it. The gate swung back far enough to allow us inside.

Gramps said, "Hold on. Need to shut the gate." Using his good foot, he kicked the gate closed. The force of the gate shutting caused a latch spring to move up and fall back onto the gate bar. A clanking sound indicated the gate locked.

Gramps led us into the paddock center. Once we were in the middle, he walked us clockwise in circles. He switched hands and made us trot counterclockwise in circles. I neighed at Grace, "What do you think he is looking for?"

She replied, "Gramps is seeing how balanced we are. Don't you remember what the trainer said about balance? Since our dressage training, have you noticed how equally developed our chest muscles have become?"

I smirked. "Right. I would have thought of that."

Gramps brought us back to the center and removed our halters. He used both hands to feel underneath our jaws. Using his fingers, he parted our mouths to inspect our teeth. He concluded, "I have seen what I need to see. Now you two go run around for a bit. I need to get back into the stable to fix up your stalls. I need to make sure soldiers brought hay to your stalls." He turned around and walked toward the gate.

After opening and securing the paddock gate, Gramps looked back at us. He waved his hand. "Now shoo! Get out and run, the both of ya. It will be dark before long. Get on now." Grace and I happily snorted, neighed, and kicked up some dirt as we chased each other around.

*****

Back in the stable, Gramps ambled over to the first two adjacent stalls. He unlatched and pulled open each stall door. He first stepped inside Tough Guy's stall. The soldiers spread out fresh hay on the floor and loaded up the metal hay nets secured to the back wall. Gramps walked over to the far wall. He mumbled, "The net is too high, dag nabbit. Ole Tough Guy may be seventeen hands tall, but the net is too darn high. I will need to lower it. Don't need him getting an eye infection from the hay he pulls out."

Gramps walked slowly over to the tack room to retrieve a wrench. He returned to the stall and lowered the net down a couple of feet. Satisfied with his work, he proclaimed, "There. Now the hay will remain dry and out of his eyes." He repeated the same inspection for Grace's stall.

Before sundown, Gramps walked back out to the paddock holding two horse leads. He carried a handful of oats in each jacket pocket. After opening the gate, he stepped inside, then closed the gate behind him. He whistled twice. "Come on over here. I got someth'n for ya."

Grace and Tough Guy galloped from the opposite side of the paddock to his position. Gramps had two leads on his left shoulder. With this right hand, he reached into his pocket and pulled out a handful of oats.

While he fed Tough Guy oats, he used his left hand to pull one lead off his shoulder. With two fingers, he pulled open the lead snap and connected it to the halter. He repeated the same for Grace. While walking toward the stable, he said, "Tough Guy and Grace, I understand the former president Roosevelt donated your services to the United States Army. Well, I can assure you both, the army will take good care of you. The only thing we can't do is continue that fancy European training the president called dress age, or dressage— well, something like that. We will figure something out."

*****

Our first night at the depot was a quiet one. Grace and I stood silently in the stalls trying to stay warm. Even though our winter coats were in, we both shivered. I was glad he closed the stable doors to cut down the chill swirling around outside. Before nodding off to sleep, Grace neighed over at me. "Tough Guy, I miss our little ones. A mare always worries. Do you think we will ever see them again?"

"I don't know, Grace. I detected their scents during our trip over here. I lost it back at the Shenandoah River. After we crossed over, the direction of their scents told me they went south. I suppose the army will put them to good service. I am hopeful they end up as cavalry horses and not pulling artillery."

"Why do you say that?'

"Trust me, I have seen horses pull artillery at the army's equestrian training center back in 1902. The strain ruined their balance and in some cases caused lameness. But no worries. Once the army concludes how well trained we are, our job will be producing the best cavalry horses, not wheel horses. Now. Let us get some sleep. I am sure tomorrow will be busy for us."

"What do you think we will be doing?"

"Picking back up our dressage training. Gramps mentioned that more horses would be coming in. Maybe a horse we know shows up. We shall see."

*****

The winter passed by without much training getting done. The cold weather pretty much kept horse and men inside. Once spring came, Tough Guy and Grace had acclimated to the depot and its occupants. Construction workers began to thin out. By summer's end in 1911, the army's Front Royal Remount Depot's first stable construction was completed.

President William H. Taft requested former president Teddy Roosevelt to make a special trip from Washington to assess the U.S. Army Front Royal Remount Depot operations. The president wanted an inspection completed by the end of September. Roosevelt accepted the offer. He himself was very interested in the army's progress toward breeding the perfect warhorse.

President Taft's chief of staff cabled a site visit date and time to the depot commander. The cable read…expect a visit during the last week of September. Given plenty of time to prepare, the depot commander ordered site-visit preparations tied to the cabled date. However, former president Roosevelt was known not to adhere to anyone's schedule other than his own.

Much to the depot commander's dismay, former president Teddy Roosevelt arrived at the depot's front gates unannounced during the first week of September. Roosevelt had cause to do so. He had received a private cable from his informant on the inside. Roosevelt had a different agenda.

It was early in the morning when Roosevelt's motorcade arrived at the Front Royal Remount Depot entrance. Roosevelt drove the lead car himself, but he was not alone. He leaned over to his guest passenger and spoke. He said, "No soldiers are in sight. They must be getting an early march in." He waited for a reply from the large black man sitting in the passenger seat. He asked again, "Well, Jeremiah Bates, looks like the army has taken a likin' to this country living. There were no guards on duty. Do you think they are on a march or on holiday?"

"Sir, I reckon they must be up in the stables getting the horses ready."

Roosevelt took off his spectacles, looked at Jeremiah, and smirked. "I hope so, for their sake."

Jeremiah nodded in agreement.

Roosevelt's security detail worked in unison to protect the president's movements. Once his car stopped, the lead protective-detail agent was already in place to swing open the depot's main gates. After doing a quick visual, the agent signaled that all was clear. Roosevelt put his car in gear and drove inside the depot.

Once inside, the security detail parked just behind the president's. The lead agent got out and quickly walked to the back of Roosevelt's car. He tapped on the rear window. Roosevelt rolled down his door window. Stuck his head and asked, "What do you think Mister Townsend?"

"Sir, if you would, please, I will send two of my men to clear those buildings. Just give us a few minutes, sir."

Roosevelt understood the agents had to do their job.

"Agent Townsend, I do appreciate your dedication to my safety. But it is an army camp."

"Sir, all due respect. Just ten minutes."

"Oh, all right. Very well. Just be quick about it."

The president's security detail divided into four teams of two to cover more ground. Agent Townsend chose to secure the first stable. He ran up to the stable and halted within inches of the double doors. Grasping the right door handle, he slid it a couple of feet to the right. He peeked in. With the help of the stable lights, he stepped inside to scan the right and left stalls. Curious horses stuck out their necks over the stall doors and began neighing. Some horses used their front hooves to paw at their stall doors.

Agent Townsend stepped in to begin his search. At the end of the stable, he noticed one closed door. He wasted no time getting to the opposite side of it. Grasping the doorknob, he turned it enough to verify it was not locked. As Agent Townsend carefully pulled the door open, it creaked. Then out of nowhere, an old leathery hand suddenly reached through the open door and gripped the agent's right hand.

Agent Townsend winced. The power of a vice grip–like hand squeezed his fingers together. He grumbled, "Sir, I am Mr. Roosevelt's security detail. Please release my hand. I have a pistol in my left. You will be shot."

Gramps pulled the tack-room door open to see who was trying to break in. He looked at the young man wearing a gray suit, white shirt, and short black tie. He released the agent's hand and then stepped back and said, "I reckon you look like a fancy man not interested in riding horses out of here. What is your business here?"

"Mister, just doing my job. Is there anyone else in this stable?"

"No. Just me and twenty horses."

"Fine. I need to get back to report to the president. He is waiting."

"Hold on, young fella. President Roosevelt is not supposed to be here for another two weeks. Besides, he is former President Roosevelt."

"Well, he is here today, and wants to inspect the horses. In addition, it is protocol to refer to former U.S. presidents as President. Now I need to get back and make our reports. He is waiting. I suggest you get yourself cleaned up."

Gramps reached down to pull up his suspenders. He limped over to the cracked wall mirror and mumbled, "Dang it. I was hoping to have a couple of more weeks to work with the horses. He is not going to be happy."

*****

Roosevelt's motorcade had stopped in front of the commanding officer's office. Jeremiah and Roosevelt walked up to the office door. Roosevelt peeked through the front window. No lights were on. He turned to Jeremiah. "Well, looks like we came too early for the commander."

Roosevelt stepped back on the porch and gave way to Jeremiah. He asked, "Give it a go, Jeremiah. Give a knock will you?"

Jeremiah nodded. He tapped his knuckles at the door. "Hello in there." He put his left ear to the door, trying to make out any noise behind it. He turned around and shook his head. "Mr. Roosevelt. Maybe the commander is out with his troops on a march."

"I hope that is the case. Give it another rap," Roosevelt commanded. Jeremiah knocked three times on the doorframe. The porch vibrated that time. A man's voice rang out from inside. "Muster is not for some time. Go away, or you will be court-martialed." Jeremiah turned to Roosevelt and laughed. "Well, sir. Looks like you are going to be court-martialed."

Roosevelt removed his glasses to wipe off the dust. He looked at Jeremiah. "Excuse me. My turn."

After a few hard raps on the door, the man inside could be heard stomping across the floor. When the door opened, a disheveled-looking officer, half dressed, stood before the former president. The commanding officer's face turned ashen white. The blood ran out from Colonel Laws' face, as did the lack of words.

Roosevelt was not smiling. He demanded to know, "Where is your commanding officer?"

The anxious officer spoke in a low tone. Trying to keep his head up, the colonel said, "Well, sir—that would be me."

Roosevelt replied, using terse language, "Not anymore, mister. You are relieved of your duties effective immediately."

"Sir, we were not expecting you for another couple of weeks. I—"

Roosevelt interrupted him. "Do not speak another word."

Gramps watched the commotion from the bottom of the porch steps. Standing with Agent Townsend, he spoke with respect, "President Roosevelt. Good to see you, sir. It has been awhile."

Roosevelt turned away from the office door and bellowed, "Well, I'll be." He walked down the steps to hug the man he knew as Sergeant John Martin Adair, the Cherokee.[29]

Roosevelt embraced his old sergeant. He placed both hands square on each of Gramps shoulders and stared directly into the eyes. Roosevelt said, "I thought you would need some help. I brought someone along. The big fella there. His name is Jeremiah Bates. He trained many horses I sent over here." The president glanced at Jeremiah and then waved him down. "Mister Bates, let me introduce you to Sergeant John Martin Adair, another cavalry friend of mine. Most folks around here call him Gramps."

Jeremiah stood near Roosevelt waiting for the formal introduction. He looked at Gramps, then extended his hand. "Very glad to meet you, sir. Colonel Roosevelt told me several stories about you and him at the Battle of San Juan Hill." Gramps nodded. "Yep. Those were the good ole days. Glad they are behind me. How about you, mister?"

Roosevelt interrupted, "Men, you will have plenty of time to catch up on trooper stories later. John, the army hired Mr. Bates to be your assistant trainer. He will be working for you, and you only. He trained my horses back on the Winchester farm. He will get the job done for you."

Gramps nodded and asked him, "Then you got my cable. That old cus of a commanding officer cares less about the horses around here. I don't care if he was a senator's son. The army never should have assigned a city fella."

"John, as of today, the captain is no longer your commanding officer," Gramps quipped. "Colonel."

"After today, he will be lucky to retire as a captain." Gramps laughed. He turned toward Jeremiah. "Mister Bates, looks like the young colonel has finally met his waterloo. His empty bunk will be a welcome sight. Hey! While I am thinking about it, we have an extra bunk in the stable you can use while you are here."

Jeremiah stood looking at Roosevelt, waiting for an assertion.

"John," Roosevelt added, "Mister Bates has a family to move here. Any ideas?"

Looking a little bit surprised, Gramps stepped back, thinking. *Well, I reckon he can use the executive officer quarters over there in the north forty. Been vacated for some time. The colonel never filled it, since the last officer resigned. And ...*

"Sorry to interrupt you, John, but I don't have much time. Please take care of Jeremiah. See to it the army gets his family moved and settled in here. Who is next down in the chain-of-command?"

"Captain Livingston. He is out marching with the rest of the men. He is also our only veterinarian."

"I will have a cable sent from the Department informing the captain of his officer-in-charge assignment. I will also leave one of my security details here to ensure Colonel Laws is properly escorted back to Washington DC Army Headquarters."

Gramps responded, "I will inform the captain of his additional duty."

"Make it so. Now, John, Mister Bates is professionally schooled in the art of equine dressage training. Those horses need the kind of battle training he knows all too well. Horses trained to fight on European terrain."

"Yes, sir. Just one quick question, Mister Roosevelt. Why Europe?"

"Let me just say, the monarchs are getting restless. Now if you would excuse me, I need to return to Washington and have a chat with the Army Chief of Staff, Major General Wood, about Colonel Laws." Roosevelt added, "Gentlemen, the world will once again be riding on the backs of horses before long. The army remount program has to step it up. And, John, remember what you said in your last cable to me. You want to go back home to Oklahoma."

"Sir, you know my loyalty to our country is unmatched. I am at your service."

Leather to Steel

"Very well, then. Give me two more years. At least until mid-summer 1914."

Gramps paused before replying. He rubbed his chin, appearing to be deep in thought. He looked at Roosevelt with intent eyes. "Well. You drive a hard bargain. I said one year. Now you want two?"

"Trust me, John. Two years, and no more. I will make sure the government pays you a little extra in your monthly retirement."

"We need to shake on it." Both men shook hands, which was the most honorable and socially binding agreement between two men. Before parting ways, all three men exchanged handshakes and good-byes.

The security detail quickly ushered Roosevelt back into the lead car's back seat. All three vehicles started up simultaneously, as if on cue. The drivers revved the engines and circled toward the main gate. The lead agent's car took first position. Roosevelt's vehicle followed, leaving a thick trail of lingering red dust.

*****

Gramps turned toward his new partner Jeremiah Bates and said, "Mister Bates, I think you have some old friends to meet. Follow me." The men walked through the main stable where neighing and snorting drowned out the chanting soldiers returning from their long march through the Blue Ridge Mountains.

Once inside, Gramps asked, "Mister Bates—"

Jeremiah interrupted. "Sorry, but would you mind calling me Jeremiah? I am not one for formal things. How should I address you? Boss?"

"Thank you for asking. I do appreciate the consideration. However, we are out here in God's country. No uppities to muck up our ways. You can just call me Gramps. Everyone else does."

Jeremiah replied, "Then Gramps it shall be. Now what was it you wanted to show me?"

Gramps tugged on Jeremiah's elbo. "Come on. Grab that old empty water barrel and pull up a seat. I have a document in my back pocket I want to share with you. Mister Roosevelt gave it to me.

Here, look at it. Jeremiah flipped through the report, and then back to the cover. He read the words aloud. "It says, 'December 15, 1910. The U. S. Department of Agriculture, Bureau of Animal Industry. Circular 186. A. D. Melvin. Chief of Bureau. George M. Rommel, Chief of the Animal Husbandry Division Reprinted from the Twenty-seventh Annual Report of the Bureau of Animal Industry.'"[30]

Jeremiah asked, "What are we supposed to do with this?"

Gramps grinned. "That document lays out why we must train our stallions and mares to the new battle standards. The Front Royal Remount Depot is chartered to produce the best cavalry horses the world has ever seen."

"Sounds like a tall order. Uhm. I am sure we can do it. What does one breed horses to produce and train the best cavalry horse?"

"Turn to page 103. The section title says 'Horse-breeding Methods in Europe.' Read it to me. Start with the first paragraph."

Jeremiah pulled out a pair of reading glasses. He put them on and began to read. "It says here, Germany probably makes larger total expenditures for the encouragement of horse breeding than any other country, and of all the German states where most attention is devoted to the subject in Prussia. Where is Prussia located?"

"Europe somewhere. Keep reading."

"'The Prussian provinces not only supply horses used in the army in Prussia, but in—having a tough time with these words—Bav...aria, Sax...ony, Wurtem...burg, and other parts of the empire. There are five breeding farms and eighteen stallion depots in the Kingdom of Prussia, the farms containing a total of over twenty-thousand acres. The breeding work of the government is partly to encourage livestock raising in general, as well as for military purposes, although there are two provinces in Prussia known as the "remount Provinces," where only the military object is considered by the government. The stallion depots (Landgestiite) are most important from a numerical standpoint. It contained 3,315 stallions in 1907. These stallions, quote 'make the circuit' unquote from February to June, at fees ranging from $1.19 to $4.76. I will be dang. They are serious about their horses."

"Darn right they are. Our government started our remount program with only one hundred and fifty stallions. The Germans own over three thousand. Keep on reading. It gets better."

"'The Prussian government does not permit expense to stand in the way of acquiring the services of a valuable stallion. Large sums are, sorry I don't understand the word, appro...pri...ated annually for such purposes, and Derby winners are bought if needed. The budget of 1907 for the purchase of horses amounted to $440,000, with a special fund of $47,600. Among noted English Thoroughbreds— which the Prussian government bought—was none other than Galtee More, the 1897 Derby.'" Jeremiah was shocked. "Well, I will be dang. So! That is where Galtee More ended up at. I remember reading about him. One heck of a fast Thoroughbred. What does this all mean?"

"What this means, Mister Bates—excuse me, Jeremiah— we have much work ahead of us. The United States has to catch up with Europe's horse-breeding programs. You and I will help make that goal a reality.

"However, that is not the only problem I see, Gramps. Someth'n is brewing over there by God. Why would Germans need so many cavalry horses, unless they were going to war?"

"Exactly my thoughts, Jeremiah. I figure the folks in Washington know what is come'n."

*****

Jeremiah moved Mary and their five children into their new home just before the new school year began. The three-bedroom home was new. There was electrical, plumbing, and sewage hookups considered modern for the time. The army even installed a new telephone line.

They thoughtfully built the house on high ground, away from the depot's main stables and soldiers' barracks. The Bates' living room bay windows overlooked the main buildings, stables, and paddocks. The kitchen window provided a direct view of the main entrance to the compound.

During the first morning in the new home, Mary sat with Jeremiah sipping coffee at the kitchen table. She reached over and placed her hand on Jeremiah's. "Thank you. Between you and the Lord, our family will be all right. The kids will start fresh in new schools." Jeremiah stepped toward Mary and said, "It all has to do with faith and a little bit of luck. Did I ever tell you the definition of luck?" Mary shook her head no. "Luck is defined as the crossroad of preparation and opportunity. I had the right skills, at the right time a position opened up on this depot. That is luck," Jeremiah proclaimed.

Every morning before going to work, Jeremiah sat at the kitchen table drinking his coffee while looking out the window. Mary always got up early to join him, and eventually get the kids ready for school. Jeremiah and Mary counted their blessings. They were very thankful to be living at the army depot. The years to come would bring the best of times for the Bates family. The oldest son, Abraham, would graduate from high school and attend college. Thanks to ole Silas, Abraham would attend the Virginia Commonwealth University in Richmond. Jeremiah and Mary were proud knowing that their first child would get a college education.

Indeed, patience and perseverance paid off for the Bates family. Consider their time living in the Oklahoma Territory. They endured poverty, discrimination, and other personal hardships that would discourage most others from dreaming. However, the Bateses dreamed, and dreamed they did.

Life at the Front Royal Remount Depot seemed to blissfully stand still for them. Jeremiah often said, "No news is good news." Nevertheless, as with the world, time would eventually become unforgiving. Unbeknownst to Jeremiah and his family, troubled world events would shape their future. Events that would change the course of history.

In May 1908, Congress authorized the establishment of a U.S. Army remount service. The War Department transferred the Fort Reno, Oklahoma reservation to the U.S. Army Quartermaster Department to build the first regional remount depot. Two additional regional depots opened in 1911: one in Fort Keogh, Montana and one in Front Royal, Virginia. An auxiliary remount depot opened at Fort Bliss in El Paso, Texas. One purchasing headquarters opened in Kansas City, Missouri.[31]

In addition to the existing three regional remount depots, the U.S. Army established thirty-three additional auxiliary remount depots and two animal embarkation depots. Four hundred officers and nineteen men supported the remount depot system.[32]

"Considering the Army's dependence on horses and mules for transportation in the nineteenth century, it is surprising how little attention was paid to insure an adequate supply of remounts. The outbreak of the Civil War and the accompanying demand for many animals showed a need for centralized procurement. By the end of the conflict, the Quartermaster General's Office was obtaining draft horses and mules while the Cavalry Bureau secured riding horses. To insure that remounts remained in good condition, the transfer of men and even entire units from the cavalry to the infantry was allowed if inspectors found evidence of animal abuse or neglect.

After the struggle ended, the earlier indifference toward remounts again prevailed until Maj. Gen. James B. Aleshire, Quartermaster General, recommended a separate office solely responsible for procurement and issue of horses and mules. He also urged the establishment of regional remount depots. Congress responded and passed an act in 1908 authorizing a system of remount depots. General Order 59, April 1908, created the first depot at abandoned Fort Reno,

Oklahoma.

Captain Letcher H. Hardeman of the 10th Cavalry took command of the depot. Civilian cowboys, farm hands, and former soldiers purchased, trained, and issued the animals. Hardeman received specific instructions to see "that the horses were well fed and cared for, gently and kindly handled at all times, and properly exercised and broken.

The Great War Begins

The effect of the war upon the United States will depend upon what American citizens say and do. Every man who really loves America will act and speak in the true spirit of neutrality, which is the spirit of impartiality and fairness and friendliness to all concerned.
—President Woodrow Wilson
Speech to the 63rd U.S.
Congress, 2nd Sess.,
(Washington, 1914)

On August 10, 1914, war broke out in Europe. President Woodrow Wilson vowed to keep America out of the war. With that said, President Wilson understood the political necessity and moral obligation to provide support to the USA's international partners. He initially did so for the Triple Entente (Britain, France, and Russia) in the form of munitions, money, and horses.

The "initial" Triple Alliance of Austria-Hungary, Germany, and Italy presented no threat to U.S. interests. Therefore, the United States adopted neutrality to allay public unrest yielded to profits to be made in America's capitalistic society. Through behind-the-scenes negotiations, the federal government and private industry negotiated deals with Britain for loans, humanitarian support, and embedding U.S. military liaison officers with British forces. The U.S. officers were charged with reporting Germany's deployment of innovative military weaponry on the Western Front.

President Wilson's administration worked on behalf of senior British government officials to recruit American doctors, nurses, and veterinarians desperately needed to serve with British government volunteer aid detachments (VADs).[33] The United States offered free passage for Americans wishing to provide humanitarian assistance on the Western Front. The British government would provide subsistence and field housing.

American volunteers clearly understood the risks associated with Imperial German Army debilitating weapons of war. Regardless, thousands of American professionals signed up to go. Many replacements would be needed in the years to come.

Newspaper headlines reported, on a daily basis, horrific German army attacks on unarmed civilians that, in many cases, had occurred months before. International opinion formed weeks, if not months, after the fact. Such was the case in the massacre of Louvain.

On August 25, 1914, Imperial German infantry divisions marched unchallenged across the Belgium countryside, burning and blowing up villages without mercy. Such was the case in the town of Louvain. The Germans committed unholy depredations against the town's civilian population. The British Prime Minister at the time was Henry Herbert Asquith. He learned of the German atrocities from several, credible eyewitness accounts and rumor. American newspapers made the reports front-page news, exciting the American public toward war with Germany.

Months later, distressful eye-witness accounts prompted Prime Minister Asquith to appoint Lord James Bryce to establish the *Committee on Alleged German Outrages* in December 1914. Lord Bryce charged the committee to investigate alleged German war crimes. Five months later, the Bryce Report was released in May 1915. The report assessed that the Imperial German Army committed excesses against Belgian civilians as part of a conscious strategy of terror.[34] The world could not stomach the idea of human atrocities. Yet, many did not believe genocide was possible in the modern era.

*****

Tough Guy

At the Front Royal Remount Depot, the summer morning offered forage unmatched by most pastures in Virginia. I grazed without a worry in the world. Periodically, I raised my head up to clear my throat, extend my nose up to smell the air, and clear my area for predators—none detected. I turned my head from side-to-side to view rolling green pastures extending to the eastern horizon. Jeremiah said they stopped at the banks of Chesapeake Bay.

Behind me, the Blue Ridge Mountains wore a veil of gray mist. For four years, the same seasonal breeze blew down from those mountains, teasing my nose and tickling my ears. The same breeze flipped Grace's mane over her neck. She looked peaceful. I neighed at her. "We need to head back. I heard Jeremiah calling." She followed me along the lone worn trail back to the stable.

*****

For four years, the depot provided for our every need. As it was on the Winchester farm, we trained, ate, and slept. Grace and I embraced the routine. Since leaving Winchester, we expected to remain together until the end of days. Life on the depot did not change, however, the world beyond our gates did. Jeremiah said Europe was at war. I knew cavalry horses played a key role in war. What the war in Europe meant to us depot horses remained to be seen.

Jeremiah said the United States would abstain from contributing soldiers. However, that did not mean horses. Soon, the demand would grow for the depot's new generation of fillies and colts—bred for the battlefield—I watched the little ones grow up on the depot. Each understood their future depended upon learning how to move on the battlefield. The army saw to it they were prepared to survive. I taught them undaunted courage. The rest would depend upon their own innate abilities and will to survive.

Many mares came and left in my life; only one mare captured my heart from the beginning—Grace. I took for granted that she would always be with me. I had no reason to believe life would be otherwise. However, as with most animals, our futures are decided by mankind. The summer of 1914 ended with peace's swan song. We sensed change was coming. Jeremiah even said troubled waters were coming. We had to prepare.

During the past couple of weeks, Gramps repeatedly told the soldiers his old bones could not keep up with the extensive training demands required of himself and the "new breed" of cavalry horses being "manufactured to European standards." He grumbled many times around us horses that he could only take us so far with what the army wanted from him. He said the new cavalry horse deserved better. If only he knew how we depended upon him. Gramps's equestrian expertise helped the army redefine modern horse management. He led the way.

Jeremiah said that with a war escalating in Europe, Britain and France quickly realized the need for acquiring capable warhorses to replace countless cavalry horses killed in action. British and French militaries needed horses trained to perform more than just battlefield movements. They needed horses and mules to haul weapons to the front, and return the dead and wounded to the rear.

President Wilson sympathized with British and French government leaders clamoring for more weapons, ammunition, supplies, and horses. In response to the latter, Wilson ordered the U.S. Army to expand acquisitions of top-notch horses for all U.S. Army Remount Depots. The army depots responded without delay. Engineers constructed more stables on every depot. Experienced horse trainers were recruited and hired to sustain elevated remount operations. All done accommodate international demands for well-trained cavalry horses.

*****

Tough Guy

During the ensuing months, the Front Royal Remount Depot received construction of new stables and increased civilian and army staff. Dozens of green horses were trailered in and indoctrinated to enhanced training techniques. Young horses were given enough training to make them competent beasts of burden. Their care and welfare depended upon many trainers, veterinarians, and farriers, who labored until winter solstice. The reduced daylight hours did not

Leather to Steel

deter the depot's work. Even with winter coming, the depot construction continued.

Our winter coats started to grow out in early December. Sooner than usual. Mother Nature's way of saying it was going to be a cold one. However, my winter coat's early arrival was not the subject of conversation on the first December Saturday morning. The depot rhythm had changed that day.

Only a few soldiers remained on duty at the depot to oversee the herds. What struck me as different was the presence of Jeremiah and Gramps. They were usually off Saturdays visiting private horse farms looking for prospective buys. December 5 was not the case. Their behavior change proved me right. My life would soon change.

Jeremiah and Gramps walked inside our stable and toward our stalls. They carried our halters in their hands. Alarmed, my ears went up. I snorted at them as they got closer to us. Grace neighed at me. "What are they doing here? This is not part of the weekly routine."

I looked at Gramps holding Grace's halter. Jeremiah had mine. I neighed back, "I am not sure."

Leaning against my stall door, Jeremiah looked at Gramps. "I will take Tough Guy out into the back paddock first. Once we are out the door, go ahead and get Grace ready." Gramps scratched his beard. "That would be best." Before leaving the stable, Jeremiah shook his head at Grace. He then led me through the rear stable door. After closing the door, he rubbed my nose and looked directly into my eyes. "Tough Guy, this is for your own good. You will understand."

I did not understand why Jeremiah put me into the paddock by myself. Within the hour, Grace answered the question with her distressed neighing. I neighed back but could barely hear her above the mechanized sounds of a diesel truck engine that started up. I observed the black smoke rising up on the other side of the stable. The black-to-gray exhaust eventually dissipated into the sky. Concerned, I ran over to the opposite side of the paddock to get a better look.

I could hear Grace's hooves clomping on an aluminum ramp, then she stopped. Grace neighed out loudly. The clanking rear trailer door was shut. The door lever clanked as it latched into a locking position. I heard the safety chain rattle across the deadbolt. Gramps call out, "All right, boys. Let us get this tin bucket on down the road. Move out!" The truck slowly shifted into gear.

I could no longer stand it. I ran to the rear of the paddock to give myself some distance. I ran toward the top rail of the paddock fence and jumped. I almost lost my footing landing on the slope outside the fence. Focused on getting to Grace, I retained my balance. My wobbly legs got me to the main gate as the army truck pulled out. The gate guard called out. "Close the gates quick. Here comes Tough Guy." Two soldiers immediately closed the swing gates.

Undeterred by the gate, I shifted my direction toward the road running parallel to the fence. I caught up and ran parallel with the truck. Gramps looked at me. He turned and said something to the driver. The truck stopped. I dug my hind legs into the dirt and stopped. Gramps sat in the main cab. The truck was hooked up to a drab-green covered doublewide horse trailer with a large white star painted on the side. Grace looked at me through the barred side opening. She was not alone. Seven other horses were loaded up with her.

Grace blinked at me with her brown eyes and softly whinnied at me. I understood her sadness. I shook my head up and down, attempting to reassure her that everything would be okay. Tears flowed from her eyes.

Gramps yelled at me, "Tough Guy. She is going home with me. My family and I will take good care of her."

Gramps extended his hand out the cab's window and waved at the soldiers who had lined up along the fence line in front of me to see him off. Before the truck pulled away, Jeremiah was already standing by my side. He hooked a lead to my halter. Gramps yelled out at Jeremiah. "Take care of them ponies, mister. Drop me a cable once in a while."

Jeremiah replied, "You bet! Take care, old man. Pass my regards to the missus." Gramps pulled his hand back inside the cab and rolled up the window.

Leather to Steel

    The truck driver started back up the engine and shifted into a low gear. Diesel smoke rumbled out of the exhaust pipes. The cab jerked forward, and then slowly pulled the horse trailer down the main road. I kept my eyes on Grace as the trailer turned toward the main road. She neighed aloud one more time, perhaps with the hope of stopping the trailer. Her efforts were to no avail. The truck picked up speed, leaving a dust cloud in its wake. Only I could faintly hear her cries.

    The truck disappeared over the hill. I turned to Jeremiah and stomped my front hooves. He patted my withers. As he rubbed my neck, Jeremiah spoke. "Tough Guy, I know she was your favorite. You must remember we both have work to do. There is a higher calling right now."

    I did not understand what he meant about a "higher calling." All I knew at that moment was Grace would no longer be here. Grace and I witnessed many seasons pass without the sound of war. At least until August when war shattered the world's silence.

    Standing by the fence, Jeremiah turned to me and said, "Well, boy, I suppose time tells. Never thought you and Grace would be separated, but it was for the best."

    I neighed back, "Do not take me for granted. My days are numbered."

    Jeremiah patted my withers. He took out a fistful of oats mixed with molasses. I stuck my nose into his hand and almost bit his fingers—by accident, of course. Jeremiah swatted at my nose. "Knock it off, boy. Don't blame me for Grace's departure. Blame President Wilson. Better yet, blame the dang German soldiers cutting down all those poor horses in Europe. We wanted to protect her from being sold."

    Jeremiah led me back to the stable. He continued, "On a positive note, I want you to know our oldest son Abraham will be going to the university. Yep, he is going to be schooled on how to take care of animals like you, Tough Guy. He will graduate by the spring of 1917, Lord willing." I snorted not really wanting to be with any human. I remained in my stall alone for the rest of the day. The longest day in my life.

Over the next several years, Jeremiah and hundreds of civilian and military trainers like him would prepare tens of thousands of horses across the country to become warhorses. Since the days of Ranse, what began with Jeremiah and Welford became the training standard—the art of dressage. Former president Roosevelt recognized that traditional cavalry horse training regimen was dated. He was, after all, an expert horseman who rode into battle during the Spanish American War. The U.S. Army cavalry training had to evolve with modern warfare. That is why Roosevelt chose Jeremiah and others like him to play a role in the scheme of preparation.

*****

Jeremiah Bates was a man of routine. Every morning, he left his house at five o'clock. He walked down to the main stable to take care of the horses. After replenishing the feed and water buckets, he left the stable. Ten minutes later, he would return with crumpled-up white paper in his hands. The tack room was his office. He used an empty wooden water barrel as a seat. While leaning his back against the wall, he unfolded and flattened out each message. The first time he retrieved the cables, he smirked. "I need to tell those boys to stop throwing away these cables in the trash buckets. Anyone can get them."

As he read, Jeremiah often mumbled to himself, while reading overseas reporting. One morning, an urgent cable read the German Empire declared war on Britain, France, and Russia. He spoke aloud through the open tack room door to Tough Guy. "Get this boy. Because of the war going on in Europe, the Department of War warns all U.S. military installations to be on alert for suspicious activity. That includes the depot commanders."

Jeremiah continued reading. "Tough Guy, the fighting is across the Atlantic Ocean in Europe located three thousand miles across from here to the east. Thank goodness, President Wilson has already come out and proclaimed America's neutrality. We do not need another war. No one wants war."

Initial foreign newspaper and government reporting indicated the war would be over by Christmas. One report stated that the German

Leather to Steel

Kaiser, Wilhelm II, publicly proclaimed hostilities would end by November, or the latest in December. The Bates family shared the same sentiments. Jeremiah and Mary had seen what past wars do to nations. They wanted their children to grow up during a time of peace. After all, their son Abraham would be graduating from Front Royal High School next year, Class of 1915. Abraham would be the first person in the family to do so. Thanks to Mr. Silas Addison, Abraham would be going to college. Another first in the Bates family.

Tough Guy listened to Jeremiah speak about the war in Europe. Jeremiah added his own personal commentary to each report. He told Tough Guy, "If America gets involved, there will be drastic changes in America as we know it today. A military draft will surely be brought into play. Millions of Americans will see battle. Perhaps millions will die."

Tough Guy neighed back with a similar response. "Our fillies and colts will be the first to go to war since Stonewall rode in battle during the Comanche's Wars." Jeremiah kept his self-conversation going. He continued on talking. "Abraham wants to study veterinarian science." Jeremiah looked through the tack room door at Tough Guy. "He wants to helps horses just like you. Aint' that someth'n, Tough Guy?"

Tough Guy neighed back with a similar message. "Yes. My No-Name son will probably end up on the receiving end of Abraham's work."

War was cause for worry. More so for veterans of war—veterans like Jeremiah Bates. The news did not sit well with him. He dropped the army messages and started rubbing his knuckles. Perspiration beaded up on his brow. He wiped the sweat off with his hands and then took a deep breath of air. The tingle that ran up his left arm lingered behind the back of his neck. His heart was racing.

Jeremiah tried to stand up, but slight nausea prevailed. The wobbly legs underneath him cautioned him from doing so. He reluctantly sat back down and let out a heavy sigh. He had seen this before in older men, like himself. His blood flow was in trouble. He promptly sat up straight on the barrel to reduce the tingling sensations traveling around his body.

Jeremiah arched his back in to push his chest out. He created more space for his lungs to expand. He then lifted both arms over his head. He stuck his chin up and took another deep breath of air and slowly exhaled. He said to Tough Guy, "Whew. That was interesting. Better back off from the fried chicken. Tough Guy, say nothing of this to the missus. She will think I am working too little and worrying too hard."

*****

Jeremiah was a veteran of war. He and millions of fellow Americans had good reason to believe the hostilities would not end too soon. The indications were in place. Kaiser Wilhelm amassed together divisions of Imperial German and Austrian army infantry, weapons, and planes superior in number to Alliance Powers capabilities. The only saving grace was Britain's maritime dominance. Royal Navy maritime dominance kept Germany's shipping in check.

Within the first few months of the war, over 3 million lives were given in exchange for a few thousand yards of dirt bordering France and Belgium. Why? Jeremiah said the American diplomats concluded the war was about German monarchy pride. The German people demanded retribution for past wars and territories lost to the French and the English. Territorial wars spanning hundreds of years in Europe.

Newspaper accounts reported Kaiser Wilhelm's plan to occupy France once again to reclaim German land surrendered to the French in 1871. Media giants like Joseph Pulitzer and William Randolph Hearst helped shape President Wilson's desire to honor the American public will to stay out of it. The president indicated as much before his Congressional testimonies during the fall of 1914. His sentiments would soon change when the neutral state would become the victim.

*****

For the next four years, horses and mules became rare commodities on the battlefields. Millions perished on the Western Front. Bullets, bombs, chemicals, and disease killed them. Britain and France resorted to requisitioning drafts and mules from local farms. Without formal training, those beasts of burden either ran away from the explosions, or went crazy.

Properly trained and conditioned replacements were shipped in from North America. Canada and the United States sold hundreds of thousands of horses and mules to the Entente, a word representing the political bonds of three countries—Britain, France, and Russia—though only Britain and France had the money to purchase horses and mules. America took note.

One year into the war, the United States Army directed depot commanders to acquire, train, and sell tens of thousands of cavalry horses to the British and the French. Civilian horse farms stepped up the operations, such as the Magnolia Horse Farm. The growing demand relocated horses like Tough Guy from one place to another with little notice.

*****

At the depot, Gramp's old age and wisdom enabled him to proselytize how the world repeated history without learning from it. He said one man held the fate of America's peaceful existence. That man was U.S. President Woodrow Wilson. The extent of President Wilson's support to the war was limited to food, bullets, horses, and loans. He knew the American will was not yet there. A full-scale military presence was not an option. The U.S. Congress restricted military support to advisory capacities only.

*****

Tough Guy

The Front Royal Remount Depot indoctrinated green horses with daily conditioning and training under the guise of Jeremiah's instruction. He worked me and several geldings through classic high school dressage movements in the paddock, even when it snowed. I neighed to the young ones that the inclement training conditions were necessary. Jeremiah said the war in Europe was being fought in muddy, cold, and dark conditions. He knew we had to get used to it. The Western Front was a nasty place to fight. Our survival depended upon our ability to adapt to the fog of war.

Before the year's end, the depot soldiers were getting restless. I sensed something unsettling in their moods. They marched from place to place chanting talk about killing German soldiers. Jeremiah said during his Saturday morning news report, "The Great War will not end." I had not known war. However, my desires to battle conflicted with my father's wisdom. He told me no one wants war. I could not help myself. I wanted to carry a trooper across the battlefield, like he did during the Battle of San Juan Hill. I wanted to feel the same relentless drive to defeat the enemy. The same drive my father, Stonewall, and his father, Lucky, was born with. Then there was my son, No-Name. I did not want him to see battle. I was torn.

All the talk of war raised my concerns for No-Name. I knew he was serving our U.S. Army cavalry; I just did not know where. Like Grace and me, No-Name and one hundred and fifty stallions became property of several U.S. Army Regional Remount depots.

On the day No-Name left the Winchester Farm, I had no idea where his journey would end. Years later, his whereabouts would no longer be a mystery. He showed up at the Front Royal Remount Depot. I will never forget the day of his return. He was no longer No-Name. His trooper named him Jubal Early.

*****

On Saturday, January 7, 1915 another army trailer full of horses arrived at the depot's main gate. Several soldiers offloaded one stallion and a dozen mares from the double-wide horse trailer. A makeshift corral provided temporary containment. I watched from the paddock the last horse being unloaded. It was No-Name. I tried to get his attention, but with the truck's diesel engine, the loud rumbling sound made it difficult to communicate with him. I could only reply upon my nose and eyesight. No name stood nearest to the trailer gate. He looked magnificent.

He had grown into a fine-looking black stallion. Jeremiah stood on the other side of the trailer, keeping watch over the offloading. He yelled out at the men, "Soldiers! Take the mares to the front pasture over there."

Jeremiah pointed to the north-field entrance. A soldier saluted and yelled back, "Do you want their halters removed?"

"No. Leave them on for now. I will change them out later!"

"Yes, sir," the sergeant replied. "Where do you want the black stallion?"

"Take him up into the stable. Once inside, put him in the first stall to the right."

The soldier agreed and spoke to the other soldier, who was actually an officer. "Major Hazzard. You heard the man. Secure Jubal and take him up to the stable. First stall to the right." The officer nodded. "Okay, Sergeant. I will make it so." Major Hazzard added, "I should have worn the gold oak leafs."

The officer took Jubal's lead and led him toward the stable entrance. Jeremiah looked over at me. "Looks like it will be old home week here on the depot."

I snorted and neighed out to Jubal. My heart was glad to see my son again. He was no longer a horse with no name. Though his name had changed, his behavior did not. He was still the silent one.

The officer leading Jubal to the stable looked toward me, then at his mount. He spoke to Jubal. "Boy, looks like you got some competition here."

Jubal raised his head up and sniffed the air. Interestingly enough, Jubal looked in my direction and pulled his ears back. Making eye contact with me, my heart filled with gladness. Yet his eyes did not reciprocate.

It had been several years since Grace and I watched him leave the Roosevelt farm. He alone stood in the open one-horse trailer. We knew not where it was going. I do recall the colt only nodded at us. He did not neigh or snort, as he was doing the same now, except with his ears pulled back. Perhaps it was instincts, or perhaps too much time had passed between us. Jubal Early seemed different, in a troubling way.

Before sunset, Jeremiah came back to the paddock. He whistled me over, and hooked the lead to me. We slowly walked back into the stable. He said to me, "Even though you are the ripe age of sixteen, I know you can hold your own against any stallion. I am sure you recognized the new stallion the army trailered in today? He now has a name. His trooper calls him, Jubal Early." Jeremiah opened the stable doors wider to get us both inside.

As we walked towards my stall, he continued, "Funny, the boys back in Oklahoma named him after a Confederate general. You would think the civil war was over by now?"

I neighed back, "My father was named Stonewall. A common Confederate name for Magnolia horses; that is except for me. A Yankee named me Tough Guy because of my behavior, not for where I was born."

*****

Tough Guy

I told the colts many times, "All animals understand why Mother Nature dictates life. Fundamentally, the strongest survive for a reason. Mankind tries to control nature. It is Mother Nature that governs our ability to draw upon unadulterated animal instincts. The kind of instincts that underpin one's will to survive."

Mother Nature's test eventually came for Jubal Early and me. Perhaps familial respect would intervene and all troubles would be avoided. I remember how it played out, like it was yesterday.

Jeremiah controlled our first muzzle-to-muzzle meeting, while the unknown army officer watched from the stable door. Jeremiah secured Jubal's lead to a paddock rail near the gate. A lung line secured me to the opposite side of the paddock. Jeremiah walked out to the center and stood between us. He yelled out, "Gentlemen, the U.S. Army selected you both—two of one hundred and fifty stallions—to produce the perfect cavalry horse. Though you have yet to serve on the battlefield, it is time for you both to get your minds

Leather to Steel

right." Jeremiah held a training aid in his right hand. Jubal and I understood what the crop meant to our backsides. We calmed down the snorting exchanges.

Jeremiah looked serious. Jubal and I were father and son in blood only. Jeremiah knew it. I was not confident our reunion would be like that between Stonewall and myself. Granted, Stonewall was not part of my everyday life growing up, but at least we made amends before he died.

Jubal had grown into a magnificent black stallion. He clearly wanted nothing to do with me. I looked into his coal-black eyes and saw his heart—a heart that longed for full charge into the battlefield. At that moment, he did remind me of me. My ears pointed forward.

Jeremiah first called out to Jubal. The young black stallion raised his right leg and pawed at the ground. Jeremiah looked at me. He yelled out a dressage command that snapped my mind back into focus. I neighed back and knelt down on my front knees. He turned to Jubal and commanded the same. Clearly, Jubal remembered his battle training.

Jeremiah said, "Boys, now that I have your attention, you will both remember that you are not here to fight each other, but to train together." Looking at Jubal, he said, "Your trooper has orders to liaison with the Royal Canadian Mounted Artillery up in Canada. Tough Guy, this may be the last time you see your son. Time is not your friend right now."

The paddock moment created cause for respect and honor between us. Jeremiah's commands released me from my position. I stood up. Jeremiah unhooked my lead. He then guided me over to Jubal, who was still in the kneeling position. I got to within ten feet of Jubal when Jeremiah bellowed out, "Jubal, you may never bow down to your father, or any other stallion. But you will show respect to your father."

Jeremiah released Jubal and led us to the center while he maintained control of Jubal's halter.

Once unhooked, Jubal raised his neck into a high carriage and pressed his ears forward. I was relieved and replied the same in kind. He snorted once. I neighed in peace. Jeremiah observed, "I don't know what you two exchanged, but at least it was not blows. If I could understand, he would know that I said, "I love ya, son."

Jubal had replied, "You too, Father."

From that point on, we kept our distance when not training in the mud shoots together. The army was keen on keeping our stamina in top condition. Physical toughness with purpose for a future place, date, and time.

*****

Major Oliver Hazzard

January 1915, Jubal and his trooper had a predetermined purpose. Soon after the breakout of war, the United States Army ordered Major Oliver Hazzard to depart Fort Sill and report to the Royal Canadian Horse Artillery Brigade, in garrison, near Davenport, England. His charge, Jubal, would travel with him.

Hearing of the major's pending transfer, Jeremiah made an effort to provide more contact time between Tough Guy and Jubal. During an early-morning feeding, Jeremiah broke the news to Tough Guy.

Holding Tough Guy's muzzle, Jeremiah looked him in the eye. "Old boy, your son will be leaving us soon. I understand the U.S. Army Second Cavalry Regiment selected the major to liaison with the Canadians attached to the British First Cavalry Division led by General Edmund H. H. Allenby."[35] He continued, "The Canadian brigade was in England to drill and train before going into battle.[36] You may never see him again. So make things right with your boy."

Major Hazzard had his orders. He clearly understood the importance of effectively executing orders to observe, advise, and report back to command during the war. He would do so as others who came before him. It was in the best interest of the United States to dispatch top-notch military officers to Allied countries during major conflicts. The intelligence gained helped protect America's national security interests. Major Hazzard carefully considered one more important goal on the battlefield—to keep himself and his charge alive.

Tough Guy

Jeremiah showed consideration. Telling me Jubal would be leaving the depot gave me cause to rethink my judgments of my mysterious son. Jeremiah understood my troubled history with Jubal. He said, "Tough Guy. I reckon you know Jubal is leaving for Europe tomorrow."

I neighed back, shaking my head from side to side. "I am not sad to see Jubal Early leave. For the few days he trained with us, he did little to show me respect."

I was glad Grace did not witness how her offspring remained the quiet, prideful, and stubborn colt we watched grow up. Perhaps it was for the best. A piece of my heart remained hopeful for Jubal's interest in getting to know me. Perhaps he would ask me for advice before he ships out. My instincts help me conclude that would not be the case.

Toward the end of the day, Major Hazzard returned to the stables. He hurriedly walked up to Jeremiah, who was leaning against my stall door. The major stopped within a few steps of Jeremiah. He seemed nervous. The major looked back and forth between me and Jeremiah. The major stuttered somewhat. "Mister Bates, uhm—you know I will be departing with Jubal the day after morrow. I am to report to the Port of Norfolk. From there, we load up on a transport ship and steam three thousand miles across the Atlantic Ocean to Dover, England."

"Sounds like a long trip."

"According to my orders, the Canadian First Regiment commander, Lieutenant General Alderson, recommends bringing two mounts. As you have read in the papers, the Brits are short on horses."

Jeremiah looked at the major with curious intent and asked him, "I see. What are you saying?"

While looking at me, the major said, "Mister Bates, I need to bring another horse. A horse well trained like Tough Guy here."

"Major. I am not sure, I—"

"Well, what I mean is—do you think the depot can spare Tough Guy? I noticed he spends most of his time alone in the pasture. You have kept him well trained. I know you both have a history. But...but—I would feel better knowing I was going to war with the best under my saddle."

Jeremiah turned his head away from the major and coughed. He looked back at me and then at the major. "Major Hazzard. When do you need an answer?" The major looked up at the stable's rafters, as if he was searching for an answer. "Sorry, but I need to know by tomorrow morning."

Jeremiah shook his head. "I don't know major. He is not a spring chicken."

The major added, "My request is not about just any horse. It is about *this* horse, Mister Bates. You fought in war. You understand I will need the best warhorse under me. Should Jubal get shot, another horse must take his place. The Canadians and British are short on horses and—"

"Stop right there, sir. I understand. No need to explain any further. Tough Guy is your best option."

"Thank you, Mister Bates. I appreciate your understanding."

I looked at Jeremiah and really did not understand what was happening. Jeremiah leaned over my stall door. He looked into my eyes. "Tough Guy, you have an opportunity to do what you were born to do. Carry your trooper into battle. You will not be alone. Your son will be at your side. The major needs you."

I neighed back, shaking my head up and down. Jeremiah turned toward the major and said, "I will have him ready for you in the morning." I could see Jeremiah's eyes begin to water. The last time I saw those tears was when Grace and I left the Winchester farm. I did not fully understand war, but I was willing to serve. I wished Grace would have been here. She would have been proud of me.

*****

That evening, I grazed in the depot's north forty pasture. The winter dusk felt brisk upon my withers. The cold air coming down the Blue Ridge Mountains smelled sweet to my nose. I lowered my muzzle to

Leather to Steel

the ground to lick the frost beaded up on the grass. The water crystals tasted so good with every bite I took. I savored every moment in that pasture, knowing it was my last eve at the depot.

While I grazed, the breeze pushed itself against the tall willow trees defining the field's eastern border. Each time I lifted my head up, the wind blew familiar scents of dried oak leaves across my nose. The wind bent my silver whiskers against my nostrils with every gust.

The wind picked up. I watched dried leaves tumble across the pasture towards the clutches of dormant blackberry vines sprawling across the fence. The relentless rustling of leaves sent shivers down my back. At that moment, my perfect life, felt imperfect. Something uncomfortable stirred inside me.

Before long, dusk turned into night. I heard Jeremiah calling from the stable. I was not ready to go in. I ignored him; opting to stay in the pasture. My legs took me over to the western corner of the field near a natural windbreak. Standing behind a copse of bushes, I enjoyed peace and quiet. Standing still and listening to silence helped calm my nerves. Before long, my eyes grew heavy with sleep. I dozed off and dreamed.

*****

The quiet would not last. I heard the hoof steps of a single horse galloping up the hill behind me. I looked up, turned around, and saw my son, Jubal, stopping just in front me. I snorted a cheery "Good morning" to him. Then, when I looked into his eyes, my senses told me something was weighing heavy on his heart. He approached me and said, "Dad, we have talked about the day would come where I would leave this place. That day has come. However, it is not me leaving. It is you."

Looking into his eyes, I felt his emotion when he explained to me how he overhead the farrier talking with President Roosevelt. The war in Europe was getting worse. President Wilson said there would be no doubt the war would eventually draw America into the mix. The British and French armies were running out of horses. The United States would answer the call.

I replied to my son, "It will be my first war."

Jubal replied, "Father. You will not be fighting. I don't understand."

"My trooper, Major Oliver Hazzard, said President Wilson wanted a U.S. Army liaison with the Royal Canadian Mounted Horse Artillery Brigade. They are near the war."

"When will you leave?"

"Tomorrow."

"Son, I hope you do not go. Your grandfather and his father passed on the words. 'Nobody wants war.' War has bound our family for three generations. My grandfather, Lucky; my father, Stonewall; and now you. I have yet to fight."

"Jubal Early, your grandfather, Stonewall, told me to serve our country with all my heart. That is what we do."

"Father, I know I am only two years old, but I am ready. You taught me how to zig and zig when the rifles and canons blow smoke and roar like lions."

Tough Guy laughed. "Son, you know your great-grandfather Lucky learned that move on the battlefields on Antietam, Fredericksburg, Brandy Station, Gettysburg, and the siege of St. Petersburg. He passed those skills down to my father, Stonewall. I suspect they will work in Europe."

"You mean Great-Grandpa served during the Civil War?"

"Indeed he did. He was one of the bravest cavalry horses to ride into battle."

"Was he hurt?"

"Yes. He was wounded several times in battle. A Yankee saber crossed his withers many a time." Tough Guy shook his head up and down, neighing, "Come on, son. We need to get back to the barn. I can hear the farrier's wagon coming up the road."

I woke up to the sound of Jeremiah calling me. The dream I just had seemed real. I shook my head back and forth to get the sleep out of my eyes. The cool breeze again blew across my muzzle. A sense of calm and peace overwhelmed my senses. I fell back asleep and dreamt.

Jubal Early looked into my eyes with great pride, and complied with a deep-sounding grunt. Though we were both familial black stallions, only I had the Magnolia Brand on my left rear quarter. Jubal Early did not. My father's owner, Manny, told the army his sire would produce strong, smart, and obedient foals. However, he neglected to mention the family brand would never burn the hide of my future generations.

"Son, President Wilson is sending me to serve on the Western Front with the Royal Canadian Horse Artillery Brigade. Your orders are to report to the U.S. Army Second Cavalry Regiment Headquarters in Fort Myer, Virginia. While there, you will prepare, train, and wait for further orders."

Those orders did come, and I was on my way to serve in the Royal Canadian Horse Artillery Brigade. My trooper was Major Oliver Hazzard. The U.S. Army commanding general assigned the major as a liaison and observer of war operations. His job was to report enemy cavalry operations back to the Army commanding general.

I woke up feeling my wet cheeks. I shook my head from side to side to lose sleep's hold of my eyes. I focused on the north forty pond. I was thirsty and headed over to its edge. I stood by the pond's edge, gazing upon the calm water reflecting sunrays on the big drooping cottonwoods. The sparkling light moved shadows on the shore. The shadows danced with each gust of wind. A sign perhaps? One that predicted my future. Perhaps not, but a sign from my father that life spent in the shadows earns no glory.

*****

The Zapatas and Eilenbergs

The Great War exacted sacrifice from all walks of life. Tough Guy and Jubal were not alone on that score. North of the Front Royal Remount Depot, civilians wrestled with the disparaging news and unforeseen consequences living in a world at war. Tough Guy's familial connection to his father Stonewall were not immune from the effects of war.

Lucinda and Manny Zapata argued over a life-changing decision, with Lucinda contemplating how to support the war effort. After a traditional Sunday dinner of fried chicken, mashed potatoes, brown gravy, homemade biscuits, green beans, and sweet iced tea, the Zapatas and their neighbors Max and Kate Eilenberg read together stories printed in the *Washington Post* newspaper.

Every major newspaper in the United States reported on horrific battles fought in Austria, France, and Belgium. During the last few months of 1914, the Germans rolled through Belgium on their way to Paris, France. Numerous reports told of great losses of life on both sides. Men and horses were dying on battlefields in countries unrecognizable by Americans. Manny read a troubling newspaper story to Lucinda and their friends Kate and Max.

"You won't believe this. The German army is killing unarmed civilians. Mothers, wives, babies, and the elderly were slaughtered. My God."

Lucinda asked, "Where?"

"Says here in a place called Dinant. Die not, I guess."

Kate chimed in. "Manny, that is French. Sounds like Duh No."

Max corrected him. "Say it like *do nigh*."

Kate said, "*Duh No, Do Nigh*—regardless of how we say it, the devil placed his hand on the town."

Manny continued reading. "The Germans forced the defenseless citizens of Do Nigh into the town's center and shot over six hundred people."

Lucinda looked at Manny and said, "I think I read something similar a couple weeks ago in the *Post*. Happened in a Belgium town."

Kate asserted, "I can't believe those horrible Germans shot innocent children! My God."

Max looked at Manny and asked, "What else does the story say?"

Manny rubbed his eyes and sighed. He said, "The town center was looted and burned."

Pointing at a hand-drawn picture in the paper, Manny said, "Here it is. Do Nigh is just one of many towns standing in the way of Germany's objective—Paris, France."

Manny and Lucinda excused themselves for the evening. After saying their good-byes, they walked back to their house. Holding hands, Lucinda squeezed Manny's and said, "We try so hard to have a baby, yet there are people in the world having them and not caring for them. The Germans are so heartless not to respect a baby's life."

Manny said, "I know that story upset you. I am sorry."

*****

Lucinda and Kate could not have children. The idea that innocent children were being killed or injured made both women noticeably angered. Christians killing one another rubbed them the wrong way. Both women were natural caregivers. These personal attributes led Lucinda and Kate Gherty to pursue an education in nursing at the University of Texas in 1894.

As the war escalated, their nursing skills became high in demand toward the end of 1914. During the annual church Christmas potluck, Lucinda and Kate looked at each other as sisters do when the minds are connected. Lucinda said to Kate, "You know what we have to do? The Western Front needs us."

Lucinda and Kate wanted to serve with the British Red Cross. The newspapers advertised free transportation, room, and board in exchange for humanitarian services. The women made plans that were not wholly endorsed by their husbands. Manny and Max suspected their wives' good intentions overlooked the dangers. The couples would cross that bridge at another time.

*****

Major Oliver Hazzard

The Royal Canadian Horse Artillery Brigade commander ordered Sergeant Ovilla Gigeurre to pick up Major Hazzard at a debarkation site near Warehouse Number 4 located just outside the main gate at the Dover shipyard. Getting to the warehouse was not easy. Sergeant Gigeurre had to navigate his twenty-foot military transport on congested roads near staging areas busy with military transport trucks, soldiers, sailors, and civilians scurrying about from one warehouse to another.

Sergeant Gigeurre located the warehouse and backed the truck in, as close as he could get to the loading dock. He put the truck in park and waited. Within the hour, he spotted a lone American soldier walking in the rain near a quay wall. Recognizing the odds were pretty good the officer was his pickup, Sergeant Gigeurre stepped out of the cab and donned his slicker. He quickly walked toward the American holding a green duffle sack over his shoulder.

The sergeant waved at the American. Gigeurre yelled, "Sir, are you Major Oliver Hazzard, United States Army?"

Major Hazzard looked towards the stocky soldier approaching him. He noticed the sergeant was wearing a cavalry hat resembling a Mexican sombrero. The major–answered, "Yes. Are you with the Royal Canadian Horse Artillery Brigade?"

Now standing in front of the major, Gigeurre saluted and replied, "Yes, sir. Welcome to the war. We hope you enjoy your stay."

The major did not smile, nor knew how to characterize a reply. Seeing the sergeant rendering a salute, the major clicked his heels together and returned a sharp right-hand salute. "My name is Major Oliver Hazzard, United States Army Second Regiment Dragoons." The major lowered his hand; the sergeant followed suit.

"Sir," Sergeant Gigeurre replied, "We need to fetch your gear and get out of here." He pointed at Warehouse Number 4 and added, "Another supply ship is porting soon. That warehouse needs to be cleared out for the next rotation of shipments. We need to move out smartly, sir."

The major asked him, "Where do we pick up my horses?"

"Aye," the sergeant said, pointing at the warehouse loading dock. "I have the unit's lorry, a brand-new Crossley parked over there by the loading dock. The horses and their tack are waiting for you. Sir, if you prefer, you can wait in the cab while I load up the ponies. The Crossley has a covered truck bed to keep them dry." [37]

"Very well. I sure would like to get out of this rain." The major adjusted his hat to drain the water away from his uniform. He asked, "Sergeant, where do we go from here?"

"Sir, we are camped near the Salisbury Plain. Over ninety thousand acres of the best chalky, muddy soil, and rolling hills old England has to offer."

"Sergeant, how long will it take us to get there?"

"Not long. We will get there before dinner."

"Thank you. Will Captain Boak be there? My orders made note to check in with him before introductions to your commanding officer."

"Aye. The captain sent me to pick you up. His is looking forward to your arrival, sir."

*****

Tough Guy

Jubal and I stood just inside the dock warehouse sliding doors. The dockworker had secured us to a railing extended alongside the loading dock. We watched Major Hazzard exchange words with the soldier. I could tell the major was indifferent with whatever was being said. After a few minutes, the soldier walked toward us. He hummed an unfamiliar song. I turned to Jubal and neighed, "The man wearing the green uniform coming toward us—he appears to be in a good mood."

"I don't see any reason to be in a good mood about around this place. This rain has not stopped since we got off the wretched transport ship."

"Jubal, perhaps he is just glad to be alive. He is not being shot at. You know there is a war going on over here."

"I don't see no war."

"Son, you and I don't know what war looks like. However, I am sure that will change, once we get to what the major calls... the Western Front."

Sergeant Gigeurre stepped up onto the dock, and quickened his pace toward a stack of crates. Still humming, he walked over to one particular crate stenciled with the words "Hazzard Tack." He pried open the crate's top with a shimmy bar lying on the top. The sergeant pulled off the oiled tarp used to protect one McLellan saddle and several bridles, leads, pads, and small white-cotton bags filled with leather tools, cleaners, and one labeled O&M in three-inch block black letters.

Out of curiosity, Sergeant Gigeurre put the O&M bag to his nose and took a whiff. He mumbled, "Aye. The Yank brought molasses and oats. Maybe for special occasions." He chuckled as he placed the small bags into a large toad sack.

He hauled the gear and stowed it in the truck's rear storage compartments. When he returned to the dock, he looked at Tough Guy and Jubal and proclaimed, "Now it is your turn, boys." The sergeant approached the nearest big black stallion. "Aye, you a big'n. 'Suspect you can cover some ground, ole boy."

Jubal overhead the comment and snorted. "Dad, he obviously does not know how old you are."

"Pipe down, son. I can still get the best of you," Tough Guy snorted back.

The sergeant spoke. "Come on now, you ninnies. Need to get you both loaded up."

Major Hazzard sat in the truck's cab out of the rain, while Sergeant Gigeurre loaded up the truck. He rolled down the driver's-side window and yelled out, "Sergeant, do you need a hand?"

There was silence. The major yelled out again, "Sergeant, do you need some help?"

The sergeant stepped down from the dock and walked over to the side of the truck. He looked at the major. "Major, did you say something?"

"Yes. I was asking if you needed help."

"Aye. Already done. However, it would be a good idea for you to double-check your horses and gear. I sure don't want you thinking something did not make it. We are not coming back here to Dover for some time."

"Good idea, Sergeant."

Major Hazzard opened the passenger door and stepped outside. He ran up the dock loading ramp. Standing behind the truck, he opened the tarp flap to see two large horse rears swishing their tails around. He announced himself. "Coming in, boys. Don't be kick'n."

He slid by Tough Guy's left side, saying, "Okay, boy, coming up on your left." He kept contact with his right hand on Tough Guy while walking toward the front. He opened the overhead cabinet and took inventory of the saddles, leathers, and farrier tools. Satisfied, he turned and walked back to the rear of the truck and out onto the dock.

Now standing on the dock with the major, Sergeant Gigeurre asked, "Everything to your satisfaction, sir?" Major Hazzard nodded, "Yes. Thank you."

"Oh yes. Sir, may I ask what the feed bags are used for?"

The major paused for a moment. "Indeed. Those bags were given to me by these horses' trainer. His name is Mister Jerimiah Bates. He told me that there may be moments when Jubal and Tough Guy might need a little convincing. A handful of oats and molasses will set them straight."

The sergeant shook his head. "Hmm. Hmm—well we best be going major."

*****

Major Oliver Hazzard

Thousands of white army tents dotted the countryside. Driving down from the hill, the major looked across at a massive assembly of artillery, soldiers, and horses. He turned to Sergeant Gigeurre and asked, "How long has your brigade been here?"

"Since October last year."

"How long has your brigade been in garrison?"

The sergeant looked at the major and smirked. "Sir, one of two ways. When the war is over, or when we are all dead." He sighed. A few moments of silence had passed. The sergeant said, "Me apologies, sir. I have lost several friends who transported several of our horses to the front. They were killed within the first week."

Major Hazzard responded in a lower voice, "Sorry to hear that."

The sergeant parked the Crossley at the largest white tent surrounded by temporary-looking wooden structures. A two-by-three-foot sign secured on a mound of dirt marked the brigade's senior officer-in-charge's tent. The white sign with black lettering read "Commanding Officer, Lt. Col. Henri Alexandre." Sergeant Gigeurre ushered the major inside the tent.

Inside, Captain Henry Eversley Boak was standing by a three-foot stack of wooden pallets covered with sackcloth. The crates served as the commander's desk. Colonel Alexandre sat behind the battlefield desk with his knees to the side. Once inside the tent, Major Hazzard took a couple of steps toward the colonel and Captain Boak.

The colonel stood up from his chair. He said, "Welcome major." Now facing the colonel, the major saluted. "Sir, Major Oliver Hazzard, United States Army Second Cavalry Regiment reporting for duty, sir." The colonel returned the salute.

"Please, Major. No need for formalities here in the tent, and especially not on the battlefield. If a Jerry sees a salute, they will drop the poor boy in front of it.

The major returned his hand to his right side.

"Yes, sir. Thank you. I appreciate the warning."

"Major. Please. As you are."

The major relaxed his arms in position. Captain Boak nodded at him and said, "Welcome, major, sir." The major deferred the expected return salute based upon recent guidance and simply accepted the captain's handshake. The captain added, "Sir, welcome to the Royal Canadian Horse Artillery Brigade. We are here at the pleasure of His Majesty King George V."[38]

Major Hazzard replied. "I am here serving at the pleasure of the President of the United States, Woodrow Wilson. He is pleased to honor the King's request." The colonel asserted himself in the conversation. "Major, I take it you brought your own mounts?"

"Yes, sir. I was told to bring two, in case one became unavailable."

The colonel nodded his head. "Very good. We are having a bugger of a time keeping our mounts upright." The colonel looked over at the captain. "Please take care of President Wilson's major during his assignment. I am sure the first thing Mr. Hazzard needs is a dry cot to rest and some warm food." Major Hazzard reached into his black leather satchel. He pulled out a rolled-up sheet of parchment paper and handed it to the colonel. The paper was secured with a blue wax seal embossed with the words "Unites States Army Official Business."

Colonel Alexandre broke the seal and pulled the paper open. It read, "To Royal Canadian Horse Artillery Brigade, Commanding Officer. From United States Army Chief of Staff. Assignment is two years from January 1915." The colonel added, "Let us hope the war does not pervade our existence much longer." He placed the major's orders down on the desk.

Captain Boak looked at the colonel, and then glanced at the sergeant. He ordered, "Sergeant, see to it the major's mounts are transported to quarantine. I will get the major settled in."

The sergeant popped to attention and rendered a salute. "Yes, sir. Where do you want me to drop off his personal effects?"

"Just put them in my tent for now," Sergeant Gigeurre responded with a firm, sharp response. "Aye, sir. My pleasure."

The sergeant saluted again, and then did an about-face. He marched out of the tent, taking long strides.

The captain yelled, "Sergeant! Stop stepping out like those damn Tommies." Captain Boak then turned toward Major Hazzard. "You have to give the old chap some slack. War has a way of making men act oddly."

Captain Boak turned to the colonel. "Sir. Permission to leave." The colonel nodded his head. "Dismissed." The captain looked at the major. "Major Hazzard, sir. Your mounts will need to be cleared by our veterinarian officer. If your horses pass the exams, the handlers will put them into one of the paddocks."

"Sure. I understand the protocol, Captain. Do you know how long they will be in quarantine?"

"Only a day or two. Our vet has to perform several tests on them."

The major's brows furrowed. He asked, "Why the caution? Looks like the worst horses are going to get here are hoof rot."

The captain laughed. "I wish that was the case. There are reports of Germans trying to infiltrate our lines to spread the Glanders virus in the horse supply chain."

The major raised his eyebrows again and said, "How interesting. There was a case in the United States on the East Coast, where a German plot of a similar nature was uncovered."

"Indeed. We are very aware of the sabotaging efforts of sympathetic German Americans. Our British intelligence told your State Department. Fortunately, those Jerrys were eliminated—excuse me, intercepted, before they could infect the horse supply we desperately depend upon."

"Yes. I think those attempts will not be the last. Let us get these horses over to the Q area."

The captain nodded in agreement.

Major Hazzard grasped Jubal Early's halter to double-check the lead connection. Satisfied with the hookup, he led Jubal Early toward the stables, where the quarantine area abutted to the stable's right entrance. Captain Boak gave the major some distance before moving. He pulled on Tough Guy's halter and said, "Okay, boy. We need a good checkup."

Tough Guy neighed. "I feel pretty good. I'm more concerned about my son, Jubal."

The captain leading Jubal added, "Old chap, I do think you and that black stallion in front of us must be related. I need to remember to ask the major."

Suffering in Every Trench

I stopped a Jack Johnson with my head and my skull is slightly cracked. But I am getting on splendidly.[39]

—Captain John Grenfell, British Expeditionary Force
Letter to his mother from a Casualty Clearing Station
Western Front, 1915

Cavalry horses perished by the thousands on the Western Front. Modern military technologies created the demand for replacement horses the British and French armies coveted. It was a romantic notion perhaps. However, the German machine gun was unforgiving to the soldier and his mount.

The mucked trenches wore down the spirits of soldiers, horses, and mules enduring indescribable suffering. War was hell. The need for replacements was a battlefield problem to be solved only by drafting more men to fight. Getting trained horse replacements was not that easy, nor timely. Canada and the United States stepped in to help.

*****

Major Oliver Hazzard

Major Hazzard awoke to sharpened bugle played by a British chap standing too close to the officer's tents. He played with great enthusiasm. The player should have been performing his duty outside the brigade's common area.

Rubbing his eyes, Hazzard mumbled to himself. "Need some coffee. Not that instant George stuff." The major looked up at the tent ceiling and could see dawn's faint light piercing through the worn tent seams. Just enough light to contrast between large objects stowed in his tent. Space was limited, considering he shared his tent with another officer.

The major's roommate slept on a cot twenty feet away, exhaling a squall of heavy snoring. The major whispered to himself, "My first two weeks in country and I end up with a snorer. When do I get my own tent?" Pushing the olive-green wool blanket aside, he sat up and pulled one leg around to find the cold wooden pallets buffering mud from the occupants. He whispered to himself, "Dang pallets got splinters. Where are my slippers? Where are my smokes?"

Major Hazzard reached up and pulled his civilian shirt off a hanger—one of many affixed to wire ties securing the tent canvass to its wooden frame. The Woodbine cigarette pack fell into his left hand. He whispered, "God is good." He flipped open the pack and shook out a butt. He kept a book of matches conveniently tucked inside the cigarette box. Within seconds of striking the match, he held the flame to the cigarette end—or fag, as the British called them. He puffed until the fag's tip glowed red. He took a few more puffs before standing up. The nicotine quickly worked its way into his brain.

The overcast sky diminished the rising sun's light. The major did not want to strike a lamp too soon, fearing he would bring unwanted outside attention to his self-serving intentions. The best thing to do was to stand up and slowly move about to stretch. He planted both feet on the pallet and grimaced from the pinewood's cold touch. Shoes were needed. He sat back down.

The major reached underneath his cot, trying to locate his leather slippers. Eventually, his fingers found one sheep-wool–lined slipper, then the other. He slipped each on his cold feet and sighed. "Nothing like a pair of sheepskin slippers." He wiggled his toes to ensure the fleece was snug around his toes and mumbled, "The Brits know how to make a good pair of slippers."

Major Hazzard stood up and stretched out his arms above his head and yawned. On the other side of the tent, British officer Captain Henry Boak soundly slept. Disregarding the captain's deep sleep, the major shuffled over to the tent's center and lit the oil lamp hanging down from the tent's high-cross ties.

Leather to Steel

He shook the lamp to listen and feel for fuel inside. Satisfied, he grasped the lamp's brass pump plunger to create pressure within its fuel reservoir. He slipped up the glass housing to access the pilot hole. He struck a match and lit the oil-soaked wick. After he had adjusted the flame's volume knob, the light steadied in the tent.

The major stepped over to the captain's bunk. He placed his right hand on the captain's left shoulder and gave him a good shake. The captain turned over in his cot and grunted. The major whispered, "Time to get up, Mr. Boak."

The captain pulled his pillow over his head and groaned. "What time is it?"

"Time for you to get up, mister. Revile was five minutes ago."

The consummate professional, Captain Boak quickly sat up. "Come again?"

"Revile just sounded off. Judging from your snoring, I am afraid you would not have woken up. Too much ale consumption last eve Mister Boak?"

"Yes, sir. I had a jolly good time at the pub last night. Now I will pay for it. Too much to do today. What was I thinking." The major did not respond. He just chuckled at his young sponsor.

Boak's rank of captain earned himself the charge of the Royal Canadian Horse Artillery Brigade administrative affairs for what the men affectionately called the Rock HAB. Captain Boak loved his work. Always willing to please, the captain tirelessly toiled to ensure Lieutenant General E. A. Alderson and his senior officers were kept informed of administrative matters.

His additional duty of assimilating Major Hazzard to English customs and military protocol was his least stressful assignment as a sponsor. His preferred duty took advantage of his love for the regiment's horses. The captain took great pride in supervising quartermaster supply and support for the several hundred dedicated Canadian soldiers and British horses assigned to the Rock HAB.

Major Hazzard's duty assignment would be much different than that of Captain Boak's. The United States Army responded to a request from King George V to President Wilson. Within weeks of notification, the army hastily deployed several mid-grade officers to

Europe to observe ally and enemy military operations on the Western Front. The major was one of several dozen officers selected to perform that function as a military liaison officer.

Like most officers selected, Major Hazzard was chosen because of his distinguished military service record. However, it did not hurt to have his upper-class family's political ties to President Wilson. Friendly political connections ushered in his European assignment. The American class system was alive and well after the U.S. Civil War.

Through official British eyes, Major Hazzard and his two mounts, Tough Guy and Jubal Early, were only there for show-and-tell. However, the major knew better. His assignment was much more than riding sidesaddle with the Canadians and the British. His real job was to collect intelligence on the enemy and report back to the U.S. Army's General Black Jack Pershing. The general sensed the war would expand and eventually include the United States military on the ground. The general was smart enough to know early intelligence drove preparation.

Major Hazzard sat back down on the edge of his bunk to finish smoking his fag. He inhaled one long drag after the other. The last puff provided entertainment. He blew a grayish-white smoke circle across the tent and said, "Captain, are you awake?" The circle settled over the captain's head.

Sitting up on his cot, Captain Boak rubbed his eyes. Yawning, he entwined his fingers and cracked his knuckles. He replied, "Yes, sir. I am good. Thank you for asking. I consumed a bit too much drink last night at the pub—what! Mary, Joseph, and Jesus. Am I in heaven?" The smoke circle looked like a halo. It dissipated.

"Relax, Captain. Just a smoke circle."

The captain sighed with relief. "For a moment, I thought I had died and gone to heaven. Major, I am surprised you are up early and so chipper this morning, sir. You were bending the elbow as much as I."

"Captain, I feel fine. Drank with plenty of sailors in my time."

The captain laughed. The major continued, "Now, please remind me. The king's review is scheduled for today, February 4. What is the prescribed uniform of the day?"

Captain Boak lit a fag and inhaled. He blew a perfect smoke ring that rose to the tent's height without breaking form. "Yes, sir. We will muster up after breakfast in the commons. The Rock HAB commander wants all horses and men arrayed down on Salisbury Plain by nine o'clock. King George will arrive promptly at ten o'clock. He and the colonel will be inspecting our troopers."

"Yes, I understand that. What is the uniform of the day?"

"Oh yes, sorry. We are to wear the olive-green winter service dress uniform, or the equivalent for you. I might suggest we get into uniform after checking up on the horse orderlies. They are pretty good about preparing the horses in the morning, but one needs to validate. After that, you and I stroll over to the officer's mess tent to enjoy a spot of tea with breakfast. I think breakfast is—"

The major interrupted. "Captain, I agree. To change the subject, I have been here two weeks. We have not seen the sun once. When does the sun come out around here?"

The captain snickered after taking another drag. "Indeed. It gets a bit dreary here during the winter months. If it is not raining, it is misting well into the spring. However, the summer months can be quit pleasant here on the island."

While the major dressed, he looked at the captain. "I see. Reminds me of the Northwest states back in American."

"A lovely region. Yes."

"Correct. Right on the Pacific. My favorite state is Oregon. Highway 101 runs up and down the coast. When you can visit, we will take a spin up the coast."

Captain Boak nodded. "Thank you for the offer. I read about Oregon in travel magazines. The Northwest—I think it is called—stays green all year while the people rust."

The major paused while buttoning up his blouse. He looked at the captain and grinned. "You might say that. They certainly don't tan." Both men laughed.

The officers spent the next ten minutes getting dressed and self-inspecting their work uniforms. The major looked at Captain Boak and asked, "Are you ready to go?"

The captain brushed off some lint sticking to his front blouse pocket and then pulled his gig line into order. The tucked-in blouse right seam was in line with the right side of his brass belt buckle. The captain stood at attention. "Major, is this gig line straight?"

"You are looking squared away, Mister Boak. Shall we go?"

"Indeed, Major Hazzard."

Stepping outside the tent, the major looked up to the sky. He mumbled to himself, "I will be glad to get back to Virginia, sunshine, and fried chicken."

The captain, staying in step with the major, asked him, "What did you say, sir?"

"Oh, nothing. I was just talking to myself."

"Sir, with all due respect, mumbling to oneself—well, it is not socially permitted here in the Royal Army."

The major looked at the captain and said sarcastically, "Yes. I noticed there is strict adherence to formalities stoically British. My American independence will need some refining."

The captain laughed. "You will catch on. We English have a long history of pomp, circumstance, and dry humor. You might say quiet desperation is the English way."

Major Hazzard slapped the side of his pants. "I reckon so, captain. Americans always adjust to the circumstance, like we did on July 4, 1776. Remember? I suppose we will not get the Fourth of July holiday off in England?"

The captain did not know how to reply. He was searching for words. "Well, sir. I…never thought of it that way. I guess we English have something to learn from you Americans."

"Captain Boak, I am just kidding. Americans have a tendency to embrace levity in the face of adversity."

"I see, sir. But there is only adversity in the trenches. Well, as you said, the English have a dry sense of humor. So if we don't laugh, please do not take it personal, Major."

Leather to Steel

"No worries, Captain. I will take note and remember that when the bombs start falling."

The captain said, "Yes. I suppose those circumstances will bring out the best of us, when it is at its worst."

The major adjusted his hat and turned to the captain. "I like what you just said. Meaning we are at our best when it is at its worst. Very good. I will write that down in my diary."

"Sir, please follow me over to the stables. We need to double-time over to the stables and check in with the quartermaster farrier. A delightful chap, Sergeant McIntyre. He does a bang-up job shoeing the horses. He changed up the shoes on Jubal and Tough Guy."

*****

Captain Boak and the major walked a half mile over three muddy roads and a soaked parade field to reach the horse training complex. The army engineers built four stables capable of housing one hundred and twenty horses. A small veterinarian clinic was built next to Stable One. The engineers constructed Building B between Stables Two and Three to house the blacksmith-farrier and tack shops. The idea of which was to make it easier for grooms and farrier to access tack and shoes. Two paddocks were built behind the stables to accommodate daily horse training.

It took ten minutes for the captain and the major to reach Building B. Standing at the main door entrance, the major said, "Interesting. Captain, I have been contemplating during our trek. What was wrong with the shoes on my horses?"

"Well, sir, the terrain around here can get a bit sticky. We devised a lighter horseshoe that is as durable as the old iron shoes, but has better traction in the muck."

"I think, captain, what works best is ensuring each hoof is trimmed to retain its balanced vertical and horizontal orientation to the ground."

"Yes, sir. That is important. However, the flat-bottom design does not bode well in the mud. Angular edges are filed on the shoe's bottom. This gives the horse better traction."

The major rubbed his chin. "Makes sense to me."

Once the officers walked inside Stable 1, the major's horses began neighing loudly. The captain commented, "Your horses must smell you coming."

Major Hazzard replied, "It is the uniform. Virginian sheep wool was used to make army winter uniforms. Virginia is their home. Perhaps they smell home, or the oats I have in my pants pockets."

The major stood in between Tough Guy and Jubal's stalls. Both horses acknowledged his presence. Major Hazzard extended his right hand to rub Jubal's nose. He said, "How was your evening, Jubal?"

Jubal neighed back and nodded his head up and down.

The captain observed, "Now, I can't believe your horse understood what you said."

"Captain, Jubal, and Tough Guy clearly understand me." The major extended his left hand over to the next stall and rubbed Tough Guy's nose. He asked, "And how are you doing this morning, mister?"

Tough Guy neighed and snorted, affirming Jubal's sentiments. The captain looked at the major and asked, "Since your arrival, I have wondered, are these horses related?"

"Yes." While touching Tough Guy's silver whiskers, the major added. "Captain, this fella is the descendant of a great warhorse. His father, Stonewall, served on America's western frontier carrying troopers to fight the Comanche and other renegade tribes. Fighting runs in his blood. Stonewall's father fought in the U.S. Civil War—on the wrong side, I might add.

The captain inquired, "What do you mean by the wrong side?"

"The South. The losing side. The states that sold cotton to your country."

"Do you mean the Confederate States of America?"

The major looked at the captain with a raised eyebrow and said, "I see you are a student of military history."

"Yes, sir, I am. As a matter of Royal British Officer training, we are instructed in cavalry battlefield tactics used by the greatest horsemen from around the world—both past and present. In the case of the U.S. Civil War, that cavalryman was called Jubal Early

Leather to Steel

Bedford Stewart, or Jeb Stewart for short. The same man your mount here is named after. Yes?"

Major Hazzard sighed. "Well, I suppose one should not correct history. General Stewart was known to win a few cavalry battles. In particular, the largest cavalry engagement during the Civil War—the Battle of Brandy Station."

Captain Boak added, "You mentioned that Tough Guy's father was called Stonewall. General Stonewall Jackson was another—"

"Please stop there, Captain. I get your point."

The captain nodded his head. "Very well, sir. Shall we take them out to the paddock?"

"Yes. They need a good lunging before they eat. Captain, I am curious. Where do you stable your horse?"

"Daisy is penned with the other drafts in the north stable, Stable Three. Nearest to the artillery limbers. Makes it easier to hook the light drafts up for training."

"Say again? What kind of horse did the army issue to you?"

"The army did not issue Daisy to me. All of our cavalrymen and artillery had to beg and borrow from the locals. We were not permitted to bring our Canadian horses over to here. There was fear the German U-boats would torpedo our transport ships. Better to only lose the men and save the horses."

"I have surmised the English adore their horses. In any case, what breed is she?"

"Daisy is a beautiful rough-haired blond, light draught horse I acquired her from a farmer living near here. She is fifteen hands high and weighs about twelve hundred pounds."

"Captain, what do you use her for?"

"She serves many different roles for the regiment. She has shorter, strong muscular legs that are ideal for pulling wagons to carry supplies and munitions. If the occasion presents itself, she will serve as an ambulance to transport injured soldiers from the front to aid stations, when the lorries get bogged down in the mud. If need be, she can also pull light artillery limbers by herself, or in teams. Major, our draught horses are the backbone of the British Expeditionary Force."

"Captain, as they are in the United States Army."

"Here, here. Well said! I would only add to that a dash of the real warhorse's instincts to make 'em perfect."

"What warhorse are you referring?"

"Yes. Sorry. *Warrior*. Warrior is Lieutenant Colonel Jack Seeley's battle horse. They recently rode into camp back on January 30. You just missed them."

> Excerpt from Official Royal Canadian Horse Artillery Brigade War Diary. On January 30, 1915 the diary reads, "Routine work. Half holiday. Visited by new Bgd. Commander LtCol. Seeley... Weather fine."

"Major, I am sure you will have a chance to meet Colonel Seeley and Warrior during your stay. The colonel stays mobile between the Western Front and headquarters. A true cavalryman he is. They say he is up for promotion. I am sure he will be awarded command of the Canadian cavalry regiment soon."

"Thanks for the information, captain. I will keep my eye out for 'em."

The major made a clucking sound. He called out, "Come on, Jubal. Let us go show the good captain your good battle instincts."

The captain followed behind. He tugged on Tough Guy's lead and clucked. "Come on, mister. You too."

Tough Guy stood his ground at first. The major added, "Come on Tough Guy. Don't be stubborn. I reckon you have something to say about that as well." Tough Guy neighed and kicked out.

The captain looked back and yelled out, "Hold on, mister. You can strut your stuff once we are in the paddock."

The officers led Tough Guy and Jubal out through the back side of the stable into the paddock. The horse's leads were disconnected from the halters. Now free, Jubal and Tough Guy ran together toward the opposite side of the paddock. They stopped to face each other. Both kept their necks in high carriage.

The captain noticed the proper stance and form. He turned to Major Hazzard and commented, "I beg your pardon, sir. Are your horses trained in dressage?"

"Captain, you are correct. Both were professionally schooled back at the U.S. Army remount depots. Strike that—both were schooled at President Roosevelt's horse farm in Virginia. From there, they were transferred to the U.S. Army to perform Mother Nature's job. Jubal and Tough Guy continued dressage training while attached to the depots."

The captain said, "European tradition requires cavalry horses to be schooled in dressage. A technique used for hundreds of years. How interesting it is to know Americans recognized the training method."

"I am sold on the training. Our remount depots are producing some of the best cavalry horses the army quartermaster has acquired since the birth of our nation."

"How did you end up with both horses?"

"Long story, Mister Boak. I will save that story for another time. Perhaps when we are stuck in a trench on the Western Front?"

The captain shook his head is disagreement. "I do hope not."

Jubal and Tough Guy neighed back and forth, jerking their heads from side to side. Tough Guy made the first move. Using his front shoulder, he took two steps to nudge Jubal against the pole fence. Jubal responded with a twisted left rear kick out that barely missed Tough Guy's nose.

The captain and the major quickly traversed the paddock. They split into opposite directions to draw attention of the horses. The major whistled. Then he yelled out, "Knock it off, Jubal."

The captain made his way along the pole fence to within ten feet of Tough Guy, who had reared up on his hind legs. The captain clapped his hands and then commanded, "Down. Down."

Tough Guy quickly complied. The captain secured the lead to Tough Guy's halter and led him to the center of the paddock.

The major walked Jubal to the center of the paddock and stopped twenty feet from Tough Guy. The captain observed, "Well, looks like we have some assimilation to do with your horses. I suspect they need some exercise."

"They were pretty good before the ship voyage. I think being cramped up for two weeks at sea has made them a little feisty."

"Major, we have seen that behavior many times. Shipments of horses coming from American and Canada are coming in on a weekly basis. Some harbor-fever phenomena spreads across the herd in the ship's cargo hold. Like sailors, it takes a couple of weeks for them to get their land legs back—and their sensibilities."

"Captain, that is an interesting point. It never would have occurred to me. I thought their rude behavior was because Tough Guy is Jubal's sire."

The captain spat on the ground and proclaimed, "I knew it. I knew there was something common between those black boys. The only difference between them is the odd-looking brand on Tough Guy's left flank." The captain moved toward Tough Guy's rear quarter and rubbed the raised magnolia brand.

Running his fingers over the raised brand, the captain asked, "Major, what is this symbol supposed to represent? I see a tree with a quarter moon above it."

"Mister Boak. The brand represents a Southern family's economic past prior and during the U.S. Civil War. The brand originated at the Magnolia Plantation located just outside Charleston, South Carolina."

"Why does not Jubal have the brand?"

"I don't know. I never knew the story until I was told by a horse trainer who worked at the U.S. Army's regional remount depot in Front Royal, Virginia. Evidently, this old fella served with a Buffalo Soldier who worked at the plantation. An interesting story."

"Major, what is a Buffalo Soldier?"

"Well, if we are ever sitting in a muddy trench, you will tell the story in between bombardments." Both men laughed. The horses stopped neighing. The brief moment of silence was broken by distant echoes of explosions. The men's smiles quickly changed to a look of thin-lipped soldiers who understood the battlefields were not far away.

Tough Guy and Jubal

While the major and captain chatted in the paddock's center, Jubal neighed at Tough Guy, "Father. Why did they separate us? You were just showing me an opposing horse's push-move on the battlefield. I responded like you taught me."

Tough Guy raised his head and arched his neck. He snorted at Jubal and neighed, "Son. I think the major and the captain perceived us as fighting, which is why they separated us. I am not sure what they meant by us feeling the effects of harbor fever. I've never felt any better."

Jubal and Tough Guy walked toward each other, straining the lead lines held by the major and captain. Captain Boak made one wrap around his hands. The major did the same. The captain said, "Looks like they want to go at it again."

The officers dug their riding boot heels in the dirt. Surprisingly, the fight did not transpire. Both Jubal and Tough Guy lowered their front right legs to the ground toward each other. The captain and the major looked at each other, shaking their heads. The major concluded, "Captain, it looks like we have some schooling to do on our own. These horses are showing respect to one another. I was wrong about them."

"Apparently, we overreacted pulling them apart. They are now showing us how smart they are."

"These horses never cease to amaze me. I hope they sustain the same clearness of mind, should we ever see battle."

The major and the captain released the leads.

Tough Guy snorted at Jubal. "You see, son, our troopers will connect with us better with more saddle time on our backs. Their lives—stop. Our lives depend upon horse and rider working together. That is what your grandfather, Stonewall, told me."

"Do you think we will see battle?"

"Son, I hope not. But if we do, we will be ready."

The major and the captain connected the leads to take the horses back to the stables. While walking back, the captain asked the major, "Have you been in battle?"

The major kicked a dirt clod on the ground. He stopped and looked at the captain. "Yes, I would prefer not to talk about it."

The captain nodded to abide by the major's wishes. They resumed walking. Once inside the stable, the horse walked into their stalls on their own.

After shutting the stall doors, the captain looked at his watch, then at the major. "Major, the mess tent is still serving breakfast. Are you famished? We have time to eat and get a hot cup of George, as you Americans say."

The major hung the lead over Jubal's stall door. He turned to the captain and replied. "Chow sounds good. What are they serving?"

The captain frowned, giving the appearance of one who did not know. He answered, "Well, sir, pretty much the same thing we eat every day—fried bread and oats."

"Well then, Captain," the major asserted, "let us go get some friend bread and oats. Perhaps they will have some brown sugar on hand."

The captain recognized the major's levity. "Indeed. Perhaps the old mess cooks came up with something new. At least it will be hot."

The major nodded in agreement.

*****

Tough Guy and Jubal

While the officers pursued breakfast, Corporal Strain and several other saddlers tacked us up in preparation for the king's review. The corporal took charge of dressing me out. Jubal stuck his head out of his stall. Looking left, he watched me tethered down by crossties in the center aisle, while the corporal brushed off the mud from my coat. Corporal Strain hummed an upbeat soldier's hymn. I neighed at Jubal. "Sounds like he is in a good mood."

"He is cheery just like me right now." Shaking his head up and down, Jubal continued, "I don't have to stand out in the middle of the parade ground for hours on end. I remember how it was back at the Oklahoma depot. The depot commander, Captain Hardeman, frequently paraded us around for the politicians."

"Jubal. You got the next royal review. I think I might throw a shoe just before the event."

"Now, Dad, that is not the spirit you taught me."

"You are right. But I did teach you not to put yourself in a situation you are not the primary beneficiary."

Jubal neighed and snorted loudly in response. The corporal picked Tough Guy's front hooves looked up. He bellowed, "Now you boys knock off the jabber. I am trying to concentrate here."

Both Tough Guy and Jubal shook their heads up and down, and snorted.

*****

Major Oliver Hazzard

At the parade field, all mounted officers lined up in the front row. While King George V rode by, each soldier would raise their swords to solute the king and his royal party. When the king reached Major Hazzard's position, he raised his right hand to halt the procession. The king and the Royal Canadian Horse Artillery Brigade commander, Lieutenant Colonel Henri Alexandre, turned their mounts toward the major. The king reined in his mount and stopped within one length of Tough Guy's nose. Colonel Alexandre did the same, careful to stay a one-half horse length behind King George V.

King George asked Major Hazzard, "Who are you, mister?"

The major was about to speak, but the colonel quickly asserted himself. "Your Highness, this is Major Oliver Hazzard. He is an American officer assigned to our brigade."

"Very good. I offered President Wilson the opportunity to embed military officers within our military services—restricted to observer roles, of course."

"Your Highness, Major Hazzard is—"

King George held his left hand up toward the colonel, who stopped talking. The king added, "Colonel Alexandre, I am sure Major Hazzard can speak."

The major fought off the urge to smile. With a straight face, the major extended an approving look toward the colonel to ensure no ill feelings were at play. Major Hazzard then looked King George in the eye. "Sir—I mean, Your Highness, it is the pleasure of the United States Army that I serve. I am honored with the opportunity to serve his Royal Highness's army." The major bowed his head.

The king replied, "Major, please pass my regards to your President Wilson. I am sure he will send more liaison officers at some point, I believe. Or should I say—after England pays her freight."[40]

The king's humor went unnoticed by the major.

The major squeezed Tough Guy's side and tapped his withers twice. Tough Guy lowered his left knee to the ground to give the appearance of bowing before King George.

The king commented, "To receive such formal reverence from a horse. Major, you and your horse may be at ease."

The major tapped Tough Guy's withers once, while gently squeezed with his legs. Tough Guy rose back up into a high carriage form.

The king commented, "Major, you have a fine-looking horse. What is his name?"

"Your Highness, his name is Tough Guy. He is a Thoroughbred and warm blood mix."

"I see. Very well, Major. I would like to give him a go someday."

King George turned his mount to resume his inspection. Once the king was two lengths ahead, the colonel looked at the major. "Very good, Major. Well done. Thank you."

The colonel looked at Tough Guy. "And thank you, old boy. Very impressive."

*****

King George's review finished just before noon. Once the king and his royal party departed, Lieutenant Colonel Alexandre dismissed the soldiers to resume their daily routine work schedule.

Captain Boak and Major Hazzard rode back together to the stables. Major Hazzard turned to the captain and asked, "Why did the colonel speak on my behalf, at first?"

"Major, he was doing you a favor."

"What do you mean?"

"Did you really know how to address King George?"

The major hesitated and said, "Well…no. I guess not. I did pick up on the 'Your Highness' part."

"There you go, sir. You learned a bit more of English customs."

"Captain, I suppose you are right. I learned how to drink warm beer, eat fried bread, and say Your Highness. I am off to a good start."

The captain added, "Not only are you off to a good start, your charge performed an amazing gesture for the king, who was clearly pleased. Now enough of this protocol debrief. Let us get these horses back to the stables. Corporal Strain said the men made final preparations of the mud shoots. Time for the horses to get their workouts."

Arriving at the stables, the stable handlers received the horses. The major and the captain dismounted and started walking back to their tent. The major asked. "Are you hungry? I am ready for dinner."

The captain contemplated a response. He raised his right finger. "Major, I am starting to think you like English food."

The major agreed. "You bet. Much better than the dried food we ate on patrol in Mexico."

The captain's eyes furrowed. He said, "Mexico."

The major replied, "Sorry. Another story for the trenches."

The officers continued riding.

*****

The European war extended beyond the battle lines drawn amongst kings and men. Countries not beholden to either the Triple Alliance, or Triple Entente, could be bought. Germany, in particular swayed Turkey with promises of new borders in the Balkans. Britain pushed through Middle East countries to deny Germany access to resources. Treaties were struck along the way. The war, in fact, grew into a complicated exchange and promises of wealth, land, and political power that stressed civilians around the world.

Broken European borders divided families and traditions in America. German Americans' loyalty to America became targets of discriminating harassments. To some degree, first-generation German Americans were torn. Some attempted to return to the Fatherland and fight. Others denounced Germany's actions, wanting only to be left alone during the war. Some Americans chose neither side, wanting only to provide humanitarian assistance to all of God's suffering children. Such was the case with the Eilenberg family back in Virginia.

*****

The Eilenbergs

Kate Eilenberg's nightmares became more frequent during the winter. Max could not understand why she had become emotionally distant in their marriage. Little did Max know, his wife Kate had suffered a traumatic experience growing up in Texas. Kate insisted Lucinda never mention the killing to Max. What Kate kept private for years affected her intimacy with Max. The distance grew wider the day after the doctor informed Kate she could not have children. She did not have the courage to tell Max about her barren womb, nor could she tell him about her traumatic experience as a child.

Kate tried to forget that awful day the Comanche raided her home in Littleton Springs, Texas. The Comanche depredations took her mother's life and her father's hope. The screams, smells, and touch of dirty Indian hands never left Kate's mind. Subconscious self-preservation conveniently tucked away the horrid memories. She mastered denial to function in life. The idea of not having children opened the gates to the past.

To escape, Kate convinced Lucinda to serve with her as volunteer aid detachment (VAD) nurse on the Western Front. Train and ship transportation arrangements were confirmed for an April departure. Both convinced their husbands it was the right thing to do. Men and horses were suffering. They had the skills to relieve their pains. However, the unpredictable nature of life interviewed. The day before their departure, Kate found out she would have to travel alone. Lucinda would not be going.

Kate and Lucinda sat in their special chairs under the old oak tree. The tea and crumb cakes on the tray had yet to be consumed. Lucinda took Kate's hand. "Before we begin our weekly gossip session, I want to share some good and bad news with you. You know we have been like sisters forever. Always will be. I love you like a sister. I have some good news to tell you that I have not told Manny."

Kate saw a twitch of a smile on Lucinda's face. Holding her right finger up to her own lips, she jokingly asked. "Let us see, sister. You can't be smiling because you and Manny have to plow the farm next week? It can't be because you are baking ten pies for the church potluck tomorrow? Okay. How about you got our tickets from the British Embassy?"

"Sorry, Kate. None of those. The most blessed news comes from my doctor. He said I am pregnant. Finally, after all these years, Manny and I are going to have a baby." Kate's smile faded, in its place a sincere grin.

"Oh. I don't understand. Excuse me. How terrible of me. Congratulations. I am so happy for you both. But...I thought you were like me—could never pregnant?"

"Kate. It is a miracle. We are just thanking God."

Lucinda paused for a few moments. Then she reached for Kate's hands. Tears welled up in Kate's eyes. Lucinda spoke softly. "But you must know now, I cannot go with you next week to England. You will have to go alone."

Holding Lucinda's hand, Kate kept a brave smile on. "Of course not! We have to go shopping for some baby clothes. I am so happy for you and Manny. When does the doctor think the baby is due?"

"He says I am three months along. I thought pregnant women get morning sickness every day. That never happened to me. Instead, I spotted some and knew that was not normal. The spotting is what got me to the doctor's office. I never told Manny. I did not want to get him upset." Kate squeezed Lucinda's hand.

"So now you are going to be a momma! I am so excited for you. I love you, Lucinda." Tears started falling from her face. Lucinda reached over to grab Kate's other hand. "I know you are happy for me, but those tears come from something else. What is going on?"

Kate wiped her eyes. "No, I am fine. Just so happy for you and Manny. So when is the baby due?"

"Doctor says just in time for Thanksgiving."

"Could not have picked a better day, sister. That is close to my own birthday, which is November 20. Mark my words. I will make sure I am back in time to help you during the birthing. You know how men can be such big babies."

Lucinda looked into Kate's bloodshot eyes. "You know…maybe you should not go alone to England."

Kate remained silent for a few seconds to think. "Lucinda, I have to go on without you. The trip was not so much about us showing women are just as brave as men can be on the battlefields. It was also for me to get away. You know Max and I have been having a time of it. The nightmares came back. Our intimacy has suffered. I have not told him we cannot have children. That was just one more stake into the cellar door."

"Kate, everything will be fine for you both. Keep praying."

"I do. But some days are harder than others. I wake up sweating and crying in the middle of the night. Max does not know what to do. I am unable to tell him about the Comanche raid when I was a little girl. I can't revisit those moments I desperately want to forget."

Lucinda did not reply. They sat silently drinking their black tea and just being together.

*****

Kate sat at the kitchen table with Max. They had just finished eating the week's leftovers; Saturday supper family tradition. Max took a sip of his nightly toddy of scotch whiskey. He glanced at Kate, and then back to his drink. He said, "Kate. What is wrong? You have been different lately? Can I help you Ehefrau?"

Kate replied, "Please look at me."

Leather to Steel

He slowly lifted his head. Kate's sad green eyes locked onto his. She remained collected while speaking calmly to her husband. "The war needs skilled women like me who have nursing skills. I must go on without Lucinda. She is with child now."

Max protested, "But darl'n. You are a woman. Going by herself. That would not be proper!"

"Max, I think *proper* can give way to saving soldier's lives. Besides, there are few nurses to take care of the boys fighting for us. You know I was trained as a nurse at the University of Texas. I even know how to doctor horses."

"I remember that school'n."

"You know that is what Lucinda and I learned to do. Those skills have saved lives here. They will save lives over there."

"But, Kate, I just don't think you should go by yourself. I would go with you, but the business can't be left alone. You know that," Max pleaded.

Kate's red face softened. She took a deep breath. "Mr. Max Eilenberg, I love you. This is the other truth. This trip is more than just about saving lives. It is about saving our marriage. I have some things to work out—she reached out to grab Max's hand—"which has nothing to do with you. Trust me."

Max tried to rub out the tension in the back of his neck. He relaxed, then took a deep breath and talked softly. "The nightmares. Your dreams have been waking you up in the middle of the night. I know. I lay there and watch you, praying they would go away." Kate lowered her chin and then lifted her eyes back up to Max. "That is my business. None for you to be concerned about."

Max did not appreciate Kate's irritable tone of voice. He was simply trying to comfort her. He abruptly sat back in his chair. He elevated his voice. "Go then. You need to go. But promise me one thing: Send me a cable every week letting me know you are alive. I can wire you money when you need it. I love you, Kate."

Kate closed her eyes and took three deep breaths. When she opened her eyes, she saw Max had stood up and was walking out of the kitchen. She got up and attempted to follow him, but then hesitated. She let him go.

One week later, Kate boarded the passenger train scheduled for a morning seven o'clock departure from the Richmond Main Street Station. She and Max did not part on pleasant terms. She hoped Max would accompany her to the platform. Since he was still angry, Max was undecided how to see her off. He simply opened the door for her and got back into his car.

Kate made her way to the station platform carrying one bag. She showed her train ticket to the conductor. He pointed her to the first-class car where fancy people were sipping coffee and smoking big cigars. Once on board, she found her window seat. She stored her bag up in the overhead. Once settled in her seat, Kate resisted looking through the horizontal sliding window.

She could not resist the urge. She quickly glanced to see the platform filling up with well-wishers. Eventually, there were dozens of people standing on the platform waving good-bye to their loved ones, families, and friends. Kate periodically glanced out of curiosity. Then she saw him. A tall, good-looking man standing near the end of the platform. He smiled at Kate. Max took off his Fedora hat and bowed his head toward her. He mouthed the words, *I love you, Kate.* He then placed the hat back on his head and waved good-bye.

Kate sat back in her seat and cried tears of joy.

The train conductor yelled out. "All aboard!" A few seconds later, the main engine released steam from its undercarriage. The train slowly lurched forward, pulling three passenger cars and ten flat cars loaded up with crates stenciled with large block letters: PROPERTY OF U.S. ARMY.

Kate's love for her husband overruled her stubborn Irish blood. She slid back the window and yelled out, "I love you, Max! I will write you once I am in England!"

Max's German blue eyes widened. He grinned at Kate. "I will wait for you!"

Kate wiped away the tears running down her cheeks. Max threw kisses to her as the train left.

The train soon picked up full speed on the track going north. Kate pulled a white lacy handkerchief from her purse. She carefully wiped away the tears from under her eyes and cheeks. She mumbled to herself, "Focus. Focus. Focus. I am on my way. Within five hours, final destination—New York Grand Central Station."

She looked down at her blue-gored skirt and brushed down its pleats. She whispered to herself, "Oh goodness. I do hope what I am wearing is proper." Kate wore her favorite dress with a wide black leather waster belt. The skirt's length ran to just above her ankles. She was wearing a warm peach-colored, button-down cashmere sweater to compliment the blue. The sweater was very special to Kate. Max had given it to her last Christmas. He told her it was imported from France. She always wanted to see France. The fashion capital of the world. She mumbled, "If the Germans don't bomb it."

In her luggage bag, she packed a minimum amount of personal effects, per the recommendation of the official British Red Cross papers she received in the mail. The written communication provided a list of recommend items to bring, stating that personal hygiene supplies were scarce in England. The war was already diminishing the availability of goods.

The five-hour trip gave Kate time to commit her orders to memory. She read and reread each piece of parchment paper. The official blue British Royal Seal occupied the letter's top center margin. The directions read, "Once at the New York Grand Central Station, meet British Red Cross representative, Misses Marie Kelly, at the Grand Central Station main ticket office." She tucked the orders back into her purses. Until then, the train ride to New York gave Kate time to reflect on Max.

Max and Kate's marital circumstances were not devoid of love, but empty of a child she could not conceive. Max's German heritage reinforced his demands for having a baby boy. But neither sex would be an option for the childless couple. Instead, Kate would satisfy her nurturing nature during the Great War.

Max was not the only person she left. Sadly, Kate had to say good-bye to her best friend Lucinda. The one and only person who understood why Kate had to leave. The friend who stood by her over many years. Lucinda Zapata creatively protested the idea of Kate's lone journey. However, she understood Kate's reasons. Reasons that haunted Kate since she was the little girl swooped up from the ground and tied to the back of a Comanche mustang. Nevertheless, Kate was determined, stubborn, and rarely uncompromising.

*****

Kate's prospective voyage to Europe would be the second time she would cross the Atlantic to a new life. The last time she sailed was back in 1872 when Kate and her family emigrated from Ireland to the United States. She was a very happy toddler then. But that changed in Texas. The day she and her brother escaped and hid from the Comanche warriors.

*****

The train pulled into the station platform on time. Kate stepped down from the train's last passenger car onto a newly constructed Grand Central Station platform. She looked for signs to the upper levels, anything with directions. Before stepping toward one of three exit signs, a middle-aged train conductor appeared from her right. He almost startled her. With his hand extended, he asked, "Madam. May I." Kate grinned and nodded.

"Of course." She took his hand to help keep her balanced while stepping over a serrated metal strip. She released the conductor's hand. "Thank you. I appreciate the assistance." She took a few steps toward the center off the platform and stood in bewilderment. The station was so expansive. Several tracks came in and out. Several exits and entrances were not well lit.

The conductor noticed she was in need of directions. He yelled out over several noisy train engines and squealing brakes. "Madam, can I assist you with directions? I see you are not sure which way to take."

Kate yelled back, "Yes, I need to meet a group of people at the station's main ticket office. Where do I go?"

"Lifting his right hand, the conductor pointed toward the green-lighted exit lamp to the right. "That way, madam."

Kate replied, "Thank you. I appreciate it."

Leather to Steel

Kate gripped her handbag and hurriedly walked toward the green exit sign. She mumbled to herself. "Here we go."

Standing at the station's ticket office, Kate noticed several other women milling about near the passenger waiting area. Several wooden benches separated the ticket counters from a waiting area occupied by women chatting about a prospective voyage. Kate overheard them. She spoke aloud, "Must be in the right place. What are the odds of a few women talking about a voyage to England here at Grand Central?"

Kate identified a large sign hanging above the glass-enclosed office. The sign read, Main Ticket Office in bold white letters. She was in the right place. Now all she had to do was keep an eye out for the Ms. Kelly.

Kate stood alone by the office window for about twenty minutes. She directed herself. "Better go ask the women. Or maybe, maybe I am in the wrong spot." She took one step toward the benches. A tall redheaded woman approached her. "Excuse me, miss. Are you meeting up with the British Red Cross contingent?"

Kate breathed a sigh of relief. She extended her hand to the stranger. "Yes, yes. My name is Kate Eilenberg. I was beginning to think I had missed the boat—literally speaking, of course."

The redhead confirmed, "No worries. You are at the right place. My name is Marie Kelly."

Marie held a clipboard close to her face. She used her right index finger to scan the list of names. Talking to herself, she whispered. "See here. I have Aitkin, Anderson, uhm…here you are. Kate Eilenberg." Marie looked at Kate. "If you will, I need to confirm your identity. May I please see your passport."

Kate reached into her purse and produced her passport.

The young woman took the passport and read the specifics. She handed the passport back to Kate. "On behalf of the British War Office and the Red Cross, we are grateful for your selfless willingness to care for those who are in need. My name is Marie Kelly. Miss Marie Kelly. Please address me as Marie."

Kate slid her passport back into her purse and replied, "Thank you, Marie. I am looking forward to the journey."

The British Red Cross volunteers taxied together over to the New York Harbor Port Terminal. It was May 1, 1915. Her transportation would set sail just before evening. During the ride over, Kate reread her orders. The transport ship would dock in Liverpool, England, on or about May 8.

Sitting next to Marie in the taxi, Kate asked, "Are you from Ireland?"

"Why, yes. How could you tell?

"I happen to be from Ireland myself. My family and I immigrated over to the States back in 1872. We were from the Port of Cork City, Ireland."

"We must be related." Marie chuckled, and Kate laughed with her.

*****

Marie, Kate, and eight other women volunteers stood on the ship's fantail looking across the New York harbor. White smoke billowed from four aligned black smokestacks protruding from the ship's centerline. Looking over the side, Kate watched the dockworkers cast off the mooring lines. The ship's crew stood on the forward and aft main decks pulling in the lines.

On the bridge, the ship's captain, William Thomas Turner, ordered four whistles blown. Free from the pier, the Canard Ocean Liner was under way. Within a few hours, she was beyond view of the eastern coast. The crew, passengers, and the secret cargo were assured a smooth sail. At least until May 7.

The volunteers got to know each other during the first few days under way. Since following seas bode well for smooth sailing, their favorite past time was spent lounging on the main deck. The crew put out dozens of lounge chairs lined up amidships on the leeward side. The women were provided blankets to stay warm and dry in case of errant waves.

The women talked about their pasts and hopes for the future. Two of them hit it off on the first day and quickly became close, like they were related. Kate and Marie both had Irish blood running through their veins. Both left a past behind for the betterment of humanity. They felt at peace with each other.

When sitting outside, Kate loved watching the blue-gray waves slowly roll past the ship's hull. She smelled the salty air mist fly up over the bow. She could taste it. Kate extended her hand to Marie. "Darling, tell me again. Where is this ship going into port?"

"Liverpool, England. From there we take a train to Devonport."

"Is that place in England?"

"Yes, silly."

"Well, I never was that good with geography. I always relied upon my husband for that."

Marie arched her eyebrows. After a few moments of silence, she asked, "Are you married? You never said you were married."

Before Kate could respond, the ship's rudders vibrated as they shifted the ship to a northeast course. The breeze coming from the north became colder. Kate pulled up the dark-gray wool blanket up to her chest for more warmth. "Marie. No. I guess I have not…I really don't want to talk about it."

Sensing an uncomfortable story, Marie changed the subject. "Well, you know, after we've completed our training at Devonport, we travel to Torquay, England. Just up the road from Devon. We are to work at the Town Hall Hospital located near the Torquay town center. I was told the nurses care for many wounded soldiers there."

Kate asked, "Marie. Will we have a sponsor assigned to us there?"

"Yes. Her name is Nurse Agatha Christie. She will prepare us for future assignments to one of several Military Royal Army Medical Corps hospitals, in France, near the Western Front."

Kate repositioned herself in the lounge chair. She loudly exhaled. "I hope we go together. It would be a shame to be separated."

"As long as we don't die together," Marie said, using a twist of sarcasm.

Both quietly laughed. Kate pulled the wool blanket over her chest and up to her chin. She said, "I think I will take a nap."

Marie said, "Great idea. I think I will do the same. An afternoon nap sounds good right now." Marie adjusted her rear to get more comfortable in the lounge chair. She said, "Kate...if I have not said it, I want you to know how glad I am we are friends. I fretted making this journey alone." She lifted her head and pulled her long curly red hair around her neck to let it fall on her chest. Kate pulled up the blanket up over her head and fell asleep. Marie eventually did the same.

*****

The ship's captain and crew knew there were risks cruising in war-challenged waters. The British intelligence report indicated German submarine would attack supply ships disguised as passenger liners cruising through the North Sea and the Atlantic sea lanes to England, Ireland, and France. The company received the same information warning the ship would be targeted by German U-boats. The ship's captain was not told. He never knew what was to come.

The ship's charted waypoints tracked around the south coast of Ireland, then over to Liverpool. A mistake the captain could not reverse. On the morning of May 8, 1915, the world's headline read, "On May 7, the Royal Merchant Ship *Lusitania* neared the coast of Ireland. At ten minutes after three o'clock in the afternoon, the unthinkable happened. German Submarine U 20 fired one torpedo into the amidships of the unarmed *Lusitania*."

News of the merciless sinking shook the American conscience with anger. The British hoped the attack would spark the United States to declare war.

The German torpedo slammed into the ship and exploded. Combined with secondary cargo explosions, the attack sealed her fate. Within eighteen minutes, the Lusitania sank to the bottom of the sea. One thousand one hundred ninety-eight on board died. One hundred and fourteen Americans perished. Marie and Kate were among the kindred souls lost at sea.[41]

Leather to Steel

Max Eilenberg opened his Richmond store on time every Saturday morning at nine o'clock. He had done so for the past ten years. He always parked his Model-T Ford next to his business on the corner of North Twenty-Fourth and East Main Streets. He had purchased the building because of its location near heavy foot traffic. He also liked the fact it was close to this church. The oldest German American church in Richmond—Saint John's Episcopal Church—was only four blocks away from the store.[42]

Max shut and locked the car door. He pulled out his pocket watch from his vest pocket. He only had five minutes to open the store. He stepped up his pace. Max was never late opening the store. He turned the street corner onto East Main and hurried toward his store. However, a boy's voice stopped him midstride on the sidewalk. He heard the paperboy in the middle of the street yelling out, "Extra. Extra. Read all about it!"

Max rarely questioned his gut feelings. He immediately reached into his pants pocket and pulled out two copper pennies. He yelled out, "Boy, come here. I will take one." The boy ran over and gave Max a folded *Washington Times* Saturday newspaper edition. Max placed two copper coins into the boy's hand. The newspaper boy expressed great appreciation. "Wow! Thanks, mister! Have a nice day."

Max made it to his store minutes before the clock bells struck nine in the church tower. He pulled the keys from his vest pocket. The key ring shook as Max flipped through each key to find the right one. He breathed out once he had unlocked the front door. He opened the door and stepped inside the store. Scents of new leather, peppermint candies, spun cotton, and silk fabrics permeated the store.

He closed the front door. Cowbells hanging off the top doorframe jingled. Max reached over to the OPEN/CLOSED sign hanging in the window and flipped it to OPEN facing the street. He spoke to himself in broken German, "Gibt. Offen für Unternehmen." There. Open for business.

Max did a quick about-face on the waxed oak floor. He hurried to get behind the display cases and the customer counter. He walked near the back wall toward the L-shaped end of the counter. The small set of green hanging curtains mounted on the wall were closed. He pulled back the curtains. Behind them was a cash register occupying a recessed space he built to hide it. For additional security, Max bolted the Model 349 National Cash Register machine into steel angle-iron hidden behind wallboard and plaster. When not in use, the machine was out of plain sight. At the end of the day, he simply closed the curtains to conceal the cash register.

Max needed both hands to set up the register. He tucked the newspaper under his armpit to free up both hands. He pulled back the curtains. Fumbling with his key chain again, he finally located the right one to unlock and open up the cash drawer. Inside the register were his previous day's sales receipts, working cash, and coin safely stored in the four-hundred-pound machine. He pulled out the till to reconcile Friday's business. He made note of the cash balance on a piece of paper and then inserted it back in the register. After he had shut the register door, he proclaimed, "Guten Morgen Welt. Zeit für die Arbeit." Good morning, world. Time to work.

Then Max turned around and walked slowly toward his office by the rear-door fire exit. He was in no hurry now. All he wanted to do was heat up some water and make a cup of tea. His mind elsewhere, he walked by the Saturday newspaper still sitting on the counter. He stopped and took two steps backward. "Oops." He picked up the newspaper and slapped it on his thigh. "Can't forget this." He walked back to his office and waited for customers.

Sitting in his leather swivel chair, Max plopped his feet up on his oak roll-top desk. He unrolled the newspaper. The front-page headline stopped him cold. Taking a deep breath, he reread it. He reread with disbelief. Max's shaking hands caused the left fold of the newspaper to tear. Max tried to calm down. Within a few minutes, sweat beaded up on his forehead. He laid the newspaper down in his lap. Leaning back in his chair, he gazed at the ceiling.

Feeling lightheaded, he loosened his tie and opened his shirt. He took a few more deep breaths. The white handkerchief tucked into in his front jacket pocket served its purpose. Max wiped away salty perspiration running into his eyes. He blinked. The salt burned his eyes. He read the story's details. He wiped his eyes several times

Leather to Steel

until his heart slowed down. The words he read robbed him of all hope and future with his loving wife, Kate.

*****

After staring at the front page for a good thirty minutes, Max stood up and laid the newspaper on the desk. Feeling weak, he sat back in his chair. Looking up at the ceiling, he asked, "Warum Gott. Warum?" Why God?

Max Eilenberg did not leave his store that day. He turned the front window sign around to 'CLOSED' and locked the front door. He stepped slowly back toward his office. By his desk, he spun the swivel chair around and around until it stopped. He sat down and leaned back to stare at the ceiling.

The ceiling's ornate plaster—he himself designed and painted it—mesmerized his mind. His eyes traced the customized wooden trim he cut from a fallen mahogany tree near his home in Arlington. Max was indeed a talented and highly motivated artisan, businessman, and what he believed was a good husband. The newspaper headlines created room for doubt.

Until the previous week, Max's life was perfect in his mind—at least until Kate left for Europe. He even told his friend Manny Zapata that Kate would come back within six months. However, the paperboy's message on Saturday, May 8, 1915, told him otherwise. The news only filled his heart with grief and heartache knowing Kate would never come back. The war took his wife. The *Lusitania* tragedy caused him overwhelming grief.

Max would not hold on to the pain. He would act like a stoic German and vow revenge. Revenge against the Fatherland. Little did he know all the facts were not reported. The real enemy was elsewhere. The British knew of the pending attack. The information was shared with the Americans. He would learn that his enemy was not his homeland. It was the Americans and the British.

2d EXTRA　The Washington Times　2d EXTRA

LINER LUSITANIA SUNK BY GERMAN SUBMARINE FLEET RUSHES TO AID

PASSENGERS SAVED EARLY CABLES SAY

Reports Received From Liverpool Are All Fragmentary, But All Agree Steamer Began Calling For Help at 2:33—Was Said to Be Listing Badly—Fishing Fleet Rushed to Her Aid.

Washington Times Headline May 7, 1915. (Photo: U.S. Congressional Archives Newspaper.)

*****

The Zapatas

The tragic news of Kate's untimely death sent Lucinda Zapata into weeks of depression. Her husband, Manny, tried several times to provide cheer and positive distractions. But to no avail. He helplessly watched his wife slip into a silent state of mind. She could not deal with her best friend's death. To cope, she spent the month of May staying at home.

 Every day, Lucinda walked outside to sit under the old oak tree she and Kate met under every Saturday for tea and crumb cakes. They'd talked endlessly about how they would change the world. Sadly, the world changed them.

 Manny knew grief and grieving all too well. He felt for Lucinda. His own mother had died too early. Her consumption had no cure. He and his father, Colonel Clementi Zapata, learned to live with death. When Manny's father died of a broken heart, Manny learned to live with it. When his childhood friend and trusted mount, Stonewall, passed, Manny learned to live with it. But this time, he did something about it.

He refused to let Lucinda live with it. God answered his prayers. A black colt was born on the Zapata farm. A colt that would eventually grow up and, hopefully, bring joy to Lucinda. But the stallion was not enough. She did not react when Manny brought Sonny to her side. She glanced up from her chair, then back to staring at the empty seat Kate should be sitting in. Her grieving was expected. But as with all things, her grieving would pass. She would change.

Lucinda's transformation came at church services later that summer. While the priest spoke of embracing every good and bad thing in life as a lesson, she blinked her eyes and stared at the large wooden cross suspended from the ceiling. A realistic plaster sculpture of Jesus was nailed to the cross. She grabbed Manny's hand and said, "We can move on now."

Manny put his arm around her and slightly squeezed her shoulder. He looked at Jesus and whispered. "His love is with us. Let him take our burdens and feel our joys."

Lucinda lifted Manny's hand and placed it on her pregnant stomach. "She is kicking. Feel her?"

Manny rubbed her belly and said, "Looking forward to teaching you how to ride, son."

Lucinda quickly said, "You mean *our daughter*."

*****

Early in the morning of November 6, 1915 the doctor held up the crying newborn. He told Lucinda and Manny their baby was a perfect nine-pound boy. Then he laid the baby on Lucinda's chest and asked, "I need a name for the birth certificate."

Lucinda looked at Manny, then back at the doctor. She said, "Clemente Manuel Zapata."

The doctor said, "Handsome name. Clemente Manuel Zapata it is." He motioned to the midwife to take over. He left the room. Lucinda and Manny admired their son. He had a head of black hair that went everywhere. The midwife stepped forward. She said, "Let me wrap the baby in a warm blanket." She picked up Clemente and wrapped a blue blanket around his legs and chest. Then she carefully laid the baby upon Lucinda's chest.

Manny placed his hand on his wife's shoulder and said, "We did it." Lucinda took her eyes off of Clemente and looked up at Manny. She corrected him, "No. God did it."

As the baby nursed, he cooed while his mother and his father lay in their bed. Before the doctor left, he had said, "When you are up to it, Lucinda, you and Manny need to bring him down to my Arlington office for a checkup and birth certificate foot stamp."

Manny looked over at the doctor and asked, "Will the black ink come off his feet?"

The doctor chuckled. "After a few years of bathing."

Manny had on a sarcastic expression, recognizing the doctor's valiant attempt at humor, which failed.

Manny, Lucinda, and Clemente remained at the Zapata Horse Farm throughout the war. The Zapata stallion, Sonny, and his warmblood brood mares produced dozens of fillies and colts. The ideal breed mixture for creating genetic endurance and stamina. The horses did not go unnoticed by their army neighbor—the United States Army training grounds commander, Colonel William S. Stout.

The colonel rode the post perimeter every Saturday morning. He knew of the Zapata farm where a small number of horses were raised. One morning, the colonel noticed the farm's owner lowering hay from the barn loft onto a wagon. The colonel stopped at the fence line near Manny's position. He yelled out, "Excuse me, sir!"

Manny concentrated on holding the lines while lowering at seventy-pound hay bale. Once the bale was resting on the buckboard, he released the rope. He turned around and responded to an officer he did not recognize. He waved. "Wait a minute. Coming right over."

Standing on his property line, Manny looked over the pole fence. "How can I help you, colonel? I think that is what the silver eagles on your collar mean."

"Please call me by my first name. My name is Bill. Yes, I am the colonel commanding this post. A training ground for experienced

U.S. Army cavalry mounts and troopers. The reason I am here is to talk about those fine looking horses you have grazing over yonder."

"Colonel—I mean, Bill. We raised those horses for several types of buyers: farmers, showmen, and, believe it or not, polo players."

"I see. Has the army ever approached you?"

"Nope. The only contact we have had with the United States Government was back maybe ten years ago when a U.S. Army mount named Tough Guy met his father—my old stallion—Stonewall. That stallion has since passed away."

"Well, I noticed you have a black stallion over there. Is he related?"

"Indeed he is. His mother, Luna—she is standing over there near the creek, was bred with Tough Guy. He is the product of their union. We named him Sonny."

"How old is he?"

"Sonny is about ten years old now. Perfect age for breeding. Why do you ask, Bill?"

"Well, I just admire the animal. He looks like a special horse. By the way, what is that brand on his left rear quarter?"

Manny shook his head. "I guess that is part of his and my family's history. Kind of a long story, but in short, the brand represents the Magnolia Plantation down in South Carolina, north of Charleston."

Bill said, "Funny. I know that place. The United States Army has purchased breeders from the woman who owns it. I think her last name is Drayton. Not sure of her first name."

"Well, in any case, the brand represents the memory of Sonny's father; his father, Stonewall; and my childhood memories growing up in southeast Texas."

The colonel pulled out a gold watch from his front pants pocket. He clicked it open to tell time. He looked back at Manny. "Well, Mister Zapata, I need to get back to the troops and ponies. It has been a pleasure talking with you. Perhaps we can do business in the near future."

"Perhaps. Good day, Bill."

Colonel Stout mounted back up on his horse. He clucked while lightly pulling the reins to the left. His horse responded to the gentle rein. A light spurring from the colonel's boot heels nudged the horse into a trot. Within a few minutes, the colonel was back at the stable and dismounted.

The private serving as Stable A's groom and orderly of the day took charge of the colonel's horse. He asked him, "Sir, did you have a good ride?"

The colonel acted somewhat smug toward the young private, but responded. "Yes, I did. Please ensure this gilding gets a good brush-down and hay. I ran him for some time."

The private rendered a salute and replied with enthusiasm. "Yes, sir. He will get the best, sir." Summer student Abraham Bates turned around and led the horse back to Stable A.

*****

The Western Front emerged from a confluence of battlefields defined daily by friend and foe. Rolling German barrages pushed forward, not backward. The Imperial German Army pressed harder and harder each day during the spring of 1915 with the three main goals—capture Paris, occupy London, and, at the same time, move in and occupy Russian territories. Germany could not occupy Russia without help. Which is why Austria-Hungary aligned itself with German interests.

The German and Austro-Hungarian armies defined the Eastern Front battle lines that moved at will against the Russians. Germany wanted Poland, the Balkans, and Russian governments brought to their knees. The Kaiser was not stopping in Europe; he had other international colony-building aspirations.

The Kaiser also wanted to protect Germany's territorial interests that included expansion and domination in Africa, Persia, Japan, and China. To do so would require mass production of naval weaponry that exceeded the capabilities of the His Majesty Ship (HMS) Royal Navy. Evidence of which rested on the decks of German super-dreadnought class battleships moored in German harbors. The same

Leather to Steel

battleships Germany built only a few years before declaring war on France and England. Was it a coincidence?

Military technology quickly transformed the German navy into an oceangoing force to be reckoned with on the sea. German families were deprived of basic living necessities as a result of Allied naval blockades that denied German seaports the ability to receive shipments of much-needed food, petrol, and natural resources. The German necessity bred solutions such as the design and production of the German submersibles known as the German U-boat, which earned the reputation as Germany's hallmark of death and destruction on oceans, seas, and ports.

Never has mankind witnessed the destructive capabilities of an enduring modern naval weaponry the Germans possessed during the Great War. The German navy was not the only service that employed brilliant German scientists who designed weapons of war.

The Imperial German Army experienced a military transformation on the battlefield. A transformation that included modernized lightweight machine guns, aeroplanes, chemical weapons, flamethrowers, and long-range artillery. Ground artillery that shot a one-ton exploding shell over a distance of four miles to reach its target. Combined, these weapons of war provided Germany a debilitating capability to advance their ground forces across Europe.

Painfully, military tradition trumped practicality. British and French cavalry charges were devastated by German Maschinengewehr 08 (MG 08) machinegun nests. Similarly, German cavalries were not immune to British Lewis and Vickers machine guns. These weapons minimized the cavalry role by virtue of simple survivability.

However, the cavalryman's forward intelligence-gathering role expanded during the Great War. Foot soldiers could not move quick enough behind enemy lines to get in and get out without discovery. Horses such as Tough Guy and Jubal Early proved their invaluable capabilities. Early warning information was key for military leaders who dictated the moves and countermoves of large armies and supply trains across terrains not familiar to the invader or defender.

Horses and mules excelled in their transportation roles on European battlefields. The muddy fields, rugged mountain terrains, and waterways deterred or halted war machines built on wheels and axles bogged down in mud or broken by jagged rocks covering a mountain trail. Horses like Jubal, Tough Guy, and Daisy saved the soldier. They were built to pull or carry armaments needed by their soldiers in the muddy trenches on the Western Front, or encamped in the high Ypres Mountains of France. The demand for horse would not diminish throughout the war. However, replacements were limited for both sides of the war. Depleted European horse and mule populations left only one option—purchase the four-legged animals across the ocean. British and French government relied upon their allies, the United States and Canada to save the day.

For the next three years, laughter was hard to summon from the heart. The events taking place on the battle lines drawn in France, Belgium, and Russia exacted hundreds of thousands of lives using weapons of war not ever seen by mankind. Weapons such as chemical munitions, flamethrowers, plane-delivered bombs, tanks, U-Boats, and massive subterranean-concentrated explosive devices. Weapons designed to bring hell upon man and animal. The death tolls continued to rise.

The Replacements

> And Ahab said unto Obadiah, go into the land, unto all fountains of water, and unto all brooks: peradventure we may find grass to save the horses and mules alive, that we lose not all the beasts.
> —Kings, Chapter 8, Verse 5, KJV

Allison Drayton

During the war, the Magnolia Horse Farm business exploded. The demand for quality horses drove British and French military departments to look beyond their borders for replacements. The war quickly exhausted local sources of both horse and mule. The Allied Powers needed over one hundred thousand beasts of burden to support the Western Front.

To acquire the horses and mules, buyers sailed from England to the United States and Canada with an open checkbook. Horse purveyors like Ms. Allison Drayton would accommodate buyers, for a price.

On May 30, Allison Drayton made her monthly trip to the Charleston livestock auction held every Saturday near the city market. The market was conveniently located near the Ashley River wharfs off Murray Boulevard.[43] The river provided farmers easy water transportation access for delivery of their crops and livestock. The Magnolia Horse Farm abutted Ashley's north bank, which Allison used to ferry her horses to the market. Water transportation simplified movement through swamps surrounding the Magnolia property.

While in town, Allison got word an English buyer was in town looking to purchase many horses and mules. A possible good payday for Allison, if all went well with negotiations. She had a large herd of horses to move. Well, over one hundred mares and geldings available for the right price. Of course, she would never let go of her prized black stallion, Wayward, and brood mare, Anna. Those two horses were the mainstay of her business.

*****

British Ambassador Sir Cecil Spring Rice worked tirelessly in his Washington DC office reviewing daily cables received from British prime minister Herbert Henry Asquith and minister of munitions David Lloyd George.[44] Both British leaders promoted positive relations with sympathetic nations to acquire supplies, bank loans, bullets, and horses needed on the Western Front. The United States and the Commonwealth countries were at top of their list.[45]

When England needed more money, Sir Cecil made phone calls to one of the richest financial dynasties in the world. American John P. Morgan's family gladly extended loans in exchange for reasonable interest rates. Once English banks received spend authorizations, Ambassador Rice dispatched diplomatic staff members to negotiate purchases with factories and farms. His most successful purchaser was Mr. Colin George. His charming wit, business acumen, and expert U.S. and Canadian horse business insights greatly benefited his king and country.[46]

Mr. George dispatched cables all over the United States and Canada to well-known horse and mule sellers, who replied with bids. He divided the cable replies among his junior staff to validate potential sellers. Of the cables received, he took special interest in a communication received from the mayor of Charleston, Tristram Tupper Hyde.[47] Mayor Hyde recommended the British embassy dispatch, a representative to the Charleston Market on any Saturday morning. The cable claimed the Market auctioned the best-trained workhorses for reasonable prices. Collin George also suspected the honorable Mayor Hyde was quick to gain an economic windfall, as other U.S. city mayors. Each benefiting from the war.

With the Charleston cable in hand, Mr. George departed New York City for the South. Ambassador Sir Cecil Rice cautioned him,

"Please be careful in your quest, Mr. George. Once you purchase the three hundred horses and mules, make arrangements for passage directly to the Port of Devon." Mr. George agreed to do as ordered. The ambassador continued, "I want you to personally ensure the animals are properly cared for during the voyage. I also need you to hand-carry official correspondence for me." He handed Mr. George a sealed envelope.

After securing the message, Colin committed to the ambassador. "Sir, I will do my duty." He excused himself from the office. Once outside the door, he made a passing comment to the secretary. "Horses and mules are not the only resources desperately needed. Our country and king needs medical professionals. The soldiers are suffering. The horses are suffering."

She looked up and said, "Excuse me, did you say something?"

Colin shook his head no and kept on walking down the hall.

*****

Colin's British buyers traveled up and down the East Coast searching for the best horses and mules they could find. Colin took it upon himself to respond to the Charleston mayor's invitation. All he had to do was get there.

A Washington DC friend told him to find rail transportation that connected to the Seaboard Air Line servicing Charleston, South Carolina. He also said once down there, to inquire about a woman who bred and trained the best horses to suit multiple purposes. Her name was Allison Drayton of the Magnolia Horse Farm. Cecil George looked forward to meeting with her.

*****

The Bateses

The Front Royal Remount Depot celebrated its fifth year of operation transferring its five hundredth horse to the United States Army. Ready for battle, the horse would be assigned a trooper as part of a ceremony the depot commander organized to tout the achievements of all depot personnel contributing to number 500.

The Bates family sat in front of a temporary stage constructed for the occasion. They were not alone. Twenty other depot staff civilians and officers sat with them, while the commander made his introductions. Jeremiah took great pride just being asked to participate in the ceremony. He had no idea he would be called onstage.

The commander first recognized the depot's top trainer and said, "Mr. Jeremiah Bates, will you please come up onstage?"

Surprised, Jeremiah looked at Mary. He rose from his seat and walked up to stand near the commander, who handed him a plaque. The presentation of an accommodation to Jeremiah was heartfelt. During his acceptance, he thanked his family for their unwavering support. He thanked the United States Army for trusting his judgment, and, lastly, he spoke of his oldest son, Abraham, pursuing his university studies in science. Standing on the stage in front of his family, friends, and peers was a very proud moment for Jeremiah.

Abraham Bates worked hard studying during his sophomore year at the university. The son of a retired U.S. Army cavalryman, working with animals was in his blood. He loved animals so, that he committed to earning his degree in veterinarian medicine. His unyielding efforts were noted by family, friends, and the Front Royal depot commanding officer. Abraham swore to himself that nothing would keep him from getting his sheepskin. The college projected a May 1918 graduation. He would stay the course, barring unforeseen circumstances.

In college, Abraham excelled in his science classes. He was fortunate to have worked all those summers during high school with the depot's senior veterinarian, Dr. William Spencer. A man who also held the rank of major in the United States Army.

Abraham believed what his father taught him. The definition of luck is when the road called Preparation intersects with the road called Opportunity. He prepared early. Before going off to college, Abraham spent weekends working with depot trainers and doctors performing a variety of treatments for bloating, colic, lameness, boils, floating teeth, hoof corning, pink eye, and unknown ailments. He eagerly learned all he could before setting foot in veterinary school.

During his second Christmas break, Abraham worked closely with the depot's Dr. Howard Spencer. The doctor treated a broad spectrum of equestrian illnesses, which made for a perfect internship. Abraham proudly tells a story of how Dr. Spencer constantly tested his attention.

During a winter storm, Abraham stayed with the sick mare lying down on a pile of hay Abraham pitched into the stall. He sat cross-legged on the floor near the mare's head. While stroking the mare's forelock, he looked up at Dr. Spencer leaning over the stall door. The doctor asked, "Abraham, what is wrong with her?"

Abraham said, "I have my suspicions. The mare is having difficulty swallowing. She is sweating, has muscle tremors every few hours, and the worst symptom she has experienced—rapid weight loss this week." Abraham rubbed his chin. He shook his head, not knowing the answer.

The doctor said, "My initial diagnosis is she has grass sickness. I read several medical reports of British remount depots reporting similar symptoms. The doctors over there think there is a toxin developed in the stomach. Something in the grass."

"Dr. Spencer, then that means horses on a strict hay diet are not getting the disease."

"Very good, Abraham. Your inference is most likely correct. Understanding that the horses working near the Western Front trenches are not showing those symptoms, since most all of the grassland is burned up on the Western Front where the warhorses live."

Abraham nodded. "Then one can conclude the disease occurs almost exclusively in horses eating only grass."

"Abraham," the doctor exclaimed, "you are going to make a fine veterinarian. You have good reasoning skills. Perhaps you should consider a commission in the U.S. Army Veterinarian Service. You would make a good officer. Then you can work with me at the depot."

Abraham realized his future was indeed full of promise. "We shall see, Dr. Spencer. Thank you for the recommendation."

*****

Allison Drayton

Englishman Colin George debarked from the Sea Air Line train in Charleston. The first thing on his agenda was to secure a hotel room to freshen up and change clothes. A traditionalist, Colin insisted English business transactions be conducted in clean proper attire. He coached his staff to understand that everyone liked to negotiate with a smart-dressed man.

Before leaving the train, the conductor recommended he check in to the Argyle Hotel located just off Meeting Street. Satisfied with the recommendation, Colin picked up his bag and walked over to the taxi stand. A Model-T Ford with "Taxi" painted in white letters on the doors was parked in front of several other taxis lined up behind him.

The colored driver stepped out of his taxi. He yelled out using a low Southern accent. "Mista! Need a ride to a hotel, or diner?"

Colin replied cordially, "Why, thank you, my dear man. I need a ride over to the Argyle Hotel."

"No problem, mista. Go ahead and get in."

The driver got back in the taxi and started up the engine. He used the floorboard shifter to engage first gear. He eased off the clutch, and the taxi moved forward. The driver didn't time stepping on the gas and clutch. The front wheels jumped some. Sitting in the back, Colin commented. "Little bit jumpy today, Mr.—what is your name, sir?"

"Last name is Shingler. Dick Shingler. Sometimes these new automobiles need a couple of kicks to the wheel."

"What do you mean by that?"

"Just an American slang for getting the car started."

"I see."

Leather to Steel

The driver looked in the review mirror and noted his passenger was writing in a small black notebook. "Mister, based upon your accent, I figure you are not from these parts."

"No, I am not. I am from England."

"What brings ya here to Charleston?"

"Just doing some sightseeing." Colin was careful not to disclose the real purpose for his Charleston trip. Realizing his passenger was being evasive; Shingler shut up and drove on.

They pulled up in front of the Argyle Hotel. The driver had to break hard to stop. Colin quickly grabbed the door handle to brace himself in the back seat. "Checking your brakes out?"

The taxi driver said, "Yes, sa. Just making sure my passengers are safe."

A hotel bellhop standing in front of the hotel wasted no time getting to the taxi. Dressed in a red tuxedo and wearing a black top hat, the young bellhop rushed to open the passenger door. Colin stepped out of the taxi. Seeing a piece of luggage in the seat, he tried to get the bag to carry up to the hotel front desk. Without hesitation, Colin waved him off. "No, thank you, my dear fellow. I have it."

The bellhop nodded and waved his hand toward the hotel entrance. Colin had U.S. money in his hand. He reached into the cab to pay the cabbie. The driver said, "Mister, this a one-dollar greenback, which is twice the fare."

Colin saluted the driver with two fingers. He turned around walked up ten steps and through the hotel's revolving glass door.

*****

Allison awoke earlier than usual on Market Saturday. She got out of bed and rushed to clean up and dressed within minutes. She did not have much time to get the horses onto the stock barge. She had to have them corralled on the market dwarfs by seven o'clock, just before the larger produce barges moored for unloading.

Allison knew it was going to be an eventful day. She was excited. The market prices for horses increased 20 percent over the last few months. The Charleston mayor told business leaders international trade opportunities were imminent. Charleston would soon realize economic benefits from European purchasers. The mayor said, "If John Pierpont Morgan Jr. can provide the money, we can provide the goods."[48]

The Market Day organizers paid a dozen local teenagers to monitor the wharf for farmers and merchants needing assistance with their goods and animals. Once Allison's barge was moored at the pier, four farm boys came down to offer their assistance. Allison gladly accepted. She handed the boys four leads to begin unloading the horses and lead them into the market's warehouse complex. The locals affectionately called the largest warehouse, *The Barn*.

Once inside the Barn, Allison's horses were tagged, numbered, and listed on the auction manifest with the horse's breed, sex, coloring, height, and minimum bidding price. Allison used her own notebook to record the tag number assigned to each horse.

The auctioneer was a potbellied middle-aged farmer the locals called Bubba. He took his time climbing up a wooden stand elevated twenty feet above the arena. The waist-high lectern attached to the stand provided an area Bubba would use to place the list of auction items. The market coordinators prepositioned a gavel and a megaphone on the stand.

The Market Day organizers built stadium seating opposite the auctioneer. Designed to handle a capacity of one hundred, the seats were already filled with prospective buyers. Each man held a small wooden paddle painted with their assigned auction number. While waiting for the auctioneer to slam the gavel down, the men talked loudly and cajoled one another.

Standing to the side of the cattle shoot, Allison put one boot on the lower fence rail and rested her forearms on the top. She looked across the arena toward the buyers' bleachers. She scanned the audience for anyone who looked different. Town scuttlebutt indicated an English buyer was in town—with money in hand—to bid on horses.

She made a smart move to bring only twenty of her best horses to get his attention. She had her farrier brush them down and tie up their manes and tails for show. The horses looked magnificent. Not

Leather to Steel

one of her geldings stood less than sixteen hands high. The Magnolia brand was visually prominent on the left rear quarter of every horse.

The gavel came down, and the auction started at exactly eight o'clock. Two hundred head of cattle would go first. Around ten o'clock, the last Herford walked off the block. The horses were next.

Bubba directed the barn boys to prepare the Magnolia horses for auction. They entered the corral containing Allison's steeds and attempted to hook leads to their halters. Her heart skipped a few beats when one of her mares side kicked one of the handlers. She hoped the English buyer in the stands did not witness the spirited bay—called Witch—get out of control. She scanned the bleachers and noted all were carrying on about their cattle purchases. Satisfied, she went back to her notebook to mark the first horse number led out of the gate.

*****

Colin George showed up at the auction just before the cattle sales ended. It took some time locating an open seat. Just before the horse auction began, he found a seat just vacated by a large cattleman—a man who did not look happy. Colin could not resist asking, "My dear fellow, what the bloody hell made you despair the time preceding you?" The cattleman looked down at Colin with a quizzical face. He spoke in a low baritone to Colin. "Excuse me, mister. I don't recognize what in the Sam Hill you just said. But if you are thinking I am not happy with the inflated price of beef—because of the dang war in Europe—then you are darn right."

Colin remained calm. The rancher continued his rant. "Dang foreigners are buying up everything, leaving little for us locals to buy in our own markets." Recognizing the cattleman's unsettling opinion of foreigners, Colin replied in a hastily manufactured Southern drawl. "I reckon you are right about that, partner. Have a better day, friend." The cattlemen sidestepped down the bleacher toward the entrance steps to leave. Colin took his seat.

*****

The auctioneer slammed his gavel down to draw buyers' attention to the next stockyard attraction—the horse. The first horse led out into the arena was one of Allison's favorite geldings. She called him Iron Horse. She had seen few horses that could run so fast without getting winded lungs. Allison knew he would be the best Thoroughbred to get out in front first.

Bubba spoke loudly for all to hear. "Gentlemen, we have twenty prime horses from the Magnolia Horse Farm across the Ashley River. Our local royalty, Ms. Allison Drayton, is the proud owner and trainer of the best horses found on this side of the Mississippi. She is looking for a good price now. You men show some respect. Her daddy and his daddy were part of the Revolution around here."

The men clapped lightly. Allison stepped out from the gate into the arena and waved her hand. The men clapped some more.

Iron Horse had a number 1 tag secured to his halter. The handler led him into the center of the arena and stopped. Bubba read from the manifest. "Gentlemen, we have a Thoroughbred-warmblood mix gilding. He is two years of age. He is seventeen hands high. Good teeth. Do I hear one hundred dollars?"

A silver-bearded farmer wearing coveralls raised his bidding paddle. The auctioneer nodded his head and started speaking faster. "Do I hear one twenty now, one twenty now—come on, give me a bid. One twenty!" Colin raised his paddle. The auctioneer continued, "Do I have one thirty, now one thirty, one thirty, come on now." The farmer looked back at Colin, and then toward the auctioneer. Bubba repeated, "Do I have one thirty. One twenty going once. One twenty going twice—"

The farmer raised his paddle. The auctioneer nodded. "We have one thirty. Do we have one hundred forty now, come on, one forty."

Colin raised his paddle and yelled out. "Two hundred!" Bubba grinned and yelled out, "By golly, we have two hundred to the gentlemen in the tweed suit. Do we have two twenty? Come on now, two twenty."

The farmer glanced at Bubba and shook his head left and right. The auctioneer yelled out, "Two hundred going once. Two hundred going twice. Sold! To the gentleman in the fancy suit." Bubba looked at Colin mouthing, "What is your number, sir?" Colin was aware not to speak proper English. "Number is one, zero, one, good ole buddy." Bubba acknowledged the number–had been properly recorded. He then spoke through the megaphone. "Dinner break. Come back at noon!"

Colin put down his bidding paddle. He had acquired his first lot of horses.

*****

Colin was unaware curious female eyes closely watched him during the bidding. Standing by the cattle shoot, Allison took note of the single buyer of her horses. She looked down and kicked the mud and manure off her boots. Brushed off the dust on her shoulders. Adjusted her ponytail, and then walked over to introduce herself to the horses' new owner.

Colin had a trained eye. He noticed an attractive, middle-aged woman walking across the arena toward his position. Her features were rugged yet elegant in his eyes. As the woman got closer, he felt a twinge of fate. She waved at him to come down to the arena. He obliged her.

Allison extended a hand to Colin and said, "Mister, I did not catch your name?"

Colin removed his hat and bowed. "Let me introduce myself as Colin George. And you, missus?"

Allison answered, "I raised the horses you purchased. I am also *Misses* Allison Drayton."

"I see. I represent the British War Department purchasing unit. It is my pleasure to meet you, Misses Drayton. If you don't mind, after I make payment for the horses, would you please join the men for lunch? We can discuss business. Agree?"

Allison looked at the clock and noted that it was time for dinner. She replied, "I would be glad to do so. While you are at the purser's table, I will go talk with the boys to make sure they look after the horses while we are at dinner. By the way, us southerners call lunch... dinner."

"Sounds like a delightful plan. I will meet you back at this spot."

As Allison walked away, she turned around and asked Colin. "By the way, what kind of business?"

"Why, horse business, of course. I am interested in buying more horses."

Allison nodded her head. "See you back here in ten minutes. Before I go, did you have a place to keep your horses?"

"I actually did not think of that. Any ideas?"

"Leave it to me."

Colin tipped his hat forward. "See you soon. Cheers."

*****

After lunch, Allison invited Colin back to the Magnolia for a tour of the farm. Colin gladly accepted the offer. They used a water taxi to cross the Ashley River. Once at the Magnolia dock, Allison said, "Now, watch out for snakes. They like to nest up in the Spanish moss hanging down from the trees."

"Don't believe I like snakes," Colin replied.

In his next breath, he said, "I will certainly follow your lead. No worries about me going off the trail."

Allison said, "Takes some time to get used to these parts."

As they walked down a narrow trail, Colin asked, "Misses Drayton—"

"Please call me Allison."

Colin continued, "By the way, what about my horses?"

"Don't worry about them. I had the boys bring 'em back over here until you figure out your transatlantic transportation options."

"Very good. Much appreciated. That was very considerate of you. Considerate Americans, I say."

Allison turned her head around and glanced at Colin. She smiled. Ten minutes later, she and Colin were standing on the front porch of her mansion. Colin looked across the expansive Magnolia estate and said, "I must say, a rather big house—for one, I assume?"

"Yes. I choose to live alone. Too many good memories to let go of here."

"I can understand that, Allison. I still own my home back in England. My family had lived there for several generations."

"Colin, do you live alone?"

"Yes. I have been a bachelor for some time. My work has been my marriage. However, I do plan on retiring as soon as this war is over."

Allison pointed Colin to a bench seat backing against the right porch rail. He sat down while Allison excused herself. "I will go inside and get us some refreshments. We can talk business over a couple of mint juleps."

Colin removed his hat. "Sounds wonderfully perfect, Allison."

She politely excused herself from her guest, but promptly returned with two tall glasses filled with a yellowish-green mixture. She handed Colin a glass and then sat down by him. She held her glass out. "Cheers," she said, using an imitated English accent.

Colin extended his glass in return. "Cheers. To good horses and company." He took one sip and asked, "What is in this drink? It has a unique taste."

Allison replied, "One teaspoon of sugar, two teaspoons of water, two ounces of Kentucky bourbon whiskey, and four mint leaves."

Colin took another sip. "Thank you."

Allison and Colin talked for hours. She provided several referrals to help Colin fulfill his order requirements. Colin asked, "If you don't mind, I would like to return tomorrow to further look at your other horses. I really need to get back to the hotel. If you would like to join me for dinner, I would be honored."

"No, thank you, Colin. That is very nice of you to offer, but I need to get the horses ready for the evening."

"No worries. What time can I be here tomorrow, assuming you can fit me in?"

"Sure. How about eight o'clock. I will have the horses fed and let out. You can view the rest of my horses in the front pasture."

*****

Colin returned Sunday morning and was pleasantly surprised to see thirty magnificent horses grazing in the front pasture on the Magnolia. Allison stood by him as he carefully studied each horse moving across the field. Allison asked, "Do you want to go into the pasture and get a closer look?"

"No, thank you. I can make a judgment from here. You have thirty horses out there."

"They are half and half. Fifteen geldings and fifteen mares. Ages two to four years. I have paperwork on each. What do you think?"

"Are they for sale?"

"They are."

"Then the British government would like to extend you an offer for them."

"How much is the British government willing to pay?"

"Depends. How much are you asking?"

Allison paused to think about her answer. She looked at Colin and said, "Two hundred per head."

Colin did not waste any time responding. "Sold. To the gentlemen in the gray tweed suit."

Allison and Colin shook hands. She pulled out a bill of sale and noted the price of six thousand dollars. She signed it and handed it to Colin. Colin tipped his hat toward her and said, "Pleasure doing business with you, Allison. Fifty down and only two hundred and fifty more horses to go."

"Just follow up with the names I gave you. They can be reached by the hotel operator. She can connect you to their homes. Everyone knows everyone around these parts."

Collin returned to his hotel and made several telephone calls to the farmers Allison recommended. Allison told Colin to reference her name during the introductions. Colin did and each farmer agreed to sell horses, though most were green.

By week's end, the British government had acquired two hundred and fifty horses from regional Charleston horse farms. It took a few days to complete the transactions. After meeting his quota, he focused on shipping the horses back to England. Fortunately, several cargo vessels were docked in the Port of Philadelphia. One ship was scheduled to get under way for Liverpool the following week. Colin telegrammed the S.S. *Haverford* captain, who agreed to take on the cargo, for a lucrative price and, of course, a personal financial consideration.

Colin paid for the two hundred and fifty horses to be trained up to Philadelphia and temporarily corralled in a warehouse near the ship's berth. Colin was thinking it would be easiest to load them all up at once, except for the fifty horses he intentionally left with Allison. He planned on returning to the Magnolia on Wednesday to pick up the rest of the horses. Most importantly, to visit with a woman—unbeknownst to her—he had become smitten with.

*****

During their first meeting, Allison agreed to keep Colin's twenty horses on her property for the week until Colin arranged for transporting the horses from the Magnolia.

Collin sent word to Allison that he would be checking out of the hotel on Wednesday morning. In his message, he asked Allison if he could pick up his horses on the same day. She replied that his return would be welcome and accommodated. Colin was pleased to know he would see her one more time.

He checked out of the hotel early Wednesday morning. He stood outside the hotel and waved a taxi down. The taxi stopped, and the driver asked, "Need a ride, mister?"

"I do," Colin replied. Colin recognized the man sitting in the driver's seat. It was Dick Shingler, the same cabbie who picked him up from the train in the previous week. Colin opened the rear door and got in.

The cabbie asked, "Where you going?"

"Down to the wharf."

"Yes, sir. You know you could have walked it."

"Perhaps. But I have this large suitcase."

"Understood." The cab pulled into the wharf area by the market. Colin handed a one-dollar silver certificate to the driver and said, "Thank you. Much appreciated."

The cabbie nodded and tucked Abraham and Ulysses into his front pocket. He then sped away.

Colin walked down to the main pier where a line of water taxis waited for their passengers to return from church. Colin approached the first one. Two teenage farm boys sat on the bow. The old man at the helm asked, "Look'n for a ride, sonny?"

"Just over to the Magnolia," Colin replied.

The old man said, "Two bits will get you there."

Colin agreed and walked on board. After handing the money to the man, he said, "All right, boys, get those poles going."

Colin stood on the water taxi's aft deck looking across the Ashley River toward the Magnolia farm. The smooth river's surface made for an uneventful quiet run. Since the tide ebbed, the river flowed with little resistance. The boys used long poles to push the boat forward.

It was quiet on the river. The only sounds Colin heard were a push pole occasionally hitting the taxi bow, and several church bells ringing from the Charleston city center. As the taxi got closer to the Magnolia property, he recognized Allison standing on the dock. He also noticed she had changed from britches to a blue dress. He mumbled, "Impressive." She waved at Colin. He returned the gesture.

Once moored to the Magnolia dock, the old man positioned a narrow wooden ramp between the dock and the taxi's foredeck. Colin picked up his luggage and carefully walked across a shaky ramp. He struggled to keep his balance while carrying one piece of luggage. Allison stood on the dock near the ramp. She said, "Here, let me help you."

"Oh. Thank you, but I have it," Colin said.

Allison smirked and asked, "You are not one of those fellas who think a woman's place is in the kitchen."

Colin was quick to respond. "Of course not! It is quite clear you can manage on your own. However, I do have my sense of pride."

Allison laughed.

Colin faced the old man. "Mister, thank you for the ride."

Colin took a quarter out of his pocket and flipped it toward the old man, who was quick to catch it.

"You're welcome, sonny. Anytime." He turned to his boys and ordered, "Push back from the dock. Time is money."

Colin and Allison turned around and proceeded to walk side by side toward the mansion. The front porch seats were already positioned out of the sun. Allison was prepared.

Allison and Colin sat together on the padded west bench chatting and drinking mint juleps. Colin mentioned to Allison the livestock water barge would be at the Magnolia dock by four o'clock. From there, the horses would be loaded up and taken to a warehouse near the railway station for the night. She said, "Good. We have plenty of time for drinks and sandwiches. I will make us lunch."

Their time together was well spent. Colin and Allison talked about their families, countries, and what they believed in. They came closer to knowing each other. If one believes in love at first sight, then perhaps this was one of those moments. Sitting close to Allison, Colin handed one J.P. Morgan bank note to Allison.

She asked, "Colin, what is this for?"

"My dear, the British government would like you to consider this money as a retainer payment for future horse purchases."

"I will not have the colts ready for another year."

"No worries. I am sure the war will still be going. Unfortunately, there appears to be no end in sight."

"That is sad to know." Allison shook her head in disbelief.

"Indeed. Perhaps the United States will join us in the near future."

"I am afraid us Americans are tired of war and have no desire. President Wilson understands this. Right now it is America's will. Until then, the best we can do for Britain is provide materials support."

Colin nodded that he understood. Then his expression turned serious. He touched Allison's arm. He said, "Misses Drayton. Would you happen to know of any chaps medically trained and willing to come over and "support" England? Please let me know. The British Red Cross needs caring souls to staff mobile comfort stations set up near the Western Front. Do you know of anyone here in Charleston?" Allison looked at Colin's face and saw compassion in his eyes. A few moments passed. She placed her right index finger on her temple.

A few moments passed, and she replied, "Why, yes. Yes, I do. How does one get from here to there, and how long does it take?"

"Glad you asked. My government recently leased the American Line steamship, S.S. *Haverford* to transport troops, supplies, and horses.[49] She is set to sail out of Philadelphia to Liverpool next Monday, June 7. I will be a passenger on that ship with three hundred horses and mules. They will take six days to cross the Atlantic. Why do you ask?" Allison replied. "I will do it. I will go with you. Why not? Life is too short."

Colin did not expect her response. Allison said she was free to make her own calculated decisions. She had trusted friends, who would jump at the chance to take care of her horses in exchange for living in the big house. Money was no object. She was not getting any younger. She repeated the same two words to herself while she packed, "Why not. Why not me?"

*****

Allison packed one bag full of britches, blouses, undergarments, a long-sleeved white cotton skirt, one pair of white leather dress shoes, and several pairs of socks. She decided to take a frilly dress just in case. Standing rigid in front of her mother's full-length mirror, she said to herself, "Allison Drayton, you are out of your mind doing this. Sailing to Europe with a stranger, three hundred horses, and the idea of helping wounded soldiers and horses. I know the horse farm will be safe while I am gone for the year. It is only a year. Surely, the war will be over with before then. It does not matter. I am compelled to prove women can handle war equally as a man. I am that kind of woman."

*****

The S.S. *Haverford* sailed for seven days to get halfway to England. Another seven days to go. The Atlantic Ocean's surface remained mostly calm for smooth sailing—good conditions for three hundred horses secured five decks below the main. Colin paid a deck hand to ensure they were provided ample food and water during the transit.

Once under way, Allison and Colin ventured out of their staterooms onto the main deck. Standing near the transom, they chatted about England, horses, and the war. The ship's brass propeller blades turned up the ocean below them. They watched as the ship carved a white serpentine design on the ocean's surface.

Five days into the trip, the S.S. *Haverford* continued to maintain twenty knots on a course bearing zero, three, nine. The North Atlantic's partly cloudy sky gave no reason for the ship's captain to be concerned. Weather forecasters predicted clear sailing all the way to the English Channel.

Colin and Allison took advantage of the good weather. They met each day after breakfast on the ship's main deck, aft. They continued to talk about life. Colin strove to impress Allison about all that he knew. One morning, he stood next to her, looking out at the western horizon. He asked her, "Did you know the horizon is twelve visual miles from where we stand?"

"I did not know that? Why do we care?"

"Sailors use that distance to estimate how far away an object on the horizon is from the ship."

"How do you know so much about the navy? Did you ever serve in the Royal Navy?"

Colin gently touched Allison's shoulder to turn her around. "I want to be honest with you Allison. I care about you—I mean, our friendship. The truth is, I am actually a senior naval officer in the Royal Navy. The Royal Navy assigned me to the British Embassy to liaison with the United States military. I am, of course, subject to the pleasure of our British ambassador, Sir Cecil Rice."

"So what is your concern? I don't think anything different of you. Don't matter to this Southern girl. So what is a sailor boy doing on land?"

"Let me say, there are unfriendly persons living in the United States working on behalf of Germany's interest. It can be a dangerous game. My adopted identify is for my own protection. In the case of my friends, their safety."

"Is your name not Colin?"

"My real name is Colin. I just want you to know the true me."

Allison turned toward the ship's fantail to look at the ship's wake. She said, "Well, Mr. Colin George, that does not change how I feel about you." He extended his hand to her shoulder and turned her around. "From now on, it is *always* Colin to you."

Allison accepted his hand to hold.

They remained silent for some time. Allison spoke up to reveal her secret. "Colin," she said, "I need to be honest and tell you. There are actually three hundred and one horses in the cargo hold. I had to bring my thoroughbred mare, Anna. Would you like to meet her?" Colin said, "Why, certainly, my dear Allison?"

They both walked back to the door hatch leading into the ladderwell. From there they stepped down four ladders and four hatches until they reached the main cargo hold. Once inside, the deck-space floodlights cast moving shadows of horses stepping about their hay and tether lines. The black mare in the far end whinnied.

Allison said, "See, that is my girl. Anna."

*****

The S.S. *Haverford* moored at the Dartmouth pier on June 21. Both Allison and Colin positioned themselves near the starboard gangway, as the ship's bowlines were lowered down to several watermen standing by to receive the ship. The men secured the mooring lines to several large stations bolted into the pier. They whistled up at the ship's captain. Giving him a thumbs-up, the captain acknowledged them.

Allison looked across the quay wall and observed two dozen green military trucks lining up behind one another. She turned to Colin. "What are those military trucks waiting for?"

"My dear." Colin cleared his throat while putting his arms around Allison's waist. "Those trucks are here to haul out the special cargo."

Allison's eyebrows arched. She said, "You mean there are explosives on this ship! What if we were hit by a German torpedo? We all would have died."

"Now, don't fret. The contents are just barrels of acetone. Our munitions experts need it to manufacture cordite, the explosive component of shells. It is produced almost entirely by the chemical breakdown of U.S. wood. As it is, the United States and Canada are exploiting escalating timber market prices to make acetone for us. But then we have no choice. Eighty tons of birch, beech, or maple trees is needed to produce one ton of acetone.[50] We just don't have enough trees here in England to make our bombs."

The longshoremen secured two brows to the ship's main decks forward and aft. One wider brow was positioned from the pier to the lower cargo hold. Collin turned to Allison and extended his arm to her. "The horses will be unloaded after the special cargo has been cleared from the pier. Shall we go, my lady?"

Allison nodded her head and slipped her arm inside his. She said, "You know, I kind of like this lady treatment."

They walked down to the end of the brow and stopped. Colin touched Allison's arm. She looked at him and said, "I am absolutely mad about you. You know this?"

Allison tugged on Collin's arm. "Me too. Now come on. When will they offload the horses?"

"In an hour or two. They need to get the acetone unloaded first. Why don't we go over to the port captain's office and get a cup of Black Earl tea while we wait."

"Sounds like a perfect idea. But what about our luggage?"

"Do not fret about that, Allison. I took care of it. I made arrangements for two rooms at my friend's quintessentially English residence just outside Exeter, not far from here. You will enjoy sightseeing in Exeter. Several old cathedrals dot the hillsides."

"Sounds fabulous." Allison turned her brown cashmere coat collar up over her neck. She said, "Gets a bit cool and wet around here." Colin nodded in agreement. "Indeed it does. Indeed it does. Come now. Let us get our hot tea before we make our way to Exeter. Tomorrow will be a long day traveling to the Romsey Remount Depot in Hampshire. The horses you trained will be there. Along with Anna. She will have free stay while you are here."

Major Oliver Hazzard

Major Hazzard and Captain Boak readied for the Sunday church parade. Afterward, the men would settle on the benches to listen to the brigade chaplain, Reverend John A. Fortier. He delivered another inspiring service message. One message the chaplain preached about was the 1914 Christmas Miracle. On December 25, German and British soldiers ceased fighting across five hundred miles of the Western Front. The chaplain said God spoke to the men's hearts.

After service, the major and the captain walked back to their tent to change into their working uniforms. The major kept scratching his head on the way to the tent. The captain observed this and said, "Something troubling you, Major?"

"Well, no. Uhm...actually, yes. I was thinking about the reverend's sermon."

"What about it?"

"Why would God stop the fighting and then let the soldiers continue killing one another?"

"Orders. Commanding orders from men. I need say no more, sir." Out of respect to his nation's sponsor, the major let it go.

The annals of war speak to a nation's will that wavers proportionally to news of death and destruction on the battlefield. Major Hazzard and Captain Boak read the daily cables received from the field. The Western Front casualties were measured in the tens of thousands of British and French forces. The major took note of a history lesson. Sitting across the planning table from Captain Boak, he said, "I hold here a field cable that repeats history."

"How so, sir?"

"Toward the end of the U.S. Civil War, President Lincoln put newly promoted General Ulysses S. Grant in charge of the Union armies. The president wanted a decisive man who would put an end to the war. Now, take note. President Lincoln's previous commanders failed miserably. As a result of those leadership failures, General Grant was given autonomous decision-making authority on the battlefield. To do so, he had to act aggressively in short order. His plan was to simply take the Confederate capital of

Leather to Steel

Richmond, Virginia. To do so required him to push his troops across unforgiving land between Washington and Richmond. The military called it the Overland Campaign—one of several battles like it to follow. General Grant's Overland Campaign resulted in the loss of over seventeen thousand Union soldiers over a period of two days. Your war is repeating history."

The captain thought for a minute and then said, "Yes, but the difference is us English want this war." The major's eyes widened, and his jaw dropped. He picked up the tin-coffee cup and took a sip. Steam from the hot coffee filled his nose. He looked down at his hands and then back up at the captain. The major said, "Okay, Captain Boak, you got my attention. Now why would the English want war?"

"Rather simple yet understandable, if you will. England has spent centuries defending itself from invasions that come and go. Our country ended up mastering the seas to acquire great wealth and English pride. The Germans, Russians, and French are no different. In fact, we call them the family monarchy squabbles ruining Europe."

"What do you mean by family monarchy squabbles?"

"Quite simple, I am afraid. You must understand that over the centuries, England, Germany, Russia, and Austria, to list a few, are countries run by kings and queens that are surely related to one another."

"Seriously. Family bloodlines run across the borders."

"Indeed. King George V is a first cousin of Germany's Kaiser William II. The Kaiser and Russia's Czar Nicholas II are cousins through the sister of King Edward II."

Major Hazzard raised his hand toward the captain and said, "I got it. Enough drama for one sitting. But I have one burning question to ask: if three powerful countries are run by a family of monarchs, why would they want to go to war with each other?"

"Great question. Like I said, it is the people who wanted war. Russia had diplomatic relationship and familial connection, somewhere in the bloodline—which forced Russia to defend Serbia after Austria attacked. Germany had to defend Austria because

Russia was coming after them. Belgium was the centerpiece of neutrality. That is where the Germans overstepped their territorial aspirations. Attacking Belgium forced France into play."

"Then, Captain, it is well known that England and France have been off and on at war for centuries. Why the change of heart? I am pretty sure England did not have a treaty in place with France stipulating wartime support."

"You are correct. However, France is just across the English Channel. Our war planners—in particular Winston Churchill—agreed with the politicians that coming to the aid of France would be in our national security's best interest."

"I see. The will of the people."

"Indeed. Through back channels, the German ultimatums given to England were rescinded by Kaiser Wilhelm II himself. It was too late. His war generals were thirsty for war, as were the English and French. You might say it was about pride and prejudice."

The major shook his head and let out a sigh. He looked at the map on the table. British Expeditionary Force troops were marked off by a black grease pencil. He asked the captain, "Where will the RCAB end up?"

Captain Boak replied, "Not sure, sir. I would hate to speculate. Our orders are to stay in garrison for six months. Acting as a reserve force, if you will."

"Thank you," replied the major, who added, "I would like to ride along when the orders come."

"Major, your orders do not require you to be in harm's way."

"Yes, I understand that captain. I want to truly be valued in this unit. I have tactical cavalry experience that may be of value. I also have two very well-trained warhorses that will fight."

"Impressive animals, sir. Perhaps we defer to the colonel on this. It is above my pay grade." The major continued scouring over the Western Front. As field cables came in, he marked the locations of all the militaries. The Germans were clearly taking ground against the French. Reports coming from inside sources in Austria told of great German army advances against the Russian Imperial Army.

The Austrians were rolling into the Balkans, showing no mercy to the civilians and the countryside.

The European War expanded well beyond its borders. Other countries view the war as opportunities to grab land and fill their coffers in exchange for supplies, armies, and natural resources. Such was the case between Germany and Turkey. Turkey would provide military support if the Germans gave Armenia to them.

*****

Allison Drayton

Allison Drayton and her diplomatic escort, Collin George, strolled arm in arm to the main guard house at the Romsey Remount Depot. A young soldier approached them and said, "Sir, ma'am, will you please show your identifications?"

Allison looked at Collin, who pulled out his diplomatic credentials to present to the guard. Allison followed Collin's lead. She reached into her purse and pulled out her United States passport and handed it to the guard.

The guard took his time looking at the identifications and the faces of the woman and the man who presented them. Then he asked, "Sir, ma'am, who are you here to see?"

Collin pulled out the bill of sale he received from Allison back in the States. He presented it to the guard, along with his military identification showing the rank of Royal Navy commander. The guard pulled his legs together to attention. He snapped his heels together and rendered a proper salute to the senior officer, wearing civilian clothes, as military protocol dictated.

The guard replied, "Sorry, sir. I did not know you were a senior officer."

Collin replied, "No worries, son. Please point us to the commander's office. We need to meet with him."

The soldier gladly pointed toward the gray-rock building nearest the stable complex.

The Bateses

Back in the States, Jeremiah Bates continued serving the U.S. Army as lead horse trainer at the Front Royal Remount Depot. He often thought about Tough Guy, Grace, and Jubal Early. Three horses that touched his life. Three horses that influenced his son Abraham's decision to pursue a college education. He was proud of his son. He was grateful for his wife, Mary, and his four other children's zest for living.

The depot processed hundreds of horses in a short period of time. The battlefield demands created rapid turnaround not conducive for proper horse training. The depot commander had no choice. He reluctantly shipped the horses to Europe.

Jeremiah asked, "Commander, why are so many horses being sent over to England?"

The commander did not smile, or show emotion in his response. "To replace the ones perishing on battlefields."

Jeremiah excused himself and walked away, shaking his head. He repeatedly mumbled, "Lord, help us. Lord, help us. Lord, save those poor horses."

> Now glut yourselves with conflict, nor refrain,
> But let your famished provinces be fed
> From bursting granaries of steel and lead!
> Decree the sowing of that bitter grain
> Where the great war-horse, maddened with his pain,
> Stamps on the mangled living and the dead,
> And from the entreated heavens overhead
> Falls from a brother's hand a fiery rain.
> —George Sterling, "To The Kings of This World," 1915

Those Poor Horses

Not only men but horses were the victims of this war of attrition. Franz Marc exclaimed in one of his letters, "The poor horses!" In only one day, 7,000 horses were killed by long-range French and German shelling, ninety-seven from a single shell fired by a French naval gun.
—Martin Gilbert,
Author, First World War, 1994

Protracted fighting across the trenches caused unbearable heartache for soldier, horse, and mule. Two years into the violence, civilians, soldiers, and beasts of burden existed without a moment of peace. The world did not stand on the sideline and watch. In response, the American Red Cross mobilized volunteers and resources to ease the suffering of men. The international community, in the spirit of human values, cried out to save the horses, for the leather was no match for steel.

In April, 1916, the president of the American Humane Association offered the services of this organization and its allied societies to the War Department for the purpose of rendering assistance in the event of war to wounded animals employed by the Army; furnishing base hospitals, veterinary supplies, and ambulances in a capacity similar to that in which the Blue Cross functioned for the allied foreign armies.
—Letter from the American Humane Association to the War Department April 15, 1916[51]

Citizens stepped up to provide financial assistance, which was all they could do. The displaced warhorses in Europe were three thousand miles away. Sadly, not much else could be done.

Taking Advantage

In the account book of the Great War the page recording the Russian losses has been ripped out. The figures are unknown. Five million, or eight? We ourselves do not know... All we know is that, at times, fighting the Russians, we had to remove the piles of enemy bodies from before our trenches, so as to get a clear field of fire against new waves of assault."

—Paul von Hindenburg,
German commander,
1916

Germany skillfully influenced international affairs to bolster its political advantages. Two nations directly, or indirectly, stood between victory and defeat. Russia was the immediate threat. The United States was an emerging threat. These nations represented a losing proposition if not contained. Two years into the war, Germany was successful in neutralizing the Russian government. The United States populace would be more challenging. The Germans would not relent in pursuing alliances and espionage to influence the American psyche.

The German Reich understood the value of creating public unrest among the Russian civilian populations. German and Austrian spies worked behind Russian border to finance Russian revolutionaries eager to dispose of the Russian monarchy. In short, the German investments worked.

On March 15, 1917, Czar Nicholas II became the last Emperor of Russia forced to abdicate his throne. The post-Czar Russian government struggled to contain public sentiment toward war. The end result produced a strategic political advantage for Germany. Russia could not sustain their militaries on the Eastern Front. Russia relented and sued for peace with Germany and Austria. The Kaiser's generals no longer concerned themselves with the East. The West had become their target.

The United States remained neutral with Germany, but not with Mexico. In 1916, President Wilson was forced to launch an expedition into Mexico to capture Mexican revolutionary bandit Pancho Villa. In doing so, the United States violated Mexico's sovereign nation status. The Mexican government was outraged. Germany saw a political opportunity to nurture an alliance with Mexico. German fomented distrust with the fractured Mexican government. History tells us the events prepared the United States cavalry for war. The U.S. Army Cavalry would be tested; a general would be made—General Black Jack Pershing—who would lead the American Expeditionary Force into battle on the Western Front.

*****

Unexpectedly, the United States got into the business of policing its own southwest borders. On March 29, 1916, the U.S. Army Seventh Cavalry fought an equal-sized force of supporters of Villa at Guerrero, Mexico. Men and horse pursued the murderous bandit across rugged terrains of northern Mexico, and the southern deserts of New Mexico and Arizona. History would tell, that in many ways, the Poncho Villa campaign was the last major cavalry action of the United States Army in North America.

President Wilson took tough action to eliminate America's distraction from neutrality. Texas, Arizona, and New Mexico National Guard units were called up on May 8 to establish defensive and offensive security posture on America's southwest border to deter Mexican civil war spillover into the States. The border security concerns moved the U.S. Congress on June 3 to quickly pass the approval of the National Defense Act.

The act prompted the rest of the states and the District of Columbia to mobilize National Guard units to the southwest border for added security. The government's decision did not bode well for public approval ratings. American newspapers across the country cried foul of policing the borders, while "German army atrocities marred the civility of European decency." Jeremiah and Mary Bates and 100 million American citizens shared the same sentiments.

*****

The Bateses

Reading the Sunday paper and sipping coffee became a family tradition at the Bates home. On the front porch, Jeremiah and Mary enjoyed their temporary privacy away from the children. Jeremiah sat comfortably on a straight-backed chair he inherited from his father, Bo. He often said sitting in the chair spoke to him. On his right, Mary rocked in her new, padded black oak rocker Jeremiah bought her for Christmas. He claimed to have negotiated a good price from a Richmond imports store owned by a young German-speaking man.

Jeremiah crossed his legs and propped his right elbow on his knee to spread out the *Washington Times* newspaper pages. Mary loved to rock and crochet while Jeremiah read. Her latest project was a colorful blanket. Her Seminole heritage was reflected in the colors she chose.

Mary purchased several different colors of yarn to make the blanket. Colors such as red, white, lavender, several shades of blues, yellow, green, pumpkin yellow, and purple. Jeremiah was able to purchase most of the prime colors from the Richmond importer. Mary had to make special dyes to get the other colors she needed. On this Sunday, she crocheted a blanket to donate to their church, which was collecting humanitarian goods for war victims in Europe.

Jeremiah scanned through the newspaper to check out want ads and for-sale items. Not finding anything of interest, he turned the paper over to view the front page. He folded the paper in half. He read the headline aloud and said, "Mary. Look at this." Mary stopped rocking and put down her crochet hooks. She turned toward Jeremiah. She read the headline, "Who is this Villa?"

Jeremiah put his paper down and explained. "Bad Mexican whose bandits wreaked havoc on a New Mexico town, then, like cowards, ran back across the border to hide out in Mexico."

"Did he kill anyone?"

Leather to Steel

"Yes. Pancho and his bandits committed unforgivable acts that caught the attention of our government. Looks like several National Guard units are being mobilized to the southwest border."

"Why so many soldiers for one man?"

"It is not just one man. It is also the tens of thousands revolutionaries who believe he represents freedom of oppression. The poor Mexican peasants. Those people want to overthrow the Mexican government. Another civil war."

"Why do we care, Jeremiah?"

"Because there is a sour history between our countries. I am sure President Wilson will not tolerate it. It says here that old John J. Pershing has assembled several U.S. Army cavalry units to search, kill, and/or capture Villa. One of those units is my old regiment—the Tenth Cavalry. Well, I be dang."

"Jeremiah, I remember the Tenth back at Fort Sill. That was some time ago. Best you not be in the army now."

"Don't worry about me doing that again. I did my time and want nothing to do with fighting. Too many people die. In some cases, for no reason. To change the subject, what do you think about going for a walk? The church bus will be dropping off the kids in an hour. That will give us time to walk and spend some alone time together."

Mary added, "You are such a romantic. Even after all these years. Let us take a walk, husband."

Jeremiah stood up and walked to help Mary out of her rocker. The two held hands as they stepped off the porch onto a trodden trail leading around the house, then down to a small creek. The afternoon sun shined brightly down on the Bates family, as it did that day on the United States Army Cavalry Regiment.

The April 2, 1916 Washington Times Newspaper headlines read, "Poncho Villa's hit-and-run tactics from Mexico into the United States drew the attention of the United States Army."

In addition to the large numbers of National Guard troops sent to the border, two Regular Army cavalry regiments, the Sixteenth and Seventeenth, were formed up to track down and arrest Poncho Villa. Pershing added several additional cavalry units to rotate in and out of Mexico. The Tenth Cavalry Regiment would answer the call again. Its black officers and enlisted knew of its herald history.[52]

The U.S. Army hunted Pancho Villa for nine months. No general was more frustrated than Brigadier General John J. Pershing who assembled cavalry units to pursue Villa, not just within the United States borders. Determined to capture Villa, General Pershing crossed the border into the sovereign country of Mexico, without diplomatic permission. He searched nine months for the illusive Pancho Villa. Pershing's troopers engaged and killed many Villa followers, but not Villa himself, who evaded capture.

During the fall of 1916, under advisement of the Secretary of War Baker, President Wilson ordered General Pershing to withdraw all troops from searching for one criminal. It was an election year, and the Great War drew America deeper into its grasps. The possibility of war with Germany became a political reality, trumping any security concerns south of the border, at least until the Zimmerman telegram reminded Americans that staying neutral could not be sustained.

The German politic reached out to Mexico to negotiate an alliance.[53] The encrypted Zimmerman telegram suggested Mexico should go declare war on the United States because it violated Mexico's sovereign nation status during its search for Pancho Villa. However, Mexico was not the only recipient of the message. The United States military decoded the message. Germany's ill intentions angered the U.S. Congress and the peoples of these United States. America's disgust with Germany cemented within retribution and vengeance.

*****

The Eilenbergs

Six months had passed since Kate's memorial service. Max Eilenberg dearly missed his wife. He tried to take his mind off her by working twelve-hour days at his Richmond store. The idea of

Leather to Steel

burying his memories through work did not relieve his pain. Outside the store, reminders of the Great War discriminated between American-born and immigrants. A war that increasingly made Max's life as a German American in Virginia more difficult. The National Security League made sure of it.[54]

Zealous American-born youths bought into the idea that a safe America must be suspicious of all German Americans whose loyalties were questioned. Citizen behaviors not consistent with the American way were judged by National Security League members as traitors.

Max's self-sequestered behavior was because of his wife's death, not because he missed the Hinterland. Richmond National Security League chapter members suspected he was hiding pro-German business dealings. For months, he was harassed and threatened.

Between August and October, Max replaced several broken storefront windows at his business. The first attacks were not claimed by any particular person or group. The last aggression broke all the store's windows except one, the front-center window. Painted in red, white, and blue letters, the message read, "Go home, hun. Do not stay here, traitor."

A white eight-square inch paper flyer had been taped to the bottom of the window. The solicitor was recruiting Americans to join the cause to combat German propaganda. Max would act upon the flyer's request. He pulled the flyer off his window, folded it in half, and then stuck it in his front short pocket. He mumbled to himself, "Perhaps the Americans are right." He had enough. He became fed up with American ideals. The Germans called him home.

*****

Sitting alone at the kitchen table, Max stared at an empty chair where Kate once sat. They should have been making plans for Thanksgiving dinner with the Zapatas. Kate always made a big deal about the holidays and celebrations. She put much effort into decorating the house and preparing holiday meals. Max always appreciated her efforts of love. However, there would be no more

Thanksgivings nor Christmas celebrations. The war took the love of his life away from him.

An outside noise made Max turn his head to look through the kitchen window. He could see no movement beyond the alder hedges. Shaking his head, he looked back down at his leftover sauerkraut and sausage. He clasped his hands and closed his eyes to pray.

At every meal, Kate would smile at Max and say, "Okay, husband, time to pray. Let's bow our heads." Max tried to pray again, but he could not finish. He lifted his head and stared at the empty chair. His heart burned with anger toward Kate's God and the country he was forced not to love. At that moment, a cold darkness descended upon his soul. A change in his life was needed. He had to decide.

Max dropped his fork on the plate of food, then shoved it across the table. He quickly stood up from this chair. As he turned around, the chair fell, crashing against the kitchen floor. He disregarded the chair and walked out the back kitchen door to breathe some fresh air. Max took a deep breath and sighed. He looked across the fields extending beyond his property line. The sun had just gone down over the horizon. Brilliant red and orange colors painted the clouds, while casting shadows on the ground.

A dark silhouette moved across the pasture. It neighed loudly. The Zapatas' black stallion paced back and forth along the fence line. He then stopped and looked back at Max in the lighted kitchen.

Max made eye contact with the stallion and mumbled, "I wish I was free like you, old boy." The horse neighed and snorted again. The stallion rose up on his hind legs, pawing toward Max. Max paused in thought. His eyes lit up. Max shook his head back and forth. He looked up to the ceiling. "If there is a God, he has spoken to me. I must fight to free this aching pain in my heart."

*****

January 1916, brought bright hopes of making New Year's resolutions for millions of people around the world. If a resolution was a wish, then most resolved to have good health and, most of all, peace. Max had good health, but no peace. He wanted change. He needed Germany.

The Eilenberg farm sold within the month. Manny and Lucinda offered to help him move, but Max insisted none was needed. He told Manny that he could not live in the house without Kate. Her scents attached to every room. The reminders caused much sadness within Max. Before he moved, he asked Manny and Lucinda to come over and take what they wanted.

Lucinda took Kate's death hard. She reminded herself that God's plan for Kate did not include Lucinda's life. If Lucinda had not been blessed with a child, she too would have been on that ship with Kate. Instead, she gave birth to a baby boy. The proud mother and father thanked God each day for their lives.

Max stood at the front door, watching the Zapatas walk up the front porch steps. In anticipation, he opened the door. "Manny, Lucinda, and little Clemente. Please come in. It is cold out here."

Manny looked Max in the eyes. "Dear friend, Max. We would not miss seeing you off."

Lucinda stepped inside first. She kept her baby boy wrapped in a warm blanket. Manny stepped inside just behind her.

Max closed the front door. "Please. Come sit in the living room. The fireplace is putting out very good heat. Can I take your coats?"

Manny replied, "No, thank you. We can't stay long."

Max nodded. "I understand. It is hard for me to be in this house without Kate."

Manny and Lucinda sat on the blue settee Kate asked Max to import from England. Max had stepped into the kitchen and brought out a tray of English tea and crumb cakes. He presented the tray. "Lucinda, I did this in honor of Kate. I know how much you and her enjoyed your Saturday mornings under the oak."

Lucinda grinned and then started to tear up.

Max said, "I am sorry, Lucinda. I did not mean to upset you."

"You are so sweet to do so in her memory. No, I am not upset. This is what we all should have done after her memorial service."

"I guess you're right," Max added. "But I was not in a good place."

Manny spoke. "Completely understandable, Max. You have much on your plate. I know the stresses of the war have been personal for you."

"I suppose you are right. The National Security League bastards have not made it easy on us German Americans. In fact, I am very disappointed in my country. Which is why I am leaving."

Lucinda asked, "What will you do?"

"I am moving to Florida. I can start over,"

Manny said, "We will miss you. Will you stay in touch?"

"I hope. My grief consumes me. I just need a change of scenery."

Max sat down in his chair to enjoy his tea and crumb cakes with Manny and Lucinda. The baby woke up and started to whimper. She rocked him some, but his cry grew a little louder. Lucinda turned to Manny. "I think we need to get home. Little Clemente is hungry."

Manny nodded and stood to face Max, who had already risen from his chair. "Max, we wish you the best life has to offer. You will be missed. If you will, Lucinda and I need to get the baby home."

"Of course, Manny," Max replied with saddened eyes.

Manny helped Lucinda to her feet. Max escorted them to the front door. "Adiós, mi amigo. Dios sea contigo." Good-bye, my friend. God be with you.

Max did not have a chance to offer Kate's clothes to Lucinda. He closed the closet door, all the while talking to himself. "Let the new owners sort through all this." He walked over to the dresser draw and picked up a framed picture of Kate. He held the picture in his trembling hands. The only possession of Kate's he would keep would be the picture he slid out of its frame.

He picked up his derby and turned it over. Using his pocketknife, he cut enough threads from the inside seem to insert Kate's picture. Then he sewed the seam back up with a needle and thread Kate had left in a spool on her nightstand. Satisfied, he put his hat on and walked back into the foyer to grab his coat.

After shutting the front door, he locked it and placed the key under the front mat. He would telephone the real estate agent of its location, once he was back in his Richmond office later in the day.

He walked down the steps and took one last look at the house and the property. He sighed and walked to his motorcar parked under the carport. As he opened the driver's door, the Zapatas' black stallion neighed and snorted loudly to get his attention. Max turned and saw the stallion standing by the fence. He was shaking his head up and down at Max.

Max shut the door and walked over to look into the horse's eyes. The black stallion was an impressive-looking animal. Standing at the fence, Max spoke to the horse. "I remember when you were born. You have grown into a fine-looking animal. Even with that Magnolia brand scarring your hind quarter. I suppose there is a mark of ownership on all of us."

The black horse stuck his nose out towards Max, who ran his hands over the horse's muzzle. Kissing the horse's nose, Max mumbled, "Adiós, mi amigo . Dios sea contigo."

*****

Max Eilenberg

Max sold his Richmond import-export business to a fellow German who immigrated on the same ship with Max and his mother back in 1888. The man said he grew up with Max's mother in Dusseldorf. Max was convinced it was all meant to be. He thought the man was the only connection to Germany. Turned out, that was not the case. He handed the store keys over to the elderly German who said the business would continue. The elderly man said, "Your mother's brother will take care of you."

Max walked away from another life. Max did not trust American banks. Instead of investing his money he made from the sales of his house and business, he converted the bank notes into gold. He knew precious metal coinage would be the only thing of value should a worldwide depression hit. He was risk averse. The world war made Max smart enough to know that a world at war was unsafe—and worse yet, unpredictable. He vowed to play it safe getting to Europe. To get to his new life would require money, training, and clever travel arrangements. His mother's brother, Uncle Ademaro, offered to handle those arrangements for Max. After all, the old Germanic saying rings true: "German Blood is thicker than water."

Mid-January, Max began his journey on a train to Tampa, Florida. The first leg of his trip took two days. Once in Tampa, he met with Uncle Ademaro's business contacts from the old country. They arranged for Max to sail on the three-mast schooner *Elsie*. She transited in and out of ports between Tampa, Miami, and Cuba. Her registered cargo was nude hardwoods, Cuban cigars, and Puerto Rican rum. The *Elsie* would not draw the attention of the authorities. The added insurance of traveling disguised as a seaman helped Max avoid curious crewman.

In exchange for ten one-dollar gold coins, the *Elsie*'s captain provided the official seaman papers Max needed for the trip from Cuba to Europe. Max did not have any additional information regarding his ultimate destination. He had to trust Uncle Ademaro. The last cable received read, "Once you are in Havana, stay for three days at the Hotel Habana Vieja. You will receive further instructions once you've checked in." The cable provided the hotel address and nothing else.

The *Elsie* maintained an average speed of twenty-five knots from the Miami River to Cuba. The southwesterly winds dipped way down into the Gulf of Mexico. The winds propelled the schooner across the Straits of Florida around near the Keys. By mid-eve, the *Elsie* anchored in the Port of Mariel, Cuba.

Max stood in complete darkness on the ship's fantail, waiting for water transportation. The only lights he could see were near the wharf. He was not alone. Several deckhands waited with him. They appeared to be guarding four, two-foot-square wooden crates waiting to be unloaded.

Within thirty minutes at anchor, a narrow sixteen-foot ketch pulled up to the leeward side of the ship. Two *Elsie* deckhands tossed rope lines down to the ketch's driver and a deckhand who tied the lines to the ketch's forward and after cleats. The largest fella threw out an oak boarding ladder down to the ketch. He yelled down, "Haken Sie die beiden Enden zu Ihrem Geländer. Eile!" Hook the two ends to your railing. Hurry!

Leather to Steel

That was Max's cue to get off the ship.

The ketch pulled up near the pier to offload Max and other cargo destined for Havana. Max walked to the end of the pier with the longshoreman, who pulled a dolly loaded with four wooden crates stamped with "Fragile. Handle with Care" in big red block letters. He asked the worker, "What is inside the box?"

The longshoreman did not reply.

Max asked again, "What is in the boxes?"

The longshoreman turned toward Max. He shook his head. "No speak English." Max shrugged his shoulders and let it go.

The transportation to Havana idled at the end of the pier. The Ford F-100 truck's gasoline engine pipe blew out white and black smoke from its tailpipe. The engine sounded as though it was making hiccup sounds that irritated the security guard standing inside a shack near the gas-lamp pole. The guard stepped halfway out of the shack and yelled, "Ponerse en marcha!" Get going. The truck's lone occupant rolled down the passenger window. He stuck his arm out and waved.

"Sí, sí. Un momento." Yes, yes. One moment. The man waved Max and the longshoreman to come quickly. Max walked past the guard without making eye contact. Max noticed the guard had a single-shot military rifle slung around the left shoulder. Max made a mental note that he had to keep to himself.

The longshoreman loaded the four wooden boxes into the truck bed. He then threw a thick, oiled burlap tarp over the truck bed to cover the boxes. While he tied down the tarp's edges, Max opened the front truck's front passenger door and jumped in. After shutting the door, Max looked at the old man sitting behind the steering wheel.

The driver was wearing a dirty white sleeveless shirt and smelled of rum. He turned to Max and patted the seat. Max nodded and continued to hold his one travel bag in his lap. The old man said, "Señor. Havana?" Max sat back into the worn leather seat that smelled of stale beer and cigars. He shifted his overstuffed bag on his lap to get more comfortable.

The driver asked in broken English, "Dinero. You dinero?" Max did not understand. He pulled out the wrinkled white paper from his front shirt pocket. He read the cable again, then tucked it back into his pocket.

Max replied, "Hotel Habana Vieja."

The old man's face contorted somewhat. He asked again, "No. Money."

Max shook his head realizing he had to pay again. He reached down into his front pants pocket to get one five-dollar gold piece. He handed the shiny coin to the old man. The old man put the coin in the side of this mouth to bite down on the coin to test it. He said, "Good gold." Max could not help notice the old man was missing several front teeth. The remaining teeth were stained and chipped.

The ship's captain said the trip would take only an hour. He was right. The old man dropped Max off in front of the Hotel Habana Vieja. Max stood for a moment to watch the truck leave. He took note of the truck's direction of travel toward the bay, where a large cargo ship was anchored. The ship that would set sail in three days.

The Habana Viejo hotel looked old. Signs of aging scarred the four-story building. The salty air had turned the painted iron security window covers into bars of rust. The siding looked worse. Max studied the outside. He mumbled, "A fresh coat of paint, and this place would not look so bad." The pinks and the greens had faded. Paint peeled on every wooden slat.

Max stepped through a spinning revolving door that was not spinning minutes before. Once inside, a small Cuban boy greeted him in the foyer. The boy placed his hands on Max's bag. He looked up and said, "Carry bag, Señor?" Max shook his head no. The small boy tugged at the bag again. "Señor. Me help." Max reluctantly let the boy carry the bag toward the hotel counter where a heavyset middle-aged woman waited. Max asked her, "Room for three days?"

The woman shook her head, not understanding Max.

He held three fingers up. "Three days please."

The woman understood. She pointed at a sign that read, "2 Pesos," which Max had no Cuban money to pay with. He reached into this pocket and pulled out one five-dollar gold piece. He handed

Leather to Steel

it to her, and she put the coin in between her teeth. She bit down on the coin to test it. She said, "Good. Good. You stay."

She handed Max a room key that had the number *404* burned into a decorative wooden paddle attached to the key. Max looked kindly at the woman and thanked her. While he fiddled with his bag, a door slammed behind him. He turned from the counter to see what it was. The front revolving door had jammed against the outer frame. The wind was kicking up. He was spooked and a little nervous.

He wanted to get into his room soon. He was tired and needed to clean up. Before he took one step away from the counter, the woman's voice rose in pitch. "Señor. Your change." She reached out and handed him three gold pesos and five silver centavos.

Max replied, "Thank you. I am so tired. I would not have remembered." He rolled the coins in his hands. He studied the money that looked freshly minted and mumbled, "That is odd. I wonder—"

The boy standing next to Max tugged at the bag. Max looked down at the boy, and handed one U.S. penny to him. The little boy ran over behind the counter and handed the coin to the woman. She spoke softly to him. "Eres un buen hijo." You are a good son.

Max mumbled, "At least I made three people happy today—the driver, the desk clerk, and now the boy."

Getting up to his room was a physical ordeal. There was no elevator to lessen his toil. Certainly not like the one he carried Kate in at the Waldorf Hotel. One of several romantic weekends they spent in New York City trying to make a baby. Instead, he found himself alone, unhappy, and a very tired man looking at the only way up and down the stairs. He climbed four stories to get to the fourth floor, during which he could have easily slipped and fell. The stairwell had little lighting, which made each step a guess in the shadows.

Max held on to the railing to keep his balance. Then he stopped just outside the stairwell door on the fourth floor. He worked up a noticeable sweat getting there. He wiped his forehead with his shirt sleeve. Taking a deep breath, he mumbled, "Now, where is my room?" Walking the hallway, he counted room numbers beginning with 400. Turning one corner, he found room 404. He pulled the room key out of his pants to unlock the door. Once inside, he flipped on the wall switch that lit one lone electric bulb affixed to the room's ceiling. He traced the exposed electric line running from the light to the light switch. The room's designer tacked bent nails over the thin white wire against the wall and ceiling. A rough solution used to keep electric wire from falling on a guest.

Max looked around the room to locate a washbasin, a chair, and a single bed. The first thing he needed was sleep. A long hot bath with a fresh meal to follow appealed to Max, but first things first, Max dropped his duffel bag on the floor and collapsed on the bed face-first. He slept peacefully until the next morning. He probably would have slept all the next day, if he was not woken up by three hard raps on the room door.

The attractive hotel maid standing in front of him did not show any signs that she had climbed four floors to his room. She had not a drop of perspiration on her forehead. She extended her right hand out, with a dirty white envelope to Max. She apologized. "Sorry to wake you, Señor. This cable came in for you last night. I brought it to you thinking it was important." Max took the envelope and said, "Gracias, senorita. By the way, you speak very good English. The first I have heard since my arrival." The maid blushed. "Thank you, mister señor." Max chuckled at her use of a double noun." He took one step backward to shut the door.

Max noticed she did not turn and leave. She remained silently in place near the door's entrance. Max looked curiously at her. He concluded she waited for a tip and said, "So sorry." He reached into his pocket and gave her two bits. The attractive maid started to walk inside his room. Max then realized he had sent the wrong message. He put his hand out to stop her. "Another time. Too tired. Thank you," he said as he slowly closed the door behind her. The maid winked at Max just before the door shut. She stood outside his door with her hands on her hips. The maid spoke under her breath. "Gute Herr Eilenberg. Sie sind konzentriert und abiding nach unseren Regeln." Good, Mr. Eilenberg. You are focused and abiding by our rules.

Olga von Marx reluctantly turned and walked away.[55]

Max sat down on the edge of his bed. Holding the envelope, he slit it open with his trimmed thumbnail. He slipped the paper out and started reading. The cable was from Uncle Ademaro. It read,

> Begin. Pay for a three-day stay. During those three days, I will contact you again. Transatlantic travel arrangements will be completed. *SS Moro Castle* provide passage to Monaco. End Message.

Max folded up the cable and slipped it back into his pocket. All he could do now was wait for the next cable message. Until then, he would walk the streets of Havana, looking for Olga. It would be a year before they could leave Cuba.

*****

Tough Guy

Throughout most of 1915, the Royal Canadian Horse Artillery Brigade remained in garrison in England, training for the battles to come—and come they would. My trooper, Major Oliver Hazzard, committed Jubal and me to stay the course. He had no intention of returning to the States. He told me and Jubal that the service was before self. Soon enough, the course would change during the first part of 1916. Command made preparations for battle.

Standing tethered to a tie line, Jubal and I observed a command inspection. We stood nearest to Major Hazzard and Captain Boak standing at attention in the front row. I overheard the Canadian commander reply to something Captain Boak asked during quarters. The commander said. "I have decided to move my command closer to the battle. We are going to Neuve-Église."

Tough Guy

We crossed over the English Channel on transport ships in early September to the Port of Calais situated on the Opal Coast in Northern France. From Calais, we were transported by rail toward the Western Front—the term soldiers used to describe the region of Northern France and Belgium.

The first way point would be La Petite Douve France. The staging area for battle preparations. From there, the Royal Canadian Artillery Brigade relieved battle-worn troops fighting across battle lines in Flanders, a region in Belgium. Before month's end, the horror of war would impress itself upon man's soul and a horse's heart.

Major Hazzard and Captain Boak traveled with quartermaster supply vehicles, horses and mules packed. Ammunition teams, mobile command, and control communication motorcars, and ambulances stayed in the rear. The artillery batteries moved forward toward prepositioned markers the scouts secured to fence posts to help sight in distances. The Canadians would use the fence markers to plan and execute rolling barrages against the entrenched Germans.[56]

Muddy fields slowed any advancement of troops and weaponry. Rain had been falling for several days prior to our arrival. In preparation, the battalion engineers moved under the previous eve's cover of darkness to lay fascine on the road. They used brush, wood, and whatever else would not sink into the mud. The engineers sent word back not to veer off the road. The rain-soaked fields were unforgiving to heavy loads.

The Germans, nicknamed the Huns, or Tommies, strung serpentine barbed wire across the muddied fields to impede our cavalry's ability to conduct nighttime reconnaissance. Our mounted troopers knew not to gallop us across a tree line. Precautions were necessary in light of several dead horses lying cut to the bone below the tangled barbed wire.

The command order was given on September 23 to cut all wires stretching two miles across trench lines previously occupied by German forces. The commander would not advance machine, man, and horse without fully understanding the terrain ahead. Major Hazzard said euphemistically the fog of war remained translucent until the cavalryman's horse stomped and the sword was swung. Solid ground and clear skies were the preferred conditions.

We trailed four ambulances slowly following the supply trucks. Captain Boak rode Daisy alongside us most of the time. We followed the ambulances for several miles until a safe exit could be made toward an old farmhouse noted on the captain's map. I snickered at Jubal, who resisted Daisy's nipping. She was a feisty horse who, in my opinion, was sweet on Jubal. He was too serious about himself to think otherwise.

The major and the captain made every effort to keep us in the center of the fascine road. The bundles of brush and wood used to harden the road's surface helped keep our hooves out of the muck. I would not call it a road. It was more like a wide muddy trail scarred by wheel ruts left by heavy-laden artillery limbers, supply, and fuel trucks.

Major Hazzard and Captain Boak kept a healthy distance from the big thirteen-pounder guns. Those guns were loud and served a German target of choice. The major said the closer we were to the big guns, the more likely we would die. He was right. The red explosions near the horizon told us of relentless shelling on both sides. We continued to move forward until daylight.

A few hours after sunrise, the commander ordered all batteries to array themselves parallel to the trenches for a two-mile stretch. The main British Expeditionary Forces occupied the trenches. The major said the British fought hard to gain a thousand yards to press forward; the gain of a thousand yards would exact thousands of lives. A price measured in the numbers of humans, mules, and horses killed and wounded.

The first dead horse I saw was a testament to the kind of war being fought. The poor horse was buried up to his neck in mud. He looked as though he had lost his footing and slid into a mud-filled trench. The pair of panniers he carried was loaded with eight rounds of 18-pound shells for a field gun. His load weighed over two hundred pounds. The panniers often became imbalanced, causing ammunition teams to lose their footing in the mud. In this horse's case, the panniers were removed.[57] A humane bullet hole in the center of his head put him at peace.

After slogging through another mile in the pouring rain, the major and the captain steered us to a partially blown-up farmhouse in the La Petite Douve. Captain Boak leaned over his saddle. He said, "Major. The commander would like to use that farmhouse as his command post for the next few days. We need to get the horses over to the barn and see what we can drum up for feed." The major replied, "I see the turnoff point to the farm."

I could feel the major wiggle his seat in the saddle. Every time he did that, I had to adjust my own footing in the sloping muddy field we were crossing. Off the road, I could feel the sticky mud trying to suck my hooves into the ground. Jubal neighed at me from behind. "I am having a heck of a time keeping my balance in this stuff."

"Son, you see that farmhouse ahead of us?"

"Is that where we are going?"

"The major is keeping steady reins. It is slippery. I am just trying to focus on getting from point A to point B"

The major spoke out. "Captain, I reckon that sounds like a good plan. I would like to find some dry ground in this godforsaken place."

The captain cleared his throat. "Not sure if that is possible. But we shall give it a go."

"Are you catching a cold?"

"No, sir. It is just the air. The musty air is making my eyes water."

The major replied, "There is mist in the air. However, I think it is just normal morning mist. Maybe there's some leftover German chlorine gas floating around?"

The captain quickly pulled out his bandanna to cover his face. The major smirked.

At the farmhouse, the captain and the major halted us. They dismounted from our backs. The major said, "Captain, looks like it is abandoned. The front windows are all blown out from top to bottom." Shaking his head, the captain added, "But we can hang some canvas over those openings. What do you think?"

"I agree. As long as the draft is kept out, I think the commander will approve. Don't you?"

"Indeed. It is not expected to secure the best of accommodations under these conditions. Perhaps the barn is in better shape. We should check it out."

The major and the captain slowly led us over to a broken barn structure casting a long dark shadow on the ground in front of us. Combined with the low gray clouds above us, the place looked eerie and sounded alarming to us. One door hinge kept the left door hanging against the front side of the barn. The door moved on its own. The hayloft opening above the door was untouched. As we stepped closer to the structure, I concluded it was only half a barn. The front right side was partially damaged.

The major and the captain would not lead us forward to the right. A ten-foot-wide bomb crater, half filled with soiled water, blocked the right-side entrance. The major sarcastically complained. "Looks like the Huns could not finish the job. They must have turned tail."

The captain quipped, "No doubt our soldiers gave them something to think about."

Once inside, I looked through the barn backside and noticed the doors were wide open. Walking up the center, to the right of me, I saw several pig carcasses lying in what were fenced-in pigpens. I admit, I was a bit spooked by the sight of dead and decaying animals.

I blinked my eyes several times, trying to focus a crouching dark shape that vanished in the shadows. My eyes were getting old. However, my sense of smell and hearing were as sharp as ever. I neighed at Jubal and Daisy. "Smells pretty bad around here. Wood ash and unusual animal scents I do not recognize. Do you both smell the same?"

Daisy answered, "Tough Guy. Not sure if this is a safe place. It was hard to make out what ran behind the barn. I can see right through to the other side."

Jubal neighed loudly, "I see some movement on the outside near the rubble. Wait. I can also hear a low growl."

Alarmed, Daisy stopped in her tracks. She snorted to get the captain's attention.

Major Hazzard nudged the captain. "You know. I used to hunt up in the Blue Ridge Mountains back in Virginia. I would see deer, elk, pumas, and, occasionally, gray wolves." Eyes wide open now, the captain responded in a whisper, "You thinking what I am thinking?"

The major and the captain pulled out their pistols and chambered rounds. The major regained control of our leads, moving us farther into the barn.

Four undamaged stalls lined the far left back side of the barn. The major spoke softly. "Captain, we need to secure the horses in those stalls first."

The captain nodded in agreement. They led us into the stalls and closed the stall door hasps. The major scanned the area Jubal and me. He said, "Boys. You need to stay put here. Keep Daisy company." The captain had to back Daisy into her stall. Her girth prevented her from turning once inside.

The major and the captain left us alone while they searched for the intruder. I neighed at Jubal, "Son, do you remember our days back on the Roosevelt Farm in Virginia?"

"I sort of do."

"Jubal Early, you were born there. Your mother, Grace, and I raised quite a few babies there. In the year you were born, there was a hard winter. The extreme cold pushed out much of the small game into the warmer valleys. The predators usually stayed in the high country. They consumed small game to survive the winter. When spring came during your first year of life, the predators were pretty darn hungry. Hungry enough to swim across the Shenandoah River onto the riverbanks running along the Roosevelt farm. You and nine other of your siblings were their prey."

"I am sorry. I don't remember."

"I suspect you would not. You were maybe a couple of months old. As you will, you and four other colts were running about the property without a care in the world. The mares usually kept a good watch on all of you. There were four bays that turned to chase you down. I watched a young black colt draw them toward the riverbank. We lost sight of you and the four bays. I smelled and heard a predator near your position. I called out to your mother, and another mare herded the rest of the fillies and colts safely back to the barn.

All the little ones were accounted for, except one. That one was you, Jubal Early. Your mother and I called you No-Name then."

"Where was I?"

"By yourself near the riverbank standing in a thicket. When I got to you, all heck broke loose."

"So what is the point of this story?"

"The point is, a big mountain lion positioned himself in a tree near where you were standing. The mountain lion was within seconds of springing on you until I arrived. There was a struggle. He did not want to give up his prospective dinner. I did not want to give up my son. In the end, he lost out, and you lived. You were not the same after that. You did not neigh or socialize with our herd. Which is why we called you the no-name silent one."

"Dad, I never knew. Looking back, maybe that explains why I don't overreact to danger. Maybe that is why I never showed affection, which I have been accused of by many a mare."

"Perhaps, son. Perhaps not. But the point is, you need to respect danger. You need to be scared because fear will keep you alive."

Gunshots cracked the air outside the barn. I heard what sounded like a large dog yelping at a distance. I heard one more shot, and the yelping stopped. The captain yelled out, "Good shooting, Major. Shooting an animal on the run with a pistol is quite an accomplishment."

The major grunted, "Thank you, but no, thank you. I don't care to kill anything if I don't have to. The wolf clearly presented a danger to the horses, and maybe us." They walked up to the animal to make sure it was dead. Looking down at the kill, the major grimaced. "He looks emaciated. His ribcage is sticking out. The wolf was only hungry."

While placing his pistol back into its holster, the captain added, "That may be so. However, I did not care to be included in his food chain."

*****

The old barn stalls provided little sound protection from the persistent shelling of the German lines. The artillery explosions eventually moved away. However, there was an occasional stray German shell. One landed near the barn.[58]

I was thankful for my depot training. Jeremiah Bates exposed all horses to controlled ordnance explosions and rapid gunfire. The intent was to acclimate horses to the sounds of war. Wisely, he eased us into it. This proved to be Jubal Early's and my saving grace. Not for Daisy. She almost kicked out her stall door. Jubal calmed her down. He neighed, "Stop kicking and whining, Daisy. The shelling is not close enough, yet. The major said that the hit was random. We will be fine." Jubal obviously had sense for protecting her. Perhaps he did care about others.

Jubal warmed up to Daisy over the past ten months in the country. He was a young stallion. Jubal's disciplined temperament rooted itself from years of U.S. Army dressage training and preparation. Like me, he was prepared for battle, but not for love. A distraction he did not need. I had to step in.

"Jubal, let her be." Jubal snorted and shook his head at me. He neighed, "Daisy obviously has a case of high spirits. I am just trying to calm her down." Daisy kept stomping her front legs against the stall door. The hinges were breaking away.

"Jubal, let her be. That mare has a mind of her own." Tough Guy and Jubal watched the light-draft horse smash her large front hooves through the stall door. Broken pieces of wood flew across the barn aisle. A stall hinge bounced off the ceiling. Her powerful chest pushed through what was left of the stall door.

Commotion in the barn caught Captain Boak's attention. Fortunately, he was standing close enough to witness Daisy's escape. She trotted toward the front barn entrance, looking to escape. Captain Boak stepped in front of her. He yelled out, "Stop, Daisy! Stop!" Holding both hands up toward her, he vigorously waved his hands and yelled at her. Daisy's large hooves stopped within a foot of Captain Boak's boots. She snorted and shook her head up and down. By that time, Major Hazzard showed up. Captain Boak grabbed her halter. He then began petting the top of her nostril. She continued to whine, but with less frequency. Eventually, Daisy stopped snorting.

One thing Major Hazzard knew about us horses was our affinity for a cup of oats laced with molasses. The strong smell of burnt sugar always stopped me in my tracks. It should have the same effect on Daisy, which it did. The major extended a handful to Daisy. She took a few deep breaths and then lowered her thick neck down toward the major long enough for Captain Boak to secure a lead to Daisy's halter. She ate from the major's hand. All was calm.

Captain Boak congratulated the major. "Thank you, sir. I almost lost her."

"You would have done the same for me."

"I would like to say so, but never thought to keep spare oats in my side pocket."

"Captain, I learned that trick from an old horse trainer back at the Front Royal Remount Depot in Virginia. *Mister* Jeremiah Bates. An old Buffalo Soldier."

Captain Boak nodded his head. "Next time you see him, tell him thanks for me. I have grown quite attached to this old girl. Many English call them dumb animals. However, I completely disagree. She is my girl. You see, us English sing about the gals and home. Since I am not married, she is the next best thing for me."

"Captain, let us hope she does not break your heart. Women have the power to do so."

"How would you know." Major Hazzard shook his head from side to side. "I reckon that is a story for another day. Come on, we need to get back to the regiment."

American Expeditionary Force Men and Horses

> I haven't had a wink of sleep since I left Wilhelmshohe. I'm gradually cracking up. The troops continue to retreat. I have lost all confidence in them.
> —German Imperial Navy, Admiral Georg Alexander von Müller diary entry, September 9, 1918

Three years of war passed. The kings of Europe cried afoul struggling in the Great War that honored neither schedule nor end date. The November 1914 proclamation was simply German Kaiser Wilhelm's wishful thinking predicting his armies would roll into Paris and end the war before Christmas. However, that prophesy prediction did not come to its fruition. Two years later, over three million soldiers on both sides of the Western Front were killed or injured. The Great War on land and sea caused much suffering for the living.

By the end of 1916, the Alliance lost more battles than won. The Imperial German Army advanced closer and closer to Paris because they had more troops. German troops redirected to the west, thanks to the Russians retreating from the Eastern Front. Germany's military success against the beleaguered Russians forced the troubled Red government to sue for peace. The great Russian Empire's agreement to fight with the Alliance became null and void by the stroke of a pen. A simple signature took the Eastern Front out of play for the Central Powers.

The Russian betrayal, in essence, turned the tide of war. The Austrian, German, and Ottoman armies had only one front to fight. The expanded German movements on the Western Front caused great concern for British and French military leaders. Recognizing the need for more resources, the Alliance appealed again to U.S. President Wilson for increased military assistance, beyond the money, ammunition, and horses already shipped to the warfront. That is if —the transport ships— were not sunk by German U-Boats.

The combination of unrestricted submarine attacks and killing of innocent civilians at sea pressed President Wilson yield to public will for retaliation against the Germans. He could no longer justify keeping America out of the war. Too many neutral ships were being sunk. The loss of over nineteen hundred American lives on the *Lusitania* burned into the American conscience. The United States citizenry demanded retribution for the indiscriminate sinking of civilian ships in the North Atlantic. Declaration of war was imminent.

*****

The United States Congress and President Wilson responded decidedly to the American public will. On April 6, 1917, the United States declared war on Germany. On December 7 in the same year, the United States later declared war on German ally Austro-Hungary, and enacted the draft.[59] Declaring war was not enough. More soldiers, horses, and mules were needed.

On May 18, 1917, Congress passed the Selective Service Act, which authorized President Wilson to increase, temporarily, the military services of the United States. Draftees would come from all forty-eight states, the District of Columbia, and the territories of Alaska, Hawaii, and Puerto Rico.[60] Of the 24 million men drafted, a broad-shouldered man like Abraham Bates would surely be a promising soldier in the field. The United States Army drafted Abraham Bates in May of 1917.

*****

Abraham Bates

At the age of twenty-one, Abraham Bates stood six foot two, weighing over two hundred pounds. Like his mother, he had a chestnut complexion. His wavy jet black hair did not curl like his dad's, nor did it go straight like his mother's Seminole locks. The most distinguishing features on his face were a straight nose and high cheeks he inherited from his mother. A noble young man, Abraham prepared to be immersed in the troubled waters of war. The U.S. Army Boot Camp would help him shape his mind to do so.

Four weeks into boot camp, a flyer circulated around the mess tent. Private Bates picked up a copy and read about the U.S. Second Cavalry's call for soldiers with veterinary experience. He told a friend standing next to him that the flyer presented an opportunity to use his hands to heal wounded horses and mules. Private Bates always said, "With good horse shoes, you have no good horse to carry. Without a healthy horse, you have no bullets. Without bullets, you cannot shoot. If you cannot shoot, you will die."

Holding the flyer in his hand, Private Bates returned to his tent to share it with his friend, Private Freddie Stowers, who asked, "Whatcha go'n to do with that piece of paper?"

"Freddie, this is my ticket to better things. I am going to be an army veterinarian. I am hoping my parents sent my college transcripts to the base commanding officer. The Second Cavalry is already in the country. They need veterinarians."

"I suppose'n that would be best for you. Given all that school'n you have and all."

"You are right. The army needs more veterinarians over there. I read in the newspapers that the Western Front was a hellhole. Many men, horses, and mules were get'n injured or killed. I can help them."

"Bates, you have been good to me. I hate to see you leave, but I understand why."

"Freddie, I am sure we will run into each other in some muddy trench in France."

"I hope not. I will make darn sure the Germans are sleeping in the trenches, not us. You can count on it. I will die honorably trying."

One week later, after Private Bates had put in his request, the company drill sergeant informed Private Bates that his request to transfer to the U.S. Army veterinarian service was denied. Much to his displeasure, Private Abraham Bates accepted his fate, for the moment.

Leather to Steel

After completing basic army training in June 1917, at Fort Jackson, South Carolina, Private Bates reported to the U.S. Army 371 Infantry Regiment in garrison at Camp Stewart near Newport News, Virginia.[61] He committed to working hard for his command leadership, with the hopes the officers would notice.

During the first two months of his assignment, Abraham proved himself worthy of being called a U.S. soldier. His platoon sergeant and regimental officers lauded his work ethic. He made it known he would keep his head high, as his father did during the Red River Wars.

Abraham wanted more from the army. He was not satisfied with being an enlisted soldier. His desire to become a veterinarian gnawed at his gut. He wanted to work with warhorses. Fortunately, a senior enlisted man in his chain of command agreed with him.

*****

After attending church services on July 8, Private Bates returned to his tent. He changed out of his U.S. Army Model 1912 service wool tunic uniform and back into his drab olive cotton working britches and blouse. He picked up his Bible and sat down on the edge of his cot to read. He opened the sacred book to a random page. Private Bates closed his eyes and placed his right index finger in the center. He opened his eyes and read the verse:

> So do not fear, for I am with you; do not be dismayed, for I am your God. I will strengthen you and help you; I will uphold you with my righteous right hand. (Isaiah 41:10 KJV)

Private Bates looked up to the sky and asked God what to do. After a few minutes of reflection, he placed his Bible back on the pillow for which he kept it. He stood up and walked outside his tent. Private Bates briefly stopped to look up into the sky. The sun temporarily blinded him. He rubbed his eyes, sighed, and mumbled, "Lord willing. Give me strength." He walked over to the sergeant's tent and stood outside at attention. He said loudly, "Sergeant, Private Bates request permission to enter, sir."

Sergeant Gunny replied, "Permission granted." Abraham pushed the tent flap aside and walked in. The sergeant stood up and faced Abraham. He said, "Quit calling me sir. I know who my parents are." Private Bates stood at attention. The sergeant asked, "What do you want, Private?"

"Sir, I would like to request an audience with our regiment's commanding officer."

Sergeant Gunny looked at Private Bates with a quizzical look in his face. He said, "Private Bates, you speak like an educated man. Not like most of us Southern boys around here."

Abraham remained at attention. He looked at the sergeant and respectfully asked, "Request permission to stand at ease?"

"And a respectful educated one you are, at that. Permission granted. What is on your mind, Private Bates?"

"Sir, I would like to use my university schooling to provide medical care for cavalry horses. I believe I can better serve the army on the battlefield getting sick and injured horses fixed up and back into action."

"Private Bates, that sounds like a reasonable proposition. I am an old cavalry man myself." The sergeant leaned back in his chair and then kicked up his boots on a stack of wooden pallets serving as his desk. Sergeant Gunny put his hands behind his head and said, "Yep, I remember those days as a young trooper riding back west. Fought many an Injun."

Abraham's eyes sank a little lower, but he did not let on that his mother was born a Seminole.

Private Bates said, "My father retired from the U.S. Army back in 1898. He was a trooper out of Fort Sill. Not sure where else he served. Texas, Oklahoma, I am not sure."

"Do you know what company he served in?"

"Yes, sir. He was with the Tenth served during the Red River battles."

Leather to Steel

Sergeant Gunny looked at Private Bates and bellowed a jolly laugh. He said, "Well, I be dang. I was a youngster working the Fort Sill stables." The sergeant took a sip of coffee.

"Sergeant Gunny, if you don't mind, I would appreciate permission and—"

The sergeant stopped him in midsentence. "Enough young man. Go ahead. Permission granted. Just give me a day to get with the captain. He doesn't like surprises. We have a chain-of-command to follow."

Two days later, with his chain of command's endorsements, Private Bates spoke with the 371st commanding officer, Colonel Charles J. Bailey. The colonel gave Private Bates five minutes. Private Bates presented his case. Afterward, he respectfully requested permission to leave, with the hopes of a compassionate leader who cared.

After taking time to contemplate the request, Colonel Bailey approved Private Bates' transfer to the U.S. Army Veterinary Service, pending a professional board's approval. He told Sergeant Gunny the colonel's aide would follow up with the paperwork.

Two weeks later, the aide, Captain Stedman summoned Private Bates into his office. Captain Stedman, himself a Southern white officer, said, "Boy, the U.S. Army cavalry has all the troopers they need. The real problem facing the army in Europe is the lack of replacement horses. Did you know our country sends over one hundred thousand horses each year to the Allied Forces? None come back. We need more Doughboys and horses."

Private Bates replied, "Yes, sir. Indeed. The war's attrition rates are very high."

The captain asked, "Your clear speech sounds educated. Did you go to college?"

"Yes, sir. My parents sent me to the Virginia Commonwealth University in Richmond, Virginia."

"How did you get into that school?"

"My father trained horses for a bigwig in Washington DC. I learned how to train horses from working with him. In any case, after I graduated with honors in all my science classes, my plan was to become a veterinarian. Part of that plan included working and learning from the U.S. Army Front Royal Remount Depot veterinarian. Well, the war draft put a hold on veterinarian school."

"The captain said, "I see. Well then, I can see why the colonel is transferring you to the veterinary service. Good for you."

Private Bates requested permission to leave the captain's office. The captain approved. As Private Bates stepped through the office door, the captain said, "Private, one more thing. Your parents need to get your college transcripts forwarded to the school and our office."

Private Bates stood at attention. He rendered a salute. "I will take care of it. Thank you, sir. I appreciate it."

The captain ordered, "Carry on, Private Bates. And good luck to you."

Private Bates wasted no time getting back to his tent. He knelt down by his cot and prayed. "God, give me strength and patience. Bless my new journey. Walk with me. Lord, I beseech thee."

*****

The day he received his official orders, he sent a telegram to his parents asking them if they would send his college transcripts to Colonel Bailey's staff secretary. She needed the paperwork for Abraham's selection package. In the cable, Abraham was realistic. He explained there were several hurdles he had to get over. He closed his message to his parent's with, "I will not be deterred."

The first step to becoming a U.S. Army veterinarian required the officer candidate to stand in front of veterinary service, qualifications review board and answer senior officer questions. The board consisted of three veterinarian officers holding the rank of colonel. Their prepared questions did not focus on serving the army. Instead, the officers assessed the candidate's abilities and genuine concern for health and welfare of animals. Private Bates was one of eight men selected to be interviewed. Not all would make the cut.

Private Bates traveled to Washington DC on July 31 to participate in the qualifications board. If he was confirmed, Private Bates would complete a series of schools designed to make the best veterinarian and army officer within a short period of time. The army urgently needed in its officer ranks to be filled on the Western Front.

At the end of the interview day, Private Bates completed one grueling sixty-minute interview with stone-faced selection board members. When exiting the conference room, a young lieutenant — acting as the board's secretary— thanked Private Bates for his interest. The officer handed Bates his orders to return to his command, the 371st. The board said they would make their decisions by week's end.

Private Bates returned to Camp Stewart that same day. For the rest of the week, he anxiously awaited the board's results. To reduce anxiety, he worked harder at his job to distract himself from the anticipation. He remained calm and collected.

On August 3, the veterinarian qualification review board communicated the selection of four candidates of the six interviewed. The cable delivered to Private Bates read,

> BEGIN TRANSMISSION (BT). Orders. Private Abraham Bates, Private, United States Army. It is the opinion of the United States Army Surgeon General, your application and qualifications were thoroughly reviewed and considered in your selection as a United State Army Veterinary Officer. Congratulations. You are to report no later than On August 26, 1917, to Commanding Officer, United States Army, Meat and Dairy Hygiene and Forage Inspection Course, General Supply Depot, Chicago, Illinois. Course convenes on August 27, 1917. Upon successful completion of the MDHFI course, report no later than September 23, 1917, to Commanding Officer, Fort Des Moines Officer Candidate School. Upon graduation, you will be commissioned as a First Lieutenant, United States Army Veterinary Officer. END TRANSMISSION (ET).[62]

Private Bates dropped the message on the tent floor. He rubbed his eyes, picked the message back up, and reread it. His heartbeat sped up. The selection was unexpected. Being a colored soldier was a disadvantage for the infantry. He knew it going in. However, science turned a different eye. His love of animals was what mattered.

Army Veterinary Corps officer candidate Bates shared the selection board news with his chain-of-command, whose endorsement was validated. Sergeant Gunny was so proud of Private Bates. He said, "Mister Bates, should my body and horse get injured in battle, fix my horse first."

Private Bates smiled. "You can count on it sergeant. If you will, please excuse me. I need to get over to the radioman's tent and telegraph my family."

Sergeant Gunny stood up and saluted Private Bates. "Good luck, son. Make us proud."

Private Bates saluted and said, "Please don't salute me. I know who my parents are."

Sergeant Gunny laughed. Private Bates turned around and left the tent, knowing the salutes would come before long. He would be on the receiving end.

*****

Jeremiah and Mary were sitting on their front porch when a depot-duty soldier ran up to the Bates house. The soldier stepped up and onto the front porch, breathing heavily from running. Jeremiah stood up from his rocking chair.

"Soldier, catch your breath." The young man was bent over panting trying to breathe. He straightened up and took one deep breath. After exhaling, he turned to Mrs. Bates and took his hat off. He then looked at Jeremiah. A big smile widened across the soldier's face. "Mister Bates, the commanding officer wanted you and Missus Bates to have this cable, soonest."

The soldier handed the folded cable to Jeremiah, who read the first line. "Mary, it is from Abraham. Camp Stewart hasn't killed him yet." He continued reading. "Mary. Oh my Lord."

"What does it say, dear husband? Everything all right?"

"More than all right. Our son was selected to attend veterinary and officer candidate schools. He is going to be a United States Army veterinarian."

Mary patted her chest. "Oh my! Good Lord. Our son is—"

The soldier looked at Jeremiah and Mary. "Mister and Missus Bates, please excuse me."

"Of course, of course. Thank you, corporal. Thank you."

Jeremiah and Mary sat back in their rocking chairs, taking turns reading the cable bringing them good news. Their pride and excitement abounded that day. Their oldest son would become First Lieutenant Abraham Bates, doctor of veterinary medicine.

*****

After successfully completing an arduous four-week animal care training course in Chicago, Private Bates transferred to Fort De Moines, Iowa, to begin his officer-candidate training. The training took sixty-five days to complete. On December 21, 1917, Private Abraham Bates graduated with honors. He and twenty-nine other colored men were commissioned as first lieutenants. Unlike his classmates, his military service would lead to the U.S. Second Cavalry headquarters in France. The rest of his classmates would end up leading only enlisted infantryman of color.

Lieutenant Bates' future changed with a colonel's simple signature. The question now remained, how long could he live to do his job? The Germans were not his only enemy. First, Lieutenant Bates soon discovered that even colored officers were treated differently. He reminded himself, *I will not be deterred. I will persevere.* Words he chose to live by.

*****

Tough Guy and Jubal

Major Hazzard periodically received headquarter communications from the United States Army general staff in Washington DC. He did not always get into specifics with us horses. Most of the time, he summarized complicated military planning into a few sentences. The last message he received said the U.S. Army Second Cavalry Regiment was formed up by attaching cavalry units from Fort Ethan

Allan and Fort Myers. Those horses and troopers received orders from General Pershing. He ordered the U.S. Army Second Regiment to serve in the American Expeditionary Force shipping out to Europe in April 1917. The Second Cavalry would become the only American dragoon unit to fight during the Great War.

*****

Tough Guy

During the summer of 1917, Major Hazzard, Jubal, and I were no longer the American minority. The United States Army Second Regiment deployed with the American Expeditionary Force to France. Major Hazzard was told to remain with the Royal Canadian Horse Artillery Brigade until further notice. Disappointed, the major expressed many times who he would rather be riding with the Second Cavalry performing reconnaissance, or screening enemy positions on the Western Front. I was comforted knowing my fellow Second Cavalry horses were in country and ready for the fight.

Major Hazzard said the American Expeditionary Force (AEF) Headquarters did battle damage assessments on a continual basis. During the summer offensive, the Second Cavalry worked as dismounted troopers to hold key terrain along the borders of France and Belgium. Major Hazzard said through these actions, the horse-mounted cavalry provided extraordinary value on the modern battlefield.

*****

With the U.S. Second Cavalry Regiment in country, the army wasted no time assigning newly commissioned Veterinarian Corps First Lieutenant Bates to the Second Cavalry. Within two months of graduating officer's candidate school, First Lieutenant Bates found himself leading a team of orderlies vigorously working to save horses, mules, and dogs brought to his mobile veterinary field station set up just out of reach of the German big guns on the Western Front.

Leather to Steel

At no-man's land, where the soldier's view of life would forever change, the boy would become the man. The soldier became the warrior, and the living would become the dead. Lieutenant Bates learned quickly how fast life could disappear before one's eyes. For two more years, he would witness suffering never before known by mankind.

Lieutenant Bates met familiar faces on the Western Front. A particular road traveled led him back to a friend he met during boot camp—a soldier who demonstrated great heroism during combat. A man named Corporal Freddie Stowers, who grew up in Sandy Springs, South Carolina. A friend whose grandfather fought in the U.S. Civil War as a Confederate. A soldier who would receive the Congressional Medal of Honor.

By the end of WWI, more than 200,000 African Americans served with the AEF. [63] Most black men survived the Great War. However, many did not come home.

*****

The muddy trenches smelled of death and despair. The winter months were brutal in the north country. The overcast skies rarely gave the soldiers a break from the wet and cold. If the fog and mist did not hide the sun, the grey and white swirls of smoke certainly blocked the sunlight rarely seen during the winter months on the Western Front.

Lieutenant Abraham Bates adjusted to the battle preparation tempo. He did not live in a warm tent. His living quarters took the shape of a trench dug near the mobile veterinary hospitals he traveled and trained with. Lieutenant Bates was indebted to the infantrymen whom helped the veterinary teams prepare temporary quarters for the staff, and camouflaged dugouts for horses.

Lieutenant Bates did not put himself above others. He worked side-by-side with other soldiers to brace the trench walls. They used wooden planks as vertical braces to keep mud from caving on their sleeping holes. Lieutenant Bates figured out through trial and error to dig holes sloping upward to allow rainwater to drain away.

There was no sense of permanence. He knew his veterinary ambulances would soon be transported across the channel to collect and treat injured mules and horses. His team's job was to keep the artillery horses and pack mules alive. No easy task. The men often sang songs to get through a barrage. As the German shells echoed from a distance in quick succession, he would start to sing:

> Lord take my soul
> In the night I willingly go
> Lord I am not alone
> Because I know you're carrying me home
>
> Lord close my ears
> To the sounds of my fears
> Lord take my hand and
> Lead me to the promise land.

*****

Max Eilenberg

The S.S. *Moro Castle* received its last load of coal from the fuel barge. The first boatswain mate directed the barge lines released from the stanchions. The ship's forward lookout kept watch from the starboard bridge wing. He looked down at the first boatswain mate and ordered the anchor pulled and all topside gear secured. Two special passengers watched the captain and the boatswain mate exchange pleasantries when an order was properly executed.

The *Moro Castle* got under way on a Monday morning. The weather conditions were perfect, with a slight offshore wind blowing over the Cuban isles. The sea state was zero. Wave heights were almost at zero feet, or as sailors called it, glassy. All conditions were a go.

The ship's navigator plotted the *Moro Castle* waypoints for a fourteen-day journey to Monaco. The freighter would not deviate from directions. Sailing under the Cuban flag—a neutral state during the war—the commercial freighter could not be targeted by German U-boats, or by British warships. The ruse was well conceived.

Max Eilenberg and Olga von Marx stood on the ship's fantail watching preparations for getting under way. The German Americans looked forward to their journey back to the Fatherland. Both believed in "shoulder to shoulder, hand in hand, for God and *Fatherland*!"— omitting the word *Emperor*.

Twelve miles out, the island of Cuba quickly disappeared over the horizon, and faded into a distant memory. Topside, Max watched Olga's every move as she held on to the ship's railing. He stepped up beside her. They both stared at the ship's wake parting the ocean waves. White foam left by the wake slowly dissipated back into the blue water, leaving no trace of the ship's passage through the water. Max touched Olga's arm and said, "Have you ever wondered how long a ship's wake stays visible?"

"Sorry. I have never given it a thought."

"There is a specific amount of time one can see where a ship has been and where it is going. Like the wake, we must ensure no one can see where we have been and where we are going."

"When did you become so philosophical, Mister Eilenberg?"

"I was never one for euphemisms. They, in fact, simplify the truth of a complicated nature. In light of the fact we are on a one-way trip, perhaps we—"

Olga pressed her finger against Max's lips. "Shush. No need to say it. Let us keep focused on the greater good. The greater good of the Fatherland."

"Deutschland, Deutschland, über alles." Germany, Germany, overall.

The SS *Moro Castle* maintained a northeastern course for the French coast. The captain's orders were to avoid transiting into the North Sea at all cost. Germany's coasts were blocked by British warships. All cargo ships transiting in and out of the North Sea were boarded and inspected. The safest route for transporting Olga, Max, and the special cargo depended upon a navigable course well south of the war. The ship's captain favored the French Riviera, which provided the safest and most logical harbor choice.

Once docked in Monaco, the remaining five hundred miles overland would be arduous and dangerous for Max and Olga. They had to get to Freiburg midsummer. From there, the last stop would be Berlin, where Uncle Ademaro would be waiting.

Max's Uncle Ademaro committed himself to supporting antimonarchy insurgencies swelling across Europe during the war. It took time, but he convinced Max to join the movement. The movement that evolved from an underground culture embracing the necessity to survive, and overthrow the German monarchy. The movement groups were intellectuals, workers, academes, and businessmen whose collective energy drew upon German, Russian, English, and French citizens tired of war, royal monarchies, and simply starving caused by British maritime blockades and unrestricted German submarine warfare.

Max and Olga dedicated themselves to the movement. A movement that carefully selected countrymen for the honorable duty of serving the weak and poor ignored by the kings of Europe. Max and Olga would not sit in abeyance. According to Max, it was cowardly and shameful to do so. He refused to stand by and watch the world implode. He kept his motivation to fight inside his heart, and sewn inside his derby hat—a small Kodak picture of Kate—his wife, his love, and his friend. His last good memory of America.

In seven days, the *Moro Castle* berthed at Ponte Delgada islands located nine hundred miles west of Lisbon, Portugal. A prepositioned coal barge waited for the *Moro Castle*. She took on enough coal to complete the remaining fifteen hundred miles to Monaco. The provider also left several crates of dried food to sustain the passengers and crew for another five days at sea. Once in Monaco, Max and Olga would begin their trek across valleys and mountains to avoid warring factions with the Fatherland.

The May arrival in Monaco Port De Fontvieille was intentional. The mountain passes melted enough to allow motorcar traffic over roads normally inaccessible during the winter months. Max anticipated travel would be difficult in some spots near the French

Leather to Steel

Alps. The higher altitudes would be cooler, and there was a war going on.

The German Americans were prepared for the journey. Their directions were to travel by horse westward of Mont Agel, then ride north for a hundred miles through dangerous territories occupied by French, British, and German armies. They both knew their cover would practically ensure a safer transit to their destination.

Max and Olga came prepared. They each brought hiking packs filled with tins of dried food, citizenship papers, and gold currency recognized by all countries. Max could not resist. He brought good memories of his time in Havana. Memories that came in the form of Montecristo cigars—hand-rolled cured tobacco leaves—and of course, a pint of Puerto Rican rum. He knew those items would help sway one-on-one negotiations should the situation require it.

Before leaving the ship, Max and Olga dressed to look like tourists. Max wore a gentleman's blue sport coat covering a blue-striped shirt topped off with a yellow bowtie. His long white cotton pants accentuated the seasonal requirement for cooler garb in Monaco. Max complimented his white trousers with brown leather Balmoral shoes worn by fashionable gentlemen.[64]

Olga wore a peach-colored gored skirt that came up to just under her breasts. She wore a matching cashmere sweater that exposed her tanned neck and shoulders. Her jewelry consisted of a gold silk band wrapped across her forehead, a style at the time. Her shoes looked like tan slippers with small heels. She told Max it was the proper woman's day outfit.

Max held Olga's hand as they walked over the gray cobblestone sidewalk leading to the town's center. They mastered the appearance of a happily married couple walking hand in hand. Max gently squeezed Olga's arm and asked, "My dear, shall we go check in to the hotel and then get some dinner? I am a bit famished."

Olga pulled back several blonde curls slipping out from the headband. "Max, you sound so much like an Englishman. Looks like our year in Cuba was time well spent."

"Indeed, madam. How ironic we begin our journey here, in a place governed by a rich and spoiled monarch. The German people will reclaim the Fatherland."

Olga laughed. "Little do they know their world will change. The People's Worker Party will rise up around the world and be victorious. Come on, darling. I need to rest before we go shopping."

"Excuse me, dear. Shopping for what?"

"Wool riding pants, knee socks, riding boots, gloves, down coats—you know, typical garb equestrians need for a country ride."

"I should suggest we also get a better map of the French Alps. The Cuban version we have is rather dated."

Olga smirked. "I so agree. How is your French, Max?"

"Studied enough to get by. You should know. We practiced many hours together over a bottle of rum."

Max took a deep breath. "La demoiselle. Irons-nous à l'hôtel?" Lady, shall we go to the hotel?

Olga slid her arm inside the curve of Max's. "Oui, Monsieur Esquivel." Yes, Mr. Esquivel.

The Hôtel Hermitage desk clerk stood straight and proper, wearing a black tuxedo tailored to his V-shaped shoulders. His white gloves spoke to the hotel's quality guest services rendered for all temporary tenants. The desk clerk handed one nickel-plated room key to Mr. Maxwell Esquivel. In return, Mr. Esquivel tipped the clerk with a gold peso. The clerk graciously accepted the tip. He bowed once toward Mrs. Esquivel and once toward Max. He said, "Merci, monsieur. Your luggage will be waiting for you in your room."

Max and Olga took the newly installed elevator up to their room on the fifth floor. The elevator's pulleys and motors labored to pull its passengers up to the requested floor. Max commented, "Very nice. Modern technology is well established here for the rich and famous."

Olga added, "I understand British war minister Winston Churchill takes his holiday here. Perhaps we will run into him."

"Most likely not," Max grumbled. "He is too busy killing innocent people. Don't get me going, Olga."

Leather to Steel

The next morning, Max and Olga woke up in their separate beds. She slept on the queen-sized bed, while Max slept in the attached sitting room on the large red settee that pulled out into a single bed. Max did not mind accommodating Olga's needs. He preferred to keep their professional relationship at arm's length. No woman could replace Kate. Her death was the very reason why he made the change. The darkness that grasped his soul would not let go until his hunger for vengeance and thirst for justice was satisfied. The Movement guaranteed his retribution.

Olga propped herself up in bed. She yawned and mumbled, "I can use some coffee." She yelled out, "Max. You up? Max. You up."

Max pulled the blanket off his head and groaned. He wiped the sleep from his eyes and grunted. "No, I am not up. But looks like you are."

"Max, we need to get going. We have supplies to get, and you need to wire Uncle Ademaro our timeline. He is expecting us to be in Frankfurt by month's end."

"I know, I know. Let us talk about this over coffee."

Olga did not reply. She jumped out of bed and stood looking at herself in the full-length mirror. "Yes, we need to drink some coffee."

*****

Max handed the room key to the desk clerk. "Merci, mon brave homme. Nous avons apprécié notre séjour . Les logements ont été fabuleusement sélectionnés." (Thank you, my good man. We enjoyed our stay. The accommodations were fabulously selected.)

The desk clerk turned the key around to verify the room number. He flipped through several index cards until he found a match. The desk clerk double-checked the key number against the room invoice. Satisfied, he nodded. "Votre compte en dans l'ordre, monsieur. La direction et le personnel Hôtel Hermitage grandement apprécié votre patronage." (Your account is in order, sir. The Hôtel Hermitage management and staff greatly appreciated your patronage.)

Olga bent down to tuck in her cotton-lined riding jeans into her black riding boots. She stood up and looked at the desk clerk. "Nous avons adoré notre chambre. Nous reviendrons. Avez-vous appelé un taxi pour nous." (We loved our room. We will be back again. Did you call a taxi for us?)

"Oui madame. Il a des instructions pour vous emmener à l'écurie Azienda Agricola Mulino Martino." (Yes, madam. He has instructions to take you to the Azienda Agricola Mulino Martino stables.)

Satisfied, Olga turned to Max. "Husband. Are you ready to go riding?"

Max said sarcastically, "I could not be more thrilled."

The taxi drove Max and Olga twenty miles west of Monaco. The horse stables were located in the foothills of the French Alps. The motorcar pulled off an unfinished road onto a long cobblestone driveway leading to a small castle surrounded by fenced pastures and horse barns. Dozens of gray Arabs and black Thoroughbreds grazed near the fence lines.

Max turned to Olga. "This is it. Those horses are lucky." He tapped the taxi driver on the shoulder. "Chauffeur. S'il vous plaît nous déposer à la première stable." (Driver. Please drop us off at the first stable. The taxi driver slowed the motorcar to a stop.)

"Oui, monsieur." (Yes, sir.)

The taxi driver started to get out to open the doors for Max and Olga. Max touched the driver's shoulder. "Pas nécessaire. Nous pouvons gérer. Nous vous remercions de l'examen." (Not necessary. We can handle it. Thank you for the consideration.)

After paying the driver, the motorcar sped off. Max and Olga had been waiting for the stable manager for some time, but no one came. While they waited, Olga asked a question: "Max, what did you mean by the horses were lucky?"

Max scooted a stone away with his boot. He sighed. "I have always loved the horse. We—my deceased wife and I—lived near an old army horse training center in Virginia. Horses were then, and I imagine are still, being sold to the British and French armies—as replacements. Several hundred thousand horses have been killed in this war thus far. I suspect tradition will eventually give way to the reality times have changed. Those poor horses are dying, not because of the soldiers they carry, but because war has changed leather to steel."

Olga frowned. "I understand where you are coming from. My father fought on the back of a stallion during the Franco-German War of 1870.[65] His charge was shot out from underneath him. Though he escaped, he fretted many years over the loss of his charge."

Max changed the subject. "Olga, let's get our gear on and walk inside the stable. Perhaps the caretaker is in there working."

Olga asked, "Okay. Would you please help me with my backpack?"

"Sicher, Frau." Sure, woman. Max tightened the backpack straps on her waist. Olga then helped Max adjust his backpack and extra bedrolls he agreed to carry. They strolled over to the stable. The closer they got, the more the horses whinnied. The horses knew.

The caretaker limped out of the stable to greet his special visitors. Max and Olga stood quietly waiting for the old man. Max whispered to Olga. "He looks like the old fella who has seen some tough times. His tweeds look like rags."

Olga nodded. "Shush. He is almost within earshot."

The caretaker shuffled his feet to get closer to Max and Olga. His humped back caused him to look up at Max and Olga. He took off his stained floppy hat and spoke in broken English. "I have been expecting you, Americans. Yes? Your Uncle Ademaro told me of your needs. My name is Karl. Karl Klaussner."

Max studied the man for a few moments. "Yes, my name is Max. Max Eilenberg. This is my sister, Olga."

Olga curtseyed. The old man looked at Olga and laughed. "My dear. I am not an aristocrat, as you can see."

"Karl, might I ask how you know my uncle?"

"Your uncle and I served during the war back forty-five years, I think. He was a good German soldier." The old man put his hat back on his balding head. He continued. "Do you know of the 1870 Franco-German War?"

Max replied. "No, sir, I don't. A little before my time. I suppose there is a long story behind it."

"There is. The short of it is I remained in France after the war to be with my bride, Marie Louise. God rest her soul." The old man coughed. After he had caught his breath. "Now, that don't matter. She knows I am too old to serve on either side."

Olga asked. "Where are the owners of this beautiful estate?"

"Aww, yes. The LaChapelles. The family has owned this farm for a hundred years. Once the war began, the elder son insisted the family take to Paris for the duration. I remained to take care of their polo horses and watch over the place."

Olga asked, "Do you have a salle de bains [bathroom] I could use?"

"So sorry, madam. I should have offered. Please. Let us go into the house. I can offer you some tea."

Max agreed. "Sounds like a splendid idea."

Karl extended his arm to Olga. "Shall I. I don't see pretty ladies out here too often."

Olga entwined her arm with Karl's. "I would be honored."

The three walked over a worn-cobblestone path leading to the front door of a chalet-style home. Once inside, Karl pointed toward the bathroom door. Olga fast-walked over to the bathroom door. Karl turned to Max. "Shall we go into the study?"

Max followed Karl into a room. Always observant, he noted the high stained glass bay window panels etched in blues and greens. A long padded sitting bench occupied the alcove underneath the window. Green velvet curtains hung down from the ceiling. Curtain tassel tiebacks held the curtain panels to the window sides. The room's twenty-foot ceilings angled together to its center. Karl motioned Max to sit down in the red-velvet settee near the rock fireplace. "Max, please sit down."

Max sank down into the high-backed settee. "Comfortable seat."

"I suppose. I don't sit in it because of my back. Hard to get up once I sit down. I sit in the window seat. Easier for me to get up, plus, I enjoy looking outside."

Olga returned to the room, and Karl waved her over. "Please come sit by Max."

Leather to Steel

Olga nodded and walked over to the settee. She replied, "Thank you, Mr. Klaussner."

Karl quickly replied, "Please call me Karl. Young lady, I must say you are very polite."

Olga blushed, and Max added, "She is, until you get to know her. She can be a tough woman."

Olga elbowed Max. "Brother, watch it."

Max commented, "Excuse us. We have a case of sibling rivalry. Now, can we talk business?"

Karl turned the conversation around. "Please. Let us talk about the horses later. I have read about how you Americans always want to jump into business first. Here in France—well, for the most part, all of Europe prefer to socialize first."

Max gasped. "Well, I suppose you are right."

"Indeed, young Eilenberg. I will go put a kettle of water on the stove. We can have tea and talk about your journey."

Olga jumped in. "I think that is a splendid idea, Karl."

Max drew a heavy sigh. "I suppose we can delay ourselves for the occasion."

Karl stood up and pointed out the bay window. "I might suggest you both stay here for the eve. The clouds are threatening."

Max stood up and walked to stand by Karl. "I hate to delay our journey, but one more warm night and rest before the long journey would be a good idea. Olga, what do you think?"

"Max, Karl makes a good point. One more day here in France will not kill us. At least I hope not."

Karl chuckled at this young female guest. "Olga, I do have some salted beef and sauerkraut. Would you mind—"

"Of course not. It has been some time since I have had a decent German meal." The three walked out of the living room and into the kitchen. Karl pointed to the white table and high-backed chairs. "Please sit. I will get the tea. We have much to catch up on. I want to hear what is happening in American." Max and Olga took their seats.

Max looked towards Karl. "You will be surprised at what we have to say." Karl placed the tea kettle under the water faucet. As he filled up the kettle, he turned and stared at Max. "You will not believe what is going on in Germany. The reason why you are both here."

Now sitting at the table, Karl, Max, and Olga exchanged news reporting of how Germany made advances on the battlefields, but discouraging losses in public support back in Fatherland. All agreed that the casualties were counted in the millions. Soldiers and civilians were perishing from disease, starvation, and lack of faith in German leadership.

Karl took a sip of tea. He asked, "Mariage Freres. Can you taste the orange blossom scent mixed into the leaves? Madam LaChapelles ordered this custom blend Mariage Freres. The tea of the French bourgeois. Not sure where the orange flavoring came from. I do enjoy the flavor."

Olga added, "Most likely from Florida."

Max jumped in. "You know I used to own an import, export business. I shipped express orders of dried orange peels to—"

Olga interrupted. "What is your point, Max?"

Arching his right eyebrow, Max looked at Olga. "I just think you should have considered asking me first, instead of guessing."

"Max, you are so sensitive." Max abruptly placed his teacup back down in the saucer plate. "I am not."

Karl broke in. "You two. Please keep it down. I did not invite you to stay so I could bear witness to obvious conflicts you have as sister and brother. Can we please get back to discussing the war?"

Max looked at Olga. "Yes, he is right. I suppose I am just getting a little anxious. We have been traveling for so long." Olga chimed in, "And we have over five hundred more miles to go. So let us be civil. I love you, brother." Max pulled his head back. He looked at Olga. He said with passion, "I…I guess I love you too, Olga."

Karl did not care for the emotion. He said, "Yes, yes. We all love one another. Now back to the war."

German newspapers describe unflinchingly the toll immense battles took not only on the soldiers but also on the countryside in which they fought. The press circulated pictures showing what were once green Belgium forest and pastures burned and churned to the ground where not a blade of grass stood. The Western Front trenches

Leather to Steel

and no-man's land in between were splattered with dried blood, brains, and scraps of flesh. Flies gathered on the remains of the dead.

Karl inquired of Max, "Why did you want to come back to Germany and serve the democratic people?"

"Long story, Karl. Too painful to tell most of it. However, let me show you what put me over the edge." Max reached into his coat pocket and pulled out a discolored white envelope. He carefully pulled out a red-and-black-bordered square form. He handed it to Karl. "Go ahead, read it."

Karl carefully unfolded the paper and read its contents aloud. "Join the National Security League. Awaken the entire country to service. Make victory certain. Educate the people on the war. Realize your individual duty. Ensure universal military training. Combat German propaganda. And add to our fighting power."

"Now see you, Karl. I supported all the points except for the sixth point. The message was against people like me—German Americans. I have since renounced my American citizenship to return home."

"My dear Max, this is the same message being used to excite German citizenry against the German Emperor, Kaiser Wilhelm. How interesting. You jumping from one revolution into another."

Olga asserted herself. "Yes. However, there is a difference. Max and I are willing to die for the Fatherland, not the Motherland."

"Very good, Fräulein. I respect your decision. You must know that the German government is hunting down anarchists and hanging them. Not only do you have the Alliance wanting to kill Germans, but you have Germans wanting to kill Germans."

Max said, "Yes, we understand the risks. Uncle Ademaro explained a people's movement was forming up to take over after the war is over. He called them the Nationalist German Workers' assembly. They have formed small underground chapters throughout Germany."

"Max and Olga, you must realize what you pursue is very dangerous. Should the Workers' Party membership survive the war, what will they do to make peace with the world?"

"Thank you for the warning. We do. Our lives are committed to the movement. No matter how long it takes."

"Max, how do you expect to go unnoticed while traveling through the Fatherland?"

"What do you mean, Herr Klaussner?"

"Surely you know all males under sixty are drafted to serve. Most willingly do so."

"I do. My plan is to join a regimental headquarters unit in Berlin. From there I can learn from General Ludendorff. I studied German military document during my time in Cuba. I will blend in with the rest. Uncle Ademaro assured me his friend on the inside would usher my entrance and assignment to the Rechsteid."

Karl raised his teacup to Max and Olga. They in turn lifted their cups in unison. He said, "Deutschland, Deutschland über alles."

The LaChapelles horse farm provided the prefect starting point for Max and Olga's journey. The farm was hidden inside a protected valley at the foothills of the Alps. Only one road led into the property. The streams and the forest yielded nothing to prying eyes. As they walked toward the barn, Max made note of the farm's natural security.

Karl, Max, and Olga let out four bay horses from their stalls. Max attached leads to two geldings and led them out of the barn. Karl and Olga soon followed, leading the remaining two mares. Karl directed Max and Olga to the right side of the barn. "Just tie them to that hitching post. We can better organize the pack saddles and supplies on their backs. The more supplies we can carry, the better. You will need added feed for the long trek through the Swiss Alps."

Karl looked up in the sky. "Looks like you are going to have good weather." Max smirked as he led his Arabian dapple gray gelding to the fence. Max wrapped the reins a couple of times around a gatepost. He turned and walked back to the pack horse loaded up with additional supplies and bedding. Olga did the same with her mount—a small stocky bay mare. She yelled at Max, "Herr Max, please get my day pack. I left it on the stable door."

Leather to Steel

"Yes, sister." Max breathed a heavy sigh, not wanting to carry out the task. He walked into the stables with Karl. "Well, Herr Klaussner. Thank you for the hospitality."

"I wish you both safe travels. Oh yes. Before I forget, I want you to have this. You may need it." Karl handed Max a Kongsberg .45 caliber, model 1914 pistol. He then handed Max a box of ammo. "She is loaded up with a seven-round magazine. Here is a couple of empty magazines you can load up later."

"Thank you, Herr Klaussner."

"Make sure you teach Olga how to shoot it. She may need to take it out of your dead hands to defend herself."

Max nodded in agreement. "I suppose that would be wise." He tucked the pistol in the back of his waistband under his coat. He placed the bullets in the front pockets of his riding jacket.

Olga yelled out, "Max, are you coming? We need to make twelve hours today. Sun sets around six thirty this eve."

"I am coming." Once outside, Karl and Max walked over to Olga. Max handed Olga her day pack. She replied, "Danka, Herr Max."

Max and Olga mounted their horses. They double-checked their saddlebags and tack. Karl walked around each horse to ensure the stirrup length were proper and the cinch straps were tightened. Max looked down at Karl. "Herr Klaussen, thank you again for helping us."

Karl turned toward Olga. "Make sure you switch out horses every couple of days. Otherwise, their early demise will be your fault, and you will be walking."

Olga replied, "I will remind my brother."

Max sighed in frustration. "Sister, we only have a month on the trail. Don't start in on me."

Max and Olga pointed their horses' north toward Switzerland. The journey would take two months. They traveled on serpentine mountain paths followed long rivers digging deep into valleys dotted with small villages. Villages that escaped the effects of war. Most of the locals Max and Olga came across spoke French—the universal language in most of Europe. The dangers Karl mentioned never came to bear on Max and Olga's journey between remote civilizations that remained protected for centuries by the mountains and Mother Nature. Uncle Ademaro was wise to map out a secure trip that only required patience and time.

After two months on the trail, Max and Olga finally arrived in Basel, Switzerland. They stabled the horses for a couple of days. They spent their time out of the saddle resupplying their saddlebags. Max and Olga enjoyed sleeping on normal beds and taking baths in hot water. The cold creeks and the campfire food was getting tiresome. The simplest things of life sparsely available in the Alps became a welcome luxury in Basel.

Rested, Max and Olga departed Basel on July 1. They traveled over forty miles northward along the Rhine River, then cut northeast toward their first checkpoint in Freiburg im Breisgau, Germany. Olga and Max had traveled over five hundred miles. Their journey was almost complete.

Their early morning entrance to the outskirts of town proved to be a solemn affair. Max rode by Olga as they approached the city. The majestic Black Forest to the east parted low-hanging fog against the blue sky. It was a beautiful sight. Scanning the valley below, Max expressed a disdain for what the war had done. He said, "Olga, everything looks so gloomy here. The roads leading into the town were empty for the most part."

Getting closer to the village, Olga added, "Have you noticed most of the people walking on the farm roads are women and children? They look so sad."

"Olga, this is what the bloody British blockades and almost three years of war have done to our beloved Fatherland. We must change this." Olga agreed. Max said. "Look, there is a farm. Let us take the horses over there. I see a large barn. I am sure they can use the money." They pushed forward. The pack horses followed.

Once in front of the farmhouse, a middle-aged woman wearing a gray, war crinoline–style dress walked out onto the front porch. She was cradling a baby nursing on her breast. The dark circles under her eyes were noticeable from lack of sleep. Her high-waist dress draped

Leather to Steel

itself over a thin shell of a woman. She stared at Max and Olga. The young woman spoke with a lisp. "How can I help you, Herr Master?"

Max looked at Olga and back at the sad-looking woman. "I would like to speak with your husband."

Olga shook her head. "No, no. He is gone. The Kaiser took my man away." She frowned. To show a sense of compassion, Olga extended her hand toward Max to keep him silent. She then nudged her horse to take a step closer to the woman. "I am so sorry. I lost my man too. Can we talk?"

The woman nodded. Olga looked at Max. "Please let me handle this. She clearly needs some help, but you know how German women are—prideful." Max shook his head in agreement.

Max and Olga dismounted and secured the horses to the wooden fence rail. Max noticed several nails missing from the fence posts. He shook the posts to make sure the horses would not pull away. Olga walked over to the young woman and extended a hand. "My name is Olga. What is your name?"

The mother shifted her suckling child to her other arm. She then covered her breast. "I am Elsa Wollschlager."

Olga tried to tickle the little baby. "Who is the cute little one?"

"He is Angus. I named him after his father. He is up north somewhere. I have not heard from him in some time. I know he will be back."

Olga glanced at Max, then back at the young woman. "I am sure he will be back. The reason why we stopped is to offer payment for boarding our horses in your barn. If you will, what do you charge?"

Elsa rubbed her shin with her free hand. She said, "I don't need money. What I need is food. All the town's sheep were requisitioned by the German army. The trains took the stock up north. We were given government promissory notes, but we can't eat them."

Max asserted, "Hello, Mrs. Wollschlager. My name is Max. Olga is my sister." Elsa smiled back, and Max continued, "We have some extra supplies to offer. Flour, tea, and a few pounds of salted meat. Would that be enough payment?"

Elsa started to cry. She struggled to speak. "God bless you. God bless you both."

Olga reached for Max's hand, and then Elsa's. "It will be all right, Elsa."

"The war has been hard on German citizens and land. The turnips are all that we can grow. The potato crops failed last fall. You know that as well—from where you are from. Which is—"

"Dusseldorf. We grew up in Dusseldorf," Max quickly replied.

"You are northern Germans, much different from us southern Germans."

Olga jumped in to the conversation. "We only lived there for a short while. Our parents moved south to Munich. We consider ourselves just Germans."

Elsa said, "Then you are welcome to board your horses here. I will make sure they are locked up. People are hungry around here, and horses are edible."

Olga cringed. "Oh my gosh. I hope they will be okay."

"They will be fine." Elsa pointed at the pack horses. "Did you bring feed in one of those tote sacks?"

Max replied in confidence, "Yes, we did. I will unload and put them into the barn."

Elsa asked, "Can you also help me with the water well?"

Max drew a heavy breath. He looked at Olga and rolled his eyes. Olga nudged him with her arm. "Of course my brother can help you."

Max watered and fed the horses before securing them inside Elsa's barn. Olga told Elsa they would be in town for a few days taking care of some business. Max would return to fix the water pump. Elsa asked, "Will you be staying long?"

Olga said, "No. We need to head north to visit our parents."

"Oh." Elsa said, saddened. "I was hoping you could stay longer. All the men are gone."

Max said, "Elsa, we will return to pick up our horses and help you with your water well, and whatever heavy lifting you need done before we go."

Elsa reached over to touch Max's arm. "Thank you. God bless you."

Olga handed Elsa two five-pound bags of flour and a pound bag of sugar. It had been months since Elsa had flour to bake with. She was elated to have enough flour to make sweetbread for herself. Elsa had to eat all she could to make milk for baby Angus. As she did with the cornmeal, she would stretch out the flour and the sugar for as long as she could.

Max and Olga knew their time in Freiburg had to be short. For several reasons. Their presence would give cause for gossip. The kind of attention they could not afford to explain away under suspicious circumstances. They needed to be in Berlin before August. They only had two weeks to cover over two hundred miles. Freiburg had only one purpose according to plan. Dispatch cables.

The Zum Roten Bären Inn accommodations were bare basics: a bed, a washbasin, and one closet to hang clothes. The fourteenth-century building was not designed for modern comforts. The immediate problem facing Max and Olga was only one bed in each room. The desk clerk offered two rooms, but Max declined. He was getting short on bank notes Germans would recognize as legitimate payment. Using gold was not an option for payment. He had to conserve the precious coins.

Olga stood next to Max and said, "I don't mind. We will work it out." Both were so exhausted from the long trek across the Alps. The formalities of separate beds were their least concern. The morning would come soon enough. They could reevaluate at that time.

On the next day, Max got up early to get ahead of the Freiburg population still sleeping. He left Olga to sleep. She snored while in her deep sleep. She did not stir when he opened and closed the room door. He walked down the stairs to the lobby and stopped by the front desk. He asked the clerk where the nearest telegraph office was located. The clerk directed him to the local railroad station. The German army buried a cable along the train tracks all the way to Frankfurt where a transfer box connected southern to northern Germany in Berlin.

Once outside, Max stopped to smell the crisp mountain air flowing down into the valley. He walked along the sidewalk leading toward the train terminal. The town's early-morning workers began their daily tasks. Freiburg's streetlamps flittered off and on. Max observed a lamplighter walking to each street corner, turning the lamp switches off.

Looking to the east, the low-light darkness gave way to the early-morning sun rising about the Black Forest tree lines. A red hue encircled the Münster Cathedral's octagonal church tower and spire. The red light made the gargoyles' mouths drip with blood outside of Münster Cathedral. Max stopped. He closed his eyes and then opened them to see the gargoyles once again gray.

He looked beyond the church and watched the brilliant oranges and reds paint the sky brushed with gray clouds. Red streaks expanded across the sky while the moments clicked by, which gave Max cause to mumble, "Red sky in the morning, sailor take warning. Red sky at night, sailor's delight."

Max walked to the middle of Main Street to get a better view of the Black Forest. The last time he walked through the forest was with his mother, God rest her soul. The morning sun eventually broke through the clouds drifting away from the eastern horizon. The oranges turned into lighter shades of blue. He took a deep breath and looked up in the sky and sighed. "Lord God. Guten Morgen. I stopped believing in you when my dear Kate died. I think I am ready to embrace my fate." Max continued walking toward the train station.

Max climbed a set of wooden stairs that led up to the train dock. Looking at the end of the platform, he observed lights shining through a small office toward the end. He walked a good hundred feet to the office door. Max knocked three times. He mumbled, "Someone has to be in there." A desk light was on. He put his ear to the door and heard shuffling on the wooden floor. An old man's voice called out, "Who is it?"

Max replied, "Max Eilenberg."

"What do you want?"

"I need to send a cable to Berlin."

"We only send cables authorized by the Imperial German Army. Are you with the army, Herr Eilenberg?"

"Yes. I need to reach command headquarters."

The office door swung open, and a short, stout, balding man opened the door. Max studied the man wearing a black visor cap, a long-sleeved white shirt rolled up to his elbows, and an unbuttoned black leather vest. Pieces of white crumpled paper stuck out from each front pocket. The old man put the pencil he was holding just inside his top right ear. He pushed his circular reading glasses down his nose to get a better view of Max. "How can I help you Herr—"

Max finished his sentence. "Captain Max Eilenberg. I am attached to the German Fourth Cavalry Regiment."

"Captain Eilenberg, what are you doing down here so far south? You should be up in Belgium or France killing Frenchmen."

Max denied him a response and asserted instead, "And your name, sir?"

"My name is Henrik von Bergstein. I am also the mayor of Freiburg and the newspaper editor."

"Very good. I see you are doing your duty for our Fatherland."

"Yes. And then some. Now how can I help you?"

"I need to get a message back to my regiment. My colonel wants me to send him a code that only he knows. Do you understand?"

"Yes, yes. I know how secretive you people are. What is the receiver code and message you want me to send?" Max handed a preprinted message to Mr. von Bergstein, who read it over. He asked, "Do you want confirmation? I don't see a confirmation number."

"No, thank you. Just send it as written. They will know what to do."

"Very well. Now if you will excuse me, I have a very important message to transcribe for the town paper. Did you not hear? The new German minister, Theobald von Bethmann-Hollweg has pushed the Reichstag to propose a Peace Treaty with the Allies."

Max looked shaken by the news. He stammered, "No. I…I—no. I did not know that."

"No worries," von Bergstein replied. "Most of the army and the navy has been kept in the dark. In fact, General von Hindenburg is pushing back hard."

Max said, "My superiors aligned themselves with General Ludendorff."

*****

Verhandlungen des Deutschen Reichstages, July 15, 1917

> However, as long as the enemy governments refuse to agree to such a peace, as long as they threaten Germany and her allies with conquest and domination, so long will the German people stand united and unshaken, and they will fight until their right and that of their allies are made secure. Thus united, the German people remain unconquerable. The Reichstag feels that in this sentiment it is united with the men who have fought with courage to protect the Fatherland. The undying gratitude of our people goes out to them.[66]

"Nevertheless, the Kaiser will weigh in at some point. Though a powerless man he has become." Max took note of the antimonarchist attitude he shared with Herr von Bergstein. He excused himself and returned to the inn.

While Max was gone, Olga had already bathed and dressed for the day. When he walked in to the room, he caught sight of Olga wearing only a bathrobe. At that moment, Max noticed how beautiful Olga looked. He closed the door behind him and walked over to her. "Are you hungry?"

"Of course I am, *brother*."

"Olga, I think we are done with the brother-sister act. We can be Germans. Max Eilenberg and Olga von Marx."

Olga asked, "Why not Olga and Max Eilenberg?"

Max stepped back to look at Olga. He cleared his throat. "We may cross that bridge someday frau. Not now."

"What do you mean? We already crossed a couple bridges together this past year, if not built them together."

"Olga, we need to get to Berlin. Let us seriously talk about it then." Olga shook her finger at Max. "You just wait and see. You will think differently about me before long."

Voices outside the inn caught Max's attention. He turned and walked toward the bedroom window. He looked down at the

Leather to Steel

sidewalk and saw two German soldiers standing around smoking cigarettes.

"Olga." Max waved his hand at her. "Come here. Looks like we have company."

Olga looked at the two soldiers. "They are young. Most likely home on leave. We can practice our cover on them. What do you think?"

Max nodded in agreement. He reached down to his bag on the chair. Max searched through the bag for the envelope full of fake identifications. "Here it is. My German army credentials. Captain Maxwell Eilenberg." Olga continued observing the soldiers. Max walked back over to the window. He studied the two soldiers. "Those soldiers are attached to a light infantry unit."

"How can you tell?"

"Both are wearing a gray wool German Feldmütze (field cap). Both caps have a green band which are associated with light infantry. A red hat band means they are regular infantry. A black band means they move and shoot artillery."

"What else can you tell me about them?"

"The tallest soldier is a noncommissioned officer. His Feldmütze has a small leather brim. The other soldier's Feldmütze does not have a brim. Do you see the top button on their field caps?" Olga squinted against the sun to better focus on the caps. "Yes, both buttons are colored black, white, and red. Our national colors of Germany."

"Max, what does the bottom button represent?"

"The German state they hail from. These two Prussians are wearing white and black buttons. They are also wearing brown corduroy pants and laced-up ankle boots. They should be wearing knee-high jackboots. The boots and trousers they are wearing are not government-issue. The army, however, did reimburse them since the army can't replenish uniform supplies. Damn British blockade."

"Max, your attention to detail is very impressive. I think you will become very successful in your first assignment."

"Danke frau." Thank you, woman. "Come on, we need to get breakfast. The bank should open within the hour. I need to exchange gold for marks." Olga touched Max's shoulder. Keeping her hand in place, she asked in a low voice, "What did Uncle Ademaro have to say?"

"Take the first train leaving Freiburg tomorrow morning. A supply train is returning to the north. While at the station, I made arrangements for our passage to Berlin."

"What about the horses?"

"Olga, your friend will be glad to get four plow horses to work, or have for dinner."

"Stop that, Max. Those horses got us here. Don't speak of them that way."

Max put his arm around Olga. He looked down at her. "Of course not. She needs those horses more than us. Our gift to her future. I am sure her husband will return soon."

Olga remained in Berlin while Max served his tour of duty with the German Imperial Army. Assigned to the List Regiment, Max found common interests among the disenfranchised German soldiers who distrusted the Kaiser and his minions working behind the scenes to end the war. In short, surrender. Captain Eilenberg and his command staff were in no position to argue. Junior officers and the enlisted had little to say in their fate. But fate found Max.

Planning a war had been done decades before the war started. All Max and the millions of soldiers and sailors had to do was execute without question. Within the small converted war room in Alsace, the List Regiment staff planned their next moves against the Allies. The planning required sharp and eager minds. Max was introduced to a young soldier wounded during the Battle of Somme in October 1916. He needed to meet him.

The young soldier stood at perfect attention in front of Max, who remained silent for a few minutes. The young soldier moved not a muscle. Max enjoyed the tension created between superior officer and a junior enlisted man. He stared into the soldier's dark eyes, then breathed out a sigh. Max commanded, "At ease solider." Instead, the soldier went into parade rest. "At ease, soldier. Follow me into my office. We need to discuss you men's attitudes. I have heard rumors of dissent toward His Majesty."

Leather to Steel

Perspiration beads formed on the soldier's forehead, though his eyes showed no fear. He replied, "Yes, Captain. I am at the pleasure of your service."

Inside his office smelling of cigar smoke and cheap whiskey, Max sat down in an old leather swivel chair behind a black-oak desk. The young lance corporal stood in front of Max's desk at perfect attention. Max turned on the small desk lamp. He tilted the green lampshade toward the soldier who remained stoic and unemotional. The lamp shone brightly on the corporal's expressionless face. His squinting dark eyes locked onto his superior officer. Captain Eilenberg ordered the corporal to relax. The young soldier instead popped to attention. He clicked his heels together, producing a sharp metallic sound. Max leaned back in his chair and put his arms behind his head. He studied the soldier's movements.

The corporal wore a perfectly pressed uniform. Max studied the young man in silence for a good five minutes before the corporal spoke. "Sir, I am at the service of the Fatherland and the officers assigned over me." Max shook his head back and forth. He pulled out a pack of cigarettes tucked inside his tunic. He extended the pack toward the corporal. "Do you want one?" The corporal shook his head to decline the offer. "Very well then."

Max pulled out an English cigarette, stuck it in the corner of his mouth, and lit it with a struck match. Max took one puff and then blew a smoke ring toward the corporal's direction. The smoke circle enveloped the soldier's face. Max observed the circle of smoke had quickly dissipated. No halo remained. Max asked the stoic young soldier. "I see you're wearing the Iron Cross. How did you earn that badge?"

"The Battle of Somme in 1916. I was put on medical duty in Munich. Now I am here in Berlin serving you."

"I understand. What was your opinion of the social unrest in Munich?"

"The Jews are responsible for stirring antiwar attitudes."

"I understand, Corporal Adolf Hitler. We have the German people's work to get done."

Lance Corporal Hitler stood at ease. "Yes, we do. Deutschland Deutschland ueber alles."[67]

Imperial German Army Machinegun Nest During the Great War: Photo: German Federal Government Archives

*****

The discussion between Captain Eilenberg and Hitler told of great change to come. The beginnings of a nationalist-socialist movement rooted itself in a musty old office that eventually would come to destroy centuries-old monarchies and ruling houses: The Romanovs of Russia, Hapsburgs of Austria, the Ottomans and lastly, the German Empire.

Tough Guy

May 1917. General Seely's company of veterinary teams deployed just behind the Canadian Cavalry Regiment's ammunition and supply trucks motoring over rebellious muddy ruts weary soldiers fought with fascine-construction efforts. Captain Boak ensured Royal Canadian Horse Artillery Brigade veterinary officers, farriers, handlers, and aides set up two mobile veterinary field hospitals close

Leather to Steel

to the fighting. A distance of one mile separated the mobile hospitals behind the line to increase the likelihood of survival.

Captain Boak learned from the previous month's disaster. A German 17-inch razor bomb exploded between two mobile units situated in the same equine dugout. The Germans constructed the Razor to detonate just aboveground. Anything within a fifty-yard radius would be hit. Several horses and soldiers were wounded or killed by flying steel splinters, penetrating legs, abdomens, and heads.

Major Hazzard and I again witnessed the destructive nature of war. We were fortunate not to be near the field hospital when the razor bomb hit. I was horrified to see the aftermath. Several horses I befriended were cut to pieces. Their pain-felt whining encouraged my desire to fight in their place. My son Jubal was tethered in the area on the other side of the dugout. His wounds were superficial. The veterinarian pulled out a few steel splinters lodged in his right shoulder. Jubal made fun of the attention. He neighed to me. "Just a scratch, Dad." I knew then he had what it took to be on the warfront.

In June 1918, we marched toward Ypres, Belgium. On the way, I witnessed more death. Decaying horses and mules lined the roads and inside trenches that became their graves. Major Hazzard said the battles were no longer defensive. The American and British Expeditionary Forces were aggressively looking to rout the Germans once and for all.

General Haig planned to take Ypres by July. History would call it the Third Battle of Ypres. The Allies had battled with the Germans at Ypres during the first few months in the beginning of the war. We were back.

Our regiment staged itself thirty miles away as a reserve force. Until then, the units spent time cleaning weapons, patching up horses and men, and getting much-needed rest. The dwell time also provided senior officers to recognize the courageous efforts of men who led or fought during the Battle of Vimy Ridge. Captain Boak was one of those soldiers.

*****

General Seely summoned Captain Boak to the Regiment command tent. By the captain's request, Major Hazzard and I accompanied him and Daisy. Standing between me and Daisy, Captain Boak commented, "Major, so pleased you will ride with me over to the command tent. I would feel better knowing an American was by my side."

"Why so, Captain Boak?"

"If I need to blame an American, you can be my defense." Major Hazzard shook his head. "Always a clever man."

The major added. "Well. Soon there will be tens of thousands more like me coming here to do your country's bidding. The United States declared war on Germany last month. You can bet the doughboys will wreak havoc on the Tommies."

Once at the command tent, the major dismounted and tied me to the makeshift rail next to another horse I had not formally met. The captain tied Daisy to a different rail on the opposite side of the tent. I suppose he did not want her bringing unwanted attention by the bay horse standing next to me.

The major and the captain walked inside the tent. I could overhear them talking with General Seely and the Rock's commander, Lieutenant Colonel Henri Alexandre. The major and the captain clicked their boot heels together to stand at attention. The next words I heard were, "General, sir, reporting as ordered." General Seely spoke in a voice that sounded as if coming from deep in a barrel. "Men, at ease."

General Seely continued, "Captain Boak, it has been brought to my attention that the loss of horse life was minimized by your decision to physically separate the mobile veterinary units. As a result, wounded horses up and down the battlefront were able to receive quick medical attention due to the proximity of each mobile unit. It has also been brought to my attention by Lieutenant Colonel Alexandre that it was your idea to create dugouts covered with camouflage netting that concealed our cavalry horses from aerial attacks. Well done."

The general paused to pick up a letter with the official Canadian Cavalry Regiment letterhead embossed on the top. He then put on his reading glasses. The general looked at Captain Boak. "Attention to orders." All the officers present came to attention. "By my hand signed, I General Jack Seely herby meritoriously promote Captain Henry Eversley Boak to the rank of Major in the Royal Canadian Horse Artillery Brigade on this day of our Lord, May 21, 1917."

General Seely then ordered the officers to parade rest. He asked the captain to step forward and stand at attention. Captain Boak stepped toward the general. General Seely looked Captain Boak square in the eyes and proceeded to remove both Captain Boak's railroad bars. The general then pinned one gold oak leaf devise on the captain's left collar, and the same for the right. General Seely took one step back. "Attention, Major Boak. Congratulations. As you are. The next papers I present are your official orders. Orders to go home. You have served His Highness with honor. Perhaps you should take a short leave and relax your bones across the channel in Blighty?"

Major Boak made a heavy sigh. He looked at Major Hazzard and cracked a slight smile. The new major replied, "Thank you, sir. I thank you. But with all due respect, sir. I would rather stay with my men. England will have to wait."

"Major, you need not worry. You are to report to the Dover remount depot within three days. I want you to help train the new horsemen coming into theater. After you complete that assignment, tell your parents to expect you home for Christmas."

Major Boak remained silent during the reading of his new orders. The general asked, "Do you have any questions?"

"No, sir. I will do as ordered with honor and becoming of a Canadian officer." The general then stared at Major Hazzard. "I have something for the American." He glanced at Major Boak. "Mister Boak, at ease." He shifted his eyes to the American. "Except for you, Major Hazzard. I have orders from your General Pershing."

Major Hazzard remained at attention. He spoke with conviction. "Sir, yes, sir. The major waits for his orders." The general waved Major Boak to take one step back.

Major Hazzard stood motionless at attention. General Seely took a pipe out of his pocket. While the major waited for a command, the general loaded the pipe with tobacco he had pinched from a small cotton sack he kept in a small wooden humidor he kept on his desk. He packed the tobacco into the ivory pipe bowl. He held the pipe's turtle-shell stem in the corner of his mouth. After lighting the pipe, the general inhaled a sweet-smelling smoke into his lungs. He exhaled toward the major.

Major Hazzard waited for a command. The general looked at the major with steely eyes and commanded, "At ease, Major. I have a problem here."

The major remained unnerved by the seriousness of the general's tone.

The general spoke again. "At ease, Major."

The major returned to parade rest, not wanting to appear too relaxed. He replied. "Sir, you have orders for me."

General Seely handed a cable to the major. He read aloud. "From United States Army, American Expeditionary Forces Commander, General John J. Pershing to Major Oliver Hazzard, United States Army, Second Cavalry Regiment Dragoons. Action. Report to American Expeditionary Force Commander command staff. Duty location is dependent upon date receipt of orders. Point of contact is Captain George S. Patton Jr." General Seely asserted, "That means you are to rendezvous with the general at their current command location. Son, that means you need to report to Chaumont, France. A bit away from the fighting, I might add. Approximately one hundred and sixty miles southeast from Paris."

"Sir, how shall I—"

"Son, you will return with our severely injured being evacuated to Paris. From there, you will check in with the American embassy. They will guide you to your next transport."

"Thank you, sir." The general stood up. He stepped around his desk and walked over to the major. Standing in front of Major Hazzard, he said, "Major. Attention."

Major Hazzard promptly brought his boot heels together. General Seely then extended his left hand to the major's front pocket. With his right hand, the general pinned a medal on Major Hazzard's pocket flap. The general said, "On behalf of His Highness, King

George, you, Major Oliver Hazzard, United States Army, are awarded this medal—the Victoria Cross—to recognize your bravery and courage while serving with the Royal Canadian Horse Artillery Brigade during hostile actions. Your service reflects great credit upon yourself and the proud traditions of the United States Army." The general took one step back and commanded, "At ease."

*****

Tough Guy and Jubal

I heard several claps and congratulatory comments shared among the officers. I then smelled and heard hot brewed tea being poured. They were going to be in there for some time. It was now a good time to have a chat with the bay standing next to me. He was rather quiet.

"My name is Tough Guy. I am with my trooper, United States Army Major Oliver Hazzard. What is your name, friend?"

Pawing the ground in front of him, the big bay came back with a curt response. "The general calls me Warrior."

I waited for him to continue on, but his social skills were tested in some way. I added, "We have been attached to the Royal Canadian Horse Artillery Brigade since January 1915. How long have you been here?"

"Too long. Since the war started."

"My son, Jubal, and I came here to observe the war. However, the war extends beyond the safety of an observation point. We both were wounded standing near ambulances."

"My best advice to you, my American friend, is learn to listen and lay down. For me. It has saved me from getting hit. When the whizzing sounds stop, get up and race toward a tree line. Never retreat to the rear. Bloody well right."

I contemplated Warrior's words. When I returned to Jubal, I shared those insights with him. A father's duty. Hopefully, Jubal and I would avert the need to lay down by choice. The images of dead and mangled horses lying alongside the roads and ditches haunted me since the Battle of Ypres.

The wholesale destruction of the living certainly affected Jubal and Daisy's ability to function on the battlefield. Each day spent in the field affected their temperament. They were young and exhibited signs of shell shock. I could only pray for Jubal's survival. Between the two of us, he had to return home. I would do whatever it took to protect my son. I would die for him.

*****

The Allied leaders expected the AEF to be at full strength by summer's end. General Pershing wanted the U.S. Second Cavalry Regiment forward deployed along the Western Front to provide tactical flanking maneuvers and intelligence back to headquarters. Major Hazzard's in-country experience benefited the newcomers. Lieutenant Bates and twenty thousand other "first wave" soldiers needed months to become effective.

General Pershing resisted the urge to send his men into harm's way—not until they were ready. He had to organize, prepare, train, and train again. He reported to President Wilson. "Sir, good performance begs good training. Good training takes time." By July 1917, he cabled President Wilson. "The men are ready. Send them over."

The order was given. Hundreds of transport ships departed from ports between Norfolk and New Jersey. Soldiers and sailors would sail above the seas, while the darkness of death lurked below—the German U-boat. Over 2 million soldiers would answer the call to arms to participate in the Allied offensive. Not all would make it to the shores of England. On February 1, 1917, the German government discarded international law, and began their campaign of unrestricted submarine warfare.[68]

The Germans also resorted to using inhumane chemical weapons on the battlefield. Both men and horses suffered. The U.S. Army knew of the threat and made preparations to protect the cavalryman and the horse.[69] Gas masks were fitted to each horse with the hopes they would not rub it off during a gas attack. The idea created a sense of false security for both the horse and the rider.

U.S. Trooper Practicing Gas Mask Donning on Horse
(Photo: U.S. National Archives)

Jeremiah and Mary worried every day about Abraham. The newspapers were almost the only source of information about the war in Europe. American's were affected by what they read and what they wondered. Most of it was wondering. Jeremiah and Mary could only pray for their son's future in the army. Until then, home life of all Americans changed to support the war. The U.S. Government created the Department of Food and Agriculture to administer programs designed to manage limited resources such as food, metals, and petrol products. The management of food became a top priority. All Americans were asked to participate in volunteer food rationing programs.

Be Patriotic sign your country's pledge to save the food

U.S. Food Administration Food Ration Program Poster 1917. National Archives

The U.S. Food Ration cards were made available to all Americans. The ration program appealed to the patriotic sense supporting American troops fighting in Europe. The government asked Americans to put the needs of the soldiers before others. The new U.S. Food Administration circulated posters around the country to encourage patriotic service.[70] Be Patriotic… was one a several syndicated across the country between 1917 and 1919.

*****

Lieutenant Abraham Bates stood on the main deck of the U.S. Army Transport ship (USAT) *Finland* watching two tugboats carefully guide the ship into the Port of Brest France. He held onto the ship's rail looking down at the tugboat's crew handle large-girth towlines being fed through the ship's chocks. He turned to his friend Corporal Freddie Stowers. "Freddie. Soon as we get off this ship, we will part ways. I figure God will take care of the both of us. He did during boot camp."

"Lieutenant Bates. You be on top of an ol' horse getting a bird's eye view of the war."

"Eddie. Abe. Call me Abe when we are not around other soldiers. You are my friend. Remember. I was a recruit just like you back in 1914."

"You bet masta'."

"Quit messing with me Eddie."

*****

1918: The Western Front

The horses were ordered unsaddled and the equipment was placed in front of them. The men tied the reins to their legs, laid down, and in spite of the frightful din and bombardment, nearly every one fell asleep, so exhausted were the men from the marching and confusion.
—*The Cavalry Journal*, Vol. XXX, July 1921, No. 124
The Second Cavalry in the St. Mihiel Offensive, Captain Ernest N. Harmon, Second Cavalry

Captain Abraham Bates

Three thousand miles away from home, newly promoted Captain Abraham Bates worked tirelessly as a capable United States Army Second Cavalry veterinarian in the field. At the age of twenty-two, he had already accomplished much more than what his parents expected. Abraham graduated from high school, the university, and arduous army basic, officer, and veterinarian training. He was grateful for a role model to measure his life against his father, Jeremiah Bates. A noble man who died doing what he loved the most—training horses.

Sitting on his bunk in Fort Myer, Abraham reread the cable he received in France. It was two weeks ago he boarded a transport ship bound for the United States. The cable informed him of Jeremiah's passing. Abraham thought his father had at least another good twenty years to live. God had other plans. The rear hoof of a frightened horse ended Jeremiah's life.

The Front Royal Remount Depot commander cabled Abraham that Jeremiah's untimely death was simply an act of God. The commander described the accident retold by several witnesses. Jeremiah had difficulty freeing a colt's rear hoof trapped between two mud shoot support frames. He stepped down into the shoot to get a better angle for freeing the colt's rear leg. Jeremiah freed the colt's hoof and held it firmly between his hands to check for injury. During the same moment, several soldiers began rehearsing rendering military honors with their Springfield rifles.

The soldiers simultaneously shot their rifles into the air. The combined shots created a loud explosion that spooked the colt. Frightened, the colt kicked out his free rear leg so fast Jeremiah could not react quick enough to deflect the kick. Unfortunately, the colt's hooves were shoed. The colt's free hoof landed squarely on Jeremiah's left temple. His life ended in a split second. The coroner concluded that a protruding shoe nail penetrated the temple, resulting in a massive head injury, instantly killing Jeremiah Bates.

At Jeremiah's memorial service, Captain Abraham Bates stood upon a narrow pulpit in the church he worshiped in as a boy. He reached into his pocket and unfolded a piece of yellow paper showing handwritten pencil notes across its corners and center. Captain Bates looked out into the worship area filled with many friends. It was standing room only. His mother and four siblings sat together in the front pew. Several of Jeremiah's friends showed up. Men he had served with back during the Indian Wars, and men he had known as a child. Since Jeremiah was an only child, he had no other family to claim.

Standing behind the pulpit, Preacher John asked Captain Bates to approach the front. After exchanging places, Abraham took a deep breath and sighed. He scanned the church pews and aisles. Many saddened faces and sunken eyes filled with tears looked up at Abraham. He struggled to avoid making eye contact with any particular person. Abraham laid his speaking notes down on the lectern to glance at during his eulogy. Before speaking, Captain Bates adjusted his collar and tie. He made sure his dress-green uniform was in perfect alignment. He wanted to look his best.

Abraham cleared his throat, then asked for everyone to bow their heads in prayer.

Leather to Steel

Our Father. Thank you for bringing us together to celebrate the life of a man whose courage and character know no comprise. Bless those who are with us today to celebrate his life as a father, a husband, and most of all, a patriot. Amen"

Jeremiah Bates knew not defeat in his mind and heart. Raised by slaves, he appreciated the blood spilled and sacrificed to keep our people free. He loved this country. At the age of eighteen, he joined the United States Army Cavalry as a private. He fought Comanche during the Indian Wars across the Plains of Texas, and hostiles running wild in the Oklahoma Territory.

Mister Jeremiah Bates could have retired after twenty-six years of military service. Instead, he volunteered to serve and fight at the Battle of San Juan Hill in Cuba. He then returned home and retired with honor.

At the age of sixty-four, he should have been rocking in his chair, or fishing at a pond with his children. Instead, he continued to work. He worked because he wanted the money to make a better future for us kids. I am a testament to that fact. But as I got older, I realized it was not the money. It was his love. He worked with what he loved the most –horses—an animal that gave him a sense of purpose, yet in the end, tragically took his life. He would not have wanted to die any other way. He told me one time, he said, "Son. You will never work a day in your life if you love what you do." I suppose my calling in life has been the same. I followed his footsteps because the horse is what fed our family. The horse is what kept him alive during battle. So in closing, we must thank God for the opportunity to have known such a great man. I know Grandpa Bo is hugging him in Heaven right now. They are probably shoe'n a horse.

Thank you all for coming. Our family greatly appreciates the respect and kindness you have shown us during this difficult time. God Bless you.

Captain Bates picked up his notes and carefully folded them to fit inside his tunic. Taking one more deep breath, he then slowly stepped down from behind the pew to retake his seat next to his mother. Holding his mother's hand, Abraham wiped a tear from the corner of his eye. He had to stay strong. He mumbled, "No emotions. Stay strong." The preacher stood up and walked back up to the pew to conclude the memorial service.

Preacher John asked the Bates family to first stand up and form a receiving line at the front church door. Mary Bates and her children stood up and walked toward the church entrance. Once outside, Mary had the children line up by age. Abraham stood next to his mother, holding her arm to keep her steady.

The first person to pay their respects was the Front Royal Remount Depot commander, Colonel Bedford. The commander offered his support and the United States Army's deepest condolences to the Bates family.

It was the saddest day in Abraham's life when he carried his father's pine casket from the church to the cemetery, where Jeremiah's mother and father lay to rest. After the funeral, Abraham kissed his mother, Mary, and said, "Do not worry, Mother. I will help take care of the family. I will send half of my army pay to you every month until you told me otherwise." Mary hugged her oldest son.

Abraham wiped tears from his mother's cheeks and said, "It will be okay, Mama. The commander said you and the kids can stay here until you can find another place to live. It will be okay."

Mary hugged her son tight, acting as if it would be the last time she saw him.

Leather to Steel

Photo: Authentic Horse Shoe (Circa 1917) Discovered at the Front Royal Remount Depot by Mr. Jon B. Rodarmel of Front Royal, Virginia. Shoe Nail was Extended like a Weapon.

Within six months of declaring war on Germany, the U.S. Army Second Cavalry Regiment charged enemy positions on the Western Front in July 1917. Eight months later, Captain Bates found himself leading a mobile veterinarian hospital.

The sights, sounds, and smells of war changed the young captain into a different man. Everything he knew to be true in life became a distorted reality. The scars of battle changed every man and animal. Captain Bates witnessed countless soldiers, horses, and mules return from the front with shell shock. If cleared by medical, the wounded repeatedly returned to the battle. Many simply became mad.

Horses and mules experienced mental anguish. Countless horses and mules once calm, turned into nervously spirited animals. Some become numb-minded. One mule demonstrated this behavior after his handler was killed during a weapons haul to the front lines. The mule had been fitted with a six-pack rocket pannier. The mule had nowhere to go but forward to the waiting artillerymen. The soldiers that unloaded him said he returned to the supply truck for another load. Cases like this were rare. Most distraught animals escaped from the front, only to die of starvation in an unfamiliar countryside.

Captain Bates was also human. He held casualties of war between his hands nearly every day. During each battle, he sorted through injured horses to determine which to send to the rear, and which to send back to the front. In many cases, horses with superficial wounds were stitched up and covered with a disinfectant. Horses diagnosed with hoof rot, or other long-term disabling conditions, were transported to one of twenty Royal Army Veterinary Corps animal hospitals positioned well behind the fighting.

If the horse could not function, it was put down with a bullet. Captain Bates ordered his enlisted orderlies to perform the humane duty. He once confided in his best friend, John, "I have taken an oath to save animals, not kill them. However, humanitarian action is the only option to relieve their suffering. I have trouble closing the eyes of a dead horse, much less shoot one."

*****

Near the French Champagne Marne Sector, Captain Bates was working side-by-side with his British counterparts. He directed a temporary veterinary field hospital to tend horses, mules, and dogs injured during the fighting. The shortage of basic medical supplies suggested that he make do with what they had. Temporary hospitals were no different.

He directed his staff to improvise the use of partially destroyed farmhouses and barns to build shelters for the animals. There certainly were no shortages of dilapidated structures across the French countryside. A partially collapsed barn was covered with camouflaged netting to help protect the horses from aerial attacks. The nets did not always fool the German pilots.

*****

On September 26, the place of battle widened, as did the number of casualties and injured grow. The powerful American Expeditionary Force rolling barrages pounded German positions near the Argonne Forest. The fighting was intense. During the battle, dozens of injured cavalry and artillery horses, as well as tracking dogs were injured and hauled back to Captain Bates' mobile field station. He operated inside the main surgical tent. The first patient could not have been worse off.

Shrapnel had ripped open the German shepherd's lower abdomen. While sewing up the dog, another ambulance parked near the surgical tent. Inside the ambulance, the drive, an army lieutenant rolled down the window and yelled out for help. Captain Bates looked up from his surgery and asked an orderly, "Go see what is going on outside. Get the injured out of the weather and into the barn." The orderly complied.

The lieutenant spoke to the orderly. "Corporal, I have a dog that needs some help."

The orderly noticed he was an officer. "Sir, take your ambulance and back it into the barn. The doctor will meet you there in a moment."

The captain replied, "Very well. Tell him to hurry up."

The orderly nodded and returned to the surgical tent. After backing in the ambulance, the lieutenant stopped and got out. He ran to the back of the surgical tent and parted the cover flap with his bloodied hand. He stepped in and yelled out, "I need a doctor. Please!"

Captain Bates heard the loud request, but before he could turn around to answer again, the lieutenant was standing behind him.

Lieutenant John Jones stared at the back of Captain Bates' head and huffed, "I need a doctor!"

Abraham turned around and pulled down his surgical mask. He stared at the angry lieutenant. "Wait, mister. I have to close up this dog. Please step outside." Then he turned around and finished the last two sutures on the dog's abdomen. He asked his assistants to pick up the dog and put him in the recovery tent.

Captain Bates put the curved suture needle into a bowl of alcohol, then removed his gloves. He asked his second assistant to wash down the buckboard serving as a surgical table. Satisfied with his orders, Captain Bates stepped outside the tent entrance. He watched a nervous and muddied officer wipe mud off his forehead. Captain Bates interrupted him, extending a hand, "John. John Jones. It is me, Abe. Remember?"

The distraught officer replied, "I am sorry. Do I know you?"

"Yes. You and I graduated from officers' candidate school back in Fort Des Moines, Iowa. Remember?"[71]

"I don't know, sir. If you would please, my shepherd was wounded by shrapnel. Please come out and help him. He is lying in the back of the flatbed."

Abraham put his hand on Lieutenant Jones's right shoulder. "What is your name?"

"Lieutenant John Jones, U.S. Army Second Cavalry Regiment."

"I see. We can talk more later. Take me to your dog."

Abraham and John walked together toward the barn. The wagon serving as an ambulance was parked under the barn's hay loft. As they walked, Abraham took a deep breath. He grimaced from the smell of smoke and unknown odors swirling in the air. He looked up at the sky and saw small slivers of blue breaking through the clouds. The overcast parted long enough to provide a brief respite from the dreary gray hanging over the countryside. He mumbled, "Maybe today will be a better day."

Abraham asked the lieutenant, "John, where did you and your dog get wounded?"

Looking confused, Lieutenant Jones replied, "No, sir. Just my dog was injured."

Abraham studied the officer's upper body. "Lieutenant, your left arm has a flesh wound."

Jones reached for his left arm to feel the blood-soaked shirt. He stopped and looked at his left arm. He asked, "Doc, would you mind throwing a few stitches after you take care of Sonny?" Abraham replied, "You bet, Mr. Jones. After we take care of Sonny."

The large dog was lying down unsecured on the flatbed. Abraham started with examining Sonny's head. Facing Sonny, he carefully removed the dog's collar. He then placed his hands over the dog's eyes to feel his eyelashes as he blinked. Abraham then placed his hands on both sides of the dog's ears and worked his fingers down underneath the jaw. Working his way around the chest, he ran both hands down each leg to check for tender areas indicating possible fractures. Satisfied, he worked his way back and up to the neck and haunches.

Abraham asked Lieutenant Jones, "Please come hold his head. Soothe him with your voice while I need to take a closer look at these shoulder wounds."

John nodded and moved in front of Sonny.

Abraham pulled out a clean rag from his right smock pocket. It was soaked with hydrogen peroxide. He wiped dried blood from the largest cut measuring about four inches in length. A piece of shrapnel had buried itself in the first few layers of hide and under tissue. The second wound was smaller. Only a gash. Abraham looked at Lieutenant Jones to give a prognosis. He said, "Mr. Jones, he will live. There is much blood, but not from a vital organ. All from flesh."

John exhaled loudly, "Whew. I was so worried."

Abraham asked, "John. Your name is John, right?"

The lieutenant nodded yes. "Go ahead and secure this cloth around his eyes. He does not need to see this." John secured the blinders. "Okay, do your business, Doc." Abraham withdrew a pair of stainless-steel hemostats from his chest pocket, while rubbing his left hand firmly on Sonny's shoulder. He used his right hand to secure the hemostats on the shrapnel buried in Sonny's muscle.

Abraham asked John, "Please talk to him." He added, "Oh yes, before I forget." He took out a small handful of dried cow fat from a belt bag he wore under his smock. He placed the scraps into John's cupped hand. "Here, let him nibble. I will only need a minute or two."

Sonny yelped a couple of times to express his discomfort. Abraham had another trick up his sleeve to minimize Sonny's pain.

He asked, "John, so you have a pint of whiskey in under your blouse?"

The lieutenant squirmed for a bit, knowing alcohol was not permitted. "Yes, sir."

Abraham said, "Relax. This war is hell. Every man needs a temporary comfort in the field." John reached inside his blouse and pulled out a small leather flask and handed it to Abraham.

Abraham unplugged the flask and took a sip. "John, go ahead and put some on Sonny's gums. Trust me."

He pried open Sonny's mouth and let the flask drip onto Sonny's tongue. "Looks like it is working. He is licking the flask." Sonny enjoyed the libation.

While he licked his gums back and forth with this slobbering tongue, Abraham removed the shrapnel and secured several stitches to each wound. He looked at John and asked, "Let me see the flask."

John handed it over to Abraham. "Need a drink?"

"Nope. Just need to disinfect Sonny's wounds." John replied, "I guess that makes sense."

"John. We have to make do with what we got here in the field. Now, lower the bed and get Sonny on his feet. He can lay down over there under the hay nets."

John lowered the flatbed and eased Sony up to his paws. He then slowly walked Sonny over to lay with three horses tethered under a row of hay nets. He walked back over to talk with Captain Bates. "Why hang the hay?"

"Mud. The British concluded that most hay got absorbed by the mud before the horses had time to eat it. The solution was to make hay nets out of knotted rope. The result is what you see. Dry hay. However, one solution to one problem creates a different problem."

"How so?"

"The nets have to be at eye level. Net hung to high cause hay particles to get into the horse's eyes. Some were blinded by infection."

"I never would have thought."

"Nor would I have. The Brits love their horses."

The lieutenant replied, "And I love my dogs."

Fourth time was the charm. On September 28, the British General Douglass Haig's victorious large offensive against the Germans in the Ypres Salient.

*****

Second Battle of Ypres: Village of Passchendaela

> The life of a soldier, in time of war, has scarcely a compensating feature ... In campaigning against the Indians, if anxious to gain success, he must lay aside every idea of good food and comfortable lodgings ... his sole object is to strike the enemy and stick him hard.
> —Captain J. G. Bourke, Third Cavalry
> Fort Craig, New Mexico Territory, 1870

Jubal

Major Hazzard; my father, Tough Guy; and I detached from the Royal Canadian Horse Brigade to spend ten days of training with one troop of the Canadian Provisional Squadron detached from General Seely's command headquarters in Brest. We accompanied a hundred or so soldiers who marched to Menil-la-Tour France, where they reported for courier duty with the Canadian First, Forty-Second, and Eighty-Ninth Divisions. The remainder of the Provision Squadron reported to the First Division on the night of September 11, 1918. Major Hazzard told us we were in close company with American forces. The mounted United States Army cavalrymen loitered at Nonsard, about five miles behind the original enemy line. It was here that my life changed forever.

Ordered from reconnaissance duty, the Canadian cavalrymen — with Major Hazzard riding on my back— met the Germans in considerable force. We were routed. Cavalrymen who survived the Meuse-Argonne action maintained liaison between flank divisions and the remaining Provisional Squadron with three troops on the front lines.

Among the muddy trenches, which made movement of a whole troop impracticable, small patrols, sometimes riding on our backs and sometimes walking, acted as military police and couriers.

By mid-October, when withdrawn from the front, the Provisional Squadron had only 150 mounted effectives, largely because sick and wounded horses were sent to the rear. My father — Tough Guy—was one of them. Major Hazzard was another.

*****

Jubal

Several simultaneous explosions knocked Major Hazzard off my back and into a muddy trench. I stood above him looking down. He whistled. I slid down into the muddy trench to help him out of a trench barely four feet wide. The major had no room to move around to my side.

Facing him, I lowered my front legs into the mud. He slowly crawled over my neck. Once I felt his body halfway over, I gradually pushed on my front legs to let gravity do its job. The major slid himself down onto the saddle, maintain balance using my mane clutched in his hand. Once I felt his seat, I stood completely on all fours. The only problem that remained was how to get out of the trench.

Major Hazzard leaned over the saddle and moaned, "Come on, Jubal. Get us out of here." That was my cue. Since I could not turn to the left or right, the only way out was to jump up over the edge. Getting out of the mud would not be easy.

I would need forward momentum. The end of the trench in front of me was only twenty feet ahead. I needed more distance. I had to back up to put more distance between me and the jump. I backed up slowly, careful not to step on a casualty. When I stood on top, I did not see any other soldiers. Satisfied that I had made it to the rear, I looked forward. This moment was what the mud shoot training prepared me for.

Then without warning, a large-caliber German shell shot over our heads. Bullets passed near. One went through my withers. Soon after the German shell exploded, my familial instincts kicked in. Something was very wrong. I looked over the trench and saw that the shell exploded near our field hospital, a half mile away. Excited, I pushed through the muddy trench, struggled some, but broke free of the suction and made it to the top.

The major moaned. He slid off my back and on to the ground. I turned to get my loose reins closer to him. He did not have the strength to grab them. "Go, Jubal. You are a sitting duck up here." The major pushed himself back into the trench. I should have stayed with him, but could not overcome the sinking feeling in my heart. I raced back to the hospital.

*****

It took some time to cover two miles of terrain pitted with craters larger than the supply trucks. I remembered what my father said to do. Snipers would still be in the woods. I had to be careful. Even though it was dark, I zigged and zagged so as not to give a German sniper a good shot. But snipers were not my only obstacle. German caltrops and landmines presented another problem. As I ran toward the field hospital, I kept my nose to the ground. My senses could not fail me. The caltrops had to be avoided.

Major Hazzard said the Tommies used Mother Nature's design to disable horses. They were very clever at setting booby-traps design in the likeness of a weed. He said that before the Germans retreated from their positions near Ypres, the Tommies had buried many iron caltrops on roads and prominent woodland paths.

The German aeroplanes also added to the fray. The pilots deliberately dumped caltrops onto terrain that the cavalry and artillery horses would pass over. I hoped none stood between me and the hospital.

Major Hazzard showed me a caltrop. It looked like a four-spike ball stuck into wooden boards the Germans hid by a thin layer of dirt, grass, and leaves. At least one spike protruded upward. When our horses and mules pulled artillery limbers to the front, some stepped on caltrops. I heard them neigh out in great pain. Stepping on caltrops was fatal for horses and mules. Infection was certain, if mud and dirt entered the wound under the hoof.[72]

*****

Jubal's breathing labored as he neared the hospital. Many ambulances coming in from the battle line drove by him. He made it to what was previously a horse field stable. Nothing was left of it. He watched the soldiers move wounded horses and mules from the bombed-out ruins. He looked for his father, but Tough Guy was nowhere in sight.

Jubal walked behind the ambulances near the surgical tents set up by the veterinarians. He smelled for his father's scent. There was none. He made note of the bloodied hoof prints left by the injured horses leading into the tents. The handlers said several dismounted cavalrymen thought it best to walk their mounts in roadside ditches. Within minutes, their screams became another telltale sign of danger.

Like soldiers, horses and mules were bandaged up and returned to the front. A soldier passed by him and said, "As long as I got two arms and two legs, I am going back to finish the job. This is war." His emotions agreed with him, but not his instincts. Yes, the war would go on for many, but not for his father, Tough Guy.[73] A gentle breeze carrying his scent got Jubal's attention.

Jubal ran back to the other side of what was a farmer's barn. He spotted Tough Guy lying down under hay nets the soldiers attached to a makeshift shelter overhanging a twenty-foot-wide trench dug four feet deep. The field stable was the best the Canadians could do to keep the horses out of sight from the aeroplane bombers. Unfortunately, the stable could not be protected from long-range artillery. As he approached the ruins, he heard whimpering and the loud neighing of wounded horses.

To get to him, Jubal walked to the left of what was the field stable. Horror blocked his path. Body parts of several horses lay strewn about the trench and on the hill it extended into. He sniffed the air and located his father. As he walked toward Tough Guy, the stench of burnt flesh and death hindered his smelling abilities. However, his eyes did not fail him. Looking to the far right, he saw a dark horse limping away from the carnage. As the smoke cleared, he recognized the big black stallion walking away from him. It was Tough Guy. Jubal followed him.

He had a heavy limp trying to get up a small knoll. Once over, he could see his father limping toward the farmhouse obliterated by the shelling. The only structures left standing was the house foundation and a small backyard fence. Jubal was not sure his father knew he was following him. He struggled to keep upright. He looked determined to get to the scorched white picket fence in front of him.

Once inside the picket fence, Tough Guy took a few more steps toward the corner of the yard. He let his right leg drop down to his knee. He then set both hind legs down. Trying to stay upright, he rolled down to his left side, favoring his right front leg. Jubal carefully approached him and neighed, "Dad, it is me, Jubal." He lifted his head and turned his neck toward me. Blood was dripping from his neck. Several pieces of shrapnel were embedded in the meat of his withers and shoulders.

Tough Guy neighed, "Son, is that you?"

Jubal took a few more steps and put his muzzle on his father's. He grunted, trying to breathe out. He smelled blood. His father had internal injuries. He turned around to make sure they were safe, then back at him. "Yes, it is me, Jubal."

He grunted. Jubal could hear a gurgling sound coming through his chest. It was his time to die.

It was difficult for Jubal to see a once-invincible stallion become anything but. He had to turn his head away to collect himself. Jubal looked across the open fields and watched dusk cast a faint light up through the night. The time of day would divide the night. The sun would soon be up.

As the sun rose over the horizon, the familiar sight of dead soldiers, horses, and mules lay in no-man's land. Trees that stood near the forest's edge were stripped of leaves, limb, and bark. Jubal watched the battlefield turned to colors of white and green. Litter bearers, soldiers, ambulances scurried between trenches, briefly stopping to retrieve the wounded and the dead. One officer walked between the dead collecting dog tags. His left hand could barely hold all of them.

Jubal was saddened over how four years of war devastated everything. One of its casualties lay before me. By the grace of God, the morning sun and the sense of peace synchronized at that very moment. My ears tuned out the sounds of war. A sense of serenity overcame me. After a few moments, he looked down at my right front hoof. A yellow flower was pinned to the ground. Jubal took one step back. The flower rose up toward him.

As the minutes went by, the sunlight began to awaken the night sky. Gray shadows surrounding me began to fade away. With the morning light, Jubal could now see why my father chose to lie in a flower garden. He sniffed and could smell sweet, pleasant odors permeate the air. He smelled roses as well. Crosses dotted the plot.

Tough Guy laid his head back down on the ground. His chest barely lifted with each shallow breath he took. Jubal stepped around front of him and lowered his nose to his muzzle. His right eye stared at me, then blinked. His eye told me of his pain. I asked him, "What can I do for you?"

"Jubal, there is nothing you can do for me *here*, son. But there is something you can do for me. Get back home. I want you to get as far away from this place, now. Follow your nose to the sea from which we came. Go."

"I don't understand."

Tough Guy breathed out and coughed again. "Son, your service is done here. You must get back home. I can't tell you the exact way. Follow your heart and nose. Remember from which you came. Remember the stories I told you. Pass those memories on to your offspring."

"Why do you say this?"

"Son, I am not strong enough to overcome these injuries this time. I want you to know—"

Tough Guy extended his back legs and snorted again. "You have made me very proud. I never thought I would get close to you. The only good thing about this war is it brought us together."

Jubal pawed the ground in front of Tough Guy. He attempted to encourage his father. "Dad, just get your two front hooves up in front of you. Then your hind legs. Come on, you can do it."

Tough Guy lifted his head and snorted hard. He tried to roll over to his left, but his left front leg was broken. The pain was too great. He lay back down.

Jubal snorted and moved over to his father's left side. He nudged him. "Try again. I will push you up."

Tough Guy made another effort, but failed. Jubal stepped back to the front of Tough Guy and got down on his knees. I neighed, "You can't die now."

Tough Guy took another deep breath. "Jubal, you need to be gett'n on. The sunlight has exposed you. Those German aeroplanes will be making their runs again. Now. Do as I say."

Jubal reluctantly stood up. He swished his tail back and forth, snorting and grunting. He stepped back two lengths. Keeping his neck arched and chest outward, he raised his front legs to paw the air. Jubal reared up seven times before stopping. He watched Tough Guy's breaths get shallower.

Obedient to his father's wishes, Jubal turned and ran as fast as he could to the west. Tough Guy lifted his head one more time to watch his son run beyond the horizon. Once Jubal was out of sight, Tough Guy let his head fall back to the ground. Born April 13, 1892, Tough Guy took his last breath on October 1, 1918. Would his legacy continue?

*****

General Blackjack Pershing continued integrating American soldiers with French and British forces. Major Hazzard was already there. He had survived one more battle to remain in the country as an advisor. He was well aware of the fact that his time with the Royal Canadian Horse Brigade would soon come to an end. American military advisors in country were no longer advisors. They were now warriors. The warriors General Pershing reassigned to various positions across the Western Front, except for the ones awarded Wounded Chevrons. Major Hazzard wore two. It was time for him to go home. If only the war would slow down long enough for him to do so.

*****

Jubal Early never saw Major Hazzard again during the war. Distraught over the loss of his father, he roamed the French countryside foraging for food and seeking shelter. Within weeks, he would not be alone. Hundreds of horses and mules escaped the confines of their keepers. Jubal's herd had one thing in common—they were hardened by shellshock and alive. Many horses and mules that stayed simply lost their minds and were put down.

*****

Jubal chose to live. He struggled to avoid capture by farmers, or by deserters looking for a ride. It was only a matter of time. Eventually, a British cavalryman roped, tied, and hauled Jubal to a transport ship returning to Dover, England. The sergeant who captured him said, "You will make a fine sire at a remount depot."

Jubal and the sergeant made it off the ship but did not report to the remount depot together. Jubal had other ideas. Taking advantage of the low six-foot holding paddocks at the port's staging area, he decided to clear the fence and make his way to the Northern England countryside. He was determined to be free of war. He had had enough of it.

Other warhorses had the same idea. Eventually, the British army veterinarians requested permanent indoor stables built near Devonport to house the stallions and brood mares. The doctors concluded the outside paddocks were not working well enough for the horses that survived war and the horrors they endured. Jubal kept his mind and made sure he kept his freedom. The only problem he had left to solve was how to get back home to Virginia.

*****

Major Oliver Hazzard

Major Hazzard would have remained in his would-be grave if not for an alert military dog barking incessantly down at him. The dog's handler, Corporal Warburton, looked over the edge and said, "Mate, are you dead or alive?"

Major Hazzard started moving his aching body about. He wiped away clogs of mud covering his legs and chest. A broken trench timber was lying on top of his arm. He pushed it away.

The corporal yelled down at him, "Sir, stay still until we can get a litter-bearer down to you." The major raised his right arm and gave a thumbs-up.

Once the litter-bearers arrived, Major Hazzard had already pushed himself up to a sitting position. He counted the wounds on his arms and legs.

The litter-bearer looking down yelled out. "Aye, Major, don't try to remove the shrapnel. We need to get a gurney down to you. We will take care of it."

Realizing he was in a pickle, Major Hazzard wisely waited for extraction from his would-be grave.

Corporal Warburton helped the litter-bearers ease one ladder down into the trench. The ladder sank three inches into the mud. The corporal climbed down the ladder. He kept his eyes on Major Hazzard while moving toward him. Two dead soldiers lying behind Major Hazzard came into view. Warburton looked up at the litter-bearers. "Mates, we need to get the dead out first, to make room for getting the living." The litter-bearers shook their heads in silence.

Corporal Warburton alerted the regiment's field hospital to expect another patient within the half hour. Like Jubal, the ambulance had a tough time of it getting around that pitted fields that when struck, roughly shook the major's gurney. The two litter-bearers did their best to keep him still during the ride back. The younger soldier leaning against the ambulance rear door watched the major's every move. The litter-bearers were afraid small pieces of shrapnel would work their way into the major's chest, or perhaps across an artery. It had happened a hundred times before. The results were predictable—almost-certain death, since blood was in short supply in the field. The ambulance got the major to the surgical tent just in time.

Leather to Steel

The doctor and nurses removed shrapnel, cleaned out gashes, and sewed up Major Hazard's chest, arms, and shoulder to stem further blood loss. He was moved to a recovery tent for twenty-four hours of observation. At the end of the next day, the doctors made the decision to evacuate Major Hazzard back to the rear.

Now awake and alert, the major was informed of his pending transfer. Major Hazzard expressed his dissatisfaction to the doctor and nurses who were shocked to learn of the major's preference. No one wanted to go back to the front. The doctor commented, "Crazy American."

Major Hazzard told his attending nurse, "I can't leave. I have to find my horses."

The nurse placed her hand on his arm and said, "Darling, we pulled out five pieces of shrapnel from your body. You were lucky they were inches away from your arteries. You need a couple of weeks to heal. Those stitches—"

The major interrupted. "Nurse, I understand. But you don't understand. My horses need me. I have to find Jubal and Tough Guy."

The nurse continued examining the major's bandages. She placed her hand over his forehead to check for a temperature. "The good news is you only have a slight fever. But if you think you can just get up and back into the saddle, no way, mister."

Major Hazzard looked around the hospital tent. The front flap was tied back. He could see outside. Nurses, doctors, and wounded soldiers passed by. Then he caught a glimpse of a black horse led outside the tent opening. His heart raced for a moment. His face turned pale.

The nurse looked at him. "See a ghost? You look pasty."

"I am fine. I thought I saw one of my horses."

"Major, I love horses myself. Better than most humans I know. If you give me a description, I would be glad to take a peek out by the rebuilt field stable."

"Nurse, what do you mean, rebuilt field stable?"

"We were lucky. Myself, one other VAD, and the doctor were treating a severely wounded soldier in the ambulance late last night.

When we returned, the field hospital near the stables was destroyed. The Tommies obviously don't give a hoot about killing the dead again."

"Nurse, please help me. I need to know what happened to one black horse I had secured in those stables."

"The doctor would not like me moving you. Can't do as you ask. However, I tell you what I will do. During my lunch break, I will get a driver to take me over to the old field stable site. I will see what I can find out for you."

"You would do that for me?"

"No, I'll do that for the horse."

Major Hazzard clasped the nurse's hand. "Nurse, thank you."

"Don't thank me yet. If we get another rush of wounded in, I will not have the time." The nurse left him alone to rest. Other nurses scurried between patients taking temperatures and dressing bandages. One soldier lay in his cot with one leg cut off at the knee. Pinkish-white gauze covered the nub. Other patients lay in their cots moaning and crying. Major Hazzard kept his head flat on the pillow. He looked up and mumbled, "God, I am ready to go home."

The nurse looked at her watch, noting it was almost noon. She walked to the head nurse and asked to take lunch. The request was approved, since the fighting had subsided and moved northward toward Belgium.

Needing a male driver, she asked Orderly Smitty to accompany her. He also needed a break and agreed to be her chauffer and security. Once inside the truck, Smitty asked her, "Where do you want to go?"

"Back two miles are field stables that took direct hits this morning. One of my patients is desperately concerned about his horses."

"You know as well as I do, those horses are either dead, or they ran off."

"I agree. But at least we can remove all doubt about the dead part. He said his big black stallion was seventeen hands and had a unique brand on its hindquarter."

"Nurse, what did the brand look like?"

"Well, the morphine kicked in before he had not a chance to describe it. Since he is an American soldier, I suspect it will say USA."

Smitty said, "Okay, well, this darn road is pitted too badly. I am going to get us on that hill ridge to get a better view."

It was not hard to find the spot. Intensive bombardment left craters surrounding the regiment's previous day's fighting positions. They parked just above the stable timbers splintered across the ground. The protective tarp was shredded by shrapnel. The nurse looked at Smitty. "Stop the ambulance. This is the place."

As she exited the passenger door, she caught a glimpse of a farmhouse lying in ruins. The most extraordinary sight she saw was the backyard fence still standing. She looked beyond the fence and squinted at a dark shape lying in the center of the yard. She motioned to Smitty and yelled out, "Hey Smitty! Come here. I see something."

Smitty and the nurse walked together over broken timbers and glass to enter what used to be a backyard. Smitty took off his hat and said, "Mother of God, this is not a backyard. This is a small cemetery." The nurse let out a heavy sigh and then spoke softly, "And its latest guest showed up this morning." She pointed to the dead black horse lying in a flowerbed.

As they walked toward the horse carcass, the nurse's eyes began to tear up. Then without warning, a cold shiver rolled up her spine. She heard horses neighing across the field near the tree line. She looked at Smitty. She pointed at the ridgeline. "Did you hear that?"

Smitty replied, "No. Just the wind blowing."

"I swear I heard horses neighing up near that tree line."

Something moved across the field, and she grasped Smitty's arm while looking at a sight she later would not admit seeing. The white mist coming out of the forest looked like midday fog moving low across a field. This fog, however, was different. It did not hover over the hill. Instead, the gray mist took the shape of seven white horses galloping from the tree line toward the dead horse.

What looked like the lead stallion stopped and turned toward the nurse and Smitty. The majestic-looking white horse reared up on his haunches and aggressively pawed the air with his large hooves. The six horses behind him did the same in unison. The white horses turned and galloped back into the forest.

The nurse turned to Smitty and asked, "Tell me you saw that!"

"What are you talking about? All I see here is this dead horse with a unique brand on his butt. Not sure what it is?"

The nurse released Smitty's arm and walked over to the carcass. She studied the brand partially covered with dried mud. She knelt down to brush the mud off with her hands.

Once the brand became visible, she gasped and stopped moving her hand. Her breathing raced. She looked up at Smitty and began crying. Tears flowed down her cheeks. She nervously said, "I don't believe this."

Smitty asked, "What do you not believe, Nurse Drayton?"

Time stood still between Allison and Tough Guy. Sixty years of Magnolia history overwhelmed her heart.

*****

Major Hazzard eventually recovered from his battle injuries. Once well enough, he returned to General Pershing's headquarters element in Paris. He commanded much popularity among the general's command staff—in particular, the intelligence officers who debriefed him over a week's time. They wanted to know what he saw on the front. His recent brush with death did not water down the conclusion the Americans hoped to hear. He reported, "The Germans were weakened. It would only be a matter of time."

When asked how the Canadians and the British were holding up, he stated for record, "The British and Canadian expeditionary forces have endured a horrific war that showed no mercy to civilians and soldiers alike. The soldiers were not deterred from defeating the Central Powers, loosely hanging on to their gains made early on in the war back in 1914. Breakage was imminent."

The U.S. Second Cavalry regiment intelligence officers pressed him for more information about the German aeroplanes. Major Hazzard said, "The German air assaults were the deadliest. Disguising ground units with camouflage tarps did little to stop aerial bombing. The only defense was a good offense. The BEF needed to put more allied fighter aeroplanes into the air to neutralize the air threats, which were not just fixed wing aeroplanes. The German dirigibles were just as effective in dropping bombs on the civilian populations."

When asked about the effectiveness of cavalries, he bemoaned the fact his beloved warhorses were limited in their ability to achieve frontal attacks. The best use of cavalries was to get behind the enemy to gather intelligence. Major Hazzard stated, "I fear the machinegun has made the honor and tradition of riding into battle a forgone thought. Keeping the horses safe was a secondary problem. Supply trains kept up well enough to provide adequate substance for the horses; however, the thickness of their hides could not deflect splinter shards of iron and steel. Most horses and mules were killed. Many escaped with whatever faculties they could muster to stand on four legs. A sad state of affairs."

The Armistice

Nonetheless, the presence of almost 2 million American troops on the Western Front by the autumn of 1918 gave the Allies a vital edge over Germany, whose own ranks were dwindling fast. Equally important was Allied material superiority in a wide range of areas, from artillery, ammunition and machine guns to food supplies and even horses.

— General Cyril M. Wagstaff,
British Expeditionary Forces
Headquarters Report, 1918[74]

Relentless American and British force counteroffensives turned the tide against the Central Powers. Germany, Austria, Bulgaria, and Turkey were hurting; their countrymen were starving. The British and American blockades kept food and resupply from reaching citizens that no longer shared the frenzy of wanting war. The German citizens had had enough. They cried for justice.

The German people's democratic parties put pressure on Kaiser to abdicate his throne. The Russians shared the same enthusiasm for their own royalty to step down from the crown. The Kaiser's cousin, Russia's Nicholas II, got the same message. Monarchies were falling.

Disadvantaged citizens, political dissenters, and disgruntled academics no longer wanted to serve the elite minority. The combined movements set conditions ripe for a revolution in Germany and Russia. Germany's two newest citizens. Max and Olga Eilenberg stood front and center witnessing the birth of a new era. A new Germany, a Third Reich.

*****

Majors Hazzard and Boak sensed a change in the battlefield rhythm during the early summer of 1918 . The Americans landed in France,

Leather to Steel

and the battle-worn Germans took note. Unlike their Allied partners, the American Doughboy's enthusiasm suffered not from years of trench warfare and debilitating weaponry never seen by the world. The Americans were fresh, prepared, and ready to take the fight to the enemy. Thanks to General Black Jack Pershing, no soldier or horse marched on the battlefield until they were properly trained. His wisdom paid off.

*****

In the final one hundred days of the Great War, the Canadian Corps marched successfully to retake Mons, Belgium from the Germans. However, not without significant loss of life. The Canadian Corps suffered 46,000 casualties. Major Boak was fortunate not to be one of them.

He and his regiment continued moving with British and Belgium troops pushing Germans back across the Hindenburg Line on September 28. The battle lasted only two days. The Belgians retook Dixmude, and the Canadians and the British secured Messines. The losses degraded the moral of German generals, soldiers, and her allies. Bulgaria felt the pain and sued for peace.

On September 29, 1918, Bulgaria signed an armistice with the Allies. Bulgaria became the first Central Powers country to quit the war. Others soon followed suit. On October 24, 1918, the Allies crossed the Piave River to push the Austrians out of Italy. Italian armies—incorporating British, French and American divisions—attacked the remaining Austro-Hungarian armies from Trentino westward to the Gulf of Venice. In its final battle of the war, the Austro-Hungarian Army lost 30,000 soldiers. Over 400,000 were taken prisoner. Austria surrendered.

Turkey recognized the Central Powers were weakened, with no hopes of winning. On October 30, 1918, Turkey signed an armistice with the Allies, becoming the second Central Powers country to quit the war. On November 3, 1918, the only remaining ally of Germany, Austro-Hungary, signed an armistice with Italy, leaving Germany alone in the war.

*****

Since August 1914—for four long years—mankind witnessed unimaginable suffering and loss of life. The people of Germany had reached their wits' end and relented. Hunger replaced their anger. Survival dictated the end of hostilities. As such, the world celebrated the end of the Great War in November 1918. The *Evening Public Ledger* reported on November 11, 1918, the terms of Armistice:

> President Proclaims Signing of Armistice to People. Washington, Nov. 11.
> President Wilson today issued the following proclamation: "My fellow countrymen---The armistice was signed this morning. Everything for which America fought has been accomplished. It will now be our fortunate duty to assist by example, by sober, friendly counsel and by material aid in the establishment of a just democracy throughout the world.
> —WOODROW WILSON

President Woodrow Wilson, Prime Minister Lloyd George of Britain, Prime Minister Vittorio Emanuele Orlando of Italy, and Prime Minister Georges Clemenceau of France delivered the final political blow to Germany on November 11, 1918, at exactly eleven o'clock in the morning.

The terms and conditions of surrender proclaimed no mercy for the German people. Forgiveness never crossed the minds of the four political leaders who prescribed Germany's future. Though history would tell us how mercy may have been the better option at the time.

*****

The armistice provided a thirty-six-day period whereas the Germans would cease hostilities. Demands stipulated the immediate surrender of German weapons, ships, and territories, which equated to Germany's war guilt. A guilt that was amended and prolonged through several conventions convened in Paris in December 1918, January 1919, and April 1919.

According to the translated document—*Terms of Armistice with Germany*, November 11, 1918, Conditions of the Armistice Concluded with Germany—the following clauses related to the Western Front verbatim:

> I. Cessation of hostilities by land and in the air six hours after the signing of the armistice.
>
> II. Immediate evacuation of the invaded countries --- Belgium, France, Luxemburg, as well as Alsace-Lorraine--- so ordered as to be completed within 15 days from the signature of the armistice. German troops which have not left the above-mentioned territories with the period fixed shall be made prisoners of war. Occupation by the allied and United States forces jointly shall keep pace with the evacuation in these areas. All movements of evacuation and occupation shall be regulated in accordance with a note (Annex 1) determined at the time of the signing of the armistice.
>
> III. Repatriation, beginning at once, to be completed within 15 days, of all inhabitants of the countries above enumerated (including hostages, persons under trial, or condemned).
>
> IV. Surrender in good condition by the German armies of the following equipment: 5,000 guns (2,500 heavy, 2,500 field), 25,000 machine guns, 3,000 trench mortars, 1,700 aeroplanes (fighters, bombers---firstly all D,7's and night-bombing machines).

Armistice Sections V through XXXIV detailed further reductions in country wealth and military capabilities. By the time the Treaty of Versailles was signed in April 4, 1919, the reparations levied on Germany would sink its economy.

Armistice signatories representing Imperial Germany included German admiral Ernst Vanselow, German count Alfred von

Oberndorff of the foreign ministry, German general Detlof von Winterfeldt, and Matthias Erzberger, head of the German delegation. The elder statesmen insisted on submitting the following amendment to the Armistice appendix 1. Their concerns summed up Germany's future:

> The German Government will naturally endeavor with all its power to take care that the duties imposed upon it shall be carried out.
>
> The undersigned plenipotentiaries recognize that in certain points regard has been paid to their suggestions. They can regard the comments made on November 9, on the conditions of the armistice with Germany and the answer handed to them on November 10, as an essential condition of the whole agreement.
>
> They must, however, allow no doubt exist on the point that in particular the short time allowed for evacuation, as well as the surrender of indispensable means of transport, threaten to bring about a state of things which, without its being the fault of the German Government and the German people, may render impossible the further fulfillment of the conditions.
>
> The undersigned plenipotentiaries further regard is as their duty with reference to their repeated oral and written declaration once more to point out with all possible emphasis that the carrying out of this agreement must throw the German people into anarchy and famine. According to the declarations which preceded the armistice, conditioned were to be expected which, ended the sufferings of women and children who took no part in the war.
>
> The German people, which has held its own for 50 months against a world of enemies, will, in spite of any force that may be brought to bear upon it, preserve its freedom and unity.
>
> A people of 70,000,000 suffers but does not die.[75]

Britain established a Zone of Occupation on German soil. Until the Armistice terms and conditions were satisfied, 20 percent of British and American forces would occupy Germany and its Central Power partner countries through 1919. The remaining Allied Forces were sent back to their respective homelands for joyful reunions with family and friends.

The Allied Powers sent their soldiers, sailors, and marines home. They were welcomed by enthusiastic revelers and ticket parades. Indeed, the Christmas holidays bode well for the world, and for soldiers like Major Boak and Major Hazzard.

*****

Major Henry Boak

Major Boak and surviving members of the Royal Canadian Horse Artillery Brigade sailed back into Halifax, Nova Scotia. Their transport ship docked on December 20, 1918. Lining the ship's main deck railing—with one thousand other servicemen—Major Boak looked down at hundreds of people waiting on the pier. Most were dressed in their Sunday best, screaming and yelling "Welcome home" salutations. Colorful balloons and "Welcome home" signs dotted the crowd.

Cranes positioned gangplanks from the ship's fore and aft main decks to the pier. Once secured, soldiers, sailors, and marines wasted no time debarking to find their loved ones. Major Boak took his time walking down the fore brow. No one would be waiting for him; he looked not for his parents on the pier. Their last letter said they had moved west to Vancouver. Henry Senior detailed in the letter their need for putting three thousand miles between them and the Spanish flu. A pandemic sickness that made its way up into eastern Canada—a flu that by year's end killed at least 25 million people around the world.[76]

Major Boak stopped at the bottom of the brow, stepped aside, and turned around to look up and admire the ship's massive gray hull jutting toward to the sky. He noticed the ship's forward anchor had been lowered halfway down toward the waterline. A seaman began his climb down the anchor chain with a paint can attached to his harness. The major mumbled. "No rest for the weary."

After rubbing his eyes, Major Boak took a few minutes to breathe in the salty air of Canada. Sighing, he adjusted his duffel bag strap on his shoulder to begin his trek. He looked back up at the ship one last time and said, "Thank you for getting me home. Now what?" He turned around and took his first step on his beloved Canadian soil.

Tired and worn down, Major Boak was in no rush to leave the pier. He moved slowly with each step taken. He had aches and pains that would not go away. As he walked, he took deep breaths and smelled the sweet scents of fish and salt. Smells he knew as a child growing up in Halifax.

As he walked, the seagulls darted between the ships nested along the pier. He watched the birds fight over garbage sailors had dumped in steel bins on the pier. The bird's loud screeches brought back memories. Good memories. He cracked a rare smile.

The day was cloudy, misty, and cool—typical December weather for Nova Scotia. A cold breeze kicked up off the bay and brought a chill upon the major. He stepped toward the edge of the pier to make adjustments for warmth. He had to dodge several people hurrying back and forth between the ship and quay wall. Some bumped into him. For some reason, crowds made him feel uncomfortable. Cold and uncomfortable, he picked up his pace.

Standing by a pier's edge, Major Boak set his heavy green duffle bag down. He unlatched the top clip and opened it up. Inside, near the top, he hid a small whiskey flask purchased back in Dover. He unscrewed the bottle cap and took a long sip. After tightening the cap, he tossed the flask into the duffel and closed it up. Now all he needed was a smoke.

His cigarettes were always handy. He reached inside his front coat pocket and pulled out the pack. There were only three left. Using his two fingers, he slid out what would end up being five minutes of comfort. But it was enough to clear his head.

Finished with his break, he pulled the wool jacket collar up over the back of his neck. Now more relaxed, he swung his ditty bag over his left shoulder and said, "Good to go." He looked down the quay wall and saw thousands of people mingling and cheering. He looked at the road in front of him. Personal automobiles and taxis drove about, several honking horns at one another. He shook his head and mumbled, "Keep going. Better to choose a path than no path at all. Where is the train station? Why can't I remember simple things, for God's sake?"

A sailor wearing his dress bellbottoms and sporting a short red beard walked in front of the major. Major Boak asked, "Sailor, excuse me. Are you headed to the North Street train station?"

The sailor stopped and turned around. Seeing the major was an officer, he stood at attention to render a salute. The major waved off the salute, and the sailor replied, "Yes, sir. Going back home to Vancouver."

"Sailor, that is where I am going. Do you mind if I tag along?"

The sailor was startled to hear an officer ask him such a question. The sailor stood at ease in front of Major Boak. Putting down his white ditty bag, he extended his hand to the major.

"My name is Leo McDowell. My friends call me Mac."

"Well, Mac, my name is Henry Boak. My friends call me Hank, Mac. What do you say we get on home?"

Major Boak and First Class McDowell made their way to the North Street train station. They were not alone. Thousands of fellow soldiers and sailors back from the war waited for their rides. Buses circled the station looking to pick up short-run passengers. Cabdrivers followed suit, looking for their next fare. Personal automobiles crowded the roads lined with uniformed men looking to go anywhere.

*****

The major, navy Petty Officer McDowell, and over 400,000 of their countrymen served overseas. Most made it home, though not at all, whole. Many war veterans came back with all their faculties, but the body was not all there. Very few veterans had both. As with all wars, each man and woman left something on the battlefield, never to be regained. Canadian deaths on battlefields exceed 65,000 during WWI.[77]

Major Boak regretted losing his horse, Daisy. He never knew where she ran off to. The shelling at the last Battle of Ypres badly spooked her. He jokingly told Major Hazzard that she probably went off somewhere with Tough Guy. Major Boak reasoned with what the field veterinarians said about horses and mules getting shell-shocked, just like humans. And like fallen soldiers missing in action, he knew thousands of horses and mules were left behind. He carried the pain of not knowing. Throughout the rest of his life, Major Boak could only hope the horses would be saved. The war had indeed taken its toll on all living things.

The Last Ship Home

> This is not peace. It is an armistice for 20 years.
> — Ferdinand Jean Marie Foch,
> British Field Marshal
> After the Treaty of Versailles, 1919

Captain Abraham Bates

The United States Navy transported over 260,000 U.S. soldiers back to the States in July, 1919.[78] The transport ship USS *Susquehanna* (ID-3016) was one of them. Her 520-foot hull displaced over 17,000 tons. Over the past week, her bow crushed through heavy Atlantic swells to get the boys home. Today, on July 4, her hull barely made a ripple in the bay. The water was now at peace. She was bringing America's heroes home.

The *Susquehanna* slowed to five knots at sight of the first harbor channel marker. As the ship steamed passed the starboard-side buoy, the religious maker's bell rang with each rolling wake disturbing the water's surface. There was no wind. The sea state was zero. In fact, the weather was perfect for the *Susquehanna*'s final curtain and port of call.

Soldiers standing on her decks smoked cigarettes and talked war stories. Not being sailors, they wandered about topside looking to get a better view of the ship's approach to Sewell's Point. They heard the sound of many welcome bands playing across the bay. The greeting parties were not landlocked. Hundreds of personal watercraft ran up and down the ship's side as the *Susquehanna* maintained speed and course navigating the harbor channel. Sailboats and motorboats of all kinds were filled with well-wishers welcoming the soldiers and the sailor home. The soldiers leaned over the side and waved back at their fellow countrymen. One soldier turned to a sailor and asked, "Why do I feel so anxious?"

The sailor replied, "You have channel fever. We all get it when time and distance has been long and far from our loved ones."

The soldier replied, "I see. Well, then, tell the skipper to speed this bugger up. I want to get home."

The ship's mooring lines were secured to Pier 1. Dozens of sailors and longshoremen hurried cranes to position gangplanks and ship-hold ramps to offload people and cargo. Within the hour, the naval port's sea wall became a scene of great activity as the docks, cranes, and railroads absorbed more than their usual capacity. From the ship's holds were discharged boxes of provisions, ammunition, artillery pieces, baled hay, horses, trucks, gasoline, and other army property returning from the war front. Battle-worn soldiers anxiously waited to get off the ship.

Thousands of well-wishers, family members, and friends anxiously waited on the pier for their loved-ones to walk down the three forward, amidships, and aft brows. Holding red, white, and blue balloons, the crowd sang "God Bless America." Everyone was dressed in their Sunday best. They all had good reason to celebrate. Their soldiers were at last home.

When President Wilson signed the Armistice Treaty in November 1918, the expectation was for all American troops to be sent home by Christmas. Most did return. However, there were occupying force and humanitarian reasons thousands of troops could not leave. Tens of thousands who survived the war were displaced and starving.

Captain Bates was scheduled to return on the same ship with the rest of his regiment destined for New York City. However, that would not be the case. As the regiment's veterinarian officer, he was tasked to tend to the needs of several cavalry horses and ammunition team mules favored by the men who rode them into battle. Sentimental reasons, and perhaps Providence, saved the poor horses from homelessness and starvation. Thousands like them were not so lucky.

After the war, starving horses roamed freely about the French, Belgian, and German countryside, looking for food and shelter. The ones that made it back to Britain were in no better shape. Shell-

Leather to Steel

shocked, hundreds escaped temporary retaining areas loosely protected by low fences. The holding areas lacked adequate water and food. The hyper-sensed horses defeated an ultimate slow death. They followed their instincts to survive. Captain Bates and others like him knew the horses and mules without their handlers would have a tough go of it. The horses he left behind were his only regret.

The U.S. Second Cavalry and several U.S. infantry divisions remained scattered about in France and Belgium to complete their humanitarian mission. Satisfied with their performance, General Jack Pershing gave the order to bring back most U.S. troops. Standing with his friend Captain John Jenkins on the *Susquehanna*'s fantail, Abraham was almost home. He kept an eye out for this family in the sea of people coming into view on the pier. He said to his friend John,

"Won't be long now. Once she is tied up to the pier, you and I are off this boat."

John added, "And not a moment too soon. I can't wait. Just want to stand on American soil—on one leg, of course."

Captain Bates smirked at this friend. "You amaze me, John. Even though the Tommies took one of your legs, you still laugh about it."

"What other choice do I have? I am not getting my leg back."

"Good point. I think—wait a minute. There is a clicking sound coming out of the speaker system. Here comes another announcement. Listen."

"Now hear this. Now hear this. Once the ship is tied to the pier, the crane operators will put three gangplanks into position from main deck locations forward, amidships, and aft. That means that for army boys, the pointy front of the ship, the center of the ship, and tail end of the ship, respectively. Once the gangplanks are in place, a quarterdeck will be established at each. We will put up the ship's colors on the aft end of the ship. Before you leave the quarterdeck, you do not need to ask permission to leave the ship. I give you permission right now. However, you will render a salute to the colors being hoisted up as I speak."

Captain Bates looked at Captain Jenkins. "Glad I did not join the navy. Too many traditions."

"Like the army does not have its own."

Captain Bates took a deep breath of the salty air and exhaled. "I suppose you are right. The officers are always the last to leave their place of duty." The microphone clicked again on the ship's loudspeaker. "Now hear this, officers of the United States Army. You are to muster in the captain's wardroom within ten minutes!"

Captain Bates stepped over to his friend leaning on the ship's rail. "Hey John. Don't fall in."

Captain Jenkins turned around to face Abraham and said, "I would have fallen in three thousand miles back at Dover."

"Right. Come on. We need to hustle over to the wardroom for officer's call."

"Just when I was getting comfortable." Captain Bates put his right arm around his buddy to help him across the deck.

*****

The Bateses

Mary Bates and her four children: Isaiah, eighteen; Corinth, seventeen; and the twins, Luke and Daniel both sixteen, stood holding each other's hands. They waited patiently to get a glimpse of Abraham coming down one of the ship's gangplanks. Mary scanned among all three groups of soldiers filing down, one by one onto the pier. She was noticeably frustrated, not wanting to miss her oldest son.

Mary asked Isaiah, "Darl'n, please keep your eyes focused on the front end of the ship. If you see your brother coming down, let me know." She turned to Corinth. "Daughter, you keep your eyes locked on the back end of the ship, while the boys and I look for Abraham in the middle. Both Isaiah and Corinth nodded in agreement.

A good thousand soldiers had come down the ship's planks within an hour. More kept coming. The wounded were the last to debark. Mary grew concerned. It had been some time. Captain

Leather to Steel

Abraham Bates said he would be on this ship. It said so in the cable she received.

The cheers and sounds of laughter and crying filled the air on the pier. It was loud. The ship's crew started to disembark. The sailor uniforms started coming down the planks. Each sailor carrying a white sea bag over their shoulders. Corinth asked her mother, "Where is Abe? I have not seen one tall colored officer walk down from the ship."

"Nor have I," Isaiah added. Within minutes of commenting and getting restless, another group of soldiers began departing amidships. It was the colored soldiers.

Mary grasped Isaiah's and Corinth's hands. "This is it. He must be coming down soon." The remaining families on the pier began screaming the names of their sons, fathers, uncles, and brothers. One mother fainted. Isaiah stepped over to help her. The woman's daughter attempted to help, but she was not strong enough to lift her mother up. Isaiah put his hand under her head. "Mamma, open your eyes. Hello. Are you going to be okay?"

The robust woman opened her eyes. She squeezed Isaiah's hand. "Honey, I will be just fine. Now please help me up. I have a son coming home." Isaiah put his hand under her right arm while the daughter assisted with the left. The out-of-breath mother stood up and bellowed out, "Mr. Jenkins, get your butt over here to your momma."

The daughter shook her head. She looked at Isaiah and said, "Thank you, son."

Mary kept scanning the ship for Captain Abraham Bates. At least one hundred soldiers had departed the ship. Still no Abraham. She reached out to one of the lone soldiers and asked, "Excuse me, are you with the Buffalo soldiers?"

The middle-aged black soldier took off his hat. "No, ma'am, I am with the 369th Infantry Division, or you may have heard of us. They call us the Harlem Hellfighters, no disrespect intended. I wish I could help you. I myself did not come back with the fellas I served with. Most of the 369th sailed back home into New York harbor in February."[79]

"I am sorry," Mary replied. "I thought all black soldiers served as Buffalo soldiers."

"No, ma'am. None of the Buffalo Soldiers were allowed to serve. My brothers remained here in the States."[80]

"Soldier, did you come across a Captain Abraham Bates?" The harried soldier shook his head. "Ma'am, I am sorry. I do not know him. All the officers stayed together during the cruise. I am sure he will be down soon. The officers wanted us enlisted to debark the ship first."

Mary breathed a sigh of relief. The soldier excused himself and continued walking.

Mary, Isaiah, Corinth, and the twins held hands. Mary said, "He will be here soon. Keep your eyes open, kids." Within a few minutes, colored officers started walking down the gangplanks. Mary saw the tall, good-looking captain helping another officer down the plank. She yelled up, "Abraham. Abraham!" The kids started waving wildly at their brother.

Captain Bates stopped midway over the plank. He waved back with his free arm.

Mary and the kids rushed over to get closer to the end of the gangplank. Other families still tarried about on the pier giving hugs and kisses to their soldiers. She kept hold of Isaiah's hand as they pushed through the crowd, excusing themselves. Abraham took his last step down onto the pier. His best friend John limped with him over to the side. Both men stood together, smiling. As if it was synchronized, they said in unison, "Thank God we are home! Praise sweet Jesus."

Captain John Jenkins sat down on the bollard. He looked up at Abraham and said, "Abraham, go give your family some lov'n. I am fine here. Navy medical said someone would be here to pick me up. We will catch up later. God be with you, friend." Abraham shook John's hand and then saluted him. He turned and ran into his mother's open arms. Mother and son held their embrace for several minutes without saying a word.

Mary pulled back and caressed Abraham's face with her hands. "My sweet boy, where have you been?"

Leather to Steel

Captain Abraham Bates could not speak. He just let the tears fall down his cheeks. His brothers and sister looked on. Words could not describe the pure joy that was shared that moment on the pier.

Captain Abraham Bates had changed. Though he did not show it then, the horrors of war would haunt his memories and dreams for the rest of his life. The first day of his new life began the day he set foot on the naval station pier. He told his mother years later that the feeling of American soil beneath his feet was indescribable. Like Captain Bates, the tens of thousands of soldiers who returned home were forever changed by what they had seen—and worse, what they had to do—in the name of freedom.

The Bates walked together as a family reunited to the motorcar. Mary and Abraham led the way. Isaiah and Corinth stayed a few steps behind with the twin boys. Abraham turned to his mother. "Mamma. I got your last cable before I left England. You said you had a surprise for me. What is it, may I ask?"

"I can't tell you now, son. You will see." Abraham shook his head. "Now, Mamma. You always said no surprises."

"Yes, I did. But that was when you were little ones. I had to keep you five kids on a righteous path. Now, you have been keeping me in the dark. What is that surprise you have for me?"

Abraham chuckled. "I can't tell you now, Mamma. You will see." Mary shook her head back and forth. "Now, now. You always said no surprises."

Mary and the kids drove back with Abraham to their new home in Arlington County, Virginia. Sitting in back of his brother who was driving, Abraham leaned over and put his right hand on his mother's shoulder. She laid her hand on top of his. "Do you need anything, Abraham?"

"No, I am fine. Just a little hungry."

"Well, I will fix you up whatever you want when we get back to the farm—I mean, house. Oops."

"What farm? Is that the surprise you have been keeping secret?"

"Might as well tell you now. You will love it, son. The property has a four-bedroom house and a ten-stall horse stable sitting on twenty fenced-in acres."

"Is that right? How did you—"

"Your papa took care of us. No need for me to explain about the money. Just know we have a paid-for farm that needs another hand. You interested?"

"Mamma, who owned it before you?"

"An old German man lived in it for a short time. He had purchased it from a fella who lost his wife during the war. Well, sadly, he was forced to leave America like many Germans who were suspected of treason. I don't know much more than what our neighbors told us. In any case, the Lord delivered. We are now farmers. We need another hand. You interested?"

Corinth interrupted, "You will like our new neighbors. I babysit their son, who is such a cute three-year-old."

Mary said, "Now let him speak, daughter."

"Sorry, Mamma."

"I will need to think it over, Mamma. I will need some time to get adjusted to things. The army wants me to come by Fort Myer to sign my discharge papers. After that, I can take a seat in the present to figure out my future."

"Son, you take as long as you need. We are here for you. Isn't that right, kids?"

Isaiah looked in the rearview mirror at Abraham. "Got you covered, big brother."

Corinth gave a slight elbow to Abraham. "So glad you are home, Abe. We missed you."

The twins spoke in unison. "Count us in for you, Abe."

Isaiah added, "Big brother, just sit back and relax. We have another hour to go."

"No, Mamma. I was just thinking how great it is to be home. I worried about you while I was gone. You know, with Dad gone—"

Mary interrupted him. "My goodness, son, you worry about us. We were not the ones getting shot at, gassed, or bombed. It is you who deserved our concerns and prayers. I know we did plenty of that."

Abraham leaned back into his seat. "I suppose so, Mother."

Leather to Steel

Abraham stared out his backseat window. His head rarely moved from watching the trees go by as they drove up Highway 11. Corinth asked, "What are you looking at, brother?"

As if he had been woken out of a trance, Abraham said, "The trees."

"What is so special about the trees?"

Abraham paused for a moment. "They are not burned nor split in half."

Corinth stopped talking, realizing she had not seen what her brother had experienced. Silence took over in the car. It was if a light switch had been turned off and the music stopped. The remaining part of the trip home offered no answers to the motorcars' passengers. If Abraham had spoken his peace, his questions would consider why so many died and so few understood.

*****

The chaplain counseled returning soldiers on board ship. Like the other soldiers, Abraham was told that he had changed, not his family. War did that to men whose lives depended upon others. His commander reminded him, "Captain Bates, you are a combat veteran whose contributions to the care and welfare of warhorses will not be forgotten by the men who depended upon those beasts of burden to do their job. Thank you for your service."

Abraham and hundreds like him did not turn away when asked to step up and go to the front. He did not waver when the choice was made to drive the ambulance to the front and care for wounded horses. In some cases, he patched up soldiers who went back to fighting. He did not waver in adversity. Captain Abraham Bates became not just the man his father wished him to be, but the man God planned him to become. The war was over, but the battle was just beginning for Abraham and many others who did not come home in one mind or body.

*****

World War I was the first time in American history that the United States sent soldiers abroad to defend foreign soil. On April 6, 1917, when the United States declared war against Germany, the United States had a standing army of 127,500 officers and soldiers. By the end of the war, 4 million men had served in the United States Army, with an additional 800,000 in other military service branches."[81] It is astonishing to think about how many Americans would have died if President Wilson committed our United States to war in 1914. Perhaps many of us would not have been born. A thought to consider.

*****

Save the Horses

If it is so serious, what have you been doing about it? The letter of the Commander-In-Chief discloses a complete failure on the part of the Ministry of Shipping to meet its obligations and scores of thousands of horses will be left in France under extremely disadvantageous conditions.
—Winston Churchill,
Britain's Minister for War and Air,
February 1919

Postwar reconstruction attempted to address the needs of civilians who lost their families, livelihoods, and property. Unfortunately, the horse and mule were overlooked. Understandably, it was the world's priority to reestablish a sense of healing and normalcy across Europe and throughout the world. World order could only define the way forward toward peace. However, the horse and the mule were overlooked during the process.

The British military purchased more than 1 million horses from Britain, the United States, and Canada during the Great War. Those horses served in every battle. Millions perished. For the horses that survived, many ended up wandering the countryside looking for food and shelter. The plight of the homeless warhorse did not go unnoticed. Their rescuer would be one man. A man who helped Britain navigate through the Great War. A man who would lead Great Britain to victory in a future time and place. His name was Winston Churchill.

Winston Churchill loved horses. He knew the cavalry horse and the working mule helped win the war. He would not let them suffer. In fact, he ordered military leaders to scour the battlefields for horses and mules displaced and held captive by starvation.

*****

Jubal

The war-torn European landscape provided little food for the living. Four years of death and destruction yielded little hope for both man and beast, such as I. There were tens of thousands of us horses scattered across the plains, valleys, and mountains separating France and Germany. We roamed the countryside looking for food and shelter.

I had no idea where I was traveling to. The countryside was unfamiliar to me. Tough Guy told me to follow my nose, when in doubt. Fortunately, I could smell and taste salt in the wind blowing from the west. I knew I was far away, but I kept moving with other homeless horses. We became a herd.

At night, I stood watch over the herd. I listened to faint whimpers and neighs from the bad dreams they were having. I remembered Major Hazzard. Surely, he or someone from the army would come and save us. But the army had left. The big guns no longer roared. The armies pulled out without us.

*****

During the winter of 1918 and 1919, the scarcity of human food did not bode well for displaced farm animals, horses, and mules. I recall the day a gang of desperate-looking humans encircled two of my mule friends before shooting them to death. It was not for sport. The humans prepared the horses for consumption. The humans were starving. From that day forward, I had to keep the herd away from the displaced civilians scouring the countryside for relief.

As the days went by, the ocean's scent grew stronger. While we moved west, recurring bouts of nervousness and shell-shock temporarily consumed me. The consequence of what Major Hazzard said is unwittingly experienced in the fog of war. I often wondered what happened to Major Hazzard.

The last time I saw him, he had slipped back into a trench. Smoke swirled in the air above him. If he called to me, I could not hear him. He was not alone. Hundreds of wounded soldiers lying on the ground around me screaming with pain, yelling for litter bearers. I was able to make it back to the hospital, but saddened to know

I watched dissipating smoke on the battlefield uncover thousands of dead enemy soldiers, horses, and mules that lay on the ground. Many wounded horses attempting to escape the muddy trenches. There was nothing I could do for them. All I could do was neigh aloud, "Keep calm."

*****

It was estimated over ten thousand horses had remained after the war. Either their owner was a dead soldier or a deceased farmer. In either case, the horses and mules were without care. Fortunately, their suffering would not last if not for humane efforts of the selfless.

During the spring of 1919, an international movement began to save the horses. High-powered personalities such as Winston Churchill and Teddy Roosevelt would not let the warhorse be abandoned. Concerned citizens like Allison and Colin George supported an international effort to save the horses.

*****

Allison Drayton-George

The Georges survived the war and honored a commitment they made to each other during an ocean voyage back in 1915. If they survived the war, a marriage proposal would be forthcoming to celebrate their lives together. The Great War ended on November 11, 1918. On November 12, Colin George proposed to Allison Drayton. She accepted.

The Georges moved from Dover to Canterbury onto a family farm Colin inherited from his mother. The five hundred acres of cleared pasture and stands of trees had not been worked for a generation. There were many repairs needed to get the property back into working shape. Allison and Colin eagerly stood up to the challenge.

Five hired contractors worked several months to get the George Farm Field's main house livable. The twenty-stall horse barn needed a new copper roof. Miles of wooden fencing needed to be repaired. The repairs were costly. Allison and Colin watched their savings quickly depleted. With each planned repair, there was an unexpected catch. Allison had a solution for financing.

One Saturday morning, Allison said, "Colin, I need to go to town and send a few cables to the States."

Colin replied, "Very well, dear. If you would, please bring back the Saturday paper. I am always curious as to what is going on in the world."

Allison replied, "I will. Darling, while I am gone, please check in on Anna for me? I think she has a cold." "Of course I will," Colin said.

Allison returned to the farm just before sunset. Walking to the front porch, she hummed a cheerful tune that caught Colin's ear, who stood at the front door. "My dear, so glad you made it back safely. Did you run into anyone we know?"

Allison stepped onto the porch and stopped within inches of Colin's face. She stood on her toes and attempted to kiss Colin's cheek. "Yes, I met with our banker."

Colin's eyes widened with surprise. "I don't understand."

Allison reached for Colin's hand. "I sold the Magnolia. I just confirmed the money had been wired into our account. We are going to build the horse farm we always wanted, with one condition."

"What is that Allison?" Colin expressed with great interest.

"The farm has to be renamed. The George Farm Field is too old. What do you think about A&C Equestrian Manor?"

Colin stepped over to the straight-backed chair and sat down. He motioned to Allison to come and sit with him. She attempted to sit in her chair, but Colin raised his hand and said, "No. Come and sit here on my lap. I want to look into your eyes." Allison blushed and replied, "Well, Mr. George, if you insist."

Colin nodded, "I do."

Leather to Steel

Colin looked at Allison and said, "You made a big sacrifice. I know how much you loved the Magnolia. Why?"

"Darling, I am never going back to America. I have no family there. I am the last of the Drayton bloodline on that side of the Atlantic. But what I do have is you, here in England. You are my family. Anna, Sarah, and Chrissie are our children. But—"

"Oh no. Now here comes the *but*."

"Yes, I want more. I want to rescue those horses who lost their riders in the war and have no homes."

Colin shook his head in agreement. "Then we need to celebrate. We need to celebrate the christening of the A&C Equestrian Manor."

Allison added, "As you say in England, cheer, cheer."

The manor contained three hundred fenced acres of pasture and two hundred acres of hardwood trees. The largest structure on the manor property was one large stone-foundation horse barn with twenty stables attached to an indoor riding arena that displaced ten thousand square feet of property. Enough grazing pasture to support one hundred horses.

The A&C Equestrian Manor was designed to be self-sufficient. The manor drew water from an underground spring that provided fresh water from a well pump to underground pipes running to the main house and irrigation for a two-acre vegetable garden Allison plowed and seeded. Colin loved fresh eggs. He refurbished the old chicken coop into a chicken house that housed twenty Rhode Island Red hens. They kept three Angus cows on hand to supplement their beef diet.

Sunday afternoons at the A&C were quiet and pleasantly restful for the George family. After church and a quick stop at the store, Allison and Collin would return to their farm and settle in for a day's worth of reading, light conversation, and working with their children Anna and two adopted warm-blood horses.

The last Sunday in May literally blossomed into a beautiful day. Allison said to Colin, "Dear, shall we sit out on the front porch and enjoy a spot of tea and crumb cakes?"

Colin answered, "Certainly, my dear. That is a lovely idea. I will retrieve the newspaper we picked up in the village."

Allison said, "Meet you on the front porch."

Colin hurried back into the house to pick up the *London Times* rolled up and tied with brown string. He glanced at the settee and mumbled, "Could get chilly outside when the breeze kicks up." He hastily grabbed a couple of throw blankets folded up on the settee before leaving the study. Before shutting the door, Colin looked back and noticed Allison was not far behind.

She said, "Colin, would you please hold the door open? My hands are preoccupied with this tea tray."

Colin stepped aside, keeping the screen door open. He watched her gracefully walk by. Her fair complexion looked absolutely radiant. As she walked by, she pushed back her red bangs of hair, looked at Colin, and winked.

On the porch, two high-backed wicker chairs straddled an old oak table. An antique piece of furniture Colin's grandfather carved out of an oak tree felled by lightning on the George property. Colin said, "You now my grandfather made that table."

Allison replied, "Yes, darling. You had mentioned that to me a few times."

Colin shook his head. "So sorry. I only meant to—"

Allison interrupted, "I know, Colin. It is okay. You are only trying to be thoughtful and ensuring I learn all I can about your family."

Colin's eyes locked on to Allison's. "Yes, indeed. I just want you to be happy. My mother experienced a certain enjoyment telling me the same about what her father made by hand. Shall we sit, sip, and eat?"

Allison set the tea tray on the table and then sat down. Colin followed suit. They poured their tea and snacked on the buttered crumb cakes while enjoying the fresh breeze blowing over the hills and into the valleys.

Allison looked across the pasture and gazed upon the beauty of a land that experienced much change over the centuries. The young wheat sprouts had turned the pastures green. The clear sky acted as a blue backdrop against the stands of hardwoods marking the property boundaries. Allison squinted to make out thousands of new tree

Leather to Steel

leaves flickering in the sunlight. She looked back at Colin. She held the warm teacup in both hands. Her serenity was undisturbed, until she saw the herd of horses running across the property.

Allison hurriedly placed her tea cup on the tray. She looked at Colin and said, "Quick! Colin, get up. You must see this."

Colin reluctantly put down his tea before getting up. "What is it, Allison?"

She pointed at the far horizon near their pasture's north forty. "Look! Those horses. There must be at least twenty of them. And look! Look at the horse leading them!"

*****

Allison and Colin devised a low-impact approach to capture the horses while minimizing the fear surely driving the animals. The plan was simple. Lay out bales of hay and water within a circular area. A series of ropes and nets would be buried just beneath the ground's surface surrounding the hay and water. Allison looked out for the horses every evening. Some nights they would show just before dark. Other days they would meander around the north forty grazing on wheat sprouts.

Allison said, "I understand why you want to use a net. But second thought, I think I can bring them in without it."

Colin smirked, "Those are basically wild horses that experienced God knows what during the war. You know, many Englishmen are adopting those warhorses running around the French countryside, shipping them back over the channel, only to wake up to find the horses escaped the fences."

"I know, dear husband. But we need to try. You know, I have a gift with horses. Let me see what I can do."

Colin relented. "Very well, then. If it makes you happy, we will do it your way."

Allison added, "You are so good to me. I never thought I would meet a man like you. Someone who accepted me for who I am. Not what they wanted me to be. Someone—"

"Stop there," Colin said. "You are the woman I love and will cherish until death do us part. Your children are my children."

*****

Over a five-day period, Allison managed to coax most of the orphaned horses inside the farm. She secured them in the farm's indoor arena to keep them warm and dry. She was pleased with her work. Ten mares and nine geldings were secured and happily reconstituting their flesh with oats, hay, and water. However, Allison's job was not done.

The lone horse leading the herd was always standing on the edge of the woods, watching. As far as she could tell, he stood on the sidelines, not trusting to come in. He stayed near a stand of trees for cover and safety.

Allison told Colin, "You know. I have one more horse to get. I can't tell what kind of horse he is from this distance. The mud is so thick on his coat. His mane and tail are so matted up. I also think he was wounded. There is a raised piece of skin on his withers."

Colin replied, "He is probably shell-shocked, just like our poor soldiers."

Allison remained silent for a few minutes, then said, "You know, my father taught me an old trick about getting a horse's attention."

Colin asked, "What was that?"

Allison said, "Oats and molasses. My daddy taught me that trick."

"Yep, it worked with my horses on the Magnolia. It may work with him."

*****

Allison's plan worked. She took great pride in knowing she got a halter on the horse who licked every oat from the large bowl Allison placed in the north forty. The horse did not run. Allison slowly walked toward him. She noticed bits and pieces of a rope halter were tied to his face and neck. The bitter end had been broken. She extended a handful of oats toward the horse, as she slowly made her way to his side. She was careful not to lose sight of his eyes.

The horse raised his head and took notice of the handful of oats. He sniffed the air and then stepped toward Allison. He stopped within a couple of feet of her hand. She took a small step toward the horse and whispered, "It is okay, boy. You will be fine."

The horse focused on her voice and not her movement. Once she got close enough, she slipped a ketch rope over his neck. She then twisted a figure eight into the rope to secure his nose. Allison soothed him with her voice. "It is okay, boy. You look hungry." She then chuckled. "Ugh. You also smell and need a bath." She reached into her pocket and brought out another oat ball mixed with sweet molasses. The horse eagerly consumed it.

After slipping her hand over his neck, she slipped a sturdier halter connected to the short lead she kept tucked in her back pants. The horse neighed and pulled up his front hooves off the grass a couple of times. Allison found a better angle to control the horse. She kept saying, "You are going to be okay, boy. You are going to be okay." She stepped back and looked up at him. He was a massive animal standing over seventeen hands high. She said, "Seeing you up close tells me more why you are the herd's alpha male."

Allison led the muddied animal back to the horse barn. As she approached the barn's front door, every orphan horse inside started neighing louder as he got closer. He neighed back, snorting and shaking his head. Allison tugged at the lead. "Hold on. Knock it off. You will reunite with your mares soon enough." The horse neighed back to Allison, as if he understood her.

The first thing Allison wanted to do was brush off the gray mud that caked his neck to hocks. Allison shook her head. She said, "I suppose you kept yourself warm during the winter and bugs off during the spring, judging from all the mud caked up on you. I have a stiff wire scrape that will do the job. Trust me, you will like it."

Allison started scraping the horse's forelock, neck, and face. She stopped and looked at him. "Wow. You sure look handsome." She continued scarping off the mud from his neck, mane, and chest. While removing the mud off his withers, she noted the scars most likely caused by shrapnel. She was careful not to touch the area with the scraper. She continued working toward his rear quarters.

She picked up the rear left leg and examined the hock and hoof. She put the leg down and said, "Blackie, or whatever your name is, you need a serious hoof trim and shoeing, among many other things."

Allison continued working her way up on the left quarter where the mud was thick and hardened. As she scraped across the horse's left quarter, the raised scar shouted at her. She scraped faster, using her hand to wipe away any dirt and dust covering it. She stood back and dropped the scraper. After taking a deep breath, she sighed, and then stepped forward to the horse. Allison wrapped her arms around the stallion's neck. Her eyes filled with tears of joy. She cried out, "Where have you been?"

The battle-worn stallion neighed back, "I am tired and want to go home."

*****

Epilogue

I believe that the value of the horse and the opportunity for the horse in the future are likely to be as great as ever. Airplanes and tanks are only accessories to the men and horse, and I feel sure that as time goes on you will find just as much use for the horse ---the well-bred horse--- as you have ever done in the past.

—General Douglas Haig,
Britain's First World War commander-in-chief, 1927

I believe that every soldier who has anything to do with horse or mule has come to love them for what they are and the grand work they have done and are doing in and out of the death zones.

—Captain Sidney Galtrey, autumn 1918

Peace's great-great-grandfather, Jubal Early survived horrific battles fought during World War I. His training and conditioning prepared him to handle the stress of war. He did not muster out unscathed. A German bullet passed through his withers. Small pieces of shrapnel nicked his chest and hindquarters during the Third Battle of Ypres in Belgium. Yet he did not give up.

Jubal Early's unyielding desire to live tempered his heart. For many years after the war, Jubal Early would not talk with his friends about the horror he had witnessed and experienced. Jubal Early wisely kept most of those memories in the back of his mind, except for one—the memory of his father slowly dying in a grave made for man.

*****

Allison and Colin George did their duty relocating as many orphaned horses as they could in the ensuing years. However, it took a larger community to step in and save the lives of countless warhorses without a home. One woman in particular took the fight to governments. She successfully lobbied for funding to save the horses. Her name was Ms. Dorothy Brooke. She wrote a letter that captured the hearts and minds of the world. It was published in *The Morning Post*:

*****

There have been several references lately in the columns of The Morning Post as to the possibility of raising a memorial to horses killed in the War. May I make a suggestion?

Out here, in Egypt, there are still many hundreds of old Army Horses sold of necessity at the cessation of the War. They are all over twenty years of age by now, and to say that the majority of them have fallen on hard times is to express it very mildly.

Those sold at the end of the war have sunk to a very low rate of value indeed: they are past 'good work' and the majority of them drag out wretched days of toil in the ownership of masters too poor to feed them – too inured to hardship themselves to appreciate, in the faintest degree, the sufferings of animals in their hands.

These old horses were, many of them, born and bred in the green fields of England – how many years since they have seen a field, heard a stream of water, or a kind word in English?

Many are blind – all are skeletons.

A fund is being raised to buy up these old horses. As most of them are the sole means of a precarious livelihood to their owners, adequate compensation must, of necessity, be given in each case. An animal out here, who would be considered far too old and decrepit to be worked in England, will have before him several years of ceaseless toil – and there are no Sundays or days of rest in this country. Many have been condemned and destroyed by the Society for the Prevention of Cruelty to Animals (not a branch of the RSPCA), but want of funds necessitates that all not totally unfit for work should be restored to their owners after treatment.

If those who truly love horses – who realise what it can mean to be very old, very hungry and thirsty, and very tired, in a country where hard, ceaseless work has to be done in great heat – will send contributions to help in giving a merciful end to our poor old war heroes, we shall be extremely grateful; and we venture to think that, in many ways, this may be as fitting (though unspectacular) part of a War Memorial as any other that could be devised.

Signed – Dorothy E. Brooke

*****

Several international campaigns to save warhorses emerged around the world. The United States, Great Britain, and Canada coordinated funding and services to locate displaced horses that served during the Great War. In particular, the military servicemen who rode them were passionate about finding their charges, or *dumb animals* as the Canadians called them. Not meant to say their dumb in mind, but dumb enough to save a man from dying while under fire. Humanity arose where none expected. The horses that survived the transition from leather to steel lived to see one more war.

*****

Clint Goodwin

Canadian Mounted Rifles. Headquarters Hamilton, Ont. Canada's Crack Cavalry Corps. Quick Service Overseas. Canadian World War I recruitment poster.

*****

During his research, the author discovered a most interesting factoid. During the interwar period, Hollywood secured the U.S. Army 11th Cavalry to make war movies. The regiment was involved in the making of two motion pictures *Troopers Three* (1929) and *Sergeant Murphy* (1937). The latter starred a promising young actor by the name of Ronald Reagan, himself an Army Reserve Cavalryman in Troop B, 322nd Cavalry. On May 25, 1937, he was appointed a second lieutenant in the Officers' Reserve Corps of the Cavalry. Ronald Reagan was the last U.S. President who served as a mounted cavalryman and the only one to "serve" with the 11th Cavalry Regiment.

The trooper and horse galloping across the battlefield became more popular on the silver screen, than an offensive military capability. Though the horse and rider had some success during the Great War, in most cases the failures and losses of life served notice that military transformation was moving ahead without our four-footed friends.

The love and respect for horse and rider endured amongst traditional officers who maintained cavalries were essential elements of land warfare. Those ideas would fade in time with new generations and modern thinking. The cavalry had to morph from leather to steel.

Notes

Prologue

1 "Topics in Chronicling America – The Assassination of Archduke Franz Ferdinand," U.S. Library of Congress, https://www.loc.gov/rr/news/topics/archduke.html, last accessed March 16, 2016.

> Two shots in Sarajevo ignited the fires of war and drew Europe into World War I. Just hours after narrowly escaping an assassin's bomb, Archduke Franz Ferdinand, the heir to the Austro-Hungarian throne and his wife, the Duchess of Hohenberg, were killed by Gavrilo Princip. A month later, Austria-Hungary declared war on Serbia, and Europe rapidly descended into chaos. Read more about it! Archduke Ferdinand.
>
> June 28, 1914. Archduke Franz Ferdinand and his wife are killed by an assassin's bullets just hours after they escaped another assassination attempt. Gavrilo Princip is immediately arrested for the shooting and Nedjelko Cabrinovic is caught fleeing after the bomb attempt. (Pricip was a member of a secret Serbian-backed paramilitary organization called the Black Hand.)
>
> June 29, 1914. Martial law is declared in Sarajevo in the wake of the assassination. On the same day, Sir Thomas Barclay of England predicts, "The danger of war in

central Europe is greatly lessened by the assassination."

July 23, 1914. Austria Hungary issues an ultimatum to Serbia.

July 28, 1914. Austria-Hungary declares war on Serbia. The declaration of war sets off a series of cascading declarations that lead to World War I.

2 "The Eastern Front, 1914–1917," United Kingdom National Archives, http://www.nationalarchives.gov.uk/pathways/firstworldwar/document_packs/eastern.htm last accessed June 6, 2915.

After the abdication of Nicholas II in March 1917, the new Provisional Government pledged to continue the Russian war effort. But the Russian Army was no longer a viable fighting force. Two million men deserted in March and April. Bolshevik agitators—including Lenin, who had returned to Russia from exile on 3 April—spread effective anti-war propaganda. A major new Russian offensive in Galicia in July 1917 failed, and by September, the northern Russian army had collapsed.

Bloodline Reflections

3 "Staff Sergeant Reckless Monument Dedication Ceremony"

http://www.pendleton.marines.mil/News/News-Article-Display/Article/987859/camp-pendleton-unveils-staff-sgt-reckless-monument/ last accessed November 8,2016. War horse, Staff Sgt. Reckless, was known for her heroics at the Battle of Outpost Vegas during the Korean War and received many military decorations.

4 "Explosion of the Space Shuttle Challenger"

Address to the Nation, January 28, 1986, President Ronald Reagan, National Aeronautics and Space Administration, http://history.nasa.gov/reagan12886.html, last accessed May 23, 2016. A quote from the president's address: "The crew of the space shuttle Challenger honored us by the manner in which they lived their lives. We will never forget them, nor the last time we saw them, this morning as they prepared for their journey and waved good-bye and "slipped the surly bonds of earth" to "touch the face of God."

Service to the Nation

5 "Theodore Roosevelt," Whitehouse History and Grounds, https://www.whitehouse.gov/1600/presidents/theodoreroosevelt, last accessed June 6, 2015.

> With the assassination of President McKinley on September 14, 1901, Theodore Roosevelt, not quite 43, became the youngest President in the Nation's history. He brought new excitement and power to the Presidency, as he vigorously led Congress and the American public toward progressive reforms and a strong foreign policy. He took the view that the President as a "steward of the people" should take whatever action necessary for the public good unless expressly forbidden by law or the Constitution. "I did not usurp power," he wrote, "but I did greatly broaden the use of executive power." He was born in New York City in 1858 into a wealthy family, but he too struggled—against ill health—and in his triumph became an advocate of the strenuous life. During the Spanish-American War, Roosevelt was lieutenant colonel of the Rough Rider Regiment, which he led on a charge at

the battle of San Juan. He was one of the most conspicuous heroes of the war. Roosevelt emerged spectacularly as a "trust buster" by forcing the dissolution of a great railroad combination in the Northwest. Other antitrust suits under the Sherman Act followed. Roosevelt steered the United States more actively into world politics. He liked to quote a favorite proverb, "Speak softly and carry a big stick..." Aware of the strategic need for a shortcut between the Atlantic and the Pacific, Roosevelt ensured the construction of the Panama Canal. His corollary to the Monroe Doctrine prevented the establishment of foreign bases in the Caribbean and arrogated the sole right of intervention in Latin America to the United States. He won the Nobel Peace Prize for mediating in the Russo-Japanese War, reached a Gentlemen's Agreement on immigration with Japan, and sent the Great White Fleet on a goodwill tour of the world. Some of Theodore Roosevelt's most effective achievements were in conservation. He added enormously to the national forests in the West, reserved lands for public use, and fostered great irrigation projects. Leaving the presidency in 1909, Roosevelt went on an African safari, then jumped back into politics. In 1912 he ran for president on a Progressive ticket. To reporters he once remarked that he felt as fit as a bull moose, the name of his new party. While campaigning in Milwaukee, he was shot in the chest by a fanatic. Roosevelt soon recovered, but his words at that time would have been applicable at the time of his death in 1919: "No man has had a happier life than I have led; a happier life in every way."

6 Map of Loudoun County, Va., and parts of Fairfax County, Va., Jefferson County, W.Va., and Washington and Frederick counties, Md., Library of Congress,

http://www.loc.gov/resource/g3883l.cwh00044/ last accessed May 25, 2015.

Going Home

7 "Biography. Quanah Parker," U.S. Army Fort Sill History, http://sill-www.army.mil/History/_bios/qparker.htm, last accessed on March 16, 2016.

> Quanah Parker, the last chief of the Quahada Comanche Indians, son of Peta Nocona and Cynthia Ann Parker was a major figure both in Comanche resistance to white settlement and in the tribe's adjustment to reservation life. Nomadic hunter of the Llano Estacado (Staked Plains in the Northern Texas Panhandle), leader of the Quahada assault on Adobe Walls in 1874, cattle rancher, entrepreneur, and friend of American presidents, Quanah Parker was truly a man of two worlds. The name Quanah means "smell" or "odor." Though the date of his birth is recorded variously at 1845 and 1852, there is no mystery regarding his parentage. His mother was the celebrated captive of a Comanche raid on Parker's Fort (1836) and convert to the Indian way of life. His father was a noted war chief of the Noconi band of the Comanche. In 1860, however, Peta Nocona was killed defending an encampment on the Pease River against Texas Rangers under Lawrence Sullivan Ross. The raid, which resulted in the capture and incarceration gof Cynthia Ann and Quanah's sister Topasannah, also decimated the Noconis and forced Quanah, now an orphan, to take refuge with the Quahada Comanches of the Llano Estacado. (The U.S, Army pushed Quanah Parker's band out of the Llano Estacado back to the Oklahoma Indian Territory Reservation during the fall of 1874.)

8 "The Presidents, Abraham Lincoln," "Whitehouse.Gov, "https://www.whitehouse.gov/1600/presidents/abrahamlincoln, last accessed January 9, 2016.

> Lincoln warned the South in his Inaugural Address: "In your hands, my dissatisfied fellow countrymen, and not in mine, is the momentous issue of civil war. The government will not assail you...You have no oath registered in Heaven to destroy the government, while I shall have the most solemn one to preserve, protect and defend it." Lincoln thought secession illegal, and was willing to use force to defend Federal law and the Union. When Confederate batteries fired on Fort Sumter and forced its surrender, he called on the states for 75,000 volunteers. Four more slave states joined the Confederacy but four remained within the Union. The Civil War had begun. The son of a Kentucky frontiersman, Lincoln had to struggle for a living and for learning. Five months before receiving his party's nomination for President, he sketched his life:
>
>> I was born Feb. 12, 1809, in Hardin County, Kentucky. My parents were both born in Virginia, of undistinguished families--second families, perhaps I should say. My mother, who died in my tenth year, was of a family of the name of Hanks...My father...removed from Kentucky to... Indiana, in my eighth year...It was a wild region, with many bears and other wild animals still in the woods. There I grew up...Of course when I came of age I did not know much. Still somehow, I could read, write, and cipher...but that was all.

9 "Fort Myer History," Joint base Myer-Henderson Hall Homepage, http://www.jbmhh.army.mil/WEB/JBMHH/AboutJBMHH/FortMyer History.html, last accessed June 8, 2016.

> Fort Myer, Virginia, traces its origin as a military post to the Civil War. Since then it has been an important Signal Corps post, a showcase for Army cavalry and site of the first flight of an aircraft at a military installation and the first military air fatality. The acres encompassing Fort Myer and Arlington National Cemetery were called Arlington Heights when they were owned in the 1800s by Mary Anna Randolph, granddaughter of George Washington Parke Custis. Custis was Martha Washington's grandson. Mary Anna Randolph married Robert E. Lee when he was a young Army lieutenant. Lee helped rescue the estate from financial disaster in 1858, left the area in April 1861 to lead the Confederate Army, never to return.
>
> The land was confiscated by the government for military purposes when the Lees were unable to pay their property taxes in person. Part of the estate became Arlington National Cemetery and the remainder Fort Whipple, named in honor of Maj. Gen. Amiel Weeks Whipple, a division commander at Fort Cass which was established where the stables are today in August 1861. Gen. Whipple fought in the Civil War battles of Fredericksburg and Chancellorsville in Virginia. He died of his wounds from Chancellorsville in 1863.
>
> Fort Whipple, on 256 acres, was one of the stronger fortifications built to defend the Union capital across the Potomac River. Units stationed there lived in tents and temporary frame structures. The fledgling post's high

elevation made it ideal for visual communication, and the Signal Corps took it over in the late 1860s. Brig. Gen. Albert J. Myer commanded Fort Whipple and, in 1866, was appointed the Army's first chief signal officer, a post he held until his death in 1880. The post was renamed Fort Myer the next year, primarily to honor the late chief signal officer, but also to eliminate confusion created by the existence of another Fort Whipple in Arizona.

In 1887, Gen. Philip H. Sheridan, the Army's commanding general, decided Fort Myer should become the nation's cavalry showplace. Communications people moved out and cavalrymen moved in, including the 3rd Cavalry Regiment, supported by the 16th Field Artillery Regiment. As many as 1,500 horses were stabled at the fort during any given time from 1887 to 1949, and Army horsemanship became an important part of Washington's official and social life.

Most of the buildings at the north end of Fort Myer were built between 1895 and 1908. Many of those still standing have been designated historic landmarks by the U.S. Department of the Interior and the state of Virginia. Quarters One was completed in 1899 as the post commander's house, but since 1908, it has been the home of Army chiefs of staff, including Generals George C. Marshall, Omar N. Bradley, Douglas MacArthur and Dwight D. Eisenhower.

10 "Medal of Honor Recipients. Indian Wars Period," United States Army Center for Military History, http://www.history.army.mil/html/moh/indianwars.html, last accessed August 15, 2015.

11 "Sergeant Major William McBryar," The Tucson Buffalo Soldiers Memorial Project, https://www.tucsonaz.gov/files/integrated-planning/Draft_Memorial_Project_Plan_-_Oct_14.pdf, last accessed August 15, 2015.

> Sergeant Major William McBryar (February 14, 1861 – March 8,1941) was a Buffalo Soldier in the United States Army and a recipient of America's highest military decoration—the Medal of Honor—for his actions during the Cherry Creek Campaign in Arizona Territory. McBryar joined the Army from New York City and by March 7, 1890 was serving as a sergeant in Company K of the 10th Cavalry Regiment. On that day, he participated in an engagement in Arizona where he "distinguished himself for coolness, bravery and marksmanship while his troop was in pursuit of hostile Apache Indians." For his actions, Sergeant McBryar was awarded the Medal of Honor two months later, on May 15, 1890. McBryar later became a commissioned officer and left the Army as a First Lieutenant. He died at age 80 and was buried in Arlington National Cemetery.

12 "Fort Sill Old Post Cemetery," United States Army Garrison Fort Sill, http://sill-www.army.mil/USAG/DPW/cemetery_post.html, last accessed August 16, 2015.

> Established in 1869 with the founding of Fort Sill, the Post Cemetery is a hallowed burial ground for soldier, Indian and pioneer alike. Until the 1880s this was the only established cemetery in southwestern Oklahoma. Indian mission cemeteries followed, then those of towns and cities, as the country was opened to settlement. This unique cemetery serves as a landmark for the past, present, and future. It includes the Chiefs Knoll, where

prominent Indian chiefs are buried. The earliest burial was Satank or Sitting Bear, who was killed in 1871 by 4th Cavalry troopers. Many other chief graves can be found here. Many of those buried were signers of the 1867 Medicine Lodge Treaty. Reburials of chiefs from the past have occurred, bringing the former leaders in from isolated grounds to this more centralized area. To the Indians of the southern plains, it is considered the Indian Arlington.

13 "Military Funeral Honors," Department of Defense, https://www.dmdc.osd.mil/mfh/getLinks.do?tab=Services, last accessed August 16, 2018.

14 "Red Men Red Men Fear Government," The Times Dispatch., October 02, 1904, http://chroniclingamerica.loc.gov/lccn/sn85038615/1904-10-02/ed-1/seq-1/ last accessed August 27, 2015.

The Making of a War Horse

15 "The Life of Theodore Roosevelt," National Park Service, http://www.nps.gov/thri/theodorerooseveltbio.htm last accessed September 22, 2015.

> Theodore Roosevelt was born at 28 East 20th Street, New York City on October 27, 1858. He spent most of his childhood living in New York. His father, Theodore Roosevelt Sr. passed the love for nature to his son, the family nicknamed Teedie. After graduating high School, he entered Harvard shortly before his eighteenth birthday. He originally chose to study natural history and had considered a teaching career. From the day of Theodore's arrival in Cambridge, he failed to fit into the Harvard

mold. His clothes were considered too flashy for the conservatives, who also disapproved of his recently grown sideburns. His college rooms were filled with his specimens and mounted animals. Faculty members who taught Roosevelt soon learned to treat him warily. Once Roosevelt asked so many questions during a natural history lecture that the professor exclaimed, "Now look here, Roosevelt, let me talk, I'm running this course!"

In 1881 Theodore ran for public office. Entering politics as a means of public service, he embarked on a campaign that was to elect him to the assembly of New York State. He was reelected twice, once in 1882, and again in 1883. Roosevelt served a short term as Republican minority leader in 1882. Learning to rope, ride, and survive in the wilderness revitalized Roosevelt. The conviction grew within Roosevelt that the American wilderness was responsible for the strong sense of individualism, the love of liberty and the intellectual independence that had so long shaped the nation. He began writing "The Winning of the West," a study of frontier living and the character of his frontier neighbors.

In 1896, Roosevelt campaigned vigorously for Republican Presidential candidate William McKinley. Roosevelt's loyalty paid off when McKinley appointed Roosevelt the Assistant Secretary of the Navy. Knowing a strong Navy was essential for the United States to become a world power, He began building up the Navy by constructing new ships, adding modern equipment and enhancing training procedures. Roosevelt seemed to know that war with Spain was imminent, and wanted the U.S. Navy prepared for it.

With the outbreak of the Spanish-American War in 1898, Roosevelt left his job as Assistant Secretary of the Navy in order to lead a volunteer cavalry regiment as a Lt. Colonel in the Army. The regiment, known as the Rough Riders, executed a daredevil charge up San Juan and Kettle Hills in Cuba. Roosevelt was hailed as a hero and finally achieved the glory he had dreamed of as a boy. He was awarded the Medal of Honor 103 years later.

At the 1900 Republican Convention, Roosevelt was nominated for the one position he didn't want: Vice President under incumbent William McKinley. The New York party bosses wanted Roosevelt out of the governorship but Mark Hanna could see the consequences beyond New York State. Exasperated, Hanna exclaimed, "Don't any of you realize there's only one life between that madman and the presidency?" Roosevelt reluctantly agreed to accept the nomination. He reasoned that perhaps he might be able to run for the presidency in 1904.

Only six months after McKinley's March, 1901 inauguration, the President was assassinated and Theodore Roosevelt became the 26th President of the United States. Roosevelt took the oath of office on September 14, 1901, at the home of Ansley Wilcox. At the age of 42, Roosevelt was the youngest man to become President of the United States.

Fast forwarding between 1901 and 1914, it was through his relations with the great powers of Europe that Roosevelt gave the American people a new understanding of their country's growing role in world affairs. Still more important was the fact that these relations caused Roosevelt to enunciate a policy that would come to be known as the "Roosevelt Corollary" to the Monroe Doctrine. Roosevelt declared, "we cannot afford to let Europe get a foothold in our backyard, so we'll have to act as policemen for the West." The policy received its first test when Venezuela lapsed in its financial obligation to Great Britain and Germany. Both Germany and Great Britain sent warships to force Venezuela to make payment. Roosevelt was willing to see that Venezuela paid her debts, but he could not allow an American nation to be threatened. The enforcement of Roosevelt Corollary forced the warships to withdraw and permitted Roosevelt to act as arbitrator for the dispute.

Roosevelt was elected to remain in office. After his election in 1904, Roosevelt declared that "under no circumstances" would he run for president in 1908 (a statement he later regretted). Roosevelt's statement gave conservative Republicans further incentive to resist Roosevelt's progressive policies. Roosevelt was undaunted.

During the 1912 presidential campaign, Roosevelt was the target of an attempted assassination on October 14, 1912. John Shrank shot Roosevelt just prior to a speech that TR was to deliver in Milwaukee. Roosevelt's spectacle case and folded speech located in his vest pocket deflected the bullet and probably saved his life. In spite of the bullet lodged in his chest, he went ahead with his speech. In only two weeks Roosevelt was fully recovered from the wound.

In 1914 Roosevelt and Kermit took part in an exploratory mission into the interior of Brazil to explore an uncharted river. While in Brazil, TR contracted jungle fever, injured his leg and lost sixty pounds. He returned weak and looking much older than his fifty-six years. Yet Roosevelt was undaunted. A wonderful book documents his journey. The book called *River of Doubt*.

The arrival of World War I found Roosevelt calling for America to prepare itself against a "strong, ruthless, ambitious, militaristic Germany." He developed an intense dislike for President Wilson because the president refused to plunge the nation into war. Roosevelt even offered to raise a division of volunteer troops to fight in France as he had done in 1898. Wilson refused the request.

Theodore Roosevelt's four sons served in Europe. On July 16, 1918, his youngest son, Quentin, was killed in an air battle over France with a German pilot. Two other sons were wounded in battle. Though Roosevelt had stressed upon his sons the importance of fighting for one's country, he himself never fully recovered from Quentin's death."

16 "On the Art of Horsemanship," Xenophon, 360 B.C.E., http://www1.hollins.edu/faculty/saloweyca/horse/onhorsemanship.htm, last accessed August 28, 2015.

It is the oldest known text on horseback riding still in existence, and the first work known to emphasize training techniques that account for the state of the horse's psyche as well as his body. The work is divided into eleven chapters, and deals with the purchase, care and training of horses. It also deals, to some extent, with the construction of stables and the equipment needed for several aspects of horsemanship.

17 "Author Interview with Mr. Ranse Leembruggen," August 27, 2015.

Mr. Leembruggen is an consummate professional with over fifty years of equine training and rehabilitating experience. The international equestrian community has long recognized and benefitted from Mister Leembruggen's dedication to equine health and welfare. Because of his proven specialty skills, Mister Leembruggen is a highly sought-after equestrian rehabilitation expert.

Mr. Leembruggen rehabilitates horses from all disciplines, but specifically those horses that have developed recurring, unspecified lameness issues. For example, he rehabilitates horses such as Rodeo Red - pictured below- to improve its ability to achieve elevation of movement, rhythm, and positive control without traditional aids. Rodeo Red, twenty-eight years of age, after completing an extensive Leembruggen rehabilitation program, won a dressage competition. Mr. Leembruggen also works with horses that sustain injuries from rodeo competitions. These injuries break down the animal's ability to live a normal life. Admittedly, he will work with any horse—unsuccessfully—treated by other means.

Mr. Leembruggen is a prior member of distinguished British Horse Society (BHS) (http://www.bhs.org.uk/). Amongst his many credentials, Ranse possesses a BHS instructor certification. An interesting fact to note: the honorable Brigadier General Friedberger facilitated Mr. Leenbruggen's BHS instructor examination. Ranse also worked as an assistant instructor for Mr. Robert Hall, a former student of the Spanish Riding School in Vienna, Austria.

(Author comment: The character Ranse Xenophon used in this book does not represent the actual horse training and rehabilitation capabilities of Mr. Ranse Leembruggen. The author's choice of the first name "Ranse" only pays respect to the living, Mr. Ranse Leembruggen.)

18 "William Cavendish Duke of Devonshire (Whig, 1756–1757)," United Kingdom Archives, https://history.blog.gov.uk/2015/01/14/william-cavendish-duke-of-devonshire-whig-1756-1757/, last accessed August 29, 2015. "Devonshire left the Commons in June 1751, taking a seat in the Lords as Baron Cavendish. He promptly was appointed to the Privy Council and became Master of Horse in the royal household."

19 "About, Royal Veterinarian College," Royal Veterinarian College, http://www.rvc.ac.uk/about last accessed September 28, 2015. "Established in 1791, RVC is the UK's longest-standing veterinary college—with a proud heritage of innovation in veterinary science, clinical practice, and education.

20 "Department of the Missouri. Brig-Gen. Theodore J. Wiat, "The Army and Navy Register, May 21, 1906, p. 19.

A Suffrage Movement

21 "The Great 1906 San Francisco Earthquake," United States Geographic Service, http://earthquake.usgs.gov/regional/nca/1906/18april/index.php, last accessed September 13, 2015.

> The California earthquake of April 18, 1906 ranks as one of the most significant earthquakes of all time.
>
> At almost precisely 5:12 a.m., local time, a foreshock occurred with sufficient force to be felt widely throughout the San Francisco Bay area. The great earthquake broke loose some 20 to 25 seconds later, with an epicenter near

San Francisco. Violent shocks punctuated the strong shaking, which lasted some 45 to 60 seconds. The earthquake was felt from southern Oregon to south of Los Angeles and inland as far as central Nevada. Areas situated in sediment-filled valleys sustained stronger shaking than nearby bedrock sites, and the strongest shaking occurred in areas where ground reclaimed from San Francisco Bay failed in the earthquake.

As a basic reference about the earthquake and the damage it caused, geologic observations of the fault rupture and shaking effects, and other consequences of the earthquake, the Lawson (1908) report remains the authoritative work, as well as arguably the most important study of a single earthquake. In the public's mind, this earthquake is perhaps remembered most for the fire it spawned in San Francisco, giving it the somewhat misleading appellation of the "San Francisco earthquake". Shaking damage, however, was equally severe in many other places along the fault rupture. The frequently quoted value of 700 deaths caused by the earthquake and fire is now believed to underestimate the total loss of life by a factor of 3 or 4. Most of the fatalities occurred in San Francisco, and 189 were reported elsewhere.

22 "SS Aller," Immigrant Ships Transcribers Guild, http://www.immigrantships.net/1800/aller881201.html , last accessed September 4, 2015. The purpose for selecting a German immigrant comes into play during 1914. During the Great War (1914–1918), many influential people in the United States suspected German immigrants of aiding and abetting Germany during the Great War. Excerpt from the manifest.

DISTRICT OF NEW YORK - PORT OF NEW YORK. {I, 1st Officer I. Hogemann, of the SS ALLER do solemnly, sincerely, and truly, declare that the following List or Manifest subscribed by me and now delivered by me to the Collector of the Customs of the Collection District of New York, is a full and perfect list of all the passengers taken on board of the said vessel at Bremen and Southampton from which port said vessel has now arrived; and that on said list is truly designated the age, the sex, and the calling of each of said passengers, the part of the vessel occupied by each during the passage, the country of citizenship of each, and also of the said vessel at Bremen and Southampton from which port said vessel has now arrived; and that on said list is truly designated the age, the sex, and the calling of each of said passengers, the part of the vessel occupied by each during the passage, the country of citizenship of each, and also destination or location intended by each; and that said List or the Manifest truly sets forth the number of said passengers who have died on said voyage and the dates and the names and ages of those who died; also the pieces of baggage of each; also a true statement, so far as can be ascertained, with reference to the intention of each alien passenger as to a protracted sojourn in this country.] [Sworn to on this date: December 1, 1888. A list of all passengers aboard the ship SS ALLER from Bremen and Southampton to New York on December 1, 1888. Master: *H. Christoffers]

23 "National Archives Co-Sponsors Conference on the Common Soldier in the Civil War", United States National Archives, http://www.archives.gov/press/press-releases/1998/nr98-136.html , last accessed July 23, 2015.

24 "19th Amendment to the U.S. Constitution: Women's Right to Vote," U.S. National Archives, http://www.archives.gov/historical-docs/document.html?doc=13&title.raw=19th+Amendment+to+the+U.S.+Constitution:+Women's+Right+to+Vote last accessed on June 6, 2015.

25 "Map. Vicinity of Brandy Station, Culpeper County, Virginia, 1863." Library of Congress, http://www.loc.gov/resource/glva01.lva00059/ last accessed September 20, 2015.

26 "Virginia Durant Young House, Allendale County (U.S. Hwy. 278, Fairfax)", South Carolina Department of Archives and History, http://www.nationalregister.sc.gov/allendale/S10817703012/ last accessed June 22, 2015.

27 "Theodore Roosevelt," White House, Home, 1600, Presidents," https://www.whitehouse.gov/1600/presidents/theodoreroosevelt last accessed September 26, 2016.

The Army Needs Men and Horses

28 "Antietam Battlefield – Blood Lane," National Park Service, http://www.nps.gov/resources/place.htm?id=61 last accessed October 11. 2015.

> The Sunken Road, as it was known to area residents prior to the Battle of Antietam, was a dirt farm lane which was used primarily by farmers to bypass Sharpsburg and been worn down over the years by rain and wagon traffic. On September 17, 1862, Confederate Maj. Gen. Daniel Harvey Hill placed his division of approximately 2,600 men along the road, piled fence rails on the embankment to further strengthen the position and waited for the

advance of the Union army. As Federal troops moved to reinforce the fighting in the West Woods, Union Maj. Gen. William H. French and his 5,500 men veered south, towards Hill's position along the Sunken Road. As French's men approached the Sunken Road, the Confederate troops staggered them with a powerful volley delivered at a range of less than one hundred yards. Union and Confederate troops dug in. For nearly four hours, from 9:30 a.m. to 1 p.m., bitter fighting raged along this road as French, supported by Gen. Israel B. Richardson's division, sought to drive the Southerners back. Outnumbered but with a well-defended position, the Confederates in the road stood their ground for most of the morning. Finally, the Federals were able to overwhelm Hill's men, successfully driving them from this strong position and piercing the center of the Confederacy's line. However, the Federals did not follow up this success with additional attacks, and confusion and sheer exhaustion ended the fighting in this part of the battlefield. In three hours of combat, 5,500 soldiers were killed or wounded and neither side gained a decisive advantage. The Sunken Road was now Bloody Lane.

Preparing for War

29 "The World of 1898: The Spanish-American War. Rough Riders," U.S. Library of Congress, http://www.loc.gov/rr/hispanic/1898/roughriders.html last accessed November 7, 2015.

> The most famous of all the units fighting in Cuba, the "Rough Riders" was the name given to the First U.S. Volunteer Cavalry under the leadership of Theodore Roosevelt. Roosevelt resigned his position as Assistant

> Secretary of the Navy in May 1898 to join the volunteer cavalry. The original plan for this unit called for filling it with men from the Indian Territory, New Mexico, Arizona, and Oklahoma. However, once Roosevelt joined the group, it quickly became the place for a mix of troops ranging from Ivy League athletes to glee-club singers to Texas Rangers and Indians.

30 "U.S. Archives. Exchange Issued December 15, 1911. U. S. Department of Agriculture, Bureau of Animal Industry. Circular 186. A. D. Melvin. Chief of Bureau. George M. Rommel, Chief of the Animal Husbandry Division Reprinted from the Twenty-seventh Annual Report of the Bureau of Animal Industry (1910).] Washington: Government Printing Office. 1911.

31 "Army Lineage Series Armor-Cavalry, Part I: Regular Army and Army Reserve," US Army of Military History, http://www.history.army.mil/, last accessed December 26, 2015.

32 "US Army Quartermaster History," U.S. Army Quartermaster Museum, http://www.qmmuseum.lee.army.mil/, last accessed December 27, 2015.

The Great War Begins

33 "Voluntary Aid Detachment," Military History, http://www.qaranc.co.uk/voluntary-aid-detachment.php, last accessed May 8, 2015.

> The Voluntary Aid Detachment worked alongside military nurses during the two World Wars. The VAD were formed in August 1909, as part of Lord Keogh's Scheme for the Organisation of Voluntary Aid, because of the fear that there was a shortage of nurses should war

come and the role of the Voluntary Aid Detachment nurses and assistants were to provide nursing and medical assistance during a time of war. They were organised by the British Red Cross Society.

34 "Bryce Report, "United Kingdom National Archives, http://www.nationalarchives.gov.uk/pathways/firstworldwar/spotlights/p_alleged_german.htm, last accessed December 27, 2015. The Bryce Report contained horrific imagery not necessary to advance the heartfelt sorrows endured by civilians during the Great War for this book. The following short narrative taken from the Bryce Report describes the lesser of evils committed by German soldiers at Louvain, Belgium: "It accused German soldiers of (among other things): raping women and girls; using civilians as 'human shields' during combat; and cutting off children's hands and ears in front of their horrified parents."

35 British Army file photo of General Allenby. H. Walter Barnett - National Portrait Gallery, London. Permission details. This image is in the public domain because its copyright has expired. This applies to the United States, Australia, the European Union and those countries with a copyright term of life of the author plus 70 years. This work is in the public domain in its country of origin and other countries and areas where the copyright term is the author's life plus 70 years or less. United States public domain in the United States published in the US before 1923 and public domain in the US.

36 "American Cavalry in World War I: Military Ignorance or Necessity," United States Army eArmor Magazine, Major John A. Regan, http://www.benning.army.mil/armor/earmor/content/Historical/Regan.html, website last updated August 9, 2013.

Among the first contingent of sixty-seven Americans who

landed in France June 13, 1917, with General John J. Pershing, thirty-five of them were cavalrymen. Thirty-one were members of 2nd Cavalry Regiment. Pershing, a former cavalryman himself, maintained a close relationship with the regiment during the war. One officer and twenty troopers were permanently detailed from A and C troops to serve as Pershing's personal-security detachment at American Expeditionary Forces (AEF) headquarters in Chaumont, France.

The 2nd Cavalry departed Hoboken, NJ, March 22, 1918, and arrived at Bordeaux April 6, 1918. Troops H and I were immediately placed in-sector with 2nd Infantry Division, who had been in-theater for a mere two days.15 When 2nd and 3rd squadrons of 2nd Cavalry arrived at Pauillac, they were ordered to various locations: Troop M moved to south France to bring up horses; Headquarters and Machine Gun troops moved to Valdehon to establish a remount station; and 42nd Division received troops F and G attached as divisional cavalry, operating in the Baccarat sector until May 6, when they rejoined the regiment at Gievres.

37 "Crossley Motors in World War I," Crossley Motors, http://www.crossley-motors.org.uk/history/WW1.html last accessed January 12, 2016.

At the outbreak of hostilities in August 1914 Crossley Motors moved almost totally to war production. The only model made was the 20/25 which was supplied to the forces in huge numbers with production running at up to 45 a week. The first had been supplied to the Royal Flying Corps (RFC) in 1913 and at the outbreak of war they had 56. By the time of the armistice this had risen to over 6000. The 20/25, known to Crossley as the WO and the War Office as Type J, became with a tourer body, one of the standard staff cars (the others being from Vauxhaul or Sunbeam) but most of the chassis were used to carry ambulances, mobile workshops, light trucks and, most importantly, the RFC Light Tenders. Every squadron in the RFC was supposed to be equipped with nine Tenders and one Staff Touring Car but it seems likely that most never had the full complement. Vehicles went to France, Belgium, Mesopotamia, Salonica, Egypt, Russia, India and several parts of Africa.

38 "George V (r. 1910-1936)," The official website of the British Monarchy," http://www.royal.gov.uk/HistoryoftheMonarchy/KingsandQueensoftheUnitedKingdom/TheHouseofWindsor/GeorgeV.aspx last access January 23, 2016.

The King made over 450 visits to troops and over 300 visits to hospitals visiting wounded servicemen, he pressed for proper treatment of German prisoners-of-war and he pressed also for more humane treatment of conscientious objectors.

In 1917, anti-German feeling led him to adopt the family name of Windsor (after the Castle of the same name). Support for home rule for Ireland had grown in the late 19th century. This was resisted by the Unionists in the north and by the Conservative Party.

The 1916 Easter Rising in Dublin, and subsequent civil war, resulted in the setting up of the Irish Free State (later to become the Irish Republic)

Suffering in Every Trench

39 "Jack Johnson struck my head" refers to a British metaphor used to describe the impact of a German 15-cm artillery shell. Jack Johnson—the man—was a popular U.S. world heavyweight boxing champion. He held the title from 1908 to 1915.

40 "England Must Pay U. S. Trade Damage, Wilson Declares," *The Evening Star*, Washington DC, December 29, 1914, front page. "President awaits answer to long, emphatic note to London Government. OBJECTS TO MOLESTATION OF NEUTRAL COMMERCE. Disputes Rule for Detention of Conditional Contraband Consigned to Non-Belligerents. SITUATION BECOMES WORSE. Declares American shippers fear to export goods and business depression here is due to attitude of England. President Wilson, referring today to the American note to Great Britain insisting on better for American commerce declared that large damages eventually would have to be paid by England for unlawful detention of American cargoes."

41 "Sinking of the RMS *Lusitania*," U.S. National Archives, Prologue: Pieces of History, http://prologue.blogs.archives.gov/2015/06/02/sinking-of-the-rms-lusitania/, last accessed January 24, 2016.

> Concerned over the international response to this declaration, the German Embassy in Washington, hoping to avoid controversy, published notices specifically warning American passengers not to travel aboard the Lusitania and other passenger liners that sailed to Britain. It had little effect.
>
> On the morning of May 7, 1915 —U-20— a German submarine, spotted the Lusitania off the Irish coast. The

submarine stalked her prey for much of the rest of the day. At 3:10 p.m. the submarine fired a single torpedo without first warning the crew, as had previously been required under the laws of war. The torpedo hit the middle of the ship. U-20's captain, Walther Schweiger, noted in the log that the torpedo caused an "extraordinarily large explosion," which tore apart "the superstructure above the point of impact and the bridge" and covered much of what was left of the Lusitania in smoke.

42 "St. John's Church History," St. John's Church, http://saintjohnsrichmond.org/about/history/, last accessed February 14, 2016.

St. John's Church traces its roots back to the founding of Henrico Parish in 1611, an outgrowth of the original church in the Jamestown settlement. Over the years the parish expanded westward from Jamestown, up the James River. As Richmond became a riverfront trading center, the Vestry of Henrico Parish began to consider building a church in the burgeoning town. The actual St. John's Church as we know it today dates almost to the beginning of the City of Richmond itself.

The Replacements

43 "Murray Boulevard: A Historic Resource Survey of The Lower Peninsula, Charleston, South Carolina," National Register South Carolina Government, http://charhttp://nationalregister.sc.gov/SurveyReports/HC10006.pdf, last accessed June 23, 2014.

44 "History. Past Prime Ministers. 73. David Lloyd George," United

Kingdom.GOV, last accessed June 28, 2015, https://www.gov.uk/government/history/past-prime-ministers/david-lloyd-george

45 "The British Embassy at Washington," The Living Age, Vol X, Non. 505. Sydney Brooks, No. 3856, June 1, 1918.

> David Lloyd George was one of the 20th century's most famous radicals. He was the first and only Welshman to hold the office of Prime Minister... His reforming budget only passed after the 1911 Parliament Act greatly weakened the power of the House of Lords to block legislation from the Commons. During the war, he threw himself into the job of Minister for Munitions, organising and inspiring the war effort. He was acclaimed as the man who had won the war, and in 1918 the coalition won a huge majority. It was the first election in which any women were allowed to vote. In 1919 he signed the Treaty of Versailles, which established the League of Nations and the war reparations settlement.

46 "Sir Cecil Spring Rice," The Spector Archive, October 12, 1929, page 23, http://archive.spectator.co.uk/article/12th-october-1929/23/sir-cecil-spring-rice, last accessed June 23, 2015.

47 "Yearbook, City of Charleston, S.C. 1916," The University of Illinois Library, 352.0757C38 1916, Copy 2. P. 405.

48 "John Pierpont Morgan Finance Capitalism," United States Department of State, http://iipdigital.usembassy.gov/st/english/publication/2008/04/20080407122011eaifas3.884524e-02.html#axzz3fI3Bu9wG, last accessed July 8, 2015.

The rise of American industry required more than great industrialists. Big industry required big amounts of capital; headlong economic growth required foreign investors. John Pierpont (J.P.) Morgan was the most important of the American financiers who underwrote both requirements.

During the late 19th and early 20th centuries, Morgan headed the nation's largest investment banking firm. It brokered American securities to wealthy elites at home and abroad. Since foreigners needed assurance that their investments were in a stable currency, Morgan had a strong interest in keeping the dollar tied to its legal value in gold. In the absence of an official U.S. central bank, he became the de facto manager of the task.

From the 1880s through the early 20th century, Morgan and Company not only managed the securities that underwrote many important corporate consolidations, it actually originated some of them. The most stunning of these was the U.S. Steel Corporation, which combined Carnegie Steel with several other companies. Its corporate stock and bonds were sold to investors at the then-unprecedented sum of $1.4 billion.

Acting as an unofficial central banker, Morgan took the lead in supporting the dollar during the economic depression of the mid-1890s by marketing a large government bond issue that raised funds to replenish Treasury gold supplies. At the same time, his firm undertook a short-term guarantee of the nation's gold reserves. In 1907, he took the lead in organizing the New York financial community to prevent a potentially ruinous string of bankruptcies. In the process, his own firm acquired a large independent steel company, which it amalgamated with U.S. Steel. President Roosevelt personally approved the action in order to avert a serious depression.

49 "S/S Haverford, American Line," Norway-Heritage, Hands Across the Sea, http://www.norwayheritage.com/p_ship.asp?sh=have1 last accessed June 23, 2014.

50 "The First World War," (New York: Martin Gilbert, Henry Holt and Company, 1194).

Those Poor Horses

51 "American Red Star Animal Relief," United States Army Medical Department, Office of Medical History, http://history.amedd.army.mil/booksdocs/wwi/VolISGO/Sec3Ch02.htm, last accessed December 30, 2016.

> It was not until June 7, 1918, that this organization was officially authorized to function with the Army, to furnish emergency aid and such supplies as were not available from the War Department, as well as special equipment unattainable through regular appropriations. The Red Star rendered valuable service and in many instances supplied medicines, dressings, and other accessories to veterinary hospitals. A leaflet on first aid for Army horses was prepared and gratuitously distributed by the Red Star to soldiers handling horses, on the request of officers and veterinarians. Over 80,000 of these pamphlets were distributed for Army use. Eleven motor veterinary ambulances of a type acceptable to the commanding general were supplied to the American Expeditionary

Forces at a cost of $57,522. Seven other ambulances, motor or horse drawn, were furnished Army cantonments and camps in the United States. Two were held in reserve by headquarters, making a total of 20 veterinary ambulances purchased by the Red Star. In this country four automobiles and 10 motor cycles (seven with side cars) were furnished for the use of camp veterinarians in order to permit them to visit sick and injured animals at distant points and to take the necessary supplies. Several supply buildings were erected, and large quantities of bandages, surgical instruments, drugs, stable supplies, etc., at the request of veterinary officers, were sent to Army camps.

Taking Advantage

52 "Black Jack in Cuba. General John J. Pershing's Service in the Spanish-American War," United States Army Center of Military History, http://www.history.army.mil/documents/Spanam/ws-Prshg.htm , last accessed January 21, 2016.

> To most Americans, San Juan Hill conjures up images of Teddy Roosevelt and his Rough Riders dashing up the hill to victory, but other soldiers also played an important role in driving the Spanish off the heights overlooking Santiago, Cuba. One such soldier was 1st Lt. John J. Pershing, the quartermaster of the 10th Cavalry, the famed "Buffalo Soldiers." Pershing's experiences in Cuba gave him important battlefield experience and showed him how an army at war behaves. This would pay off when Pershing led the American Expeditionary Forces into battle on the fields of France in World War I, less than twenty years later.

As tensions heated up between the United States and Spain, Pershing was teaching tactics at West Point. Desperate to join the action he foresaw as inevitable, he bombarded the assistant secretary of war, George Meiklejohn, with letters. Realizing the importance of combat duty, he wrote, "if I should accept any duty which would keep me from field service, indeed if I did not make every effort to obtain an opportunity for field service I should never forgive myself."[1]

Pershing was not totally unprepared for battle. An 1886 graduate of West Point, he had seen duty against the Plains Indians with both the 6th and 10th Cavalry Regiments. The 10th was one of two black cavalry regiments commanded by white officers. Pershing was called "Black Jack" in reference to his service with the 10th, and the nickname stuck long after he left it. Pershing had also taught military tactics and mathematics at the University of Nebraska and earned a law degree there.

53 Zimmermann Telegram. Received by the German Ambassador to Mexico. General Records of the Department of State National Archives Identifier: 302025. German Foreign Minister Arthur Zimmermann sent an encoded message to the President of Mexico on January 16, 1917, offering United States territory to Mexico in return for joining the German cause. British intelligence intercepted the telegram and deciphered it. In an effort to protect their intelligence from detection and to capitalize on growing anti-German sentiment in the United States, the British waited until February 24 to present the telegram to Woodrow Wilson. The American press published news of the telegram on March 1. On April 6, 1917, the United States Congress formally declared war on Germany and its allies.

54 "The National Security League and Preparedness for War," The Advocate of Peace (1894-1920), Volume 77, World Affairs Institute, July 1, 1915.

55 "Topics in Chronicling America – Female Spies in World War One," Library of Congress, https://www.loc.gov/rr/news/topics/femalespies.html, last accessed February 13m 2106. Richmond Times newspaper article published June 23, 1918.

56 "Maps of The First World War: An Illustrated Essay and List of Select Maps in The Library of Congress," Library of Congress, Geography and Map Division, Washington, D.C. Summer 2014, https://www.loc.gov/rr/geogmap/pdf/plp/occasional/OccPaper7.pdf , last accessed February 6, 2016. "An example of creeping or rolling barrage, a later tactical development in the war, whereby the artillery barrage rolled forward according to a fixed timetable, and the infantry followed behind the "fire curtain" that would be "lifted" when the final target was reached."

57 "Pack Horses Taking Up Ammunition," Library and Archives Canada, http://www.collectionscanada.gc.ca/lac-bac/results/images?module=images&action=results&Language=eng&PageNum=2&SortSpec=score%2520desc&ShowForm=show&SearchIn_1=&SearchInText_1=horses+wwi&Operator_1=AND&SearchIn_2=&SearchInText_2=&Operator_2=AND&SearchIn_3=&SearchInText_3=&Media%5B%5D=1200&Level=&MaterialDateOperator=after&MaterialDate=&DigitalImages=1&Source=&ResultCount=50&BIGipServerWEBSITE_V41XAPPS_SERVER=1345015438.20480.0000, last accessed February 10, 2016.

58 According to the Royal Canadian Horse Artillery Brigade log, Captain Boak recorded in the regiment's log, over 1000 artillery rounds shot on September 26.

American Expeditionary Force Men and Horses

59 "U.S. Entry into World War I, 1917," U. S. Department of State, Office of the Historian, https://history.state.gov/milestones/1914-1920/wwi, last accessed February 18, 2016.

> Germany's resumption of submarine attacks on passenger and merchant ships in 1917 became the primary motivation behind Wilson's decision to lead the United States into World War I. Following the sinking of an unarmed French boat, the *Sussex*, in the English Channel in March 1916, Wilson threatened to sever diplomatic relations with Germany unless the German Government refrained from attacking all passenger ships and allowed the crews of enemy merchant vessels to abandon their ships prior to any attack. On May 4, 1916, the German Government accepted these terms and conditions in what came to be known as the "*Sussex* pledge."
>
> By January 1917, however, the situation in Germany had changed. During a wartime conference that month, representatives from the German Navy convinced the military leadership and Kaiser Wilhelm II that a resumption of unrestricted submarine warfare could help defeat Great Britain within five months. German policymakers argued that they could violate the "*Sussex* pledge" since the United States could no longer be considered a neutral party after supplying munitions and financial assistance to the Allies. Germany also believed that the United States had jeopardized its neutrality by acquiescing to the Allied blockade of Germany.
>
> German Chancellor Theobald von Bethmann-Hollweg protested this decision, believing that resuming submarine

warfare would draw the United States into the war on behalf of the Allies. This, he argued, would lead to the defeat of Germany. Despite these warnings, the German Government decided to resume unrestricted submarine attacks on all Allied and neutral shipping within prescribed war zones, reckoning that German submarines would end the war long before the first U.S. troopships landed in Europe. Accordingly, on January 31, 1917, German Ambassador to the United States Count Johann von Bernstorff presented U.S. Secretary of State Robert Lansing a note declaring Germany's intention to restart unrestricted submarine warfare the following day.

60 "World War One Select Service System Draft Registration Cards, M1509" United States National Archives, last accessed May 18, 2015, http://www.archives.gov/research/military/ww1/draft-registration/.

The Selective Service System, under the office of the Provost Marshal General, was responsible for the process of selecting men for induction into the military service, from the initial registration to the actual delivery of men to military training camps. The Selective Service System was one of "supervised decentralization." The office of the Provost Marshal General in Washington was responsible for formulating policy and transmitting it to the governors of states and territories. During World War I there were three registrations. The first, on June 5, 1917, was for all men between the ages of 21 and 31. The second, on June 5, 1918, registered those who attained age 21 after June 5, 1917. (A supplemental registration was held on August 24, 1918, for those becoming 21 years old after June 5, 1918. This was included in the second registration.) The third registration was held on

September 12, 1918, for men age 18 through 45. The registration cards consist of approximately 24,000,000 cards of men who registered for the draft, (about 23% of the population in 1918). It is important to note that not all of the men who registered for the draft actually served in the military and not all men who served in the military registered for the draft.

61 "93D Division Summary of Operations in the World War, United States Government Printing Office, American Battle Monuments Commission, 1944, http://www.history.army.mil/topics/afam/93div.htm, last accessed May 16, 2015.

62 "Development of the Army Veterinary Service 1916–1940," United States Army Medical Department, Office of History, http://history.amedd.army.mil/booksdocs/wwii/vetservicewwii/chapter2.htm, last accessed April 17, 2016.

63 Mitchell Yockelson, "They Answered the Call, Military Service in the United States Army During World War I, 1917–1919." Fall 1998, Vol. 30, No. 3. http://www.archives.gov/publications/prologue/1998/fall/military-service-in-world-war-one.html, last accessed May 16, 2015. African Americans made a significant contribution to the United States Army during World War I, and they are well documented among several different series in Record Groups 120 and 391. Although the military was segregated at this time, two all-black divisions, the Ninety-second and Ninety-third, played prominent roles in the defeat of the Central Powers. More than 200,000 African Americans served with the AEF. The majority served in quartermaster labor units. Pioneer Infantry Regiments (troops employed in building roads, digging trenches, and other construction projects) consisted almost entirely of African Americans.

64 "The Collection Online, Balmorals," New York City Metropolitan Museum of Art, http://www.metmuseum.org/collection/the-collection-online/search?ft=*&what=Balmorals, last accessed February 14, 2016.

65 "The Franco-German war of 1870–71," the Library of Congress, https://archive.org/stream/francogermanwaro02molt#page/n9/mode/2up, last accessed February 15, 2016. Field Marshall Helmuth Von Moltke. Translated by Clara Bell and Henry William. (New York: London, and Harper Brothers, 1901).

66 "Bernstorff's Cousin, New German Foreign Minister; Peace Formula is Drawn. Reichstag Peace Resolution," *New York Tribune*. July 16, 1917 edition. "On July 19th, Reichstag Deputy Matthias Erzberger introduced a peace resolution which was passed, 212 votes to 126."

67 "Two world wars and tyranny." The Federal Government, German Archives, https://www.bundesregierung.de/Content/EN/StatischeSeiten/Schwerpunkte/Gedenken/Artikel/artikel_buehne_01_en.html?nn=853010, last accessed April 20,2016.

> The First World War – the "great seminal catastrophe of the 20th century" – broke out 100 years ago this year (2014). The Second World War began 75 years ago, provoked by the Nazi regime under the leadership of Adolf Hitler. Millions of people – soldiers as well as civilians – lost their lives in the two world wars. And millions fell victim to Hitler's master race delusion in the Nazi extermination camps.
>
> The consequences were devastating, especially for people in Central and Eastern Europe, who were directly affected

for decades – and whose liberation from the Nazis led them straight into new dictatorships. It was not until 1989/90 that the age of dictatorships ended in Europe.

68 Vice Admiral Albert Cleaves, United States Navy. *A History of the Transport Service. Adventures and Experiences of United States Transports and Cruisers in The World War* (New York George H. Doran Company,1921), 26.

69 "U.S. Army Soldier and Gas masks for man and horse demonstrated by American soldier, circa 1917–18," National Archives, https://catalog.archives.gov/id/516483, last accessed on December 23, 2015.

70 "Teaching With Documents: Sow the Seeds of Victory! Posters from the Food Administration During World War I." National Archives, https://www.archives.gov/education/lessons/sow-seeds/, last accessed February 15, 2016.

1918: The Western Front

71 "Fort Des Moines Historic Complex, Des Moines, Polk County, IA," Library of Congress, http://www.loc.gov/item/ia0160/, last accessed January 25, 2016.

> Significance: Fort Des Moines is significant as the site of the army training camp for black officers during World War I, the first extensive attempt to education black officer candidates for the rigors of combat leadership. During and after World War I, the post attained recognition in medical circles for innovations in the field of orthopedics research. The fort is further significant as the home of the First Women's Army Axillary Corps (WAAC) Training Center during World War II, where

more than 72,000 women completed training to assist the military mission, thereby fostering a greater role for women in the nation's military establishment.

72 *The Daily Missoulian*, Tuesday morning newspaper, March 13, 1917 edition, summed up the effects of caltrops, a reporter described while covering a battle between the Italian and Austrian armies at Gorizia.

> All fighting upon the Isonzo is in a certain sense a struggle for possession of the city and its bridges." The reported continued ... the trench systems on both sides have been elaborately developed during the late quiet months, the opposite positions sometimes approaching within half a dozen yards, the parapets seemingly separated only by impassable cocoon wire and iron caltrops colored brilliant red with rust. The most uncomfortable proximity, and the fact that the Italians are working incessantly has affected the Austrian nerves.

73 "Nothing New in Warfare," The North Platte semi-weekly tribune. (North Platte, Neb.), 22 April 1919. Chronicling America: Historic American Newspapers. Lib. of Congress. http://chroniclingamerica.loc.gov/lccn/2010270504/1919-04-22/ed-1/seq-7/, last accessed February 16, 2016. The word "caltrop" describes the star thistle, a weed whose form and function were similar to those of the weapon. A caltrop used during WWI was a iron or steel ball with four, three-inch spikes projecting outward. Three spikes made contact with the ground, or backplane. The fourth spike always pointed upward.

The Armistice

74 "The 1918 Allied counter-offensive," United Kingdom National

Archives, http://www.nationalarchives.gov.uk/pathways/firstworldwar/battles/counter.htm, last accessed February 21, 2016.

> In the spring and summer of 1918, replenished by new divisions transferred hurriedly from the East after the crushing defeat of Russia, the German army launched a bold new campaign on the Western Front. Appearances, however, were deceptive. Imperial Germany, as many army staff officers admitted, was playing its "last card," and after initial successes, the Ludendorff offensive ran out of steam.
>
> On 18 July, having rebuffed the last major German assault, French forces in the Marne area launched a surprise counter-attack. This marked the beginning of the Hundred Days, an Allied counter-offensive that finally broke the military stalemate on the Western Front and brought the First World War to a close.

75 "Armistice with Germany," 1919 For. Rel. (Paris Peace Conference, II) 1; Senate Document 147, 66th Congress, 1st Session, May 1919.

76 "Pandemic Flu History," U.S. Center for Disease Control, http://www.flu.gov/pandemic/history/, last accessed April 28, 2016.

> Illness from the 1918 flu pandemic, also known as the Spanish flu, came on quickly. Some people felt fine in the morning but died by nightfall. People who caught the Spanish Flu but did not die from it often died from complications caused by bacteria, such as pneumonia. During the 1918 pandemic: Approximately 20% to 40% of the worldwide population became ill; An estimated 50

million people died; Nearly 675,000 people died in the United States and unlike earlier pandemics and seasonal flu outbreaks, the 1918 pandemic flu saw high mortality rates among healthy adults. In fact, the illness and mortality rates were highest among adults 20 to 50 years old. The reasons for this remain unknown.

77 Colonel G.W. Nicholson, C.D., Canada Department of National Defense, Army Historical Section. *Official History of the Canadian Army in the First World War*. Queen's Printer and Controller of Stationary, Ottawa, 1962. The last Canadian Calvary battle was fought in WWI. Excerpts describes the battle.

> Before accompanying the Canadian Corps in its final operations of the war, we must turn back briefly to view the last action in which Canadian cavalry were engaged. This was the employment of the Canadian Cavalry Brigade with General Rawlinson's Fourth Army in the advance to the Selle River. The fighting took place southwest of Le Cateau on 9 October, (1918) the day on which the Canadian Corps captured Cambrai. ... increasing Allied pressure had forced the Germans to withdraw to the Hermann Position, which in the sector opposite the Third and Fourth Armies ran south from Valenciennes to Le Cateau. In falling back the enemy left a series of rearguards in a line approximately three miles east of his former positions. When British infantry encountered these early on the 9th they found a series of strong little centres of resistance which effectively slowed the advance, and allowed the German retirement to proceed without serious hindrance. On the afternoon of 8 October General Rawlinson had alerted the Cavalry Corps to "be prepared to take advantage of any break in the enemy's defence." The Canadian Cavalry Brigade, which had seen no

fighting since the Battle of Amiens, was concentrated with the rest of the 3rd Cavalry Division about seven miles north of St. Quentin, on the left flank of the Fourth Army. On the morning of the 9th the 66th Division, operating next to the boundary between the Fourth and Third Armies, had as successive objectives the village of Maretz, two miles away, and the road joining Bertry and Maurois, some three miles farther on and about the same distance short of the Selle. Advancing through heavy fog, the infantry encountered no enemy until they reached the eastern edge of Maretz. Here they came under machine-gun fire from German rearguards in the Bois de Gattigny and in Clary, which lay in Third Army territory. The defenders were members of the 72nd Regiment (8th Division) and the 413th Regiment (204th Division).

It was decided to make an organized attack, in which the 3rd Cavalry Division was called on to participate. Its G.O.C., Major-General A. E. W. Harman, planned to move forward astride the old Roman road which ran straight as an arrow north-eastward from Maretz to Bavai. He placed the 6th Cavalry Brigade on the right of the road and the Canadian Brigade on the left. The Fort Garry Horse, with four machineguns and a battery of the R.C.H.A. attached, led the Canadian advance. Lord Strathcona's Horse was given the task of protecting the left flank and reconnoitring out to the line Montigny-Inchy-Neuvilly.

The Cavalry Brigade, commanded by Brig.-Gen. R. W. Paterson, moved forward at 9:30 a.m. Soon after crossing the lateral Clary-Maretz road both regiments met machinegun fire from the same German positions that had stopped the infantry. A spirited charge over 1500 yards of open ground by Laid Strathcona's Horse cleared out the enemy rearguard near Clary. Then, in the face of scattered shelling and machine-gun fire from Montigny on their left, the Strathconas worked their way around the edge of the Bois du Mont-aux-Villes—a northern extension of the Bois de Gattigny. Meanwhile the Fort Garry Horse, supported by the attached R.C.H.A. battery, had attacked the Gattigny Wood. While one troop of the regiment successfully charged the machine-guns in the southern half of the wood-though losing more than half its men in this attempt-a squadron galloped through a gap between the northern and southern halves of the wood to take the same objective in flank. With the assistance of infantry of the South African Brigade (of the 66th Division) in mopping up, the Bois de Gattigny was cleared shortly after 11:00 a.m.

The encounter had yielded approximately 200 prisoners, a 5.9-inch howitzer and about 40 machine-guns. Success at the Bois de Gattigny and the Bois du Mont-aux-Villes prompted General Harman to make his next objectives Maurois on the Roman road and the neighbouring village of Honnechy a thousand yards to the south. He planned to encircle the latter place with a flanking move by the 6th Cavalry Brigade, while the Canadian Brigade came in on Maurois from the north. But when Brig.-Gen. Paterson went forward to relay these orders to the Fort Garry Horse he found that they had already taken Maurois.

On the Canadian left the Strathconas had worked their way into Bertry. At 1:00 p.m. the 6th Cavalry Brigade reported that it had not been able to advance beyond the Busigny-Maretz road. At the same time the Fort Garrys were being held up on the Maurois-Bertry lateral. The next village on the Roman road was Reumont, only three miles from Le Cateau and the Selle. Paterson now ordered a squadron of the Royal' Canadian Dragoons to swing wide to the left around Bertry to take the high ground north of Reumont. The reserve squadron of the Fort Garrys would make a smaller swing to enter Reumont from the northwest. Again the Strathconas were to provide flank protection by pushing northeast from Bertry to Troisvilles. All the guns of the R.C.H.A. Brigade, including an attached battery of 4.5-inch howitzers, were grouped in a valley 1000 yards west of Maurois to give the cavalry covering fire. The neatly planned little operation was entirely successful.

While dismounted Fort Garry troopers forced their way into Reumont, the Dragoons reached their objective in time to cut off a detachment of the retiring enemy. On the left the Strathconas were beyond Troisvilles shortly after 4:00 p.m. During the afternoon enemy guns and transport had been seen moving along the Cambrai-Le Cateau road, which crossed the path of the Canadians about a mile beyond Troisvilles. While the Fort Garry Horse retired into reserve the Dragoons and the Strathconas ware ordered to cut this line of retirement as soon as possible.

As night fell the Dragoons pushed forward to Montay, less than a mile from Le Cateau, and during the hours of darkness R.C.D. troopers patrolled the MontayNeuvilly road along the west bank of the Selle. On the left the Strathconas sent patrols into Inchy on the Cambrai road. Other patrols found the Germans still strongly holding Neuvilly, east of the river. In the meantime the relief of the 6th Cavalry Brigade by a cyclist battalion had left the Canadian right flank open from Reumont to Le Cateau until two squadrons of the Fort Garry Horse were brought forward to fill the gap.

Enemy shelling during the night caused several casualties to both the Fort Garrys and the Strathconas, but daylight brought an end to the Canadians' operation. They were relieved by the 7th Cavalry Brigade and withdrew west of Troisvilles. In advancing approximately eight miles on a front over three miles wide, the Canadians had captured more than 400 prisoners and many weapons, and by disrupting enemy attempts at demolition they had materially aided the infantry's progress.

The Brigade reported a total of 168 men and 171 horses killed, wounded and missing. It was gratifying that this last action by Canadian cavalry was successful. Mounted troops had too frequently met with frustration during the war. The introduction of machine-guns and tanks meant the end of their arm as a useful offensive weapon; This was particularly true, on the Western Front, where the concentration of machine-guns and rifles was far greater than in other. theatres. Nevertheless many Allied commanders either failed to recognize this trend or refused to believe it. Time and again cavalry was massed for a break-through which never occurred.

On the comparatively few occasions when active employment came it was often misdirected. Horses were impeded and horribly injured by barbed wire, and their riders' sabres proved futile against enemy bullets. In assessing the work of the cavalry it must be recognized that the greatest contribution was that made by those squadrons which served dismounted in the trenches.

The Last Ship Home

78 Vice Admiral Albert Cleaves, United States Navy. *A History of the Transport Service. Adventures and Experiences of United States Transports and Cruisers in The World War.* (New York George H. Doran Company,1921), 245. "At sea almost constantly, in the severest weather that has swept the Atlantic Ocean for many years, these Master Mariners of the United States lived up to the highest traditions of the sea, and brought credit to their country."

79 "Teaching With Documents: Photographs of the 369th Infantry and African Americans during World War I," Library of Congress, https://www.archives.gov/education/lessons/369th-infantry/, last accessed February 20, 2016.

> Among the first regiments to arrive in France, and among the most highly decorated when it returned, was the 369th Infantry (formerly the 15th Regiment New York Guard), more gallantly known as the "Harlem Hellfighters." The 369th was an all-black regiment under the command of mostly white officers including their commander, Colonel William Hayward.
>
> Participation in the war effort was problematic for African Americans. While America was on a crusade to make the world safe for democracy abroad, it was neglecting the fight for equality at home. *Plessy v. Ferguson* (1896) established that the 14th Amendment allowed for separate but equal treatment under the law. In 1913 President Wilson, in a bow to Southern pressure, even ordered the segregation of federal office workers. The U.S. Army at

this time drafted both black and white men, but they served in segregated units. After the black community organized protests, the Army finally agreed to train African American officers but it never put them in command of white troops.

During World War I, 380,000 African Americans served in the wartime Army. Approximately 200,000 of these were sent to Europe. More than half of those sent abroad were assigned to labor and stevedore battalions, but they performed essential duties nonetheless, building roads, bridges, and trenches in support of the front-line battles. Roughly 42,000 saw combat.

The 369th Infantry helped to repel the German offensive and to launch a counteroffensive. General John J. Pershing assigned the 369th to the 16th Division of the French Army. With the French, the Harlem Hellfighters fought at Chateau-Thierry and Belleau Wood. All told they spent 191 days in combat, longer than any other American unit in the war. "My men never retire, they go forward or they die," said Colonel Hayward. Indeed, the 369th was the first Allied unit to reach the Rhine.

The extraordinary valor of the 369th earned them fame in Europe and America. Newspapers headlined the feats of Corporal Henry Johnson and Private Needham Roberts. In May 1918 they were defending an isolated lookout post on the Western Front, when they were attacked by a German unit. Though wounded, they refused to surrender, fighting on with whatever weapons were at hand. They were the first Americans awarded the Croix de Guerre, and they were not the only Harlem Hellfighters to win awards; 171 of its officers and men received individual medals and the unit received a Croix de Guerre for taking Sechault.

80 "World War I and the Buffalo Soldiers," U.S. National Park Service, http://www.nps.gov/prsf/learn/historyculture/world-war-i-and-the-buffalo-soldiers.htm, lasted accessed February 2016.

African Americans felt the Buffalo Soldiers would form the nucleus of an all-Black division within the United States Army. However, "racism within the army and the Woodrow Wilson administration blocked any hope of that happening." Veteran Buffalo Soldier regiments of the Regular Army were denied service on the Western Front. The 24th Infantry had been on the Mexican border since 1916 and remained there. The 10th Cavalry was also assigned to patrol along the border. The military justified this action by saying that the country needed a dependable force on the border with Mexico. The 9th Cavalry spent the war years in the Philippines. The 25th Infantry garrisoned in Hawaii.

Black Americans would serve. African-American National Guard regiments and battalions were called to active duty and sent to fight in the Great War. Thousands of men-of-color either enlisted, or responded to the draft during the war. The separation did not stop at the enlisted ranks. Black officer candidates would be treated differently.

An officers training camp for Blacks was established at Fort Des Moines, Iowa, in the June of 1917. Several hundred men attended, including veteran non-commissioned officers from the regular army and National Guard. They were commissioned as Reserve Captains and Lieutenants. One African American National Guard regiment, the 8th Illinois (later renumbered the 370th) was entirely Black including its commander, Colonel Franklin A. Dennison.

President Wilson, in his book *History of American People*, referenced that after the Civil War, "congressional leaders were determined to put the white south under the heal of the black south (and) white men were roused by the mere instinct of self-preservation." Wilson strongly felt that Blacks should not hold high positions of authority in the army, particularly in combat. In a short time, all African-American field grade officers in the regiment, including Colonel Dennison, were sent home and replaced by Caucasian officers."

Most African American troops in the Expeditionary Forces were segregated and consolidated into two Divisions, the 92nd and the 93rd. The men of the 92nd Division were used primarily as support troops. The 93rd Division was placed under the direct command and control of the French army. These men distinguished themselves in battle, but casualties were high with dead or wounded men totaling almost 50% of the division. The men of the 93rd were recognized with 68 Croix de Guerre's and 24 Distinguished Service Crosses.

[81] "The American Expeditionary Forces," Library of Congress, Stars and Stripes xxxxx, http://memory.loc.gov/ammem/sgphtml/sashtml/aef.html, last accessed February 20, 2016.

Once war was declared, the army attempted to mobilize the troops very quickly. The fatigued British and French troops, who had been fighting since August 1914, sorely needed the relief offered by the American forces. In May 1917, General John Joseph "Black Jack" Pershing was designated the supreme commander of the American army in France, and the American Expeditionary Forces (AEF) were created. Pershing and his staff soon realized how ill-prepared the United States was to transport large numbers of soldiers and necessary equipment to the front, where supplies, rations, equipment, and trained soldiers were all in short supply. Since even the transport ships needed to bring American troops to Europe were scarce, the army pressed into service cruise ships, seized German ships, and borrowed Allied ships to transport American soldiers from New York, New Jersey, and Virginia. The mobilization effort taxed the limits of the American military and required new organizational strategies and command structures to transport great numbers of troops and supplies quickly and efficiently.

Although the first American troops arrived in Europe in June 1917, the AEF did not fully participate at the front until October, when the First Division, one of the best-trained divisions of the AEF, entered the trenches at Nancy, France. Pershing wanted an American force that could operate independently of the other Allies, but his vision could not be realized until adequately trained troops with sufficient supplies reached Europe. Training schools in America sent their best men to the front, and Pershing also established facilities in France to train new arrivals for combat.

Throughout 1917 and into 1918, American divisions were usually employed to augment French and British units in defending their lines and in staging attacks on German positions. Beginning in May 1918, with the first United States victory at Cantigny, AEF commanders increasingly assumed sole control of American forces in combat. By July 1918, French forces often were assigned to support AEF operations. During the Battle of St. Mihiel, beginning September 12, 1918, Pershing commanded the American First Army, comprising seven divisions and more than 500,000 men, in the largest offensive operation ever undertaken by United States armed forces. This successful offensive was followed by the Battle of Argonne, lasting from September 27 to October 6, 1918, during which Pershing commanded more than one million American and French soldiers. In these two military operations, Allied forces recovered more than two hundred square miles of French territory from the German army.

By the time Germany signed the Armistice on November 11, 1918, the American Expeditionary Forces had evolved into a modern, combat-tested army recognized as one of the best in the world.

The United States had sustained an estimated 360,000 casualties in the First World War, including 126,000 killed in action and 234,000 wounded. In less than two years the United States had established new motorized and combat forces, equipped them with all types of ordnance including machine guns and tanks, and created an entirely new support organization capable of moving supplies thousands of miles in a timely manner. World War I provided the United States with valuable strategic lessons and an officer corps that would become the nucleus for mobilizing and commanding sixteen million American military personnel in World War II.